THE ATLANTIS CODEX

Dean Crawford

© 2016 Dean Crawford
Published: 13th October 2016
ISBN: 1547267089
ISBN-13: 978-1547267088
Publisher: Fictum Ltd
The right of Dean Crawford to be identified as author of this Work has been asserted by him in accordance with sections 77 and 78 of the Copyright, Designs and Patents Act 1988.
All rights reserved.

www.deancrawfordbooks.com

I

Tingis, Iberian Peninsular,

2,460 BCE

'Row faster!'

Heliosa's voice rang out across the deck of the huge trireme, blue waves crashing against her hull in sparkling blooms of white foam as his crew of a hundred seventy slaves hauled glistening oars through the churning ocean. The wind whistled its song through the vast canvas sails above their heads and heaved the rigging lines as taut as the cat–gut whips that sliced across the muscular shoulders of the slaves.

Heliosa turned and looked behind him to a distant horizon already receding beneath the endless waves. Pale cliffs rose up in the distance through the haze either side of a wide channel of water, two distinct towers of rock soaring against a savage sky. He shielded his eyes against the sunlight and peered at them, knowing that no man had ever sailed this far west and lived to tell the tale.

'We shouldn't be here,' his first mate, Acklion, growled. 'We don't know what's out here, Heliosa.'

Heliosa nodded as he lowered his hand, the mysterious nature of the waters beyond the straits common knowledge among all sea farers of the Greek Islands: *No man dare sail beyond the Pillars of Hercules.*

'I know,' he replied, 'but the gods cannot tear the earth apart and expect us to sit down and die.'

Behind them the sky was stained with a vast maelstrom of roiling black clouds that soared high into the vault of the heavens as though a wave that at some point must come crashing down upon them bearing the wrath of the gods themselves. Crouched low against the horizon was a line of further dense cloud so dark that it seemed as though the night were crawling toward them across the waves.

'We cannot out run it,' Acklion snapped. 'The men can row no faster.'

Heliosa's experienced eye judged at a glance the turbulent waves, the conflicted winds and the advancing wall of hell sweeping ever further over their heads and he knew that the first mate was right. No vessel of man could escape the wrath of Poseidon, and to cheat one death was only to invite the anger of the gods and another, more gruesome fate in its place.

'Heave to!' Heliosa yelled to his crew. 'Take us in to the shore and find us shelter!'

The trireme turned as Acklion barked orders to the exhausted crew. Heliosa turned back to the hellish firmament behind them and stared in superstitious horror at the soaring pillar of ash and smoke that was even now blasting upward in the far distance, its darkened depths flickering with forks of angry lightning. The apocalyptic pillar had appeared only minutes before and yet even now the sun itself was being swallowed by the rapidly growing maw of the darkness.

'It is the end of times!' one of the crew wailed in horror. 'The sky will fall and our souls will be swallowed by Hades and...!'

Heliosa crossed the deck in three strides and hauled the sailor bodily from the bench. The odors of sweat and fear shamed his nostrils, thin and rank as he growled into the man's face.

'That will be preferable to what I will do if you don't start rowing for your life!'

Heliosa hurled the man back down onto his bench and glared at his crew as he drew a bronze sword from its sheath on his belt and waved it at them, the metal flashing like gold in the growing darkness as he yelled above the growing winds.

'Does any man wish to die here today?!' he demanded of them, and in response he heard and saw nothing save the fearful gazes of his crew. 'Then row! Row for *all* of our lives!'

Even as he said his last the sky above the trireme split asunder as a deafening blast of noise crashed past them with hammer blows that shook the very ocean. Heliosa felt the terrible din reverberate inside his chest as though his organs were being shaken loose from their moorings and he ducked down instinctively as pain seared his ears and his vision blurred.

The infernal noise passed by and Heliosa's ears rang where he crouched as he looked up and saw the crew rowing like madmen, the trireme heading toward the nearby shore at a tremendous speed and grown men weeping in terror as they rowed for their lives.

Heliosa stood and saw Acklion stagger upright, blood trickling from his ears as he turned and saw an immense pillar of fresh flame and smoke expanding outward from far behind them. Heliosa's courage failed him as he saw countless flaming projectiles soaring into the heavens above, trailing plumes of thick black smoke as they arced across the sky and began plummeting down toward the ocean.

Heliosa whirled and surveyed the shore, and at once his gaze settled upon a narrow inlet nestled between two low cliffs of rugged rock. He could see scant beaches nearby and at once he yelled to Acklion.

'There!'

The first mate spotted the inlet and nodded as he guided the trireme in, the big ship heading directly for the shore at close to maximum speed, for Heliosa and his crew knew what was coming next and how little time they had left to save themselves.

Heliosa turned and looked down into the ship's hatches where endless crates of fine silks and spices, gold and silver, jewellery and all manner of exotic goods awaited the markets of Athens. His fortune, the result of half a year's work, and now he knew that he would never be able to bring it home to his family unless he could get away from the fearsome storm that had risen so cruelly when they were so close to home.

'Beach her!' he bellowed.

The brilliant sunlight bathing the shore vanished and the air turned bitterly cold. Heliosa looked up and saw the sun vanish behind the wall of ashen cloud and he knew that their time was almost over. A deep fear poisoned his belly and weakened his legs as the ship rushed in toward the beach and then he felt the hull shudder beneath his feet and the great vessel slowed. Heliosa staggered as the ship lurched, sliding up onto the beach as the wind spilled from the great sail above his head.

'Run!' somebody yelled. 'Run for your lives!'

'Stay with the ship!' Heliosa roared, but panic had taken the crew and they fled from their posts and vaulted over the trireme's bow onto the sand and churning waves below and waded onto shore.

Acklion staggered to his captain's side and grabbed his shoulder.

'There is nothing we can do, Heliosa! We must leave the ship!'

Heliosa looked longingly at the holds of his beloved trireme and he knew that Acklion was right, but his pain at such a loss was too much to bear and tears that he would never have shed before the rest of the crew spilled down his cheeks and soaked his beard.

'This is all I have!' he gasped. 'All my family has!'

'There will be other ships and other voyages, but not if we stay here!'

Heliosa hesitated a moment longer and then the pull of his loyal first mate drew him away from the holds and together they rushed to the side of the ship and hurled themselves down onto the beach as waves crashed into the trireme's hull.

Heliosa sprinted up the beach and scrambled up onto the rocks as he followed Acklion up and away from the churning waves below. Acklion mounted the top of the bluff first and Heliosa saw a vast sea of marshy reeds and swamps spreading before them toward low hills crouched in the distance. To their left he saw the specks of fleeing figures, his crew running frantically inland and away from the shore.

Then, to their horror they they saw the river in the nearby inlet begin to flow faster.

'The gods,' Acklion whispered in fear and awe, 'they are consuming the whole world!'

Heliosa watched in disbelief as he saw the river flowing back out to sea, gathering pace as it did so. As he watched so he noticed the ocean waves receding away from the shore. The trireme's hull sagged as it settled on the surface of a rapidly growing beach as the entire ocean began to drain away from them and exposed endless miles of coast sodden with debris and foliage.

'Zeus, save us!' Acklion implored the heavens as he sank to his knees with his arms outstretched toward the turbulent heavens.

Heliosa could speak no words as he watched the waves of a once–indomitable ocean recede away as forks of savage lightning raked across the sky and flaming chunks of rock spilled from the clouds and slammed into the ground around them.

Acklion hurled himself flat against the earth and threw his hands over his head, Heliosa ducking down and flinching as fine ash poured like filthy snow from the thick clouds above and pumice slammed down around them. He was about to suggest running back to the trireme for cover when he heard screams coming from the river.

Several of the crew had been caught up in the tumultuous flow and were being dragged out to sea. Heliosa heard their terrified cries of despair fade away as Poseidon claimed his own once again. And then he saw something else that made his heart freeze in his chest.

The immense river's churning surface was swirling around a huge circular form in the center of the estuary, the flow of the water eddying and coiling around strangely symmetrical shapes standing just beneath the surface. Despite the debris raining down around him Heliosa managed to stagger to his feet and found himself staring down into a vast natural harbor concealed beneath the river. Even as he watched he saw towers and buildings emerge from the green water, immense docks and jetties, what looked like palaces and parks and roads all built into a vast system of symmetrical rings hundreds of leagues across.

'Son of Zeus,' he gasped. 'Acklion!'

Heliosa turned and saw his first mate cowering face down in the mud. He grabbed him and hauled him forcefully to his feet. 'Quick, we must get to the ship!'

Acklion saw the spectacle before them, but then his eyes filled with horror as he looked out to sea.

'There is no time, look!'

Heliosa turned and saw the immense expanses of beach strewn with debris and showered with flaming rocks, but beyond that he saw something that squeezed his heart in his chest. The ocean was returning with a vengeance, a wall of black water as high as the masts of the trireme thundering toward them with foaming white rollers rising up to tower above the beach.

'The deluge,' Acklion gasped. 'Poseidon has come for us!'

'The ship!' Heliosa yelled and sprinted toward the terrible wave bearing down upon them.

He heard Acklion's horrified cry but none the less the first mate pursued Heliosa back toward the trireme. They leaped down off the rocks and onto the beach as Heliosa heard the terrible roar of the surging wall of water thundering inward, saw debris tumbling among the waves as they rose up. He reached the bow of the ship and hauled himself aboard with Acklion to see a terrified slave girl still crouched on the deck before them, too struck with terror to leave the ship.

'Jaela!'

'Grab the helm!' Heliosa ordered Acklion as he dashed toward the girl.

He reached Jaela's side and hauled her to her feet, then dragged her to the bow of the ship and crouched down as the girl screamed and the immense wave smashed into the shore like a wall of unstoppable warriors howling the vengeance of the gods. The trireme heaved to one side as the waves blasted past either side of her hull and then she was lifted off the beach and propelled into the estuary at the head of the immense wave.

Heliosa gripped the bow of the ship and gritted his teeth as he saw the water rush into the vast natural bay that opened out before them, and for a brief moment of time he saw the vast city resplendent in all of its glory. He saw collonades and amphitheatres rush by as the ocean plunged once more into the ancient bay and swallowed the entire city whole, but as they plunged through so he saw one towering building in the heart of the city, its perfect walls staring defiantly back at the unstoppable might of the ocean, and upon its surface a series of forms carved into the walls, geometric shapes that he knew were writing of some kind that he could not understand.

The waves swallowed the city before them as they clashed with one another in a violent maelstrom that rose up before the trireme and crashed down upon it as the rest of the wave behind them smashed into the ship's stern. Heliosa heard a crack that was loud enough to drown out even the tremendous storm all around them and he knew that the ship's back was broken through.

As water plunged down all around him Heliosa turned and saw that the ship's helm was gone, torn off by the force of the impact, and then the wall of water rushed overhead and plunged down on top of them with the weight of the ages. Heliosa's consciousness was torn from him into a deep blackness that swallowed him whole.

***

II

Glavnoye razvedyvatel'noye upravleniye

Grizodubovoy str. 3, Moscow

(Present Day)

Lieutenant Colonel Konstantin Petrov strode into the headquarters of the Main Intelligence Directorate in Moscow, his uniform immaculately pressed, his belt polished to a shine that he imagined reflected some of the old glory of the Soviet Union lost so long ago. The GRU building was an ugly, angular construction that departed from the old Soviet style of architecture yet somehow retained its bleak nature. Gray steel panels were surrounded by concrete walls topped with barbed wire that glinted in the weak morning sunlight glowing behind blankets of cloud. Ordinary Russians rarely entered, or wanted to enter, this building. Even the General Secretary of the Communist Party of the Soviet Union required a security screening to enter GRU headquarters.

The floor of the foyer was emblazoned with a large image of a bat, the emblem of the *Spetsnaz* Special Forces, the agency's logo mounted on the opposite wall over an image of the earth as though Russia had already laid claim to it. The GRU's official full name was the Main Intelligence Agency of the General Staff of the Armed Forces of the Russian Federation, and it was Russia's largest foreign intelligence agency, deploying six times as many agents in foreign countries as the SVR, the successor of the KGB's foreign operations directorate. Tens of thousands of *Spetsnaz* troops were also under its command, the agency given the role of handling all military intelligence from sources outside the Soviet Union.

Petrov was more than aware of why he had been summoned to the building. He knew that the GRU operated residencies all over the world, along with a dedicated Signals Intelligence station in Lourdes, Cuba and throughout the former Soviet–bloc countries, and that it served an important role in his country's defensive structure. He knew also from the reports he had been required to read before travelling to Moscow that his predecessor, Colonel Anatoly Mishkin, had been killed in action and that he had been selected to take his place. What he had not been able to understand was what mission could conjure the extreme vetting and security that enveloped this assignment like a forcefield. He had no family, but Konstantin had been required to sign endless Non-Disclosure Agreements before reading the reports and finally understanding why; Russian covert forces had been aggressively deployed into foreign sovereign territories, potentially an act of war if their presence had been exposed at the political level.

Petrov took an elevator up to the fourth floor and followed the signs until he reached the office of the agency's director, General Sergei Olatov. Petrov checked his watch: ten in the morning in *three, two, one...* He took a breath before he knocked on the door and after a muffled "enter" he walked in.

He closed the door behind him and walked to where General Sergei Olatov sat behind a large desk which was undecorated but for a laptop computer and a framed photograph of the general's wife and two children. Craggy, white-haired and with his uniform hanging off his wiry frame, the general looked as though he should have retired a decade previously. Petrov realized he probably would have if not for the president's reliance on an "old guard" to prop up his dreams of a return to former Soviet glory.

'Sit down.'

Petrov obeyed in silence and waited for the general to speak.

'You have read the reports?'

'I have.'

'Do you understand what is being asked of you?'

Petrov raised his chin a little.

'I do,' he replied, 'but I do not know the nature of my mission. There is nothing in the reports to detail the purpose of our cause.'

Petrov deliberately described the mission in terms of "our cause", a means of fostering the General's trust in him and also a way of showing the older man that Konstantin could be trusted to undertake the task at hand on the strength of his belief and patriotism alone.

The sop worked as he saw a softening in the old man's eyes.

'The targets are all enemies of the Motherland,' Sergie explained. 'They were directly responsible for the death of Colonel Mishkin and his team in Egypt.'

Petrov felt a vague anxiety rise up in his gut.

'May I ask, general, what our comrades were doing operating inside Egypt?'

The was a long moment during which Sergie stared silently at him while remaining utterly motionless. Petrov had the sense that he was being assessed in some way, but the scrutiny went on so long that for a moment he wondered if the older man had fallen into a state of torpor.

'Our world has changed in so many ways,' Olatov finally replied. 'The political alliances forged by our leaders now present us with new allies in powerful places within the American administration that we could not possibly have envisioned even months ago. Once again, an American leader believes that we have their best interests at heart and we are determined not to let this opportunity pass for it cannot last long.'

Like most Russians Petrov had witnessed the rise of populist but dangerous leaders around the globe as the people of countries in both the east and the west used their democratic power to oust an elite they blamed for their ills. The fact that in America the people had rejected the old guard leadership, the billionaires and the Wall Street investors, and instead voted for a misogynistic billionaire who had installed many other billionaires into cabinet positions they were unqualified for was a source of amusement for many Moscovites.

'The populist uprising is a dangerous game,' Petrov agreed. 'The Arab Spring and its consequences in Syria are a clear example of how the house of cards can fall fast, despite the best intentions of the people involved.'

'It will not last,' Olatov went on. 'The people will realize their error sooner or later, but that is not the point. Right now their voices are being heard across the world. A message has been sent to the elite, to those who rule from behind the scenes in their corporations. The people will not stand idly by any longer, and their resistance is something that needs to be stamped out as soon as possible.'

Petrov's eyes narrowed.

'What are you suggesting?'

Olatov gestured to a folder that he produced from a draw in his desk and laid between them.

'Can you imagine what would happen if the people had any true power? What they would do with that power? If they suddenly knew about everything we did, about everything our governments have learned over the past decades, the past centuries? Power must remain centralized and in the hands of those who know how best to use it. The new American president is not such a man, and the American people are not such a people.'

Petrov stared at the folder as though it was alive as the general went on.

'The American president is just about crazy enough that he might send in military forces to any country in order to finally achieve what we have sought for so long. He might believe in the unbelievable, whereas most other presidents have scoffed. But if we are right, then we risk handing the greatest discoveries of modern times to a demagogue who would use them like a club to subdue the rest of the world, Russia included.'

Petrov found himself wondering what on earth could possibly be of such importance that it could drive the GRU to contemplate biting the hand now apparently feeding them from Washington DC, but protocol prevented him from just reaching out and opening the file.

'*Mat' Zemlya*, or Mother Earth, is the unit to which you have been assigned,' the general went on. 'It is a counterpart to the American Defense Intelligence Agency's ARIES program, a highly secretive unit tasked with investigating anomalous phenomena.'

'Anomalous?'

'Your unit will investigate events and locations believed by others to be impossible, the work of legends and myths,' the general explained. 'Before you fear that this assignment is some form of punishment, let me put your mind at rest. You were selected for this role because of your record and your loyalty to the Motherland, but also your ability to get results without drawing attention to yourself. Your work in both Chechnya and Syria was much admired by Moscow. They, and I, felt that you would be well suited to this role.'

Petrov inclined his head and feigned a brief smile of gratitude, but inside he was in turmoil. Given the secrecy of the mission, his lack of family and dependents and the apparent importance of whatever was in the folder before him, Petrov suspected that he had been chosen because he was expendable.

'May I?' he asked finally as he looked at the folder.

The general nodded and sat back in his seat as Petrov picked up the folder and opened it.

'This is what we have been searching for,' Olatov added.

Petrov stared at the images in the folder and for a moment he wasn't sure what to say. He kept his eyes on the pages to buy himself more time to absorb them and concoct a response of suitable gravitas but instead just one thing kept popping into his mind: *insanity*.

He looked up at Olatov over the folder's pages, having seen also images of people assigned to the DIA's ARIES unit.

'The agents we have targeted: they too are searching for this?'

'We believe so,' Olatov replied. 'The former president is believed to have shut down the ARIES program and destroyed any evidence of it in order to prevent the material falling into the hands of his successor. The last time the agents were seen was in Egypt, and they may have escaped with vital evidence we need to continue our search. Your task, Konstantin, is to find them and reacquire that which they have taken.'

'Ethan Warner and Nicola Lopez are civilian contractors and they have been missing for months. They have a long headstart on us.'

'Indeed, but they left behind weaknesses, detailed in the reports we gave you.'

Petrov nodded, reading the contents of the file. Ethan Warner had parents and a sister, Nicola Lopez had family in Guanajunato, Mexico, and Douglas Jarvis had a daughter somewhere in Chicago.

'I see,' Petrov replied, squirming slightly in his seat, 'and I understand what is required.'

'There is more,' the general added. 'We understand from a number of Russian billionaires who had dealings with a cabal of American industrialists known as Majestic Twelve that the billions of dollars recovered by the United States Government from the cabal after its collapse was only a fraction of its actual worth. We cannot be sure, but it would appear that the members of the DIA you have been briefed about absconded with the bulk of the money and that the DIA is understandably keen to recover such vast sums.' The general leaned forward on his desk. 'I too would be keen to see that money recovered for the benefit of the Motherland, along with the artefacts in question. Any officer who achieved such a goal for the GRU would be highly rewarded.'

For the first time since entering the room, Petrov smiled. The old general truly was one of the old guard and willing to bend a rule or two for his own gain rather than see a fortune go entirely to waste in the Kremlin's coffers.

'And the agents of the DIA, Warner and Lopez? They may be willing to fight for their own mission and may have gathered support from other sources.'

'They are irrelevant,' the general replied, 'abandoned and hunted by their government and an irritation to our own. If you find them, follow them until you have extracted all that you can about their mission. Then, kill them.'

Petrov stood and saluted the general briskly before he turned and marched from the office. He closed the door outside and let out a long breath as he stared at the folder in his hand. The Kremlin was keen to point out privately that they considered the new American president to be a buffoon, but the images in the folder he had been given suggested that the *Politboro* had long since lost their minds also.

He opened the folder once again and stared at an artist's impression of a city, constructed inside a large bay. Three concentric rings formed the city's structure, ringed with ports, while the central island was dominated by elaborate buildings and towering spires that made it look like a cross between Buckingham Palace and Disneyland.

Petrov closed the folder and promptly forgot about the image as he focussed instead on the general's promise: *I too would be keen to see that money recovered for the benefit of the Motherland, along with the artefact. Any officer who achieved such a goal for the GRU would be rewarded.*

Petrov doubted that the corrupt old man would share anything recovered with a lowly GRU officer. But then, if not every one of the lost billions made it back to Moscow, perhaps Petrov wouldn't need to come back either…

***

III

Sortland,

Norway

A frigid wind blustered in off a vast fjord that was entirely encrusted in sea ice, the jagged mountains a deep blue in the fading light and their icy peaks consumed by wreaths and ribbons of turbulent, bruised cloud.

'I can see something.'

Doctor Lucy Morgan turned from gazing at the distant lights of Sortland, known as the *Blue Town* by the local people after the decision some decades earlier to paint every building blue. The handful of street lights twinkled like lonely stars in the growing darkness as Lucy saw her companion crouched knee–deep in freezing mud and ice before her.

'Can you identify it?' she asked.

The man before her cast her a glance that suggested he was anything but happy about being where he was.

'I can barely see what I'm doing, let alone identify it. Bring the lights down here.'

Lucy switched on four site lamps and lowered them down into the excavation that they had been working on for the last two weeks, laboring quietly and out of sight of the settlers. The muddy, icy hollow in which they stood was six feet deep and around ten feet square and faced out toward the fjord, the icy shores nearby creaking and groaning as the ice froze. Soon the entire area would be enveloped by the ferocious grip of the Norwegian winter, the ground frozen as hard as rock, and another few months would be lost as they awaited the following years' spring thaw.

'It's probably nothing more than mammoth bones,' Professor Charles Wright complained as he worked with a shovel and a kerosene blow torch, melting chunks of permafrost and then shovelling them out of the way. 'If I never see another tusk in my life it'll be too damned soon.'

The bleak spit of land on which they stood was a quarter of a mile from the nearest settlement, a clutch of tiny homes crouched against the bitter gales that swept in from the Arctic Circle. To the north there was nothing but the mountains and fjords of northern Norway and then beyond the bleak wastes of the Norwegian and Barents Seas. There was no way that any museum or university would have funded Lucy's expedition up here, because none of them would have believed for an instant that what she sought was there, or even possible. Most would have dismissed her quest as nothing more than the ramblings of a lunatic, a fringe scientist. Hell, it wouldn't have been the first time…

'Good lord.'

Lucy's reverie broke and she looked down at Wright. 'What?'

The professor, clad in waders and Arctic clothing to protect him from the elements, backed out of an excavation he had completed and gestured to it with a small shovel in his hand.

'That's not a mammoth tusk,' he uttered, appearing quite shaken in the ghostly light from the lamps.

Lucy stepped forward and got down onto her knees, the thick waders she had bought from a local trader protecting her from the mud and the ice as she moved up against a wall of frozen black sediment that was encrusted with ice, like diamond chips lodged in a seam of coal.

Entombed within the sediment she could see the remains of something that took her breath away, something so far out of place that it seemed impossible that it could ever have surfaced where it had.

'It's not possible,' Professor Wright uttered as he looked over her shoulder. 'It just shouldn't be here.'

Lucy smiled as she stared at the artefact lodged in the sediment before her.

'It's only impossible if you're not willing to *believe* in what the evidence tells you.'

Before them both was a length of wood that had been formed perfectly by human hands many thousands of years before. The shape of the artefact was clear, revealed by the seams of ice that were threaded through the sediment like windows into an ancient past. The wood was a tiny section of a great oar, tens of feet long that stretched through the ice in the excavation and vanished into the ancient earth to either side.

Lucy knew that the level of the sediment they were observing would have been laid down more than three thousand years ago, but only actual carbon dating of the artefact would provide an accurate age range for the piece. Right now, however, the age of the artefact did not interest Lucy.

'We need to find the rest of it.'

Professor Wright baulked as he looked up at the turbulent, darkening sky above them.

'Lucy, this is one of the most exciting historical discoveries of the modern age but I have to insist that we come back tomorrow.'

'I don't do waiting,' Lucy replied as she climbed out of the excavation and began erecting a canvas sheet to protect their discovery from sleet and snow.

'This artefact has survived for the past few thousand years,' Wright pointed out. 'It's not going to get up and run away overnight.'

Lucy smiled as she drove aluminium stakes into the hard ground and began stretching the cover over them.

'It's not the oar I'm interested in.'

'It's *not?*' Wright echoed, shocked. 'Lucy, this could change the history books, re–write everything we know about how civilization rose and how we became the dominant species on this planet! You do understand what we have here, don't you? This is the remains of an oar from a Greek trireme, two thousand or more years old, buried in the ice in *Norway*!'

Lucy nodded in agreement as she worked, hauling the sheet over the site and pulling it taut so that it closed them in.

'I know, but finding this is a means to an end.'

'Good lord, *what* end? I've risked my career joining you on this wild goose chase from England. Everybody told me to avoid it, that you were a loose cannon obsessed with fringe archaeology and pseudo–science.'

Lucy barely acknowledged the criticisms, as she had heard them many times before now and refused to let them deter her from her work.

'I don't do small talk either,' she replied simply. 'Do you think this oar is the result of pseudo–science and fringe archaeology?'

Professor Wright's bluster failed him and his shoulders sank as he shook his head.

'No, Lucy, I do not. However, I have travelled a long way and risked the ridicule of my peers at Oxford merely because I shall soon be retiring and therefore I am not in risk of losing my job. Were I twenty years younger I can assure you I wouldn't be here. I don't know how you manage to get funding for these kinds of expeditions.'

'I have wealthy friends with an interest in these sorts of finds.'

'Then you owe me at least some kind of explanation,' Wright said, and folded his arms. 'You told me that we were excavating here in search of evidence of sunken Elizabethan trade ships and instead you unearth a Greek trireme. What's really behind all of this?'

Lucy stopped her work and sighed. Professor Wright was an expert in ancient maritime trade and thus had been the perfect companion for her on this covert expedition. He had initially refused, but the money she had been able to pay him had virtually doubled his forthcoming pension and he had been unable to refuse despite the consternation of his colleagues at Oxford. Now, in his late sixties and shivering from the cold, she figured that he was right – money wasn't all that he was here for.

'You're going to have a hard time believing me,' she warned him.

'I had a feeling you were going to say something like that.'

Lucy pulled from a nearby bag of her belongings a laptop computer that she opened, the glow from the screen illuminating the interior of the tent and providing a feeble sense of warmth as Wright moved alongside her and she spoke a single word.

'Pytheas.'

Wright's eyes widened and he gasped. 'No, it cannot be! Pytheas returned to Greece from his voyages. This cannot be a vessel of his!'

Pytheas had been one of ancient Greece's legendary mariners and explorers. Sent beyond the *Pillars of Hercules* to find out where the country's imports were actually coming from, Pytheas had sailed north along the coast of Portugal and then beyond, up and around the British Isles and toward the Baltic nations in search of a legendary isle known to the ancient Greeks as "Thule".

'The ancient Greeks spoke of a foreign nation of great technological prowess that lived on an island known as Thule,' Lucy said, 'and Pytheas believed that he found such a place at the northern–most extremes of his travels. Maps drawn afterward based on Pytheas's writings marked the northern isles as Thule.'

'Yes,' Wright agreed, 'but those notions have long since been proven wrong. There was little up here in those times, and Pytheas wrote only of seas filled with ice neither solid nor water, upon which one could neither walk nor sail.'

'Pancake ice,' Lucy confirmed. 'For a Greek to have witnessed such things, they must have travelled at least as far north as Scandinavia.'

'I agree, but the travels of Pytheas are well documented. What is not possible is that we should find the remains of another ship of the type that he used in this region. This vessel should not be here.'

Lucy gestured to the laptop as she replied.

'Pytheas came this far north in search of a mysterious island, and in doing so he encountered groups of people living in the wilds of Britain. He is the first person to document the existence of the Picts and other societies including Germanic barbarians. It's those encounters that interest me the most.'

'Why?' Wright asked.

'Because they and many other ancient peoples all claim that they were descended from people of great wisdom who came from across the sea,' she replied. 'Who brought them great knowledge and helped them form new societies. They all claim that they originated from elsewhere.'

'I'm not following,' Wright said softly, watching her with an uncertain gaze.

Lucy flipped a page on the screen of her laptop and turned it to face the professor. Wright read from the page and his eyes widened as he did so.

'You're not out here looking for what I think you are, are you?'

'Pytheas didn't make it up here on his own,' she replied, dodging the question a little. 'There were sceptics about his voyages even at the time and some of his measurements and claims didn't stand up to scrutiny even then. It was remarked by his peers that he seemed to have relied upon some kind of earlier writings to have completed his voyage, filling out details with information from another source, some sort of guide or codex.'

Lucy gestured to the remains before them and Wright understood immediately.

'How much earlier?' he gasped, eager now to learn more.

'The Greeks had already heard of northern lands where there was perpetual darkness and that the seas froze and veils of fire danced through the night sky,' she replied. 'Word could have come over land via trade routes and via shared stories travelling south from community to community, but what if the information had been kept from an earlier time in the same way that most myths and legends were kept alive before the advent of writing? What if some common origin of all people was not just their stories but the actual living record of how a dispersed, technologically advanced people were scattered about the globe and interacted with existing hunter–gatherer populations, forming what we think of now as the first civlizations?'

'You're talking about Atlantis,' Wright said, his voice sounding flat in the growing darkness as Lucy put the laptop away.

'I'm talking about the possibility that civilization was thriving before the period currently reconized by modern historians and archaeologists, and that it was reborn as survivors of some great calamity were dispersed around the globe. Nobody has ever been able to explain how so many advanced early cultures around the world sprung up at the same time, with similar technologies and legends, on widely separated continents that should have had no contact with each other. My assertion is that they shared a common origin for those technologies, dialects and legends, and this ship is my evidence.'

'A Greek trireme?' Wright said.

'No,' Lucy replied, 'I don't think that this ship is Greek at all.'

Wright stared at her blankly for a long moment as he digested what she was saying.

'You think that this was an *Atlantean* vessel?'

Lucy glanced over her shoulder at the ancient oar buried in the sediment.

'This fjord was created by the retreat of an ancient glacier,' she said. 'The sediment around that oar was not put down after the ship was lost here. It was put down after the glacier retreated.'

Professor Wright seemed to turn pale in the glow from the lamps. 'That's not possible. The glaciers in this region did not retreat until some twelve thousand years ago!'

'Right about when Plato and others state that a super civilization was wrecked by a colossal climatic event that wiped them out,' Lucy replied triumphantly. 'I think that this ship was left here over ten thousand years ago, and I want to know what's inside it, because if we can figure that out we might learn of where it came from.'

Lucy picked up one of the lamps, the glow from it illuminating half of her face while the rest remained in deep shadow.

'You wanna start doing some fringe research professor, or are you just going to stand there?'

***

IV

Pentagon, Washington DC

Lieutenant Colonel Foxx walked through the corridors of the most famous military complex in the world, kept his eyes fixed ahead and ignored the glances of other members of staff going about their business in offices all around him.

The Pentagon employed a large number of people, sufficient that it was unusual to see the same face twice in one visit. As Foxx rarely walked these halls the anonymity offered by the place suited him just fine. His rank would normally have guaranteed recognition but Foxx did not command divisions of infantry or armor. In fact, he had not stepped onto a parade ground in almost two decades. Foxx worked in the shadows, his department funded by a "black budget" that was now growing larger every year due to the policies of an administration built upon a fear and paranoia that now fuelled or hindered the American dream, depending on how one viewed the world.

Foxx stopped at the door of a non–descript office and checked his uniform briefly out of habit before checking his watch and knocking briskly. Once, long ago, men in his position had worn black suits, ties and hats. They were tasked with ensuring that witnesses to unusual phenomena, especially UFO sightings, remained silent about their experience and were "discouraged" from reporting them either to the media or friends. Their visits to members of the public from the late 1940s onwards had resulted in them being labelled with a strange moniker: *Men in Black*.

Those days were long gone now, and instead it was preferred for ultra–covert operatives to remain tucked out of sight in what appeared to be menial roles within the regular military. Foxx's true role as an agent of a highly classified government organization was thus perfectly concealed from all but those who served alongside him. The office he sought was likewise anonymous among the many hundreds of others that filled the Pentagon.

'Enter.'

Foxx walked in and closed the door behind him. Inside was a small office with pictures on the walls of the residing officer's family and military service. A simple filing cabinet stood in one corner of the room and the desk was cluttered with mundane paperwork.

'Please, sit.'

Foxx sat in the only other chair inside the room and waited for the older man before him to speak. A senior officer with close links to the White House, he had been quietly appointed his position while the media was focussing on whichever scandal was rocking the administration of the time. White hair, tired and rheumy eyes and slumped shoulders, Foxx had seen these kinds of appointments before given to men who could be relied upon to maintain silence about their work until reaching a grave that was not far away. There was no greater means of keeping a man's silence than death itself.

'What news of Russia?'

Foxx shifted uncomfortably in his seat as he replied. 'They are as ever among us, welcomed even.'

He could not help but express a little surprise in his response, given where they were sitting.

'They have their place,' the old man said and then finally looked up at Foxx. 'It's not like we haven't done this before.'

'The Cold War is long over,' Foxx cautioned. 'The enemy cannot be trusted.'

'And the enemy of my enemy is my friend,' came the cryptic reply. 'It is not our place to make policy. We are merely the instrument of that policy.'

Foxx said nothing. He had seen the passing of enough administrations to know that they were merely the public face of a much more powerful and labyrinthine machine that few people even knew existed. Although in recent years the powerful military industrial complex which underpinned all of western society had seen its influence eroded by the rise of people power across the globe, it still maintained control of the bulk of the media and the vast majority of the political establishment in the United States and Europe. The phase of people voting for nationalistic dictators was seen as just that; a phase that would soon pass as the populace of country after country slowly came to realize that a populist agenda only came to fruition at the hands of those with the temperament to remain popular. Inevitaby, that ability was lost in the face of their rise to power and their unwillingness to part with it.

'Why am I here?' Foxx asked.

The old man spoke quietly, using no force in his words, no emotion or sense of urgency. Instead his calm and steady tones were imbued with the authority of countless years of experience which Foxx would likely never hear about even with his level of security clearance.

'The administration is unstable to say the least, and although their cosying to the Russians appalls any sane American it does provide us with opportunities that did not exist during the previous president's tenure.'

'Such as?'

'The ear of powerful Russian figures for whom profit is of greater concern than democracy, or the lives of the people from whom they extract their fortunes.'

Foxx's eyes narrowed uncertainly. 'Where is this going?'

'The administration is being run in the manner of a business and major arms contractors and technology giants have the ear of the president. Their ability to maintain profit is largely dependent on the continuation of an American defense program overseas and the maintenance of a war footing in at least one theatre around the globe.'

'Peace is the enemy of profit,' Foxx acknowledged.

Any sane person had long become aware that the word defense as used by the administration was a deception in itself. America maintained some three thousand overseas bases around the world, whereas Russia maintained precisely three. America had never needed nor relied upon such a global presence for its own safety, but rather used it to project power across the globe along with its own insistence that other countries abide by an American Way that was as corrupt in many sectors as anything the Soviet *Politboro* had conceived during the Cold War.

'With the administration cutting international aid and public spending in order to increase our own bloated military budget by a further ten percent, most of the major arms companies are rubbing their hands together in glee at the prospect of another major regional conflict designed to line their pockets with the blood of innocent civilians. To oppose this, of course, is now referred to as "un–American", or even Communist.'

Foxx was aware of how the country's leadership was on the verge of plunging into the abyss like nothing he had ever witnessed before but like most he couldn't see what he or any federal agency could do about it.

'Our greatest concern now,' the old man went on, 'is that in return for facilitating these new conflicts, or at the very least providing minimal resistance to the next military intervention by American forces, Russia will be offered recompense in ways other than the retraction of sanctions.'

'Such as?'

'The president shares more than just his attitude with dictators of the past,' the old man said. 'He is just as interested in the conspiracy theories peddled by several right–wing radio shows and television channels and is showing a concerning habit of basing actual policy on those theories. Our concern is that in his lunacy he might inadvertently start to get a little too close to the truth.'

Foxx knew what the old man was referring to and suddenly he understood why he was in the room. Seventy years earlier, a meeting between the President of the United States and elements of the industrial and military complex had resulted in the formation of a shadowy cabal of powerful figures known only as Majestic Twelve. In continuous operation for nearly eight decades and charged with the post war takeover of the democratic process, it had been Majestic Twelve that President Eisenhower had warned against all those years ago and which overshadowed United States foreign policy to this day.

However, in a shocking breach of intelligence agency security the veil of Majestic Twelve had been brought down by a small team of civilian contractors within the DIA and the entire operation had collapsed. Exposed and hounded, the sitting council of Majestic Twelve were no more and now a new and unpredictable president was being briefed daily by a CIA hostile to other agencies and commanded by a man who was little more than a crony for the administration.

'You're concerned that the administration will trade secrets for political or business favors,' he said finally.

The old man inclined his head. 'What is the status of our work on relics recovered from the sites of previous investigations by the DIA team, before their ARIES unit was forceably disbanded?'

Foxx sighed, knowing that there was little to show for almost eight months of work.

'We're no closer to figuring out what they were chasing beyond their work in dismantling Majestic Twelve, but we're sure that they were not finished and that they stole artifacts from the ARIES building before they all disappeared from the Egyptian desert.'

'And we're sure that no nation other than Russia has any idea what occurred there before they vanished?'

'The location site was destroyed and all evidence lost or damaged. Egyptian forces did not detect the blast that destroyed the site due to an unusually powerful storm cell over the area at the time.'

The old man nodded, apparently satisfied. 'ARIES was shut down completely six months ago by the then president, presumably to prevent his successor from learning about what had occurred in case that successor turned out to be the kind of lunatic we all feared. That unfortunate eventuality has now come to pass and the CIA are being used as a weapon by the administration to uncover everything that we have fought to discover and understand.'

Now, Foxx looked up.

'Are you saying what I think you're saying?'

'Yes,' the old man assured him. 'The nature of our enemy has changed radically, in every sense. The administration's decision to encourage open relations with Russia and normalise departmental cooperation means that our rivals in Moscow may now have leverage against our intelligence services to gain access to our most classified operations.' The old man looked Foxx in the eye. 'The enemy is within us, and we must act accordingly. We must forge our own alliance with the very people we sought to destroy: the remaining members of the ARIES team.'

Foxx baulked. 'That will never happen. They sacrificed almost everything to bring down Majestic Twelve. The idea that they would even consider working with us is insane, and besides we have no leverage over them.'

'What were the names of the operatives missing in Egypt after ARIES was shut down?'

Foxx knew the names by heart, as he had spent much of the past few months monitoring watch stations around the world in the hope that one of them would surface.

'Ethan Warner, Nicola Lopez, Joseph Hellerman and Douglas Jarvis.'

The old man handed Foxx a series of photographs. The images showed a number of civilians whom Foxx recognized instantly. One was a palaeontologist by the name of Doctor Lucy Morgan.

'Where is Morgan now?' the old man asked.

'She works at the Chicago museum of natural history, but I don't know that this is the best way to try to get these people to trust us let alone help us to…'

'They have been missing for months,' the old man insisted, 'essentially fugitives from justice but in actual fact victims of programs classified far beyond even my knowledge. The only weakness we have not yet exploited is the one thing that they have been forced to leave behind.'

Foxx thought for a moment. 'This could backfire badly and lose us what little manoeuvring space we have left.'

'All the manoeuvring space we had left vanished the moment our elected leader revealed himself to be a tyrant determined to advance his own agenda over the welfare of his country. Our purpose was to discover how much these missing agents knew about Majestic Twelve's intentions and take over the work while discrediting them until any testimony from them would be considered farcical. Now, the only way we can keep this information out of the hands of the demagogue in our own White House is to force them to hand over what they know on the threat of losing their families for good. Locate Warner and his people, draw them out using their loved ones, and obtain what we need. No more loose ends from this point on. Eliminate them all if you have to. Dismissed.'

Foxx stood, turned and marched from the office, pursued by the sense that the insanity enveloping the White House was already spreading out into the intelligence community and beyond like an unstoppable cancer willing to kill its host in the name of domination.

***

V

Pulau Lobobo,

Indonesia

The dawn seared the horizon like a burnished blade spilling flickering embers onto the ocean as Ethan Warner jogged along a deserted beach on the island's north coast. There were few residents on the island, mostly located in three small towns perched on isolated spits of sand that emerged from the lush forest that enveloped most of the interior. Barely ten miles long and only two miles wide, Pulau Lobobo was an island on the edge of existence, far from the tourist routes of Sulawesi to the west.

Ethan ran at a leisurely pace, not wanting to over exert himself in the cool of the dawn only to become overheated later when the sun rose swiftly over the broad expanses of ocean to his left. The golden glow of the dawn bathed the palm trees with light, the nearby rollers glistening as they surged back and forth against the pristine sand.

Ethan had been on the island for almost six months and had developed a certainty that he would not be leaving unless he was dragged kicking and screaming by a train of wild horses. The idyllic beauty of the island and the calm nature of its residents rendered any other kind of lifestyle he had ever experienced a poor alternative. The simple fishing villages were comprised of homes built on bamboo stilts over crystalline waters so clear he had never seen his own reflection on the surface. For the past two months he had even allowed himself to forget about the Defense Intelligence Agency, Majestic Twelve and just about everything else that had dominated and shaped his life these eight years passed.

Ethan ran around the island's north east tip and followed the beaches south toward a small fishing village on the east coast that had become his home. Already the sun was rising up into a powder blue sky as he jogged through the dappled shadows of palm groves and across narrow strips of white sand that felt warm beneath his feet. Within just a few minutes he joined one of the narrow tracks that travelled off the coastline to avoid a few rocky outcrops and then re–joined the beach a half mile later where it curved around the inside edge of a secluded bay. Rows of homes on stilts were perched in the sparkling water and fishermen were just rowing out toward the deeper waters to the east.

'About time.'

Ethan jogged down to the waters' edge and strolled into the cooling water as he saw a familiar face leaning on a bamboo railing on one of the elevated homes. Nicola Lopez's smile was bright, her legs long and tanned and her thick black hair flowing over her bare shoulders like glistening oil.

'I don't see you out running every morning,' Ethan pointed out as he waded across to Lopez's home, situated alongside his own.

'I've got youth on my side.'

Ethan hauled himself up a ladder and onto the balcony where Lopez handed him a glass of chilled water. 'Anything?' she asked, as she did every morning.

'Nothing,' Ethan replied. 'No new boats, no encampments, nothing.'

'Excellent. In that case I shall brace myself for another day filled with nothing but sunbathing and idle strolls along the beach.'

'You take it easy now.'

'I'll cope.'

Ethan followed her off the balcony and back down into the water as they made their way to the nearby beach where a small number of industrious islanders were already unloading the morning's first catch onto sheets made from palm fronds. They greeted the two Americans with cheery waves and smiles, having long since grown accustomed to their presence on this speck of an island. Ethan had offered his services to the islanders when they had first arrived, helping to repair machinery and tools, while Lopez had taught the younger children to read and write in English and Spanish in return for food and somewhere to live. Their efforts to integrate as seamlessly as possible into this remote little village had gone down well with the elders and they were now accepted as a part of the community.

'Which section of beach will be enduring your backside this fine morning?' Lopez asked as she selected a pristine area and tested it for crabs hiding beneath the sand, before lying down and stretching out like a cat basking in the heat of the sun.

'You don't ever worry about when they'll come back?' he asked as he sat down alongside her.

'Nope.'

'It's gonna happen one day.'

'Ethan, don't spoil my ambience.'

'Just sayin'.'

'And I'm just ignorin'. I'm not going anywhere even if Doug Jarvis comes walking up out of the water right there in the damned bay.'

Ethan lay back on the sand and put his hands behind his head. 'I just don't think you should keep ignoring what's happening in the world. We still have a job to do and it's not finished yet.'

Lopez, her eyes closed, did not look in his direction as she replied.

'Be quiet, I've got a whole lot of gratuitously unnecessary sleeping to do. I think I'm safe in saying that there's absolutely no danger of Jarvis or anybody else showing up today.'

Ethan shrugged and then heard a riotous flapping of wings as a flock of birds suddenly took flight from the forest to their right. Ethan looked up at them as a deep throbbing noise reverberated through his chest and then from behind the treeline a huge aircraft burst into view. Its long, straight wings were painted a brilliant white that flashed in the sunlight as it thundered over the bay, twin piston radial–engines mounted above the wings and clattering noisily. Ethan recognized the aircraft type straight away, a vintage PBY Catalina seaplane whose pilot was well known to both Ethan and Lopez.

'You were saying?' Ethan said as the big seaplane turned away from the beach and began circling out in preparation for a landing.

'Tell me I didn't hear all that,' Lopez uttered without opening her eyes.

Ethan stood up and watched as the big Catalina turned through a full circle, deploying her flaps and outriggers before descending and touching down on the surface of the ocean a hundred fifty yards off the beach.

The aircraft slowed and turned for one of the larger empty jetties around the bay as Ethan reluctantly walked toward it. The Catalina's big engines sounded deafeningly loud to Ethan after months of hearing nothing harsher than the occasional screech of jungle birds. Even the last serious storm they'd experienced had passed by a hundred miles to the east, the thunder and lightning mere distant rumbles across the endless ocean.

Ethan caught a pair of mooring lines tossed from the cockpit and tied them loosely to the jetty as the pilot mercifully cut the fuel to the engines and the infernal din clattered into silence. The odors of metal and grease and aviation fuel seemed harsh to Ethan, grim reminders of the life that he had left behind, and he could hear the metallic engines tinkling as they cooled and contracted.

'Warner! Damn me if there's nowhere you can't hide!'

Arnie Hackett hauled himself from a top hatch above the Catalina's heavily glazed cockpit to slide down the fuselage and onto the jetty. Ethan shook his hand as a bleary-eyed Lopez joined them and looked the pilot up and down.

'Arnie, lookin' good.'

'Not nearly as good as you, Nicola,' Arnie replied as he hugged her.

'I'll give you a million bucks to get out of here and tell nobody that you found us,' she said as she released him.

Arnie offered her an apologetic look as he gestured back toward the Catalina and they saw an old man climb out of the main hatch and step onto the jetty. Spritely for his age, Ethan felt that he saw a weariness in Doug Jarvis's expression as he walked up to them with his hands in his pockets and a smile on his face, his white hair bright in the morning sunlight.

'Ethan, Nicola, you're looking well.'

'I take it that something interesting must have occurred for you to have travelled all the way out here.' Lopez uttered, not attempting to hide her disdain for the unwelcome interruption.

'You could say that,' Jarvis replied and then looked about him at the nearby fishermen and women working on their nets. 'Is there someplace we can go?'

'Someplace secure?' Lopez snorted. 'We're a billion miles from anywhere, what do you think's going to happen? Have the CIA learned to teach birds of paradise to eavesdrop?'

'You'd be surprised,' Jarvis replied. 'They once trained ravens to deliver listening devices hidden in broken pieces of roof tile to ledges outside embassies, and surgically inserted similar mechanical bugs into a cat that lived in the Kremlin.'

Lopez didn't respond as Ethan gestured to the beach stretching around the bay, far from the prying eyes of ravens and rogue cats. They walked in silence until they were well beyond earshot of the villagers before Jarvis spoke once more, the gentle whisper of the rollers an effective foil to any listening device that might conceivably have been placed in the area.

'There's been a breakthrough in the search and we want you both to go check it out.'

Ethan felt his shoulders sag at the prospect of returning to civilization once again and confronting the dark forces that he knew were still searching for their lost billions.

'Can't Garrett hire somebody else for this?' Lopez asked. 'I mean, I know he's down to his last few trillion dollars and all but there must be other people willing to chase this down for you.'

'Not people whom we can trust,' Jarvis countered. 'We've put Lucy Morgan on this and she was in India the last time we spoke but she's been off the radar ever since.'

Ethan's eyes narrowed. 'She's missing?'

Jarvis shook his head. 'I don't think so, but you know how she likes to go off on her own.'

Ethan nodded. Doctor Lucy Morgan's disappearance eight years before in the wilds of Israel's Negev Desert had been the first time that Ethan had been contracted by Jarvis to work for the DIA and the first time he had met Lopez. In those few years they had conducted no less than eleven investigations for the secretive ARIES unit before it had been closed down by Homeland Security just months previously.

'Did she find anything?' Lopez asked, her natural curiosity peaked.

Jarvis perched himself on a rock as he replied.

'As part of her investigations conducted after you and your team were pulled out of Egypt, Lucy was pursuing something that she had noticed about the artefact we recovered from the Black Knight satellite.'

Ethan recalled the extraordinary device that they had recovered from Antarctica a couple of years previously, located inside the remains of a satellite that had been orbiting the earth for some thirteen thousand years. Dubbed the *Black Knight*, the satellite had been a staple of conspiracy theories since it had first been detected by Nikola Tesla over a century before and later classified by air forces around the globe.

'Lucy had noticed that the projection we witnessed from the artefact contained an icon that she recognized from other archaeological studies conducted around the world, and she began a search starting with the oldest examples of that icon that she could find.'

Ethan frowned. 'What does this icon look like?'

Jarvis pulled a piece of paper from his pocket and handed it to Ethan. Printed upon the page was a series of three concentric circles, with the whole being bisected by a vertical and horizontal line in the manner of an inverted Crucifix, the vertical element poking from the top of the rings.

Lopez glanced at Jarvis. 'Lucy was looking for ancient carvings of a rifle scope's sights?'

Jarvis didn't reply, instead looking at Ethan.

'What you're looking at there is one of the world's oldest surviving icons from the ruins of an ancient city in India, which is where Lucy was last headed when I spoke with her. She wasn't aware of the precise location of the city but had obtained a guide to lead her there.'

'And this icon, what does it represent?' Lopez asked.

'It is believed to be associated with a city that we now refer to as Atlantis.'

'Atlantis,' Lopez echoed, 'as in Plato's lost city, and not the one at Caesar's Palace in Vegas.'

'The same,' Jarvis confirmed. 'This could be the break we've been looking for, the final piece in the puzzle. This is what connects almost every other investigation you did under my command at ARIES with what Majestic Twelve spent so long searching for: the actual connection between mankind and the strange visitors recorded in the myths and legends of virtually every ancient civilization that ever lived. This is our end game, the discovery of this city and perhaps the answers mankind has been seeking for our entire existence.'

***

VI

The interior of the beach house was cooler than the heat of the sun outside already beating down from a flawless blue sky. Ethan revelled in the shadows of the stilted hut, the water below cooling the interior and the sea breeze maintaining a constant and cooling flow of air.

Jarvis had set up a small satellite dish connected to a display screen now standing on a table in Ethan's hut as a connection was established with Joseph Hellerman, a former DIA scientist and technology expert who had lost his job after ARIES had been shut down and was now employed by Rhys Garrett, their billionaire benefactor. The bearded youth's visage flickered into view on the screen as Jarvis stood back and Hellerman waved.

'Hi guys, hope you've been enjoying your vacation.'

Lopez smiled brightly back at him. 'Wish you were here Jo, what have you got for us?'

Hellerman's face was alive with excitement. 'Have you seen the icon yet?'

'Yeah, Doug showed us. What's the big deal?'

'This,' Hellerman replied, 'is the big deal.'

The screen changed to show an image of what looked like a large stone pillar that had clearly been shaped by human hands, standing in the middle of what looked like a jungle somewhere. Somebody had placed a metal rule alongside the structure to reveal its height as being around three feet. At the top of the rock Ethan could see a carving that matched the printed image Jarvis had handed to him on the beach, while below the carving was a series of what looked like ancient texts inscribed into the rock.

'It's a rock,' Lopez said flatly. 'With a picture on it.'

Hellerman's enthusiasm was not dulled by her dismissal of the evidence.

'It's not just the imagery that matches what we're after,' he said. 'It's the text.'

'Does it say "turn right for Atlantis"?'

'It's Hindu,' Hellerman explained, 'and it speaks of the legends of Lanka, a city described in the Hindu texts of the *Ramayana*. The saga is the story upon which Homer's *Iliad* is based, and concerns the story of many wars over a great capital city that eventually sank into the ocean. The story that we would all recognize now is that of Troy.'

'You're saying that Homer's work was plagiarised from earlier Hindu works?' Ethan asked in surprise.

'Not plagiarised,' Jarvis corrected him, 'but referenced as a myth, and that this same story is the basis and reference for virtually every cultural and religious story ever written since.'

'But that stone might not be old enough to qualify as a precursor to every other source of legend,' Lopez pointed out. 'And I thought that it was Atlantis that was destroyed by the ocean and that Troy was conquered by the Greeks?'

Now, Hellerman's true excitement began to shine through.

'Doctor Morgan tested the soils in which she found the stone, the sedimentary layers in which it was buried. The tests came back three days ago and confirmed that this artefact was located within sedimentary layers dated at some twelve thousand years old.'

Now Ethan started to take notice. Throughout their investigations, he and Lopez had repeatedly found compelling evidence that the officially recognized dawn of civilization as being some four to five thousand years ago was likely an error and that complex civilizations far older than those in the Fertile Crescent may have flourished millennia before.

Hellerman gestured to a photograph of the stele beside him as he talked.

'Homer's Troy was conquered by the Greeks but later fell into disrepair and was claimed by the ocean. Plato's Atlantis was supposedly consumed by waves commanded by an angry Zeus, whose wrath had been driven by the societal collapse of morals in mankind's civilization and the fraternizing of lesser gods with mortal women.'

'Sounds familiar,' Ethan said.

'Even the gods can't resist a good woman,' Lopez pointed out.

'It sounds familiar because it is,' Hellerman said. 'The vast majority of ancient origin stories contain a narrative involving the growth of a great civilization which then becomes too powerful for its own good and a threat to the gods, who summarily destroy that civilization with a natural disaster of one kind or another. The big issue for modern society in the west is that we tend to assume that the biblical narrative is the oldest and first instance of such legends, but in fact the opposite is true. When the Hebrews wrote their Torah, the Old Testament, they simply copied the legends of far older civlizations and adapted them for their own purposes.'

Jarvis picked up the threads of Hellerman's story.

'The *Pentateuct*, or "Five Scrolls", are the first five books of the Bible as supposedly recorded by Moses and relate the story of Genesis and the familiar legends. However even there Moses points out that he is recounting legends from a time of much greater antiquity that would have been preserved in songs and oral tales, as there was no writing at the time until the rise of Sumerian civilizations many thousands of years later.'

'Although there is no historical evidence that a man named Moses ever lived,' Hellerman added, 'it is clear that *somebody* wrote the words down and were referring to older legends which we can easily identify as coming from the far east.'

'That'll go down well in the Bible Belt,' Lopez murmured. 'What did Lucy dig up about these older versions of the legend?'

'The stories are well known to researchers,' Hellerman explained, 'but rarely revealed in education because of the influence of churches across the world, who actively campaign to keep these kinds of revelations for fear of their power being further eroded by the spread of secularism. Most religious educators in the west teach children to believe only in the bible and that all other histories, regardless of evidence, should be considered heresy and false testimony. The truth of course is that the bible is merely a copy of so many older texts, and the flood myth of Genesis is one of the most striking examples of that. The Greeks copied their legends of Atlas and Atlantis from the Hindu stories of Atalas, the sunken paradise of the Hindus. As in the Greek traditions, Atalas – whose name is Sanskrit and means "Pillar" – was deemed to be the "Pillar of the World", just as was Atlas in Greece.'

'The *Mahabharata*, the other great Hindu classical saga that completes the *Ramayana*,' Jarvis said, 'tells of the mighty empire of Krishna and its destruction in the great war between the Lunars and the Solars. Hastinapura, the capital of the Pandu empire, was the "City of the Pillars". The *Mahabharata* also tells of Dvaraka, the capital of Krishna, located in an island in the middle of the seas. Krishna's capital, Dvaraka, sunk underseas when the divine hero died in the great war, more or less in the way Atlantis went under, according to Plato.'

'And Krishna,' Hellerman added with a knowing smile, 'was born of a virgin on December 25th when a great king slew all new born sons in the region. Krishna grew to become a great leader and prophet, was captured and killed before rising from the dead three days later. That legend was recorded thousands of years before Christianity was conceived.'

'I'll cancel my church subscription,' Ethan said. 'Any more?'

'Dravidian traditions speak of a vast sunken continent towards the south–east of India called Rutas. The Dravidas claim to have moved to India from that continent when it sank underseas in a great cataclysm. The Phoenicians claimed, like the Dravidas, to have come from an "Island of Fire" located beyond the Indian Ocean. Even the Egyptians spoke of the mysterious Hanebut, a people who lived beyond the Indian Ocean in the region of Amenti. The name of the Hanebut means "People of the Haze" or "People of the Pillar". This enigmatic people was said to live under a dark haze which the light of the sun never penetrated. The Egyptians affirmed that the region of the Hanebut was real and could indeed be visited, as they often did. Most ancient nations spoke of a similar region in the overseas covered by a dark haze or mist that can only be described today as volcanic smoke.'

'So you think that Atlantis has some connection with a volcano?' Lopez hazarded.

'That's what Lucy was thinking,' Hellerman went on. 'The various Atlantis legends all describe a city that lives under a cloud of some kind and almost all of the ancients describe their version of Atlantis not as some modern marvel but as a city of flames and smoke, a city that is feared as well as revered. The Romans and their predecessors, the Etruscans, had traditions concerning their coming from an overseas land submerged under the seas in a cataclysm shortly after or during a great war. They were led by Aeneas, and came in a great fleet of ships from a region located outside the Pillars of Hercules. Even the Amerindians of the Brazilian Amazon such as the Tucanos, Desanas and Barasanas claimed to have come from a sunken Paradise, destroyed and submerged by the Flood.'

Ethan listened as Hellerman spoke of the enormous number of ancient civilizations who bore legends of their ancestors as having travelled from some distant, mysterious land consumed first by flames and then by the oceans. All over the world, from the Amazonian jungle to the plains of Babylon to the sandy deserts of Egypt and the Near East, there were mythical allusions to sunken golden realms that are often likened to Hell or Hades, the Realms of the Dead. The *Suvarna–dvipa* or "Golden Isles" of the Hindus, the *Chryse Chersonesos* or "Golden Peninsula" of the Greeks, the *Aigeia* of Poseidon, the *Aiaia* of the Argonauts, the *Eldorado* of Amerindian traditions, the *Apsu* or "House of the Apsu" of Babylonian traditions, the subterranean *Vara* of Yima, the Flood Hero of the Persians and more. They all derived from the myth of Atlantis and their true source was the Hindu traditions such as those recounted in the *Ramayana* and the *Mahabharata*, which Lucy had been investigating when she had suddenly fallen silent.

Jarvis leaned against the beach house wall as he spoke.

'We sent Lucy out under the cover of her research projects for the Chicago Natural History Museum to start searching for any common threads in the story of Atlantis that might shed some light on whether the city actually existed and if so where it might be found. Obviously, people have been searching for Atlantis for millennia and so far they've come up empty, but Lucy located this emblem in three separate locations on the coast of India and was able to tie them to actual physical towns or cities that have long since been lost to history. She went off to find them and that's where we lost contact with her.'

'When did we last hear from her and where was she?' he asked.

'Rampara, India,' Hellerman said. 'Lucy mentioned that she had made some sort of connection with an ancient Greek manuscript, some kind of codex that she was trying to unravel. Arnie's flying boat is within range of the region and it should be child's play for you to slip into the country unobserved and find out where she went. Her last contact before us is an archaeological expert who has been excavating sites around that part of India's coast for the past thirty years. I'll send his details.'

Ethan turned to Lopez expectantly. 'You up for this?'

'*No*,' Lopez uttered as though it were obvious, which he realized that it was. 'You sure it can't wait one more day?'

Jarvis smiled and pushed off the wall. 'I'm afraid that as unjust as it may seem, one of the world's greatest discoveries can't wait for you to top up your tan, Nicola. Arnie will get you out to Rampara and will fly you around for as long as you need. We'll stay in touch via Rhys Garrett's yacht which will follow you up there but remain a discreet distance away to avoid risking any connection between yourselves and the rest of our operation.'

'What about Mitchell?' Ethan asked, recalling that the towering, sepulchral former assassin who had once served Majestic Twelve was now working for Jarvis. 'Will he be helping us out with this one?'

'Mitchell is otherwise engaged,' Jarvis replied enigmatically. 'Rest assured he will join us as soon as he can. Go, now, and find Lucy. She might be about to reveal to the world something even more astounding than the remains she found in Israel all those years ago, and we're not the only ones who will want to be there when she does. Mat' Zelmya in Russia are following similar leads to us, and we suspect that they're closely allied with elements of the American government and may be willing to trade information and resources in order to locate us and the money we liberated from Majestic Twelve. Watch your backs folks, because this time *everyone's* looking for us.'

***

VII

Capitol Hill,

Washington DC

Allison Pierce pulled her jacket closer about her and yanked her collar up to protect her neck against a bitter wind gusting off the streets nearby beneath a featureless slate gray sky. She had been standing on the steps of Congress for almost an hour but still had not caught sight of the man she had been waiting for.

She glanced down the steps to where her companion awaited, tucked out of sight behind stone pillars that flanked the entrance to the Capitol. He peeked out at her but otherwise did not move, something in his grasp hidden beneath a thick winter coat.

Allison checked her watch once again. The congressional committee should have completed its final meeting and disbanded almost an hour ago. To her amazement, she was the only person on the steps of the building who seemed to have any idea of what was occurring within, that this was one of the most momentous days in modern democracy. Yet there had not been a single news piece about the meeting, not a single station carrying the story.

Allison hugged herself against the cold and for the first time that day wondered whether she had made some mistake and got the wrong day, or that perhaps this story really wasn't worth covering. Then she recalled the countless hours she had spent pursuing leads, the endless blocking of her work by her superiors and the efforts made by nameless souls to dissuade her interest in the meeting. She steeled herself against the cold once again and resolved to see it through to the…

'*He's coming out.*'

The voice of Allison's companion crackled in her ear piece and she looked up to the Capitol entrance to see Congressman Milton Keyes stride outside with his secretary on one side and a security guard on the other. Squat, overweight and embued with the arrogant air of a lawmaker above the law, Keyes struck out toward her without a care in the world. Allison waited until they were descending the steps, as far from the sanctuary of the Capitol building as they were from the glossy black limousine that was pulling up at the bottom of the steps, and then she pounced.

'Congressman Keyes, Allison Pierce, KNW news.'

Keyes glanced at her and the cameraman who leaped out from behind the stone pillars nearby, then he averted his eyes and began to hurry down the steps as he angled away from her approach.

'Congressman Keyes won't be taking questions today,' his secretary informed Allison.

Allison hurried to keep pace as her cameraman deftly walked backwards down the steps with his camera trained on the congressman.

'What has been the conclusions of the committee on the Majestic Twelve scandal congressman?' Allison demanded. 'The public were promised an open and frank review of what happened eight months ago and yet the final findings of the investigation have taken place today without any fanfare. There has been no opportunity for the people to receive an explanation as to how a group of industrialists could have made off with billions of dollars of tax–payer's money?'

'The three billion dollars of public money was returned to the people as reported last summer, Miss Pierce,' the secretary replied with a smile so forced it looked as though she were chewing a wasp. 'Everybody knows that.'

'Yes, but what they don't know is that three billion dollars is just a fraction of the money found to be missing from government coffers over the past twenty years. What happened to the rest of the money, congressman? We know it's still out there so why isn't anything now being done to recover it?'

Congressman Keyes glanced at his security guard and the muscular, shaven headed man pushed his way forward to block Allison's way.

'Is that where we are now, congressman?' Allison called as her cameraman continued to film. 'Blocking the press whenever they ask questions that you don't like? Is the administration's hatred of the media now poisoning the legislative branch too now? Or will anything I say now be dismissed as fake news, like any other inconvenient truths that the administration and its cronies don't want the people to hear or think about?'

'Congressman Keyes won't be answering any questions at this time,' the secretary repeated. 'Any further pressurisation or provocation will be considered harassment!'

'Is it harassment to ask a congressman for the very information he promised to deliver to the people of this country months ago?' Allison snapped as she pushed against the security guard. 'Or is that the free press merely doing our job and an elected official failing to do theirs?'

Congressman Keyes reached his car and the security guard moved to open it for him. Allison grabbed the opportunity the brief respite offered and she ducked left, cutting in behind the congressman and shoving her microphone between him and the vehicle's interior.

'Are the people whom you vowed to serve no longer entitled to a response to their questions, or the fulfilment of promises that you made to them on live television, congressman?'

The security guard shifted position and pushed the microphone aside as the lawmaker virtually hurled himself into the car and the guard slammed the door shut behind him. Allison made the most of the moment as she called into the glossy black mirrored window.

'Are you shutting the door on the people you promised to serve, congressman? Are you now just the lackey of a corrupt administration? Has America now become the kind of state the rest of the world fears it has become?'

The security guard climbed into the front passenger seat of the vehicle and within moments it was gone, pulling swiftly into the flow of traffic and vanishing as a squall of thin snow began to fall from the bitter sky overhead. Allison turned to her cameraman and saw him shut the camera off, his features dejected.

'You should have known better Ali, they were never going to talk to us. This whole thing has been a whitewash from day one.'

Allison grinned as she tucked her microphone away and they headed toward their car nearby.

'On the contrary, it couldn't have gone better.'

'What? They said nothing, gave us nothing. What the hell's good about that?'

'Curiosity,' Allison replied. 'If Keyes had been smart about it he would have spoken to us, hid behind some kind of legalese or just claimed that there was nothing to hide and that the findings of the meeting would be released soon. Instead, he brushed us off using force and refused to say anything, which to any sane mind means he's hiding something.'

The cameraman sighed and shook his head.

'I don't know, Ali. Ever since the new administration took power they've been cutting out broadcasters from press conferences who print anything that doesn't show them in a good light to the public. You know as well as I do that they'll do everything they can to prevent us from releasing anything that can be construed as negative press.'

'Good,' Allison replied. 'As hard as they push to silence us the harder we'll push back to be heard. This is how fascism once took hold in Europe Pete, the attempts of a governing power to pressure or coerce the free press and the sewing of the seeds of doubt in the public mind about anything they read in the news. If the people come to believe that the only truth that matters is that which they hear from the halls of power, then their democracy is already lost.'

Allison walked to their vehicle and unlocked it as Pete moved to the trunk to stow the valuable camera safely before joining her. As she got into the driver's seat she heard the camera thump heavily down.

'Hey, take it easy back there will you? That camera's this months' pay check for you and I!'

Pete moved around to the passenger door as she started the engine, and then he climbed into the car with her and she realized that it was not Pete at all. The barrel of a 9mm parabellum pressed into her side and a pair of dark eyes glared silently into hers. The man spoke with a deep, almost solemn voice, no hint of a threat in his tones and yet his voice all the more threatening for it.

'Drive, now, or your friend in the trunk will pay the consequences.'

Allison stared for a moment into the big man's eyes and she knew that the threat was serious. She pushed the vehicle into drive and then eased out into the flow of traffic as she kept her eyes straight ahead.

'Congressman Keyes won't get away with this,' she said. 'I don't care what the administration thinks it can get away with, the forceful abduction of a journalist in the process of reporting on...'

'Silence.'

The word was spoken without force and yet Allison obeyed instinctively as the car wound its way out of the district, the armed man offering monosyllabic directions as they travelled south out of Anacostia, crossing the river into Maryland toward Suitland. The gunman directed her to an anonymous spot near the Forestville center, the rear of a parking lot where trash gusted on the cold wind and where few pedestrians strayed.

Allison slowed the car down and pulled in alongside an abandoned lock up. The gunman reached across and switched the engine off before he yanked the keys from the ignition and slipped them into his pocket.

Allison kept staring straight ahead out of the windshield, the wheel held in a death grip as she blurted out more words.

'If you kill me it will only draw more attention to my work and expose even more of the corruption festering right here in the nation's capitol! Others will take my place, far more of us than you could possibly silence and they will…'

'Look at me.'

Allison hesitated, deeply aware of the gun pressed deep into her side. It nudged her a little harder and she turned her head with an effort and looked at the man. Dark skin, soulless black eyes devoid of any compassion that she could detect, salt and pepper hair cropped short above a bull neck and broad shoulders. Judging by the way he was crammed into her car, he was probably six four and weighed two hundred fifty pounds, big enough to crush her with one hand and…

'You need to learn to shut up, because right now all you're going to do is get yourself killed.'

Allison's lip trembled along with her voice but she lifted her chin a little.

'I'm not afraid of you people. I won't be stopped from doing my job and…'

'See what I mean?'

Allison stopped talking as she stared at the man and saw something now in his gaze, a bemusement perhaps, as though he were assessing her. The thought that he might simply be a drug–addled hijacker looking for cash for his next fix crossed her mind, but his clothes were smart and he was clean shaven and…

'You assume that I'm working for Congressman Keyes and you assume that you've been targeted in some way for assassination,' he rumbled at her.

'You're ex–military, dressed like a security team member, you have a gun pressed against me and you've locked my cameraman in the trunk,' Allison snapped back. 'Excuse me for jumping to *conclusions*.'

Now, the man smiled a little, still watching her with interest.

'And your reports are being broadcast but nobody's listening,' the man replied. 'You have a story but nobody wants to hear it because it doesn't stand out. It's just one more tale of corruption in the halls of power that people have come to expect. Nobody trusts a politician these days, so what difference will it make?'

Allison was about to answer the question with her usual fiery patriotism when a new thought crossed her mind.

'Who are you?'

The big man gently eased the pistol away from her side and slid it into a shoulder holster beneath his coat as he replied.

'Now you're thinking straight,' he said. 'My name is Aaron Mitchell.'

Allison frowned expectantly. 'I don't know you.'

'And that's your problem, right there. You're reporting on something and you know almost nothing about it. You don't even know about the people involved.'

Allison's eyes widened as she stared at him. 'You know about Majestic Twelve?'

Mitchell watched her for a long moment with that sombre gaze.

'I worked for them for thirty years.'

'Doing what?'

Mitchell sucked in a deep lungful of air as he glanced outside at the abandoned lot. 'Clearing up issues.'

Allison stared at the big man for a moment and then her journalist's instinct kicked in.

'Prove it.'

Mitchell smiled a faint, enigmatic smile as he returned his gaze to her. 'Note this down: Russian billionaire Yuri Polkov goes missing in Peru; Stanley Meyer's fusion cage; computers that can read minds in real–time in Japan; the Black Knight satellite.'

Allison grabbed a notebook that she always carried with her and scribbled furiously. 'I've never heard of any of this?'

'That's because the congressional committee hasn't either,' Mitchell replied. 'Congressman Keyes can't talk to you because he's as involved in what has happened over the past year as any of the cabal of Majestic Twelve. He is towing the line for others and will be hoping that people like you will eventually disappear.'

'That's bullcrap,' Allison uttered. 'Keyes is a congressman and has no history of any kind of corruption issues that…'

'He will maintain a low profile over the coming weeks and wait for it all to blow over, which it will because the White House will divert attention away from it with more conventional scandals designed to keep the press occupied with sensationalist stories instead of the really important ones.'

Allison's eyes widened with every word that Mitchell said.

'You could just be a very clever man but a fantasist none the less. I'm going to need more than this.'

'And you'll get it, but right now your job is to stop talking about Majestic Twelve. Let them think they've silenced you, that you've given up.'

'What, let them get away with it?!'

'Let them *think* they have,' Mitchell corrected her. 'Then, when they forget about you, I will hit them where it hurts and you're going to help me.'

Allison's eyes narrowed.

'A cynic might suggest that this is all a ruse to get me out of the public eye so that you can kill me and nobody will notice.'

Mitchell nodded.

'And now you're thinking straight again,' he said. 'These people, the things that you're digging into, they're extremely dangerous and you're right that if they think you're getting too close to the truths they're trying to hide, they'll seek to destroy you, literally. What will happen next is that you'll be discredited, probably ousted from your job and your reputation tarnished so that anything you do say will be ignored even if people do somehow get to hear about it.'

'This isn't some cable drama.'

Mitchell turned to look directly at her. 'How many washed–up conspiracy theorists have you heard blabbing about free energy devices or UFO encounters?'

'Tons, but...'

'Have you ever taken any of them seriously?'

'Well, no, but...'

'That's why you need to stop shouting about all this until you have something so concrete that they cannot consider taking you out, as to do so would only draw even more suspicion upon themselves.'

Allison stared at Mitchell for a long beat, but she sensed no evidence of deception.

'Are you serious?'

'What I'm saying is that you can't finish this job if you're at risk of being discredited or killed half way through it. If you're in, you're in to the end.'

Allison sensed the finality in Mitchell's tones, but she nodded once. 'I'm in.'

'Good,' Mitchell said. 'My apologies to your cameraman, who you may say nothing about this to. You were carjacked and your money and purse stolen before being left here. I will contact you soon with instructions and more evidence to support my claims and reveal what Majestic Twelve were really about. Right now, research what I've given you and one further person of great importance.'

'Who?'

'Douglas Jarvis.'

Before Allison could write the name down the car keys landed in her lap and Mitchell was out of the car and gone.

***

VIII

Kutiyana, Porbandar District,

India

Ethan could not recall a time when his senses had been so assaulted by such a variety of noises, sights and smells that swirled in a heady aroma through the streets of one of the oldest cities on the face of the planet.

Located near the Indian coast and the Arabian Sea, the district of Kutiyana was synonymous with an abandoned ancient temple building hundreds of years old, known as the Kutiyana Madresa for whom there were no builder's records or ownership paperwork. Inhabited for thousands of years, the city was a dazzling mixture of shanty towns, monumental temples and hordes of animals sharing the land with the people.

'Ethan, there's a goat in the street.'

Lopez gestured to where a small, horned goat was wandering along a narrow alley nibbling at fruits perched precariously on the edge of a market stall outside a small shop. Ethan saw the animal, and others like it, cyclists and pedestrians passing them by with barely a glance as they walked down the dusty street beneath the burning sun. Small tuk–tuk rickshaws with clattering engines rattled by in clouds of exhaust fumes that billowed on the hot air, the drivers' sounding their horns in an ever–present chorus to clear cyclists, goats and other animals from their path.

'It's this way,' Ethan said as he consulted a small map and led Lopez toward a narrow alley where the odors seemed intensified by the confined walls.

They eased their way down the alley, passing an old woman sitting on a doorstep who watched them silently as they passed, her eyes rheumy and most of her teeth missing, and then a man smoking a hookah who appeared to barely notice their presence.

Ethan spotted a battered old sign dangling above a doorframe of peeled paint and matched it to the directions he had been given.

'Apparently, that's the home of the specialist Lucy was talking to.'

Lopez regarded the tiny entrance with disdain as they approached, the door barely hanging from its hinges and the walls of the abode probably as ancient as the city itself.

'You really think that some guy living in an alley in southern India is the key to finding the city of Atlantis?'

Ethan shrugged as they walked inside. 'Lucy obviously did, and she's the scientist.'

The interior of the building smelled of dust and oil seeds and the sickly scent of a hookah that stood upon a nearby counter. The walls were smothered in painted images, some of them lithographs from what Ethan figured was the eighteenth century, the drawings featuring British infantry bearing long barrelled muskets guarding docks filled with the vessels of the Dutch East India Company.

'Man, this place has been here a while,' Lopez whispered.

Ethan had not been taught the history of the rest of the world while at school in Chicago, but he had later learned that India had been a thriving country thousands of years before the founding fathers had even set foot upon American soil, and that the British had later controlled an Empire that spanned half the globe, larger than any other in the history of mankind.

'This doesn't look like a museum,' Lopez said. 'It's more like a trinket shop they forgot to dust for a couple of decades.'

The sound of shuffling feet attracted their attention and an old man hobbled into the front of the building to meet them with his hands pressed together beneath his chin as he bowed slightly at the waist.

'Greetings,' he said in perfectly pronounced English. 'I am Professor Raz Singh, can I help you?'

Ethan stepped forward. 'We're looking for a mutual friend, Doctor Lucy Morgan.'

'Ah yes,' Raz said, 'you must be Ethan and Nicola, yes?'

'She mentioned us?' Lopez asked.

'She told me to speak only to a tall American and a little Mexican,' Raz replied matter-of-factly. 'She said that where I would find one, the other would appear as if by magic.'

Ethan smiled wryly. 'She knows us too well. Do you know where she is?'

'I do not,' Raz replied, 'I know only where she has gone.'

'I don't get it,' Lopez said.

'Come,' Raz insisted, 'there is much that Lucy wished you to know.'

Ethan exchanged glances with Lopez, who shrugged and followed the old man through a battered old muslin sheet that concealed an entrance to a narrow passage that wound its way through the building. Ethan's shoulders brushed the walls as he followed Raz out into a tiny courtyard entirely concealed by the four walls of the surrounding buildings. Above, a square of hard blue sky looked down upon a single tree inside the courtyard, upon which chirped a flock of tiny, excitable birds.

Raz walked across to an old reclining chair beside a table and eased his tired frame into it as he gestured to two more chairs nearby. Ethan and Lopez sat down as the old man leaned forward, resting his elbows on his knees as he spoke softly.

'Welcome to my museum.'

Lopez raised an eyebrow. 'The museum? We're in the courtyard.'

Raz reached up with one hand and tapped his temples. 'The greatest of all museums is the one we carry with us, Nicola. It holds all that we know, and all that we would wish others not to know.'

'Lucy came here looking for information on the whereabouts of Atlantis,' Ethan said. 'We haven't heard from her in a long time and we're concerned for her safety.'

Raz nodded as he spoke. 'Lucy is not in any danger, for where she walks is far from where the Russians will be looking for her.'

'The Russians?' Lopez uttered. 'They're here?'

'They came here two days ago,' Raz replied with a calm smile. 'They were looking for Lucy and they were looking for both of you, too.'

Ethan leaned forward. 'Did they say why?'

'No. I sent them packing with a cover story about Lucy looking for information on the Indus civilizations and such like, but I didn't specify.'

'They didn't harm or threaten you?' Ethan asked, concern in his eyes now.

'No,' Raz said with a faint smile. 'They saw me as a weak old man with little to hide and no stomach to do so. It's why I don't keep any evidence of my work on Atlantis out there in plain sight, and instead keep it all up here in my mind.'

'What happens if you lose your mind?' Lopez asked. 'It happens to Ethan all the time.'

'That's where researchers like Lucy come in, able to learn from me and continue my work, and that is what I must relate to you now. Lucy was being followed while she worked here, and for that reason she decided to do her best to disappear.'

'We're all ears,' Ethan said.

'Most people are familiar with the basic tale of Atlantis, taken as it is from Plato's *Critias*.' Raz's eyes blurred as he recounted Plato's writings from two and a half thousand years ago: "For it is related in our records how once upon a time your State stayed the course of a mighty host, which, starting from a distant point in the Atlantic Ocean, was insolently advancing to attack the whole of Europe, and Asia to boot. For the ocean there was at that time navigable; for in front of the mouth which you Greeks call, as you say, 'the Pillars of Heracles,' there lay an island which was larger than Libya and Asia together; and it was possible for the travelers of that time to cross from it to the other islands, and from the islands to the whole of the continent over against them which encompasses that veritable ocean. For all that we have here, lying within the mouth of which we speak, is evidently a haven having a narrow entrance; but that yonder is a real ocean, and the land surrounding it may most rightly be called, in the fullest and truest sense, a continent. Now in this island of Atlantis there existed a confederation of kings, of great and marvelous power, which held sway over all the island, and over many other islands also and parts of the continent."'

'So far, so abnormal,' Lopez said. 'I understood that it has long since been proven beyond any doubt that there is no such missing continent anywhere.'

'Correct,' Raz agreed with her, slapping one thigh in delight. 'There is no such continent and there never was. Plato's reference to the city of Atlantis is the first recorded instance of its mention, and the name suggests of course that it was located somewhere in the Atlantic Ocean, beyond the Pillars of Hercules, the name the ancient Greeks gave to what we now call the Straits of Gibraltar.'

'And I sense that you have a different take on all of that?' Ethan guessed.

Raz shook his head.

'No, not really. Most scholars who take the existence of an Atlantis seriously assume that Plato was somehow mistaken in his description of the city and its location. But Plato is quite precise in his description of the city itself, not just in terms of its appearance of three concentric rings but also its dimensions. No, I don't think that Plato got it wrong.'

'Well, what do you think then?' Lopez asked.

'I think that Plato was faithfully describing what he had *heard* about,' Raz said, 'and that it is modern scholars who have been making a mistake in assuming that Plato's reference is the very first time that the city is mentioned in the historical record.'

'Earlier references,' Ethan said. 'A researcher friend of ours called Hellerman told us of references to a city from which all men originated that was swallowed by the ocean.'

'That's right,' Raz enthused. 'Plato was merely recounting a legend that had already been circulating for centuries, perhaps even millennia, and he then put his own spin on it with Athen's victory over the city which was then submerged beneath the waves by vengeful gods and so on.'

'Hellerman also mentioned that many referred to the city as being beneath clouds of smoke, that it was considered a land of the dead, Hades even,' Lopez added.

'This is perhaps true,' Raz replied, 'or perhaps it is more accurate to say that it was true *at the time*. We cannot say much about geological activity around a site that we have not yet located, but we can rely upon some of the iconography associated with the city's legend to inform us of its existence deep in humanity's past. You are familiar with the symbol of the great city, which has existed since ancient times as three concentric rings with a cross in the center?'

'Yeah, Hellerman showed us that,' Lopez agreed.

'The symbol has long been associated with Atlantis, long before Plato ever mentioned its existence and it entered the common conscience. The rings appear on carved stones dated as old as ten thousand years, and were a feature of many supposedly pre–historic tribes.'

Raz leaned down to one of the aged stone flags at his feet, the cut stones worn smooth by the passage of feet over countless centuries, perhaps millennia. With his fingers he carefully prized one of the stones up and from beneath it he lifted a disc–shaped object that was wrapped in cloth, nestled alongside the edge of a storm drain beneath the table. Raz set the object on the table before them and then unfolded the cloth to reveal a circular, terracotta tablet about eight inches in diameter.

'This, is the Phaistos Disk,' Raz said grandly.

Ethan stared down at the disk, which was roughly shaped and inscribed with three concentic rings, each of which contained heiroglyphic characters of some kind that looked somewhat Egyptian but also reminded him of the pictographic writing he had witnessed at many other ancient sites over the years.

'Where did it come from?' Lopez asked.

'Well, that is the great question. It was found in 1908 by an Italian archaeologist excavating the ancient ruins of the Minoan Palace of Phaistos, on the island of Crete. The script upon it is unknown and has never been deciphered, which leads most scholars to come to two possible conclusions: either the ancient Greeks had a form of writing of which we have never known, which is unlikely as the Minoan culture is well known to historians, or alternatively the disc did not come from Crete at all but was taken there for some reason.'

Ethan frowned.

'How does this tie in with Lucy?'

'I was able to gain an understanding of what is written on this disc, and from it she has begun the search that I was unable to complete. Lucy is on the hunt for Atlantis, and the very shape and form of this disk is what guides her.'

'What does it say?' Lopez asked, intrigued.

Raz smiled. 'It's not actually so much what it says as what it represents. The three concentric rings are present once more, and with the single line extending from the center. This icon has long been associated with Atlantis but was much later appropriated by other belief systems across the world, its true meaning lost amid the warring factions of countless religions. The same symbol is also called a *Rosi–Crucis*, the Dew Cup, and is the symbol for what is now referred to in popular culture as the Holy Grail.'

Ethan blinked. 'As in the cup of Christ?'

Raz nodded.

'Lucy isn't yet searching for the city: she is following a trail that I am now too old to follow myself. She is following the grail, the symbols carved into the rocks of the world's oldest cities that prove they were aware of its existence, in the hope that they will lead her to its location. The holy grail has nothing to do with Christianity: it speaks of the true location of Atlantis itself.'

***

IX

'That's insane,' Ethan said. 'If you announced that on live television in America you'd be hounded out of the country.'

'Such is the anger of the religious right,' Raz agreed, 'but there is no escaping the historical record. This icon, that of the holy grail, existed long before the cults that comprise modern religions. We have been taught that they are the one truth, the beginning of faith, but in reality they are all just the re–hashing of far older myths and legends, and no amount of shouting to the contrary can change that.'

'I've seen the movies and read the books,' Lopez pointed out, 'and they all state that the grail is a Christian relic of some kind, whether a chalice or a person.'

'Some would believe so,' Raz said, 'but in truth the fledgling Christian cult appropriated many legends for its own use. The story of Christ's birth, life and death was stolen from the Mithraic tradition of sun–worship that preceded it, which was in turn taken from the Hindu legend of Krishna two thousand years before that. Easter was originally Eostara, a Roman celebration of the arrival of Spring and the ressurection of life as crops began to grow and a new generation of animals born after the cold and darkness of winter. All of the stories of course owed their existence not to gods but to the sun, the passage of which across the sky each year marks the path of the seasons. The sun's descent toward the horizon and midwinter, where it "died" and resided for three days at its lowest from December 21st before being reborn or "ressurected" three days later and ascending to the heavens a little more each day in the march toward spring is the foundation of all the world's religions, no matter how much they try to hide it behind violence or legends to the contrary.'

Lopez was smiling once again as she processed what Raz was telling her.

'So you're saying that the worship of the icon of the holy grail is in fact the worship of Atlantis?'

'Partly,' Raz replied, 'in that it is the meaning of the symbol in its *original* form. The icon is most often found in ancient artifacts associated with sun worship, a common theme in most ancient societies. The sun was the giver of life without which it was believed no life could exist, the only truly *holy* grail. Atlantis, if it existed as described by Plato during the time of Solon and had been present for several thousand years already, must have been built long before any of the commonly accepted earliest cities of mankind, and its construction was repeatedly described by many sources as being a natural harbor with a narrow channel leading to three rings of land in an inland water way, the layout of the icon itself.'

'What about the disc?' Ethan pressed. 'You said that you know what it says?'

'Yes,' Raz said, 'in as much as I was willing to look beyond Crete in my search for an understanding of the ideograms upon it, which are quite distinct from the local Cretan writing of the time. There are over two hundred forty symbols found on both sides of the disc, depicting everything from people, birds, plants, insects and all manner of cryptic images arranged in a manner that suggests either a list or something that should be read following a counter clockwise spiral pattern. What's most interesting about the disc is that it contains inscripted signs that match inscriptions found as far north as the Baltic Sea and as far west as Brazil, where identical carvings have been found dated to prehistoric times.'

'Seriously?' Lopez asked.

'There are also carvings of the constellations of the Pleiades, Pisces and Serpens on the surface, and that led me to deduce that their positions on the disc suggested a date of origin some ten thousand years old, when those constellations would have occupied the regions in the sky as denoted by the disc when held aloft during the summer solstice and matched to the sky.'

'That's much older than human civilization,' Ethan said.

'Far older,' Raz agreed. 'The fact that this icon was found in the palace of the Minoan civilization, which was consumed by the sea after a major volcanic event, further sheds light on how such legends could have arisen around the fate of any supposed Atlantis.'

Raz pointed at the disc.

'The symbols are syllabic, rather than letters, and they speak as follows; *"The sun in azimuth, the dawn star aloft, the eyes of the north shall gaze ever toward their goddess, where a land of fire bleeds toward the underworld."*

Lopez blinked. "Clear as day.'

'Not to us,' Ethan said, 'but perhaps to Lucy?'

'If she understood something of this,' Raz said, 'then she did not speak of it to me for fear of the Russians trying to harm me for information. I can understand the sun's azimuth and the dawn star references as they enabled me to orientate the disc and discover its age, but beyond that I am at a loss.'

'Could the land of fire be another reference to volcanism?' Ethan asked.

'Perhaps,' Raz conceded, 'but it could also be simply a poetic verse describing a sunset too, that Atlantis is behind the viewer when the disc is held aloft. I have been unable to verify a location based on that so it must mean something else.'

'Did Lucy leave any clue at all to where she might be going?' Ethan asked.

Raz leaned back in his seat once more as he replied.

'Her mission was simple. The icon or symbol for the holy grail has changed over millennia, and by following its evolution back through time as inscribed upon the rocks of ever older ancient historical sites, Lucy was hoping to be able to study the civilizations that built the sites and obtain clues and references to the existence and location of Atlantis.'

'The picture of the stellae that Hellerman sent us,' Lopez said.

Ethan nodded. 'We have an image of an artifact that Lucy sent before she disappeared.'

'Again,' Lopez interjected as she directed an innocent smile at Ethan.

'Hellerman suggested that the site she visited was dated to over eleven thousand years ago. Is that even possible?'

Raz watched them both for a long time before he replied, and the smile was no longer on his face as he did so.

'The beliefs of man were once merely our attempts to place meaning and understanding on the world around us. There is incontrovertible evidence that our ancestors, even back to the Neanderthals of tens of thousands of years ago, buried their dead alongside garlands of flowers, that they showed grief for those who had died. They had no religions, no gods, their beliefs are things we can only imagine at, but those beliefs if they existed were without bias or conflict, merely their attempts to humanize the uncaring world around them. But for the past two thousand years the beliefs of mankind have become first weapons and now big business. The fear that the falsehoods of the world's major religions might be laid bare for all to see is what drives violence against blasphemy in the Middle East, the paranoid secrecy of the Catholic Church and the attempts by the religious right in the west to infiltrate governments and schools to push their agenda and take control of children's minds.' Raz sighed softly. 'Our society is comfortable in its mythical gods. To prove beyond all reasonable doubt that religion is a myth and that all of their legends stem from a singular society far older than anything previously thought possible is something that the discovery of Atlantis would achieve. If we were building cities ten thousand years ago, then there is a huge part of the human story that has been wiped clean from our history books.'

Lopez looked at Ethan. 'But why would the Russians be chasing after this also?'

'Because they're one of the strongholds of atheism in the world,' Ethan replied, 'and the discovery of a religion shattering city that unifies all of the world's religions would also be an indirect validation of a Communist regime which championed atheism.'

Raz inclined his head in accquiessence.

'In a nutshell,' he replied. 'Russia is looking for reasons to return to the good old days and there would be nothing better than the discovery of the city of Atlantis by Russian teams to break the hold of Islamic terrorism and Catholic dogma over many countries otherwise allied to the Russian Federation.'

Ethan knew well that as well as the Russian's own patriotic reasons for locating the city for themselves there was a larger geopolitical force at work. The US administration had long been suspected of colluding with the Russians even before the current president had taken office, with the Russian president suspected of deliberately orchestrating a campaign to alter the outcome of the election in favor of a candidate with close ties to Russian business interests. Despite the bizarre nature of the revelations, it was conceivable that the current US President would be willing to orchestrate Russian assistance in hunting down those responsible for walking away from the country with the lost billions of dollars that had been hoarded by Majestic Twelve.

'You're thinking what I'm thinking,' Lopez said as she watched him.

'If the administration is heading the way we think it is, then it's not being run so much as a country and more like a business. Profit, free from government interference and all of the laws designed to protect consumers from the greed of multinational corporations, is all that concerns them.'

'And thirty billion dollars is a lot of money to have seen disappear,' Lopez agreed.

'The president can't shout about it as being a failure of the opposition in power at the time as doing so might also expose links to the Russians or whomever else they've come into contact with over the years,' Ethan went on. 'That means that any action made to recoup the lost billions would have to be done under the radar, out of the media eye.'

'And out of the eye of any congressional oversight,' Lopez said, her features now pinched with concern. 'They couldn't risk a whistleblower dropping details of any operation into the laps of the media, they can't afford another scandal.'

'So you'd outsource,' Ethan said, 'to trusted second parties, people who stood to benefit from you achieving your goal.'

They both reached the same conclusion together. 'Russia.'

Ethan looked sharply at Raz. 'How long ago were the Russians here?'

'Yesterday, they questioned me for about a half hour and then they just left.'

Suddenly the flock of small birds nestled in the nearby tree burst into motion and flocked upward in a dramatic cloud of beating wings and chirps as they flew up into the hard blue sky and vanished over the nearby rooftops.

Ethan looked up at the walls around them and somehow he knew in his gut that they'd been played. They were sitting in a tiny building in an obscure corner of India, far from civilization. If they were killed here, nobody would ever hear about it.'

'We need to move,' he said.

Lopez was already on her feet and heading for the courtyard door that led back into Raz's little museum when she saw shadows moving before her. She whirled and pointed to Ethan, signalled a warning. Ethan turned and looked around them at the courtyard but instantly he knew that they were cornered, no other exits in the sandstone walls surrounding them.

'Spread out.'

Valentin Kurov strode into the musty little building and removed his sunglasses as his men spread rapidly through the building. Valentin was tall enough that he had to stoop and twist to get into the building, his muscular physique too wide for the entrance and his cropped blond hair brushing the door frame as he moved through. By his side, cowering on his knees and with blood trickling from his nose, an aged and wiry Indian man pointed frantically deeper into the building.

Valentin showed him again the images he had carried with him from Russia, one shot each of the American man and woman he and his team had been told to look out for. The little man nodded vigorously and pointed again into the building.

Valentin shoved the man aside with his boot, hard enough that he crashed into a wall and collapsed, wimpering as Valentin hurried through a narrow passageway. He shoved an old muslin sheet aside and saw his men vanishing into a courtyard just ahead of them.

He walked out into the courtyard to see an old man sitting smoking from a hookah and watching them with an interested but unafraid gaze. Valentin looked up at the surrounding walls of the courtyard and then peered down at the old man as he held out the images with one hand while with the other he pulled a heavy pistol from a holster beneath his loose shirt.

'Where are they?'

The old man shrugged and smiled.

'They ran as soon as you arrived, up and away.'

Valentin looked up at the walls and saw instantly the ledges and window sills. His eye traced the possible routes up the pair could have taken and he whirled to his men.

'Get out there now, track them down before they get too far!'

The men, all dressed as tourists but barely able to conceal the weapons secreted upon their bodies, hurried out of the building as Valentin leaned in close to the old man and peered into his eyes.

'If you are lying to me Raz, know that I will come back for you.'

Raz regarded him for a long moment before he replied.

'Had I needed to lie to you, I would not have sat here waiting for you.'

Valentin frowned briefly and then he whirled away and stormed from the courtyard.

Raz sat for a few moments, quietly smoking the hookah as he listened to the sound of the Russian men as they searched the rooftops. Slowly, the voices trailed away into the distance and after a few minutes more he heard the soft flutter of wings as the birds returned to the tree in the courtyard.

Slowly, Raz got to his feet and pulled the chairs to one side.

'You can come out now.'

An old drainage grill in the stones at his feet rattled and was pushed aside as Ethan hauled himself out with Lopez right behind him.

'Great,' Lopez uttered as she dusted herself off. 'Four hours in this country was all it took to wind up in a sewer.'

Ethan replaced the drain cover and pulled the chairs back over it.

'I would have preferred to take to the roofs,' he said as he looked at Raz.

'They would have expected that and captured you,' Raz replied. 'The storm drains here are large because of the monsoon rains that pass over every year, and they're big enough to hide in. I gambled that the Russians would not think of that but now you must go, for they might eventually realize the deception.'

'We still don't know where Lucy is,' Lopez pointed out.

'She is already far ahead of you,' Raz replied, 'and right now that is the safest place for her.'

Ethan understood immediately. The Russians would only be able to track Lucy down by following Ethan and Lopez, and while that allowed her to work freely it also meant that Lucy was out on her own without back up.

'She will be fine,' Raz said as he saw the concern in Ethan's eyes. 'As long as the Russians have you to focus on, they will not search for Lucy and she will be free to continue her work.'

Ethan walked to the front door of the building and carefully checked the street for any sign of their Russian pursuers, but apart from the old woman sitting nearby on the doorstep there was no sign of them.

'Go, now,' Raz urged Ethan as he pressed the Phaistos Disk into his hand. 'Meet me at the Dwarkandish Temple at dawn, it is the last place that Lucy went before she disappeared.'

Ethan stepped into the alley and hurried away with Lopez to the south as Raz headed north.

'I don't like this,' Lopez said. 'Lucy's a great scientist but she's no field agent. If the Russians catch a lucky break she'll be forced to lead them straight to the prize, and I can't believe for a moment that the Russians would honor any agreement with our administration.'

'Nor do I,' Ethan agreed. 'This whole thing is based around money for the White House and nationalistic pride for the Russians and neither of them will be willing to abandon their prize when it's within their grasp. You can bet your bottom dollar that their little arrangement will go south and before you know it Russia and America will be at each other's throats.'

'You think it'll go that far?'

'You think the president's thin skin will cope with Russia taking the money and the city of Atlantis without putting up some kind of belligerent military responabouse? You and I both know that he's the kind of guy who'd blow the world up just to feel better about himself. Either we get to that city before they do or this whole thing will explode, and there's only one way we can avoid it.'

'How?'

'By giving both sides what they want,' Ethan said. 'This is where it ends, Nicola. We have to find a way to give the money stolen from Majestic Twelve back to the government and we need to find Atlantis before the Russians do.'

Lopez stopped in the hot and dusty street. 'Wait one, if we go charging in there we don't know what will happen. We could end up creating as big a problem as we have already.'

'And if we stand back and do nothing?'

Lopez rolled her eyes, and Ethan pressed his advantage.

'We have the fact that Lucy visited a place here, Dwarkadhish Temple, and that something about the place sent her on this new course. All we have to do is figure out what that something was.'

***

X

Washington DC

Allison Pierce sat in silence in the office of the *Bright & Warner* law firm on the city's east side, and waited for a meeting that she had booked the previous evening under the pretence of wanting to hire an attorney to preside over a divorce.

The law firm was only two years old, having been founded by experienced attorney Lucinda Bright and her partner in the business, Natalie Warner. Allison had learned in the limited time available that the law firm had built a small but loyal client base handling mostly small claims but also larger cases on occasion from contacts over at the Capitol. Those contacts had led Allison here, and it was Natalie she was interested in talking to.

The door to a nearby office opened and a tall, smartly suited woman of perhaps thirty years of age walked out. She had long wavy light brown hair and an easy smile beneath green eyes, a wide jaw and a firm handshake.

'Mrs Pierce, I'm so sorry to not be meeting under happier circumstances. Please, come in.'

Allison detected none of the thin and uncaring veneer normally associated with lawyers, Natalie guiding her into the office and closing the door behind them.

'Coffee?' she offered, a maker installed in the office.

'No, thanks,' Allison replied, maintaining some distance from Natalie as she suspected any grieving would–be divorcee might.

Natalie sat down with her but not on the opposite side of her desk as Allison had expected. Instead she pulled up a chair and her notepad and sat close by.

'Okay, so, obviously separation and divorce is a difficult thing to go through so I want you to understand that there's no pressure here and no need to rush things through, even if maybe you feel that you want to. Getting it right is, at least for now, more important than getting it over with.'

Allison nodded. 'I do want to get it right.'

'Good,' Natalie said. 'Can I take the name of your husband?'

Allison nodded. 'Yes, he's a government employee named Douglas Ian Jarvis and he's been missing for several months after disappearing from his place of work at the Defense Intelligence Agency. Would you happen to know anything about that?'

Natalie had started writing in her notepad but now those sharp eyes flicked up to meet hers, still clear and green but now with a steely edge to them.

'This some kind of joke?'

Allison went in hard.

'I've been covering the aftermath of the scandal surrounding the rumored collapse of a cabal of industrialists known as Majestic Twelve. Since the story broke I've seen it swept under the carpet and buried along with the thirty or so billion dollars they held in assetts. I've tried to keep the story alive but hardly anybody is interested in carrying the piece because they're all so fascinated by our president's current scandals.'

'And you're telling me this why? You want me to launch a legal action against the media or the White House? We're a small claims business and wouldn't be able to…'

'Then, guess what happens?' Allison cut across her. 'This guy comes out of nowhere, a big black dude, ex–military and abducts me in my car. He takes me to a lot over in Maryland and explains that MJ–12's billions are still out there and that I should go looking for a Doug Jarvis, DIA. So you know, due diligence and all that, I go looking and you wouldn't believe what I found on this guy!'

Natalie Warner tossed the notepad onto her desk. 'What do you want?'

Allison opened a file and began reading.

'Douglas Ian Jarvis is a decorated former United States Marine who wound up working high–level classified intelligence operations for the Defense Intelligence Agency. During the course of all that he hires another former Marine, a guy called Ethan Warner, and man does he leave trails of destruction all around him. I've got a diplomatic crisis in Israel which has forbidden Ethan ever to return on the threat of imprisonment, after he allegedly stole ancient artifacts from somewhere over there, police reports of explosions in New Mexico with Warner present at the scene and the same off the coast of Florida a year later.

He shows up again in NYC and the Nez Pierce National Forest, then Peru, here in the continental US again in Arizona, here in DC, then in Antarctica of all places and then in Egypt, and you know what?'

Natalie raised a silent, expectant eyebrow.

'Not only is there law enforcement hunting him down throughout it all, but he has a sister who was involved in the death of a colleague at the Government Accountability Office several years ago, who is now a lawyer at Bright & Warner and I'm thinking: *How can these people cause so much carnage and not be locked up for it?*'

Natalie sat for a moment in silence as Allison let the question hang between them in the air.

'You'd have to talk to either Doug or Ethan about all of that,' she said finally. 'My brother's work is none of my business, and for the record I've had many reporters ask me about things like this in the past and they always end up with nothing so I'd stop wasting my time if I were you.'

Allison smiled. 'You're not me, and I'm very interested in why it is that my mysterious informant would send me on this path that has already revealed so much. I mean, at first I thought he was a fantasist or something, but now I'm starting to think that he's really onto something here and...'

'Aaron Mitchell,' Natalie said softly.

'You know him?'

Natalie leaned her elbows on her knees and her eyes locked onto Allison's as she spoke in soft tones.

'He is an assassin and probably the most dangerous man I have ever met in my life. He was once assigned to kill me and it was only the intervention of Doug Jarvis and my brother that saved my life. I don't know what you're looking for here but I can tell you that you're already in far more danger than you could possibly realize. These people, they don't play games. They kill, Allison, without mercy, without hesitation, without remorse. I don't know what he wants with you but I can guarantee that once he's done he'll cut your throat before you even know what's happened.'

For the first time in a long time, Allison was speechless. Natalie's voice reached her as though from afar.

'By coming here with this to me, you're putting me back on his radar. I have a family now, so please don't take offence when I tell you that if you don't get the hell out of my office I swear to God that sooner than put my child in jeopardy I will kill you myself right here, do you understand?'

Allison looked into Natalie's eyes and saw a resolve there sufficient that she did not doubt that if pushed further, Natalie would probably lose control of herself. Allison stood up abrutply and made for the door, granting Natalie a breathing space before she turned to look over her shoulder.

'The man, Mitchell. Who does he work for now?'

Natalie shook her head. 'I don't know and I don't care.'

Allison left the office both relieved and frustrated. Natalie Warner's reaction to her visit had revealed all too clearly that there was a hell of a story behind whatever the administration was trying to conceal, but that same reaction had also closed a door on what should have been a deep and reliable vein of information.

Allison crossed the street to her car and opened the door. Just as she was about to drive off she noticed a tall, dark skinned man with a military bearing walking down the street toward the lawyer's office. Something about the guy made her hesitate and slip the vehicle back into park as she watched him vanish inside the building.

*

Natalie Warner stared out of her office window and cursed silently to herself. The reporter had gotten her rattled, and not for the first time she cursed her brother Ethan for the trouble he kept getting himself into. This wasn't the first time that Ethan's DIA work had burst into their lives and she was damned sure that after the last time she wouldn't let it become the danger it had been before.

Natalie picked up the phone and dialled her parents' number. Both were elderly now and were usually to be found taking it easy at their home in the Chicago suburbs. When neither of them answered by the tenth ring, she tried first her mother's cell and then her father's. When she could not reach either of them the first hint of panic sparked inside her stomach.

'Natalie Warner?'

Natalie turned to see a tall man standing in the doorway to her office. She could tell at once that he was military, or ex–military at the very least. His short cut hair, square jaw and erect posture marked him out as clearly as if he'd been wearing a uniform and not the dark suit confronting her.

'Yes?'

'I have to ask you to come with me, ma'am.'

'Who are you?'

'My name is Lieutenant Colonel Foxx.'

Natalie's eyes narrowed. 'What's going on?'

'I'll tell you on the way,' the man promised.

'On the way to *where*?'

Foxx gently pulled one lapel of his suit jacket back to reveal a shoulder holster and a pistol tucked within.

'This isn't a request, ma'am.'

Natalie considered turning and hurling her office chair through the window before following it through, but Foxx sensed her sudden fight–or–flight reaction and he stepped lithely forward, too close for her to hope to escape.

'This can be easy or it can be hard,' he said simply, his dark eyes emotionless and determined. 'It's your call.'

*

Allison saw the man emerge from the lawyer's office minutes later, Natalie Warner with him as two large black SUVs appeared as if from nowhere and slid in alongside the sidewalk. Allison, her cell phone resting on the dash, filmed it all as within moments Natalie and the mysterious man got into the vehicles and they drove away from the office, headed north towards the city.

Allison slipped her car into drive once again and set off in pursuit, following a discreet distance behind the two vehicles and hoping against hope that she would not be spotted or identified.

***

XI

Dwarkadhish Temple, India

Nicola Lopez looked up a steep flight of stairs that led to one of the most bizarre looking temples that she had ever seen. Bathed in the warm light of the sun rising over the nearby Arabian Sea, the temple towered over the narrow alleys and streets below, where toiled the local residents of one of the most ancient towns in India.

'The temple is known to the local people as Jagat Mandir,' Raz said as he guided them toward the building, all three of them wearing traditional native dress of long shawls supplied by Raz to help disguise them from any concealed Russian observers. 'It is dedicated to the god Krishna, the original inspiration for the Christian myths of Christ, and is well over two thousand years old.'

As they began to ascend the steps, Ethan was starting to realize just how much most modern religions owed to much older traditions.

'This Krishna seems to show up over and over again.'

'That's because it represents some of the earliest known references to legends that we consider assigned to so many other religions. We humans have a habit of assuming that what we hear from our elders and teachers must be the truth, and as children we rarely question that authority. That is why so many religions wish to control the education of young children but rarely bother themselves with taking over high schools: it is easier to indoctrinate the young, but by their teenage years' children are too smart to be easily indoctrinated. However, our interest here is in the building itself, which it is said that Krishna built on a piece of land that was reclaimed from the sea.'

'Unlike Atlantis,' Lopez said, 'which was consumed by the sea.'

'Dwarka has a history that goes back far further than most mainstream archaeologists and historians are prepared to admit,' Raz said as he huffed and puffed his way to the top of the steps and paused to look up at the temple before them.

Three *shikharas* dominated the building like spires, one higher than the other two and each constructed of limestone with intricate sculpturing created by the countless ruling dynasties in the region. The structure was five storeys high and stood upon seventy–two pillars called the *vimana mandapa* and the *natya mandapa*. Ethan was standing in front of the south entrance known as the Swarga Dwara, the *Gate to Heaven*, with the Gomati River now visible sprawling behind them. The crowded bazaar was far below at the bottom of the steps leading up to a decorative torana arch topped with stone garlands and snake motifs. On the highest of the shikhara spires was a huge silk flag, the Dhwaja, fifty–two yards long and stained with seven primary colors that rippled in the hot, humid dawn breeze.

'You said that this temple is two thousand years old,' Lopez said.

'It is,' Raz agreed, 'but the age of the temple is not as important as the number of pillars upon which it was built.'

'Why?' Ethan asked.

'There are seventy–two pillars, and that number has special significance for all of the very oldest civilizations on earth,' Raz explained. 'The number appears in many modern religions; there are seventy–two Divine Names in Jewish mythology's Kabbalah, said to be used as codes in creation, seventy–two languages spoken at the Tower of Babylon; the degrees of the Jacob's Ladder and the disciples of Confuscius numbered seventy–two and the Egyptian God Thoth used seventy–two portions of a day to make the intercalary day.'

'The hell does that all mean?' Lopez asked.

'The ancients worshipped not gods but the sun, and all worship of all religions is ultimately derived from that one foundation. The seventy–two pillars of the temple relate to the one degree of motion of the sun's precession against the background of star constellations associated with the twelve signs of the Zodiac.'

'So?' Ethan asked, feeling slightly dizzy from all of the revelations.

'The ancient Babylonians developed the sexigesimal method of counting much as the ancient Indians did; sixty seconds in a minute, sixty minutes in an hour, three hundred sixty degrees in a circle. Multiplying the divine number with the degrees in a circle yeilds a figure of twenty–five thousand, nine hundred twenty: the precise number of years in the procession of the equinoxes through the twelve Zodiac ages.'

Raz gestured to the entrance of the temple.

'Lucy came here to try to discover whether there was a connection here between the ancient Hindu traditions of astronomy and astrology, the originators of all religions, and an older civilization from which they might have inherited their knowledge.'

Ethan remembered what Raz had said the day before. 'A location, something she could back track to from existing relics.'

Ethan wasted no more time and walked into the interior of the temple, removing his shoes and cell phone as was the custom before advancing inside. The price of admittance was only a few lakhs, and the interior was crowded even at this early hour as locals practiced the first *Aarti* of the day, having first bathed in the nearby Gomati River.

The halls were open spaces, a huge carved tiered roof supported by carved stone pillars. The entire temple was covered with ornate inscriptions and the walls and pillars adorned with sculptures in floral and geometric motifs, countless images of gods and goddesses and decorative patterns.

The sanctum and vestibule led to a rectangular hall with porches on three sides and was surprisingly simple compared to the exquisite carvings of the exterior. Ethan looked about them, the hall echoing with the chantings of Hindus as they worshipped the elaborate shrine of Dwarkadhish at one end of the hall, a hive of color and incense and hymns of devotion.

'Krishna as the king is a majestic figure,' Raz whispered. 'The image is made of a dark stone and has four arms holding the discus sudarshana chakra, the mace Kaumodiki gada, the conch panchajanya and a lotus flower, padma.'

'Lovely, but what are *we* looking for?' Lopez asked.

Ethan scanned the room and sought something that he might recognize.

'The seal of Atlantis,' Raz answered, 'or anything that suggests this temple was orignally built to worship something other than Krishna.'

Ethan eased his way forwards through the throng of worshippers, heading instinctively for the shrine. The walls were covered with colorful decorations that concealed the bare walls of the hall, and Ethan wondered what Lucy might have seen that could have sent her out on her own in pursuit of Atlantis.

He was half way to the shrine when he saw a bulky figure through one of the open porches, a tall man with cropped blond hair and a muscular form beneath the clothes of a western tourist.

'We've got company,' he whispered as they moved, and pulled the veil of his shawl across his face to help shield it from view. 'The Russians must have picked up our trail.'

Raz moved to the shrine, within which was a small idol of polished black stone or metal, the Krishna holding various implements. Ethan stared at it for a long moment, the idol dressed in garish colors inside a square shrine walled with ornate red hanging blankets as Hindus prayed in dense ranks inside the small hall.

Ethan was about to turn away when he looked up at the ceiling and saw something among the inscriptions carved into the stone. There, faint with age, was an intricately carved image of the rising sun and the setting moon, and beyond the shore of some unknown beach was a sort of building with rays bursting forth from it.

'What's that?' he asked Raz.

The historian looked up at the image and shrugged. 'It's the old city of Dwarka that was lost to the sea due to coastal erosion. The carving commemorates the old city with the rebuilding of the temple on new land.'

'Where is this city?' Ethan asked.

'It's off shore somewhere,' Raz explained, 'beneath about a hundred feet of water. A few teams have searched for it in the past but there's no easy way out there and the tides and conditions are considered treacherous. I would have searched for the site myself back in my youth but I'm much too old to… You don't think that Lucy would have gone down there?'

'Knowing her as I do, yes,' Ethan replied as he looked again at the carvings above their heads. 'You say that this temple was rebuilt, that it is not the original construction?'

'Yes,' Raz agreed, glancing cautiously at the Russians now gathering outside the temple arches and scrutinizing each and every person who was leaving the building. 'The temple itself was enlarged a few hundred years ago, but the shrine is two thousand or more years old and so are the pillars built to support it.'

Ethan thought for a moment. The temple itself would likely not have any direct connection with a city of far greater antiquity beyond the inscriptions, but if it were in fact a replica of something that had once stood further out to sea then the carvings could have simply also been replicas…

'The three shikharas,' he said as he looked at the shrine.

'What about them?' Raz asked.

'There are three of them but they're different sizes and shapes. What's the significance of that?'

Raz appeared thoughtful for a moment.

'They signify the sun and the moon, and of Krishna's power over the heavens and earth.'

'And this temple, it is built on the foundations of something much older?'

'Yes, legends tell that a temple has stood here for thousands of years, but that even the oldest segments of this temple are built on the ruins of much older structures.'

Ethan thought of the intricate carvings on the exterior of the shikharas and of the far greater antiquity of the pillars that supported the temple and he realized what Lucy must have done.

'She didn't enter the temple,' he said. 'What she found isn't on the inside at all, it's on the outside, hidden in plain sight. It must tell her where the older temple stands, the one swallowed by the sea.'

Lopez looked over her shoulder at the Russians awaiting them.

'Yeah, and outside is one place we can't go yet.'

As Ethan watched so more Russians appeared and began filtering into the temple, closing off the exits one by one as they began hunting Ethan, Lopez and Raz down.

'There is nowhere to hide,' Raz said nervously.

Ethan turned and made his decision.

'Then let's not hide at all.'

***

THE ATLANTIS CODEX

Dean Crawford

XII

Ethan stepped through the throng inside the temple and headed directly for the nearest of the Russian agents lingering near the arches. He was taller and younger than Ethan, with broad shoulders and a bull neck. Ethan often found it amusing that the Russians, who openly showed their contempt for American forces, then emulated their *Hollywood* versions in so many ways, wearing designer sunglasses and projecting angry glares at anybody who ventured too close.

Real bodyguards and security experts tended to avoid sunglasses except when absolutely necessary as they removed detail from a scene, increasing the chances that they might miss some crucial detail. Likewise, they tended to wear local clothing to help their ability to blend in with a scene, and although invariably physically fit they rarely bulked out with muscle, again to maintain a low profile when working that made them harder to pick out in a crowd.

Ethan kept his face hidden and altered his gait, mimicking one of the local worshippers who seemed to have a damaged foot. He slumped his shoulders and made to pass close by the guard's left side, where he figured the man's weapon would be concealed beneath his shirt.

Ethan got to within a couple of feet of the guy when the guard noticed that Ethan had paler skin beneath his hood than the locals and he turned toward Ethan and reached out to pull the hood back. Ethan had been waiting for the move and responded instantly, grabbing the guard's wrist and twisting it sideways and down, the bones inside straining against the force of the move as Ethan forced his weight down behind it.

The Russian made to let out a howl of pain and a warning to his comrades that Ethan cut short with a sharp chop across the man's throat. The Russian's eyes bulged as he folded over and crashed down onto his back. The shirt flew up and as Ethan squatted down he reached over and yanked the guard's pistol from its holster.

Ethan deselected the safety catch and aimed up at the sky out of the arch as he fired two shots. The confines of the temple amplfied the gunshots and they crashed out deafeningly loud and in an instant the entire crowd inside the temple burst into panicked flight as they rushed for the exits.

Ethan leaped to his feet and saw the other Russians pulling their weapons out and shouldering their way through the fleeing crowds. Ethan made eye contact with each of them as he backed away, sure that their attention was focused entirely on him as the crowds flooded out of the temple past them. Ethan saw Lopez and Raz drawn out of the temple past the guards amid the flowing river of hoods and shawls, and then he whirled and dashed for the pair of narrow arches on the opposite side of the temple beneath the tallest shikhara.

The tumbling crowds of visitors poured past him as he ducked past the ornate shrine to Krishna and headed into the darkness of the passage beyond, following the scent of morning air that was cool on his face. A temple such as Dwarkandish would require great ventilation from the heat of the Indian sun and that generated by the crowds of worshipers inside the building. Ethan knew that the morning sea breeze was the result of the land warming faster than the sea, causing the air to rise above it and drawing in fresher, cooler air from the ocean toward the low pressure that resulted. Now, he saw a pair of arches ahead that opened out toward the vast Arabian Sea and the bright sky above it.

Russian voices behind him alerted him and he heard boots pounding the ancient stone flags as he shoved the pistol beneath the sash of his shirt and vaulted out of the archway. His boots hit the ground and he immediately turned left, putting the curved walls of the building between himself and the view from the archway as he made his way toward the throng of people still pouring from the interior.

Almost immediately he saw armed policemen rushing up to the entrance on the Gomati River side, their pistols drawn as the panicked crowd pointed back toward the temple. Ethan slipped the pistol from his sash and let it fall into an ornate stone fountain as he circled the edge of the crowd and again adopted his limping, head down gait.

Behind him he heard Russian voices and the crowd whirled as two agents sprinted around the corner of the building with their weapons in plain sight. The hordes of Hindus panicked and scattered as the policeman took aim at the two men and started screaming at them to drop their weapons.

Ethan hobbled away, staying with the crowd as the Russians were forced to drop their pistols and put their hands up to the policemen. Ethan moved among the Hindus, trying to make himself look as small as possible as he descended the steps back toward the Gomati River and saw Lopez and Raz waiting for him at the bottom, still shielding their faces somewhat from any unwanted observations.

'Nice work,' Lopez whispered as he joined them. 'Now what?'

'We need to go back.'

'We need to *what?*'

'The Russians will have their hands full for at least a while and will leave the area for fear of being arrested. We need to find out if the temple has any inscriptions remaining from the construction that stood here before the current temple was built.'

Raz nodded as he understood where Ethan was coming from.

'Some of the supporting pillars stand on the original foundations of the previous temple and I know how to get to them, but the Russians will not be held back for long and we saw at least two of them pass by here and head into the bazaar. They will be back.'

'Then we'd best be quick,' Ethan said. 'We'll head back up when things have quietened down.'

It took almost a half hour before the police led two Russian men away in handcuffs and the temple re–opened. Ethan, Raz and Lopez were at the head of the queue as pilgrims flocked back into the temple and its grounds.

Raz led them around to the side of the temple, and Ethan at once got a fresh look at the way in which the building had been constructed. Below the level at which the crowds entered the two shikharas there were two further levels beneath that were not generally visible to the public but were accessible via a flight of steps. Ethan could see more rows of pillars supporting the very bottom of the temple as Raz led them down the steps, nobody blocking their path, and Ethan found himself grateful for the relatively slack security in this country.

'Here,' Raz said in a whisper, the lower section of the building housed inside a courtyard that echoed to the sound of the crowds somewhere above them, the shadows cooler out of reach of the burning sunlight. 'These rocks are the oldest part of the building.'

Ethan stepped forward and walked among the immense stone pillars supporting the weight of the temple above them. The huge pillars were carved from solid rock and decorated with various intricate designs but there was nothing specific that marked anything that could be referred to as Atlantean in design.

'There's got to be something here,' Ethan said.

Despite searching for almost an hour none of them were able to come up with anything definitive, and Raz was getting more nervous by the moment.

'They could come back any moment and we're trapped down here if they spot us.'

Ethan glanced up to where several curious bystanders were leaning on railings above them and watching. He sighed and nodded reluctantly, then followed the archaeologist up the steps and onto the entrance level where tourists were once again milling in large numbers around the temple.

As they turned to leave, so Ethan saw again the ornate archway guarding the entrance to the temple through which visitors were flowing. As they were carried along by the crowd, so something caught his eye on the ground nearby.

Beyond the pillars of the archway were two vivid black and white discs set in the stone flags. Ethan could see that they were white discs with three distinct concentric black rings and what looked like a star in the centre that was radiating lines outward.

'What about those?' Lopez asked, pointing to the vivid symbols.

Raz looked at the symbols and frowned.

'That is the symbol of Jvalamukhi, with the goddesses Lalita and Kali representing the waxing and waning moon respectively. Jvalamukhi represents fire, which reduces all things to ashes and represents the end of time.'

Ethan looked at Lopez. 'Hellerman said that the ancients referred to Atlantis as being a land of fire.'

'I know,' Lopez replied, 'but these symbols were not placed here thousands of years ago were they?'

Raz shook his head.

'No, but their placement would have been precise in position due to the sacred positions of the seventy–two pillars supporting the temple, and will be the same at all similar temples built in the Hindu tradition.'

Ethan looked at the pillars of the archway. 'And the entrance, and archway?'

'Likewise, the same,' Raz said, and then he slapped his head as he realized what he had missed. 'Mother Shiva, it has been here all along!'

Ethan watched as Raz knelt down alongside one of the discs and looked at the archway before him. 'Beyond the Pillars of Hercules. It's a reference, something carried through from ancient times and associated with our temples now, but originally it would have had only one purpose: measurements.'

'Measurements of what?' Lopez asked.

'Distance,' Raz replied. 'The ancient Hindu used *kosh* and *yojana* as measurements of distance, four kosh equalling one yojana of distance, equivalent to a few miles. Archways are always holy places, believed to have the ability to transfer a person from one realm to another on their path to greater consciousness. This precise structure would have existed at the older site that once was here, and it may have referred to something.'

Ethan watched as Raz pulled out a notebook and hurriedly began taking measurements between the pillars of the archway and the two symbols in the flags, and then he stood back and looked at his conclusions and his eyes widened in delight.

'What is it?' Lopez asked.

Raz took one last look at his work and then he turned to them.

'According to my calculations, the symbols and the archway indicate that the location they're referencing is precisely one and a half *yojana* north east of this location.'

Ethan stepped closer to the archaeologist, keen now to get moving. 'How far is that?'

Raz inclined his head this way and that as he made a rough estimate.

'Give or take, it's about ten miles.'

'Damn it, no wonder Lucy took off so fast,' Lopez said, 'she must have thought she was on the verge of finding Atlantis already.'

'What's out that way? Anything that would interest Lucy?'

'Oh yes,' Raz nodded enthusiastically. 'It's the ocean. This must refer to the location of the submerged city.'

***

XIII

Washington DC

'This is serious!'

Allison Pierce sat in front of her editor, Daisy Harper, and was met with a disinterested glare.

'As you've said, just the same as you said the last time you marched in here asking for prime time slots for your conspiracy theory garbage.'

Allison bit her lip. Daisy was wearing a smug smile that made her puffy cheeks glow red, her squinting eyes sparkling with delight. At two hundred twenty pounds Daisy was anything but dainty and Allison fought the urge to reach across the table and slap her cheeks until they grew a little brighter still.

'I've got footage, of an abduction by US agents on our soil of an innocent lawyer connected to one of the men involved in the Majestic Twelve case. Something's going on here!'

'I agree,' Daisy purred, 'you're putting two and two together and coming up with forty–six again. You've got footage of a woman willingly joining two men in a vehicle with government plates and that vehicle driving to the headquarters of the Defense Intelligence Agency, nothing more. Maybe she's a lawyer, but maybe she's a criminal too.'

'I was abducted, and so was my cameraman! You think he's making it up too? He got shoved into the trunk of my car, in case you hadn't noticed.'

'Abducted by whom?' Daisy demanded. 'You have given no name, no real description and isn't an abduction like that something that you should be reporting to the police? I know that if some random guy jumped into my car I would report his ass right away, but not you. No, you narrowly survive a car jacking and now you're connected to a high–level, ultra classified super secret conspiracy about a congressional investigation that's already been closed and is old news even if it *hadn't been*.'

Allison sat in stony silence and glared at Daisy's immovable bulk.

'I'll take it someplace else if you tell me you're going to bury me in a small–hours slot.'

'I'm not going to bury you, honey,' Daisy smiled sweetly, 'because I'm not going to let you run with the piece at all. If you're not capable of coming up with any real investigative journalism, then you can take your conspiracy theories wherever you please. In fact, as far as I'm concerned you can take them and shove them up your…'

'*After* I get this piece on live televsion, I'll be sure that the CEO learns that it was you who blocked the biggest story this network has ever encountered.'

'Oh, don't bother yourself,' Daisy waved the threat aside as Allison got up and headed for the office door, 'I'll tell him myself in about an hour, when we have lunch.'

Allison walked out of the office and purposefully did not shut the door behind her. Daisy's voice called after her.

'And your cameraman has been reassigned to another reporter!'

Futile rage boiled beneath Allison's skin and threatened to burst like fire out of her eyes as she glared at anyone who dared to look in her direction. As soon as she was out of sight of the main offices and alone in a corridor she slumped against a wall and dragged her hands down her face. Daisy Harper had only got her job as editor after climbing the ranks of the corporation thanks to her father, who was an accountant who did a fine job of ensuring that the network's books were always clean and that taxes were mimimized. Able to mix with the heirachy, she had landed the editorial position after her predecessor retired, and promptly focussed her preferences toward celebrity gossip and scandal rather than focusing on the real issues, the real news that nobody ever got to hear about.

It was a sad truth that there was a reason that world news got so little coverage in America. Buried away on some obscure corner of the pages of the broadsheets or in broadcasts slotted for well after midnight, Americans slept soundly knowing that their own country was the only one that mattered, the only story that was worth telling. Every other country was merely a bit–part player in the movie of America. Worse, the vast majority of the country's news papers and networks were owned by just a handful of major corporations, ensuring that the people received only the kind of news the big corporations wanted them to hear. That was especially true when the government had something to hide and wanted a distraction story to drown out the bad news. She had lost count of how many times Congress had passed unfavorable laws at unsociable hours on days when some other major catastrophe or celebrity wedding was dominating the front pages and the broadcasts.

Allison's cell buzzed in her pocket and she retrieved it to see a text message.

OUTSIDE, TEN MINUTES. TELL NOBODY

Allison sighed and slipped the cell back into her pocket as she made her way down the main stairwell and into the foyer. She walked outside into the bright sunshine and a cold wind, and saw at once a tall man watching her from across the street, his features partially concealed beneath a baseball cap but his height and physique leaving her in no doubt that this was the same man who had abducted her the previous day.

The urge to call Daisy and tell her that Mitchell was right outside was overwhelming, but she knew that the editor probably wouldn't bother to even pick up the call let alone send a camera to film whatever was going to happen next. Allison left her cell phone in her pocket and followed Mitchell from the opposite side of the street as he walked toward the Memorial Park, the iconic monuments visible from the sidewalk.

Allison crossed the street as soon as Mitchell headed into the park and followed him until he reached the Memorial Wall. There were few people out in the cold this early in the morning, and Mitchell was standing alone and staring into the reflecting pool when she moved alongside him.

'Very *James Bourne*,' she said as she looked around. 'You don't need to worry about us being observed, there's no way my editor is going to take any interest in anything I do any more.'

'Good.'

Mitchell's appraising nod angered her. 'Are you kidding me? I might as well be out of a job!'

'You'll have plenty to do.'

'What the hell is *that* supposed to mean?'

Mitchell drew in a deep breath of air and expelled it in thick clouds of vapor as he replied.

'Did you investigate Doug Jarvis as I suggested?'

'Yeah, I looked into him all right and he's up to his neck in something,' Allison replied gloomily. 'Trouble is it's all behind closed doors and there's nothing more that I can do about it all. My editor won't pick up the piece and...'

'You won't be needing an editor where you're going.'

'Excuse me?' Allison snapped. 'I'm not going anywhere until you...'

'A return ticket to Indonesia,' Mitchell rumbled as he held a ticket out to her and she stared at it as though it were a poisonous insect of some kind. 'You will meet there with Douglas Jarvis.'

Allison looked up at Mitchell. 'Wait one, he's the guy they're all looking for, right? He's the one that took the money and...'

'Nobody took any money,' Mitchell replied, 'but they sure will if they can get their hands on it all. Both the Russian government and our own are both attempting to recover the cash, and trust me when I tell you that neither is interested in seeing that money returned to the countless individuals that Majestic Twelve defrauded over so many decades.'

Allison's eyes narrowed. 'You think they'll try to cut and run?'

'Why do you think that our administration would be so cosy with the Russians all of a sudden, while at the same time moving defensive and offensive troops and missile systems so close to the borders of Eastern Europe?'

Allison's eyes widened as she considered the wider aspects of the newly developing relationship between east and west. The Russians had been going backwards for years under the rule of a man who was a dictator in anything but name, while now the current administration was in one breath cosying up to the Russians while at the same time preparing for a war footing against their eastern rival.

'Mutual distrust, I get that, it's always been there. But they're not about to go to war, are they?'

Mitchell pressed the tickets into her hand.

'Not if we can help it,' he replied. 'This country's government is now running the country as though it is a business, and all businesses must make a profit to survive. The Russian government is even more corrupt now than it was in the Cold War and shows no sign of developing into a true democracy. Both of our leaders are obsessed with controlling the media and expanding an already bloated military. They say it's for defense, but in truth it's to ensure that thirty billion dollars of lost and untraceable money can't cross the borders into or out of Russia or Europe. They're each covering their own and that means only one thing.'

'They're both in it for the money.'

Mitchell nodded. 'Our president was never about this country, he's about making money. The Russian president is a dictator and is also interested in ensuring his fortune when the time finally comes for him to step down, not to mention restoring Communism and an eastern bloc alliance sufficient to challenge US global supremacy. Each leader is sufficiently self–interested and paranoid enough that they are willing to deploy their military to ensure that neither one can double–cross the other, and each of their countries sufficiently paranoid about the other that the people and the governments openly support the moves. Knowing the personalities involved, what do you think the chances are that they'll honor this agreement of theirs and not try to ensure a greater slice of Majestic Twelve's ill–gotten gains for themselves?'

'I don't have a cameraman, no way to record or document any of this except for what I can carry myself.'

'That's precisely what we want,' Mitchell assured her. 'There's only one way that you'll get to blow this story wide open, and that's to get right in the middle of it. Nobody will believe a word of it unless you can witness it and record it yourself, do you understand?'

Allison stood her ground and then shook her head.

'I'm not going anywhere,' she insisted. 'So far this little escapade of yours has cost me my job and I'm done with it. I don't know who you are, but I do know that you're not to be trusted by anybody. You're so sure that all of this can be done, then go do it yourself.'

Allison turned and walked away, and Mitchell's voice rumbled after her.

'I can give you Keyes.'

Allison stopped, closed her eyes and replied without looking back. 'How?'

'There is footage of him talking to known Russian computer hackers, three months before the elections.'

Allison turned. 'Thanks, I'll take it now.'

'I don't have it on me,' Mitchell said, 'but I know where it is. You'll need to go alone, and when you've got it we can talk again.'

'Where?'

Mitchell turned away and replied as he left.

'I will arrange the meeting and call you as soon as they're ready.'

***

XIV

Gulf of Khambat,

India

The engine of the boat upon which Ethan stood clattered and spilled puffs of oily smoke onto the brisk wind as he balanced against the rolling swells rocking the boat from side to side. He turned to one side to see Lopez leaning against a rusty railing encircling the deck, her usually perfect skin ashen and her eyes hooded with nausea.

'At least we don't have very far to go,' he offered.

Lopez nodded but didn't look at Ethan as he turned to Raz.

'What do you know about these submerged ruins?'

Raz shrugged as though it were obvious.

'These ruins are rumored to be from an ancient Indian culture, but Lucy was searching for Atlantis, not a city well known to historians unlike ancient Dwarka'

'This place has been known about for a long time?' Ethan asked as he scanned the distant coastline, one eye now always on the lookout for their Russian antagonists.

'A few years,' Raz confirmed. 'The current city of Dwarka is the reconstructed site of the old city after the original was swallowed by the waves many thousands of years ago. Historians know that it was real as it was referenced often in history, but they didn't know where it was located. What you have to understand is that the world is littered with submerged cities that were swallowed by the oceans.'

'It is?' Lopez groaned as she peered at them from the railings. 'They must've forgotten to mention that in school.'

'The world's oceans have been rising for many centuries, for many thousands of years even,' Raz explained. 'This is because of the end of the last Ice Age, when so much water was locked up in the ice caps and the sea levels around the world were far lower than they are today. When the glaciers began to melt so the sea levels rose and the cities that mankind had built on coasts and river estuaries were consumed by the oceans. Twenty thousand years ago, the Arabian Sea was a hundred meters lower than it is today.'

The site they were headed to was concealed fully thirty meters below the waves. It didn't take Ethan very long to do the math.

'That would make the site around seven thousand years old.'

'And that's why you don't hear much about such sites from mainstream archaeologists,' Raz explained. 'The dawn of human civilization is estimated to have occurred in the fertile crescent of Asia some five thousand years ago and was limited to small scale agriculture. To have a major city buried beneath the waves predating any known civilization by two thousand years would completely change our perception of human history and likely end a few careers in the process.'

'You think that this place could be a sort of Atlantis itself?' Lopez asked as she mastered her nausea and pulled on her diving suit.

'Explorations conducted in similar waters revealed sandstone walls, a grid of streets and evidence of a sea port. If this location turns out to be the true ancient site of Dwarka, then it was also the dwelling place of Krishna and old enough that every history book in the world will have to be re–written.'

'We've seen a few places like that,' Ethan replied as the boat crashed through the waves toward their destination. 'What do we know about this place?'

'I managed to find some limited reports from diving expeditions conducted in great secrecy in this area some years ago,' Raz replied. 'A large number of stone structures were detected, geometric in form and clearly not natural in their formation, and they're scattered over a vast area of several kilometres. Stone anchors have been found along with pottery shards, indicating that the settlement would have been a major port at one time or another.'

'The time being the operative factor,' Ethan said.

'Precisely. Fragments recovered in this area during marine archaeological expeditions were carbon dated by the National Geophysical Research Institute in Hyderabad and the Birbal Sahni Institute of Paleobotany in Lucknow, and returned dates of between nine and ten thousand years' old, far exceeding any other civilization currently known to man. Those same measurements were repeated on fresh fragments of microliths, wattle and daub remains and such like by laboratories at none other than Oxford University. The carbon dating again confirmed an age of between nine and ten thousand years, but the research was suppressed in all but the minor journals and so word did not get out about the discoveries. Funding was stripped and that was the end of the expedition. Nobody has been out here since except Lucy, who was brought here by Ranjit and his son just a couple of weeks ago.'

The boat's engine coughed and died down as the boat reached the area where Lucy had presumably dived. Raz called to the boat owner, Ranjit, in Hindu and the old man replied around the husk of a cigarette smoldering in his mouth and nodded as he pointed toward the sea below them.

'This is the spot,' Raz confirmed as he peered over the edge of the boat. 'This is where Lucy dove for almost an hour.'

The boat rocked on the waves and Lopez hurriedly hauled on her tanks and staggered across to the side of the boat. Ethan watched as she yanked her mask down over her face and opened his mouth to speak.

'Wait a second, I'm almost ready to...' Lopez tipped herself backwards over the side of the boat and vanished in a crash of sparkling water. '.., follow.'

'I don't think she likes being on boats so much,' Raz observed as Lopez's position drifted away from the boat, betrayed only by a swathe of bubbles breaking the surface nearby. 'Be careful, the site is known for treacherous currents that can tear you away toward the deeper water beyond, it's why it's so rarely visited.'

Ethan perched on the side of the boat and gave Raz a thumbs–up before he pulled his mask down and pitched himself backwards off the boat and into the water.

The bright blue sky was replaced with the shimmering depths of the Arabian Sea as clouds of silvery bubbles rippled past Ethan, heading toward the surface. Ethan quickly got his bearings and saw the boat's anchor chain nearby and Lopez heading past it as she dove for the mossy seabed below.

What he saw there was surprising in its clarity.

Ethan could see instantly that the seabed was scattered with uniform shapes too regular to have been formed by natural processes. Although some volcanic and erosive environmental processes could carve quite geometric shapes from the landscape they tended to be localized and rare, whereas here he could see long, straight walls of uniform height and direction stretching away from them in all directions. Chunks of stone lay at awkward angles on the seabed, but the chunks were square or rectangular and often piled in groups in a way that suggested structures had collapsed *in situ*.

Ethan spun in a circle as he hung suspended above the city and he quickly spotted a larger structure to the north of their position that Lopez was already swimming towards. Ethan kicked off in pursuit and they descended down and away from the rippling surface into gloomier water, deep blue in color but filled with a jetsam of debris that drifted with the strong currents.

Ethan noted a movement in the distance to his right and turned to see the ghostly form of a tiger shark drift like a marine phantom through the endless abyss. It seemed to watch him for a long moment with one cruel black eye, and then its tail flicked and it accelerated out of sight.

Ethan kept moving and saw the impressive site of a low temple emerge from the depths ahead, its sandstone walls still standing thousands of years after it had been built thanks to the dense layer of dark green sea moss clinging like a blanket to its surface. The moss protected the stone that otherwise would have been eroded away by currents over the millennia it had been submerged. Ethan could see arches concealed by the dense foliage, small clouds of fish zipping this way and that in perfect formation past the walls, other larger fish cruising casually and only giving cursory attention to Ethan and Lopez as they swam past. Ethan figured that was another indicator that people rarely dived here, the local wildlife unafraid of humans.

Lopez looked back at him and pointed ahead, and Ethan nodded as he saw what looked like an entrance into another temple structure that was larger but set lower than the one they were swimming past now. The seabed rose up around the temple as though it had been consumed by silt, the location and height suggesting that it was one of the older constructions on the site.

Ethan checked his depth and his watch as he followed Lopez around the perimeter of the temple, and as they rounded the south side so they both saw a dark, rectangular entrance that decended into the mysterious building. Lopez didn't hesitate, activating her head–mounted flashlight and descending toward it.

Ethan followed, switching on his own flashlight and noticing around the entrance evidence of recent excavations, dislodged rocks and pyramidial mounds of sand that might have been caused by a diver using a machine to suck sand away from the entrance and spit it out a few yards away.

The darkness swallowed them both, their flashlight beams cutting through the blackness with harsh white light that illuminated a passageway of stone. The walls to Ethan's side were inscribed with images, carvings of Hindu gods and what looked almost like Egyptian heiroglyphics. The water was thick with silt kicked up by the moving currents and their own passage, but Ethan could see enough to pull from his belt a life line that he wedged into a slim cavity in the wall. The line would unreel behind him, showing them the way out of the structure.

Lopez's flashlight beam suddenly burst out into a larger, even darker space and Ethan followed her out of the narrow passage and into what might have been some kind of gathering place. He could see a couple of pillars and part of the temple wall nearby but everything else was shrouded in darkness.

Ethan reached down to his utility belt and pulled from a pouch a pair of luminous glow sticks. He cracked them one after the other to provoke the chemical reaction that caused the glow and then dropped them near what he assumed was the center of the space. Lopez mirrored his actions, dropping her glow sticks further into the cavity than he had done.

The sticks began to glow and their combined light increased as Ethan hung back from them and looked around as the glow filled the chamber around them and revealed a temple that had not been seen by human eyes for thousands of years.

The walls of the temple were built from cut sandstone blocks, into which were embedded rows of pillars that Ethan guessed would number a total of seventy–two. The ceiling was made from horizontal blocks of sandstone braced with what might have been iron work but the metal was too encased in moss to be sure. The blocks must have weighed tons apiece but somehow these ancient people had managed to cut and place them in a temple that stood at least twenty feet high.

Ethan could see a shrine or raised area at the front of the temple, and although the shrine was empty he was about to head toward it when he looked down at the ancient stone flags beneath them and realized that the floor of the temple was filled with a vast symbol cut directly into the stones themselves.

Three concentric circles, the largest almost reaching the walls of the temple, surrounded a blazing sun icon, and inside the icon was an engraving of the Krishna himself. Ethan noted the winged appearance of the god, looking very much like the angels of the biblical tradition but portrayed here in a much older society, much like the Babylonians and others, and clear evidence of how modern religions had merely copied the myths, caricatures and legends of their pagan predecessors.

Then, quite suddenly, he realized that the Krishna in the engraving was pointing out of the center of the star and looking in the same direction. As Ethan looked at the temple around them, he saw patterns carved into the ceiling and he realized that it was an image of the stars, the belt of Orion easily recognizable even to him many thousands of years later.

He saw Lopez pointing up and down at the various icons and he nodded vigorously. The temple was what Lucy Morgan had been looking for because the temple itself was a map, a map that Ethan realized might point to Atlantis itself.

***

XV

Raz stood on the fishing boat's transom and waited for Ethan and Nicola to resurface. He knew that the area they were in was dangerous for more than just its currents and the frequent storms that rushed in across the vast expanses of the Arabian Sea. The waters of the gulf were patrolled by pirates who thought nothing of attacking private vessels and looting them of their contents, even stealing the vessels themselves and leaving their hapless owners stranded on remote spits of land or, worse, floating dead upon the endless waves.

He glanced up at Ranjit and his son, who were now lounging near the wheel, smoking and regarding him with silent gazes. Even as he watched them he realized that it had been after her dive here that Lucy had gone off the radar and vanished before sending the video of the stele that had started the whole search. He had assumed that Lucy had been spooked upon her return to the shore, but slowly it dawned on Raz that maybe it had been out here that Lucy had become concerned for her safety and had decided to flee without warning...

'How long did Doctor Morgan dive here for?' he asked the fishermen.

Ranjit shrugged non–comittally, but his son replied without concern.

'For two days,' he said. 'She said that it took her some time to find the entrance.'

Raz frowned. That meant that the fishermen would have had time to return to shore and be questioned by anybody who might have been interested in what Lucy was doing. He looked at the men's fishing nets and noted that they were folded and neatly stowed. He walked toward them on the deck and he could see that they were bone dry, the nets not having been deployed for some time.

Raz noted Ranjit's threadbare clothes and sun–weathered skin. Both were men of the sea and both were poor, and yet their nets had not been cast in days. A premonition of doom overwhelmed Raz and he was about to turn and run out of sight when Ranjit reached down and slipped an old pistol from beneath his shirt, a faint smile on his old lips as he pointed the weapon at Raz.

'You're not fishermen,' Raz said as he looked at the two men.

Ranjit smiled without warmth and the younger chuckled as he shook his head. 'You're not either.'

'What are you going to do with my friends?' Raz asked.

'Us?' the younger man asked as he stepped down, a thick plastic cable tie in his hands that he used to bind Raz's wrists together. 'Nothing. But those guys?'

The young man nodded toward the horizon, and Raz looked up to see in the distance across the endless waves a pair of fast–moving boats rushing toward them, each packed with armed men. The young man yanked the cable tie tight on Raz's wrists.

'Let's just say that your friends will be staying out here longer than they planned.'

*

Ethan surveyed the image of Krishna on the floor of the temple through the clouds of debris drifting with the currents around them. Although there was debris scattered around the site it was clear that somebody had come down and cleared the area in order to reveal the vast carving. Lucy's work had saved them valuable time and given that she had not decided to conceal the site after completing her work, Ethan figured that at this point she had not felt as though she was in any danger.

Ethan and Lopez both wore compasses and were quickly able to orientate themselves to north and get their bearings as to where the carved icon was pointing. Ethan noted that Krishna appeared to be pointing toward the south east, and as Lopez pressed a laminated map against the wall of the temple so Ethan produced a diving pen and carefully marked the precise direction on the map.

He saw that the line marked on the map travelled directly through Indonesia, through dense jungles and across vast mountain ranges. Lucy could be anywhere on that line and he knew that they were missing one vital piece of information. He looked at Lopez and placed his hands together as though in prayer and then drew them apart in an indication of distance before shrugging at her. Lopez shrugged back and turned again to the symbol on the floor of the temple.

Although the icon bore the cardinal points of the compass around its edge, allowing for reasonable accuracy in determining direction, there was little to show distance and no markers that Ethan could determine that would let him know how far the location that Lucy had travelled to was, from where they floated now inside the ancient temple.

Ethan began searching the walls, moving past the pillars as he sought some sign of where or what Krishna was portrayed as indicating. The walls were covered with engravings of Hindu gods, some of which Ethan recognized as similar to those he had seen at the Dwarkandish Temple, others less so. Some portrayed Hindus kneeling before fearsome orbs of light that seemed to be descending from the sky and radiating beams of light. He had seen such icons many times at ancient sites just like this one, scholars of archaeology claiming that they were images of men worshipping the life–giving light of the sun, others claiming the fiery orbs of light represented something else entirely less natural.

Ethan completed a full circuit of the temple and met Lopez coming the other way. Her dark eyes behind her mask offered him a helpless expression and she shook her head. Ethan sighed and then he reached down to his belt and pulled out two more glow sticks. He broke them and tossed them into the center of the temple, increasing the light around them. Then he pulled a compact waterproof camera from his utility belt and took photographs of the temple floor, walls and ceiling.

Ethan slipped the camera back into his belt and checked his watch. They only had a few minutes left and they would have to ascend once again to the surface. At this depth, they could not simply float directly up but would have to decompress on the way, allowing nitrogen that would have formed in their blood to dissipate and thus prevent the "bends".

Ethan led the way out of the temple and into the narrow corridor and was about to strike out for the exit when he saw the flash of a diver's lamp cutting through the deep blue sea at the far end of the corridor. Ethan halted in time for Lopez to collide with him, and despite being underwater he heard her muffled curse. Ethan pointed frantically back into the temple and she obeyed without question, sensing the urgency in his gesture.

They swam back into the temple and Ethan glided over the scattered glow sticks and picked them up, cradling them in his arms as he swam to the front of the temple and dropped them there before using his hands and flippers to brush debris over them. Lopez helped, and then Ethan pointed to her flashlight and drew his level hand across his throat.

Lopez switched off her flashlight, Ethan doing the same as he took one of her hands in his and with the other reached down to find his life line. The temple was plunged into absolute blackness, the water seeming suddenly colder now in the absence of light and the confines of the ancient building seeming to close in around them.

Ethan checked his watch and saw that they had only five minutes remaining before their oxygen supply would be outstripped by their ascent time. Then, in the darkness, he saw a glimmer of light as his eyes adjusted to the gloom and he spotted two beams entering the tunnel leading to the temple.

*

Sergei was not an experienced diver and he was not comfortable down here in the darkness of the seafloor. The sighting of the Americans boarding the same boat used by Doctor Morgan only days before had given them the lead that they needed, but they had not been able to mobilize quickly enough to intercept them before the boat had launched.

Fortunately, the boat owners were more than susceptible to a bribe of two hundred American dollars, and in one brief meeting with them while the Americans were sourcing their diving equipment the tables had been turned.

The problem was that Sergei and his companion were not well trained, capable of only basic diving at shallow depths, and expert divers could not reach the gulf until the following morning. Therefore, it was down to him to either capture Warner and Lopez or ensure that they never made it to the surface. Sergei was in no mood for negotiations and he knew that the two Americans would be low on oxygen by now. All he needed from them was any evidence they might have recovered and he could leave them down here to rot.

The tunnel entrance to whatever lay beyond was intensely dark. His flashlight penetrated the gloom only a few yards in front of him and he knew that anybody waiting there would see him coming long before he arrived. Sergei reached down to his side and unclipped an ADS underwater rifle that he cocked ready for use. Designed for use by Russian Navy Special Forces and *Spetsnaz*, the rifle was equipped with standard 5.45 x39mm ammunition fed from the same magazines used by the ubiquitous AK–47 rifle, along with a grenade launcher underslung beneath the barrel. With a range of anything between fifteen and thirty meters depending on depth, the rifle was a valuable weapon and a huge advantage for Sergei over his opponents, wherever they were hiding.

Sergei's flashlight broke free of the narrow walls of the corridor and he sensed rather than saw the larger cavity before them. Conscious of his bright flashlight beam he reached up and switched it off before turning on his night vision goggles.

The night vision system flickered into life and he instantly saw a hazy green image of the underwater temple before him, the water filled with floating debris as he eased his way inside. The image was grainy and without depth, detail hard to pick out but the clear vision a massive advantage and comfort when compared to the limited illumination offered by the flashlights. One finger curled over his rifle trigger as he pointed the weapon out in front of him and suddenly kicked his flippers and rushed into the temple.

Sergei whirled in a circle as his companion guarded the entrance and covered him with a second rifle, but there was nothing to be seen. The temple was ringed with pillars but there were no divers within that he could see and no sign that anybody had ever laid eyes on the temple's interior.

Sergei turned as something caught his eye, and he noticed a soft glow of light from one end of the temple. He turned toward it, the glowing light like a lure that drew him in as he aimed his rifle at it and prepared to kick aside the pile of debris partially concealing the source of the light.

Sergei checked over his shoulder and saw his companion aiming in the same direction, his rifle covering Sergei as he turned back to the light and kicked the debris off to reveal a handful of brightly shimmering glow sticks.

Panic ripped through him and he whirled to fire at anything moving inside the temple.

***

XVI

Ethan lunged forward as soon as he saw the lead diver reach down and kick the debris from the glow sticks out of the way. Light filled the temple and Ethan saw the form of a second diver just yards from where he and Lopez had concealed themselves behind one of the pillars.

Ethan saw the diver in the tunnel focussing on his partner as the light bloomed and Ethan swam toward him. The moment the light grew inside the temple the two enemy knew that they were not alone and they turned as one, wicked looking rifles turning in slow motion in the water as they tried to draw a bead on Ethan.

The diver beside the entrance tunnel spun his weapon around to point at Ethan, the man's eyes concealed behind night vision goggles. Ethan reached up and switched on his flashlight and directed the beam into the diver's face. The man threw one hand up to protect his eyes from the vicious blaze of light that assaulted him as he tried to switch off the goggles, and Ethan plunged in and pushed the rifle aside as he tore the diver's mouthpiece away.

The diver near the front of the temple took aim and fired at Ethan, who ducked down and used his victim as a shield as the bullet rocketed past his left shoulder in a trail of silvery bubbles and smacked into the wall behind him. Ethan hauled the diver from the tunnel, trapping his mouthpiece against his oxygen tank as Lopez darted past them to safety.

The second diver pushed toward them, aiming again as the diver in Ethan's grip thrashed desperately to loosen his trapped mouthpiece. Ethan yanked hard on it, throttling the diver as he pulled him over as a shield against the second man rushing toward them. He heard the diver's frantic screams, garbled and muted as he fought for his life, and then the second diver fired again.

Ethan ducked as he hauled the trapped man's body up and he heard the bullet thump into his captive's chest, felt the diver quiver in pain and horror as he was hit. Ethan reached around him and grabbed the man's rifle as he took aim at the second diver.

The second man was close enough that Ethan could see his eyes behind the oxygen mask, the night vision goggles pulled back now as he rushed in. Before Ethan could pull the trigger the diver used the barrel of his weapon to smash the rifle of his injured companion aside, and

Ethan knew that he would not be able to prevent the gunman from taking aim and shooting from point blank range.

Ethan relinquished his grip on the stricken man and instead reached out and grabbed the barrel of his assailant's rifle, pushing it aside as the diver squeezed the trigger and a bullet smashed past Ethan's ear and rocketed away into the blackness.

The diver's momentum slammed into the body between them and Ethan was pushed backward and away from the entrance to the temple as he saw the diver's eyes glaring into his. Ethan slammed onto his back on the temple flags, the dying diver on top of him and the other diver on top of them both, and Ethan knew that he could not hope to win the fight. He saw the fierce delight in his assailant's eyes, Ethan's grip on his enemy's rifle useless now as the diver pushed his feet down onto the flags and stood upright. He pushed up with such force that his rifle was torn from Ethan's grip, and with a flourish of victory the diver aimed the weapon down at Ethan and squeezed the trigger.

Ethan saw something flash behind the diver's head and suddenly the delight in the man's eyes vanished as they flew wide and a cloud of blood puffed onto the water behind him. The diver floated up from the stone flags, his eyes wide and staring and his limbs hanging uselessly by his side.

As he rose slowly up he rolled sideways and Ethan saw a thick bladed knife buried hilt–deep in the back of his neck, the diver's spine severed cleanly, paralyzing him instantly before he could pull the trigger. Behind him floated Lopez, who reached down and with Ethan's help hauled the second diver's body off him.

Ethan looked at his watch and he could see that they were out of time, the oxygen in their tanks no longer sufficient for them to make the ascent back to the boat.

*

Raz stared down into the water and felt his guts convulse as he realized that Ethan and Lopez should have surfaced by now. They could have very little air left and he should have been able to see them as they closed in on the surface.

The fishing boat was now flanked on both sides by two speedboats, each of which was manned by four Russian agents who were armed with pistols and grim expressions. Raz knew that Ethan and Nicola could not hope to prevail against such numbers, especially when they could not reach the surface without risking being shot on sight.

Valentin Kurov's enormous hand gripped his arm like a vice, the barrel of a pistol jammed against his ribs as the big Russian smiled down at him.

'Do you remember what I said I would do if I found that you lied to me?'

Raz tried to keep the terror from his voice as he replied.

'I have not lied.'

Valentin grinned and squeezed his arm harder. 'Then let's agree that this is probably going to be your unluckiest day.'

'There!'

Raz turned as one of the Russians pointed to a cloud of bubbles that burst upon the surface close to the fishing boat's bow. All at once, Raz realized that he was in the unusual position of hoping that it was Ethan or Nicola reaching the surface while at the same time hoping that it was not them, and that they had escaped their pursuers.

A second cloud of bubbles broke the surface near the first, and then Raz's heart sank as he saw the two Russian divers break the surface not ten yards from the boat. He saw both of the Russians give a hearty thumbs–up to their comrades, and heard a ripple of grim chuckles from the agents surrounding him.

'Looks like your friends have become permanent residents, Raz,' Valentin sniggered in his ear as the pistol was pressed harder against his side. 'Time for you to join them.'

Raz felt his guts churn and his legs felt weak where he knelt on the bow of the fishing boat and watched as the Russian speedboats pulled gently away to collect their comrades. Behind him, Valentin turned to Ranjit and his son with a grim smile.

'This boat cost two hundred dollars to hire but our work is complete early, therefore you'll be required to return the money paid, unless you want to give up the boat and swim home.'

Raz felt a grim satisfaction as Ranjit scowled at the Russian and began preparing to leave as his son angrily reached beneath his shirt for a pouch, presumably wherein he had stashed their ill-gotten gains.

'Slowly now,' Valentin cautioned, 'I wouldn't want you and the old man to pull out a weapon and cut us all down at once now, would we?'

More chuckles from the other Russians, and then Raz saw the two Russian divers in the water each toss something into the two speedboats. The two divers ducked back beneath the waves as he heard cries of alarm screech out from the Russian gunmen, and then two blasts shattered the silence of the ocean and Raz jerked his head away and instinctively dropped onto the boat's deck as a blast of heat and shrapnel shot out from the two vessels.

The two Russian divers popped up from the surface again, this time firing controlled shots into the Russians that hadn't been cut down by the grenades tossed into their boats. Raz saw hideously injured Russians screaming, their bodies lacerated with shrapnel and in two cases missing limbs as the divers' rifle fire cut into them and silenced them.

Valentin Kurov staggered to his feet in the wildly rocking boat and took aim at the divers, and Raz turned and shoved the big man hard in his side. The muscular Russian tumbled off balance as his shot went wide into the water, and then he whirled to point the pistol at Raz, screaming in fury and his face and chest lacerated with bloody wounds.

Valentin's shot cracked out and Raz cried out in fear but then realized that the shot had missed him and that the big Russian was staring vacantly at Raz, his legs quivering. Then, he slumped to his knees and fell face first into the boat, two large gunshot wounds in his back.

The two Russian divers swam to the fishing boat and clambered aboard one at a time, each covering the other as water streamed off their diving suits. Moments later, they hauled off their masks and Raz stared in amazement as he recognized Ethan and Nicola.

'Sweet Krishna!' he gasped. 'My friends, I am so glad you're not dead!'

Ethan said nothing as he and Lopez pumped two more rounds into the bodies of the Russians on the fishing boat and then heaved their bodies over the side and into the water. Already Raz could see tiger sharks swimming toward them, the blood in the water spreading rapidly. Ethan, his face boiling with suppressed rage, stalked closer to the two fishermen, both of whom collapsed to their knees with hands clasped before them, gabbling in desperate Hindu for mercy.

'They wish only to live,' Raz said, uncertain if his stomach could stand the sight of any more death.

Lopez glared at Raz as she replied.

'You tell them that they either tell us everything about who these people are and who sent them, or we'll leave them out here for the sharks, got it?'

Raz nodded and relayed the instruction, and instantly Ranjit and his son were nodding frantically and both trying to explain everything at once in garbled union.

'Tell them to get us out of here,' Ethan snapped as he hauled off the Russian diving suit and searched for his cell phone to call Arnie Hackett. 'We've got a plane to catch.'

***

XVII

Bellveue, Washington DC

Allison Pierce drove slowly down a street that was littered with garbage piled high in unsightly piles alongside tired and torn chainlink fences. There was little traffic at this time of night off Atlantic and 4th Street, and Allison was more than aware of the area's reputation.

One of the most dangerous areas of the city, Bellveue was a haven for violent crime and the drug trade, the kind of place that people living closer to the more gentrified areas of the city liked to pretend didn't exist. Just a couple of miles from the district and within sight of the Capitol across the Anacostia, the area was dangerous during the day and positively lethal at night, and now she was here and driving alone to meet a man who would just as likely kill her as talk to her.

Mitchell's contact had been in touch with her, all messages by text and she had no idea what he looked like. Mitchell had insisted that she tell nobody where she was going, and do nothing that might spook the supposed informant. She knew well that this whole thing could be some kind of elaborate set–up to get her killed, but if so why wouldn't Mitchell himself have committed the deed when he had first accosted her? The human foible of insatiable curiosity and the lure of a bigger story kept her following Mitchell's path.

She killed the lights on her Lincoln sedan and eased into the sidewalk. The car was facing downhill, a deliberate ploy on her part to give her better acceleration if she had to get out of dodge in a hurry. From the top of the low hill she could see the illuminated dome of the Capitol and the glittering city street lights flickering in the bitter cold around it. Her position was literally just a couple hundred yards from Anacostia–Bolling base, the home of the Defense Intelligence Agency. The fact that she could be sitting in an area of such cataclysmic social decline while simultaneously within sight of the country's beating heart of power and one of the most secretive intelligence agencies in the world spoke volumes to her about the precarious state of the nation, more than any presidential address. This was America's rotting core laid bare, right on the doorstep of the White House. The wolves at the door…

A movement in her rear view mirror caught her attention and she spotted a hooded youth walking with his hands shoved into his pockets and his head low. The youth crossed the street beneath the sickly glow of one of the few remaining street lights, looking this way and that as he closed in on her car. Allison tensed, and she reached down to her thigh and once again checked the location of a can of pepper spray lodged there. She would have preferred a gun, but even in self defense the risk of being hauled before a court for homicide was too great a fear for her, especially if Mitchell was right and the Russians were already on to her.

The youth closed in on her car and she could see that he was peering from beneath the rim of his hood, dark eyes searching the shadows as though demons were crouching and waiting to pounce. His gaze switched briefly to her license plate and then he reached out for the door and opened it.

The youth climbed in and shut the door, casting a single hostile glance at her to ensure that it wasn't a gunman awaiting him before he spoke.

'Kill the engine, you drawin' attention to us as it is.'

Allison obeyed and shut the engine off as the youth rubbed his hands together to warm them.

'I switched off my lights when I got here,' she said defensively.

The kid shot her a wince. 'You's driving last year's Lincoln. Ain't nobody on these streets owns wheels like this. Coulda turned up here in a helicopter and you wouldn't have stood out mo'.'

Allison said nothing. Although she couldn't see his face very well she judged him to be in his early twenties perhaps, a stocky Afro–American. She assumed that he was a gang–banger, a member of one of the many hardened gangs that prowled the streets south of the Anacostia plying their particular trade in drugs, violence and mayhem.

'Yo' got the money?'

The kid didn't hesitate to get down to business. His gaze rarely met hers, constantly scanning the street outside the car for any evidence of other parties that might be watching them.

'I got the money,' Allison replied, subconsciously mimicking the kid's tone and dialect, an old psychological trick known to engender trust in a stranger; *make your voice sound a little like theirs and they'll speak more easily.* 'What I don't got is the story I need.'

'You're asking a lot. I get seen here talkin' to you, I'll be wearing 9mm jewellery by tomorrow mornin' so I want assurances.'

'Assurances of what?'

'Immunity from prosecution,' the kid replied. 'For anythin' I done or might be accused of doin' for five years after.'

'I don't have any kind of power to grant that kind of legal…'

The door opened and the kid made to climb out of the car. On impulse Allison grabbed his arm to hold him back and in an instant the kid whirled and a blade flashed in the weak street lights filtering into the Lincoln. Allison felt a cold blade pressed against her throat and the kid's dark eyes bored into hers.

'Lose the piece,' he growled.

'I'm not carrying.'

'Right leg,' he snarled and pushed the blade harder.

'It's pepper spray!' Allison pleaded, suddenly aware that the kid was deadly serious and would slice into her throat in an instant if he sensed a lie.

He reached down for her thigh and grabbed the can, glanced at it and then stuffed it into his jacket pocket. He watched her for a moment longer and then he jerked the blade away from her throat and pulled back, his eyes never leaving hers as he spoke.

'This is how it's gonna go down. You're gonna give me the money, and then I'm gonna get out of this car and disappear and you're gonna forget you ever saw me. You come after me, or you send anybody else after me, we'll be having another meeting like this one and you won't be goin' home after, you feel me?'

Allison nodded, unable to speak and the sensation of the cold metal against the thread of her pulsing arteries fresh in her mind. She stared wide–eyed at the youth as she handed him a thick envelope stuffed with used fifties. The kid opened and checked the envelope, counting briefly before he closed it and shoved it into the pocket of his jacket. Allison figured that he would get out of the car and just vanish, but instead to her amazement he upheld his side of the bargain and started talking.

'They showed up last summer,' he said simply. 'We knew they were foreign, Eastern European is what they claimed to be but we figured them for Russians. They had money, most of it dirty but they offered the gang bosses as much as most of 'em could earn in a year to run for 'em.'

'Drugs?' Allison asked.

The kid shook his head. 'Computer equipment, chips, modems, all that.' Allison frowned and the kid nodded. 'Tha's what we thought, didn't get it. We figured that the stuff was hot, y'know, something that needed movin' from state to state or somethin', but they told us the stuff wasn't hot, just important to them and needed protectin' while in transit.'

'Do you know anything about what the computer equipment was for?'

'They didn't tell us anythin', we was just running the gear for them and doin' as we was told. Then the bosses hightailed it with the payments, just took off and the gang fell apart. The Russians or whoever they were disappeared too, just a few months ago, like the whole show was over and they'd gone back to wherever the hell they'd come from.'

'Did you get any names, any images or anything that could be used to track these foreigners down?'

This time, the kid nodded.

'We got nothin' on the Russian's names but they had a contact in DC, and right before the bosses took off a few of us knew something was up so we followed one of them to a meetin' they held down in Hyde Field, Maryland.'

The kid handed Allison a cell phone.

'The cell's hot, but the images on there should tell you everythin' you need to know. Don't ever call or contact me again, y'hear?'

Before Allison could answer the kid was out of the car and walking quickly away down the hill. Allison opened the cell's menu and selected the gallery, and instantly she saw a series of high resolution images depicting a man getting out of a smart black limousine surrounded by what looked like a security detail. Allison gasped as she recognized the man as Congressman Milton Keyes. The images showed him meeting with a pair of aggressive looking gang–bangers whom she assumed were the bosses the kid had worked for, and alongside them four Caucasian males who looked a little older but no less rough around the edges.

The cell's powerful camera had captured images sufficiently sharp that identifying Keyes was beyond doubt, provided she could get the assistance she required to ensure that a legal defense could not claim that the images were faked using digital artwork. Even before that, she knew that this evidence was explosive. Hyde Field sported a private airfield, and given that the congressman and his entourage were in a vehicle, that meant that there was a strong likelihood that the other participants in the meeting might have flown out of the area – the kid had said that his bosses and the Russians vanished right after the meeting and were never seen or heard from again.

Allison checked the time stamps on the images and smiled as she saw that they were correctly recorded and matched the kid's description of the meeting taking place sometime late the previous year. That meant she could call up the details of any flight that departed Hyde Field and find out who was aboard, who owned the aircraft and where it went after taking off from the airport.

Allison reached down to start the car's engine when she heard two loud claps somewhere ahead of her. She looked up sharply as she saw a vehicle turn onto the hill just as she saw the kid she'd spoken to tumble and fall in the vehicle's headlights.

Panic hit her as she saw the vehicle accelerate and to her horror it smashed over the kid's body. She heard the suspension thump as the car bounced and then turned as it headed straight toward her. The kid's words echoed in her mind as she considered ducking down in the hopes that the shooters would pass her by: *ain't nobody on these streets owns wheels like this.*

Allison fired the engine as the car screeched toward her and in the flare of its headlights she saw a youth hanging from the rear window with a pistol in his grip. Allison slammed the Lincoln into drive and rammed the accelerator down as she purposefully mounted the sidewalk and drove down it, using the other parked vehicles as a shield as she ducked down behind the wheel.

A clatter of gunshots rattled outside the Lincoln and Allison flinched as she heard glass shattering and a squeal of tires on asphalt as the shooters braked and swung around to pursue her. Allison swerved off the sidewalk between two parked vehicles and the car shuddered as it thumped back down onto the road. She turned for the bottom of the hill and accelerated wildly for the safety of the city.

The car headlights behind her flashed as the vehicle accelerated in pursuit and Allison hauled the wheel hard to the right as she skidded across the intersection and headed north with the car full of gunmen close behind her. She saw the vehicle slide onto the intersection in her mirror, the gunman still hanging out of the rear window and trying to draw a bead on her as she accelerated away from them. Another gunshot cracked the cold night air and she ducked instinctively as the shot snapped by her window just inches from her head.

Allison grabbed the cell phone the kid had given her and dialled 911 as she strove to keep the vehicle behind her and not let them past. She swerved left and right as the call connected and she heard a voice on the line.

'*Nine–one–one, what is your emergency?*'

'I'm being shot at!' Allison shrieked. 'I'm in a car on 4th Street headed north, hurry!'

The reply came through garbled as she drove down one hill and began ascending another toward a high school, the cell's signal broken intermittently as she struggled to prevent the gunmen from getting past her.

The Lincoln surged up the hill and then she was shunted forward in her seat as the gunmen's car slammed into her tailgate and she heard a crunch of smashed plastic and the clatter of metal fragments on asphalt. Allison managed not to scream as she kept the accelerator pressed to the floor and rocketed up the hillside.

The pursuing car slammed into her again and the back of the Lincoln drifted as she lost control. The car raced over the brow of the hill and straight across a broad intersection lined with chainlink fencing. Allison got a brief glimpse of a large red brick building ahead as the Lincoln's tires suddenly gripped again as the car slid sideways across the intersection.

The Lincoln tipped up on its side and Allison screamed as the wheel was snatched from her hands. The car rolled onto its roof amid a shower of bright sparks that flared all around her and then it slammed into a fire station wall at the top of the hill. Allison's head hit the window with a dull crunch and her vision blurred and filled with whorls of color.

The engine coughed into silence as she hung from her safety belt, her hair dangling and her head pounding with pain as she tried to free herself from the vehicle. She could see a faint haze of blue smoke in the car around her and could smell gasoline that she feared might be leaking from the upturned engine.

Allison reached up as she regained her senses and supported her bodyweight with one hand as with the other she released her belt and slumped down into the inverted Lincoln. The windows around her had shattered in the final impact and she crawled through the nearest of them, trying not to scrape her knees and hands on the shards of glass all over the asphalt.

The sound of sirens alerted her as two police cars rushed toward her location from the distance, their flashing lights reflecting off distant buildings and the sound of their engines rising in volume, and she heard the faint sound of the dispatcher's voice from the cell still inside the car.

'Stay on the line ma'am, can you hear me?'

Allison tried to clear her head as a noise beside her made her turn. She saw a figure silhouetted against the street lights. For a moment she was convinced that he was going to shoot her, but then he glanced in the direction of the police cars racing toward them and he whirled and sprinted into the darkness. She heard a car pull away, its headlights out as it vanished into the night.

Allison slumped onto the cold, damp ground, her head spinning and a nausea poisoning her stomach as two squad cars squealed into the fire station lot and four officers leaped out and rushed toward her with their weapons drawn. Allison felt the last vestiges of her strength fade and her consciousness slipped slowly away into darkness.

***

XVIII

Jakarta, Indonesia

The flare of the sun glittered off the surface of a large harbor and the hulls of yachts moored alongside the city as Ethan and Nicola walked down a long jetty to where two very large vessels were moored. Both were white hulled and one had a helicopter upon a landing pad on its stern, a dramatic image of opulence compared to the tin–shed slums that filled the rest of the city.

Arnie Hackett's Catalina had landed half an hour previously after a long flight south east from India, hugging the coastline down through the great continent and then crossing the expanses of the Bay of Bengal before tracking south again along the coast of Sumatra. Ethan and Lopez had managed only fitful sleep aboard the noisy, rattling vintage aircraft as it flew through the night to evade any Russian pursuit.

There was no boarding ramp, the yacht's sheer sides far too steep for the owners to have any fear of thieves getting aboard. It was only as they approached that a ramp unfolded automatically from near the stern and touched down on the jetty to allow them access.

Ethan led the way aboard into the yacht's cool interior, a bay where jet skis and diving gear was stowed neatly. A young man in blue shorts and a T–shirt met them and beckoned for them to follow as he led them through the plush interior of the yacht and out into a dining area high on the bow where a small group awaited them.

'About time,' Jarvis greeted them as they walked out into the sunshine.

Beside Jarvis was Rhys Garrett, their billionaire benefactor and the man who had helped them squirrel away Majestic Twelve's lost billions. He greeted them both with a warm handshake. Dressed in casual clothes that somehow still seemed to appear formal, Garrett's personal mission to expose and eradicate MJ–12, the people responsible for his father's murder decades before, had led him to join their crusade.

Sitting near them and working on a laptop computer was Joseph Hellerman, totally engrossed in his work as they gathered around. Ethan could see on the screen the images that he and Lopez had taken inside the submerged temple off the Dwarka coast before their Russian friends had arrived.

'Any luck, genius?' Lopez asked as she ruffled Hellerman's hair with one hand.

Hellerman nodded.

'It's fascinating,' he said in reply.

'So is Donald Trump's hair,' Jarvis pointed out, 'but do the images tell us anything about where to go next?'

Hellerman leaned back in his chair and stretched as he replied.

'The direction indicated by the engraving in the floor of the temple is clear, and passes directly through India and the Bay of Bengal, on through Indonesia and beyond across Northern Australia and the Coral Sea before extending out into the Pacific Ocean. Along that line, somewhere, is what Lucy found in her video and where her trail goes cold.'

Ethan folded his arms.

'And you haven't learned anything yet?'

'About the distance from the underwater temple to Lucy's location, no,' Hellerman admitted, 'but I have pretty much solved one of the greatest mysteries of human evolution while working on this, so y'know, you're welcome.'

'Do enlighten us,' Jarvis prompted.

Hellerman gestured to an image of the pointing Krishna found on the floor of the submerged temple.

'One of the biggest mysteries mankind has struggled to solve is not so much about how mankind suddenly began building complex cities after thousands of years of hunter–gatherer lifestyles, although that in itself is a mystery, but how they managed to do it on separate continents at almost precisely the same time. No theories exist that explain how so many ancient cultures also developed such similar scripts at the same time thousands of years ago despite being separated by vast distances, even by oceans.' He tapped the image of Krishna. 'Well, there's your answer right there.'

'Krishna?' Ethan asked.

'Not so much the person, but the fact that the god is portrayed as pointing to something despite having been created as long ago as nine thousand years. From that we can presume that the god is referencing something of great importance located to the south east of India.'

'That could just as easily be a natural formation or location,' Garrett pointed out. 'Maybe these folks worshipped a volcano, or Krishna is pointing toward the site of a great victory in battle or something.'

'Maybe,' Hellerman, 'but you have to remember that this temple is thousands of years older than any comparable site, already far more ancient than anything in the common historical record, and yet it's as if it was built by a civilization on a technological par with ancient Egypt, Rome or Greece. I'm willing to bet that the reason they went to the trouble of building an entire temple with this symbol in the middle was of far greater importance to them than merely a battle site or place of worship.'

Ethan frowned as he stared at the symbol on the screen.

'Why would they be doing this at all?' he asked. 'What would be the point of making all of these cryptic images and symbols. If they were indicating the location of Atlantis then why wouldn't they just write or indicate that? Wouldn't they have viewed the city as just another trading partner or enemy state or something?'

Hellerman smiled up at Ethan. 'You're a genius.'

Lopez coughed in amazement and shook her head. 'There's something you don't hear every day.'

Ethan was equally confused. 'I'll defer to your judgement and agree with you, even though I don't know why.'

Hellerman gestured to the symbol of Krishna again.

'They must have viewed any such site with great reverence, enough so that it would be singled out against all others. I was just saying that the great mystery of how the world's ancient civilizations could have sprung up across the world was one that modern archaeology could not solve. Well, we just solved it.'

'How?' Jarvis asked.

Hellerman switched screens, and with a rattle of the keys brought up a series of images of ancient Egypt's pyramids, the famous monoliths of Giza.

'Check these out,' he said as he pointed at them one after the other. 'These are the greatest known pyramids of Egypt, from the three largest at the Giza Plateau through the older step pyramids and on into the ancient past where there can be found pyramids deep in the desert built from broken and irregular blocks, many of them half buried by the desert sands. What do you notice about them all?'

Garrett replied first, voicing what they were all thinking.

'They get bigger and better as time moves on.'

'Exactly,' Hellerman agreed as he gestured to the images. 'The earliest pyramids are small and simple in their construction and have not stood up well to the elements over thousands of years. The largest and most impressive pyramids are the latest and last, huge monuments that still stand to this day and are built from blocks that even today's engineers would have trouble manipulating.'

'So?' Jarvis asked. 'That's just common sense. The Egyptians got better at building pyramids as they went along.'

'And that's the problem,' Hellerman replied. 'What if we *assume* that's what happened, because it's common sense, but in fact things happened the other way around?'

'What do you mean?' Lopez asked.

'What if the ancient Egyptians really didn't build the pyramids on their own, but in fact tried to copy them and got progressively worse as some kind of ancient knowledge was lost?'

'You're kidding?' Lopez uttered.

'I'm not,' Hellerman replied as he pulled up a chronology of pyramid building in ancient Egypt and showed it to them on the laptop's screen. 'It's one of the least known facts about ancient Egypt and one that conventional archaeologists bend over backwards to try to explain away but have consistently failed to do so. The giant pyramids on the Giza Plateua which were built some four and a half thousand years ago were not the last pyramids to be built by the Egyptians – they were some of the *first*.'

Ethan stared in amazement at the screen as he looked at an image of the three immense pyramids at Giza and more images of newer pyramid built in the deserts around ancient Memphis.

'The Egyptians didn't invent pyramid building,' Hellerman said. 'They copied already existing structures, but were unable to match the originals.'

***

XIX

'I take it that you have some corroborating evidence to support this?' Jarvis asked Hellerman. 'Walking in here and telling us that the most iconic monuments in Egypt were not in fact Egyptian isn't a small step to take.'

'I'm not the first to bring it up,' Hellerman said. 'A number of archeologists and meteorologists have studied patterns of weather erosion around the monuments of the Giza Plateau and have confirmed that all of them show evidence of being affected by torrential rain.'

That got everybody's attention real quick. Even the least travelled people on the planet would likely have known the location of the Egyptian pyramids and the lack of rainfall in that part of the world.

'They're smack dab in the middle of a desert,' Lopez pointed out.

'They are now,' Hellerman countered, 'and they were when the ancient Egytians ruled the region, but that area has not been desert for its entire existence and that's where the real mystery begins. The ancient Egyptians referred to the pyramids only occasionally in their texts, and when they did so their writings consider the monuments to have been ancient even to them. 'Think about it: the greatest monuments they had ever built and they barely mention them, and consider them to be ancient?'

'I thought that the Great pyramid was built as a tomb for the pharaoh Khufu,' Ethan said.

'That's what most archaeologists believe,' Hellerman agreed, 'and they reference various hieroglyphic records to support the notion. However, recent studies have revealed that most of those records refer to repair work done on the pyramids by the Egyptians rather than the actual construction of the monuments. It is even recorded in an artefact known as the *Inventory Stella* that the pharaoh Khufu engaged in a restoration project on the Sphinx, known as the *Hwran* to the ancient Egyptians, confirming that the entire site was already in existence at the time and could not have been built by the pharaoh's people.'

'So how does this tie in with the supposed location of Atlantis?' Lopez asked.

Hellerman's eyes were alive with excitement now as he replied.

'It's all about the ages,' he said. 'The records show that the last time the region of the Gaza Plateau would have seen torrential rain for prolonged periods would have been around the end of the last Glacial Maximum. That's around *ten thousand* years ago.'

Ethan let that sink in for a moment. Ten thousand years was close to the age of the submerged site at Dwarka and also tied in with a number of similarly aged sites around the world that they had visited on past expeditions. The Yonaguni site off the coast of Japan had been one of the most striking, its geometric city streets and steps clear in their arrangement. The site itself had been underwater for perhaps as long as the Giza Plateau had been enveloped in the sands of the Sahara Desert. Other sites in Turkmenistan and the Gobi Desert hinted at advanced civilization existing in regions of the world that were now unable to support such cities, and had not possessed a climate capable of doing so for many thousands of years.

'Most of the archaeological finds relating to the pyramids in Egypt show considerable links to astronomical locations,' Hellerman went on, 'which is understandable given most ancient cultures' interest in all things heavenly. The Pyramids of Giza and associated structures further out in the deserts show the entire construction to be a stellar map depicting the constellation of Orion. Many archaeologists have dismissed this as coincidence, despite the fact that the builders of these monuments had to both level the entire Giza plateau to build them, and that other major monumental structures around the world also are maps of the same constellation.'

'There are others?' Garrett asked.

'Many others,' Hellerman confirmed. 'The Giza plateau is postioned at the center of the geographical earth, the center of the planet's landmass. Teotihuacan, the ancient home of the Aztec people of central Mexico, occupies a similar location but we know that the Aztecs did not build the city itself, which predates the civilization by centuries at the very least. Their name for the city meant "Place of the Gods" although its original name and builders remain unknown. Those original builders constructed the city in very similar ways to the methods used to build the Egyptian pyramids, and the layout of the site once again mimics the constellation of Orion, with two larger pyramids and one smaller one marking the belt of Orion, precisely the same arrangement as seen at Giza. The Hopi tribe of Native Americans made their home in what is now Arizona, using three mesas that happened to match the constellation of Orion's belt. The villages they have inhabited for thousands of years are arranged in locations matching the corner stars of Orion.'

Ethan felt that he suddenly had a sense of where Hellerman was coming from. The ancient tribes of countless civilizations both large and small shared the same obsessions with cosmology and astronomy and had sprung up in wildly different locations around the globe, with their cities apparently built on similar foundations of technical and architectural prowess and yet separated by entire oceans.

'They were all working off the same instructions,' he said finally.

'That's what I think,' Hellerman agreed. 'Although modern archaeology rejects the notion out of hand, it stands up to scrutiny when we look at the evidence. These civilizations knew nothing of each other and yet they occupied areas around massive monolithic constructions that shared the same building techniques, the same mathematical precision, the same astronomical knowledge and the same legends.'

'The same legends?' Lopez asked.

'Precisely the same,' Hellerman agreed, 'with minor variations based on differences in dialect and the passing of time and word of mouth repetition. They all speak of gods who descended from the skies or from across the seas, who bore great knowledge and wisdom that they shared with the people, which allowed them to build immense structures and draw mankind out of his hunter gatherer lifestyle and begin the process of technological advancement at a tremendous pace. Their technologies were believed by our ancestors to have been little different from magic. Those legends have since metamorphosized into the great religions of today, our ancestors' mysterious benefactors likewise transforming into gods in the minds of those who witnessed them.'

'And those people would have had to have had an origin,' Lopez said as she caught on to Ethan's train of thought. 'They would have had to have come from somewhere, and these symbols and icons may point to that location.'

'As preserved by the retelling of ancient legends for millennia,' Hellerman agreed, 'and later in the symbols and carvings embedded in Neolithic sites now buried beneath the waves that have advanced since the last Glacial Maximum. The end of the last Ice Age began some twelve thousand years ago and continues to this day. At times, the rising seas would have in some locations been like a deluge, entire cities and regions flooded in very short timescales in the geological sense. The Black Sea is believed to have formed in this way some seven thousand years ago in what is termed by geologists as an Outbreak Flood, when the Aegean Sea broke through, a catastrophic regional deluge that would have eradicated countless towns and coastlines.'

'The origin of the flood legends,' Jarvis acknowledged.

'It makes sense,' Hellerman agreed, 'and Lucy may be back-tracking toward the most ancient victim of such a deluge, the mythical Atlantis. These icons that she has found in such ancient locations are a sort of codex, a means of finding the origin of the city. The further back in time Lucy goes, the closer to the origin of the symbols she will presumably get.'

'If the Russians don't get to her first,' Lopez said. 'They have access to all the same information that we do and they could get the jump on us at any time.'

'They don't have this icon,' Hellerman pointed out. 'Although when they locate the temple where their colleagues met their demise at Dwarka, it won't take them long to catch up.'

Ethan nodded as they all silently looked at the image of the Krishna pointing toward the south east, and then Lopez pointed at the top of the screen.

'Wait a minute, you said that all these ancient folks were obsessed with the stars, right?'

'Sure,' Hellerman replied.

'And the stars move over time,' she went on.

'Yeah, but only over thousands of years and...' Hellerman stared at her for a moment and then his eyes lit up. 'And we have the age of this temple down to an accuracy of a thousand years!'

'Y'see?' Lopez said as she nudged Ethan with her elbow. 'We're not just pretty faces.'

Hellerman grabbed some images of the stellar constellations from the pictures and then a star map from a website on the Internet.

'So, if we figure the temple was built some nine thousand years ago, and we wind back the star map here so it matches how the sky would have looked around that time...'

Ethan saw the star map shift slightly, and then Hellerman began manipulating an icon over a three–dimensional image of planet earth until the stars matched the position of those in the temple, and he saw a longitude and latitude appear on the screen and a glowing icon flashing.

'Bingo,' Hellerman said as he zoomed in on the map. 'The Krishna is pointing us toward a location in Indonesia, and it's flagged here as the location of a remote Neolithic site known as Gunung Padang, one of the oldest human settlements ever discovered.'

'That was where she must have been when she recorded the video of the idol,' Hellerman said as he looked at the map. 'But why didn't she let us know where she was?'

Ethan smiled ruefully as he imaged Dr Lucy Morgan, once again on the verge of perhaps one of the most explosive discoveries in the history of mankind. Both of her previous major discoveries in Israel and then Peru had been concealed either by Majestic Twelve or their own government as being too controversial to risk exposing to the general public. Ethan knew well that she had been twice robbed of tremendous acclaim and professional success and that right now she would be hoping for "third time lucky" and would not want Jarvis, the government, Majestic Twelve or anyone else to interfere.

'She's not in danger,' Lopez said, 'she's chasing her fortune and glory.'

Ethan nodded as he took one last look at the screen.

'The Russians won't be far behind us,' he said. 'We'd better move, fast.'

Lopez was about to follow him when Hellerman's laptop pinged and a new window appeared. Upon it was Aaron Mitchell, his dark eyes filled with foreboding as his video connection was established and he saw the team watching him.

'The program's changed,' Mitchell reported simply. 'Ethan, Nicola; I have some bad news.'

***

XX

Maryland, USA

Allison Pierce sat alone in a hospital ward, staring at the opposite wall and wondering how her life had gone entirely to hell in less than twenty-four hours. A brief check by paramedics and a handful of pain killers upon arrival had ensured that her accident had only briefly slowed her down, and now she was keen to get the hell out of the ward and back to DC.

She had no idea why she had been targeted and shot at by the gang bangers. She had assumed in the instant that the kid with whom she had met had been followed and that his snitching had provoked a death sentence, carried out with typical brutality by his former comrades. However, she could not shake the sense that there was a second possibility, one that haunted her now as she waited in the silent ward. She felt exposed, nervous, far from the familiar surroundings of DC.

At the far end of the hall, through an open door, she could see a nurse walking toward her flanked by two uniformed officers and one detective. The three men were led to the ward entrance by the nurse, and the two uniformed officers took up positions either side of the door as the detective walked in.

She figured him to be maybe fifty, short and overweight with beady, glistening eyes that bored into hers with something approaching malice. He smiled at her as he approached, but there was no warmth in his expression.

'Allison Pierce, my name is Detective Jason Cleaves, how are you feeling?'

Allison smiled and feigned relief as the detective sat down alongside her bed.

'I'm good now,' she said as Cleaves folded his hands together, his elbows resting on his knees as he looked at her.

'That's good to know,' he replied in a manner that suggested anything but concern for her welfare. 'I have a few questions for you. Can you tell me from the beginning what happened? Why were you in Maryland?'

Allison had already explained her story to uniformed officers at the scene, but she knew why she was being asked again: the detective would be seeking any holes in her story, anything to hint that she was lying or concealing evidence. Allison took great pride in telling her story once more, knowing that there was nothing to hide and that Cleaver would leave empty handed.

Cleaver listened intently as she explained how she had been investigating a possible story and had travelled into Maryland to interview a street kid who may have had information about a conspiracy. After the interview, the kid had been shot and she had been attacked and pursued out of the area by the same gunmen before crashing. The police had arrived just in time and the gunmen had fled before they could finish her off.

When she had finished, Cleaver watched her for a long moment before he pulled out a notepad and scanned a few details on it.

'You say that you're following up on a story lead, right?'

'That's right.'

'I called your office and was told that you were dropped yesterday,' Cleaver informed her. 'Why would you be working on a story?'

'Freelance,' Allison replied. 'I was already working the story before my boss and I had a little falling out.'

Cleaver nodded, a cursory gesture that suggested he didn't believe her. Allison began to feel a twinge of discomfort, as though this man were viewing her as a suspect of some kind.

'The victim, the kid who was shot at the scene, you knew him?'

'No, and he didn't tell me his name.'

'Then how did you know where to find him, or make contact with him?'

'I was working on a tip–off from another source.'

'And who was the other source?'

Allison hesitated. 'I can't tell you that.'

Cleaver raised an eyebrow, as though he had identified the first flaw in her story. 'Why?'

'Because I just got shot at,' Allison uttered as though it were obvious. 'Anything that happens to me could potentially work its way back to others in the chain.'

'You think that this shooting and the attack on you is part of some larger conspiracy?'

Allison's eyes narrowed. 'I'm not sure yet.'

Cleaver nodded in understanding, as though he were patronizing her in some way.

'So, these gunmen you mention,' he went on, 'they shoot your informant as he's leaving the area and then they come after you?'

'That's right.'

'Why would they do that? They presumably don't know who you are and the shooting of the kid seems like nothing more than a gang dispute. Why would they take the time to hunt you down as well?'

Allison shrugged. 'Like I said, I don't know yet, but they must have been watching us to know that I was there at all. It was a dark night and the kid I interviewed knew how to keep himself out of sight. Maybe they had him followed or something? They might have thought I was a member of another gang.'

Again, the nodding and now a furrowed brow as Cleaver looked at his notes again.

'And you're sure you didn't see the drivers of this other vehicle that you claimed chased you before the crash?'

Allison sat up in the bed. 'Claimed? What the hell do you mean *claimed*?'

Cleaver lowered his notepad and spoke calmly.

'We have no witness reports of a second vehicle, Miss Pierce, and no evidence other than the bullet holes in your vehicle that you were attacked, and that's where my problems start.'

Allison felt a volatile mixture of anger and fear rising up within her.

'What do you mean, *problems*? I just got run off the road by armed gunmen and you're questioning me as though I'm the suspect?'

Cleaver regarded her in silence for a moment before he replied.

'The gunshots directed at your vehicle are consistent with those fired from a small automatic weapon, and that weapon was the one we found in the possession of the victim shot, the one you said you met with.'

Allison stared at the detective in shock. 'They must have placed the weapon in his hands before the police arrived at the scene.'

Cleaver smiled.

'And the gun used to kill the kid was found in the back of your vehicle.'

Allison felt as though she had stopped breathing. For a moment she could not see the detective, instead focussed on an image in her mind's eye of being trapped in her upturned vehicle as the shadowy form of her attacker loomed before her. Could he have tossed the murder weapon into her car before he fled?

'The driver, he was out of the car before the police arrived,' she said softly, not looking at Cleaver. 'He could have tossed the gun into my car.'

'You didn't mention that to the officers in your original statement.'

'I'd just been in a damned accident! So sorry for not being on the ball!'

Cleaver nodded, still staring at her for long periods of time as though assessing her. Allison willed herself to hold his gaze and not show any sign that she had anything to hide, which she didn't, but despite her innocence she began to feel as though she really was guilty of something.

'And you say that you'd never met the victim before?'

'Never,' Allison confirmed.

'And yet you used a cell phone that we also have connected to the victim's movements in the hours before he died.'

Allison bolted upright in the bed as she suddenly remembered the cell phone.

'The phone, I need it!' she snapped. 'That was the whole point of the meeting! The victim gave it to me as evidence. Is it safe?'

Cleaver appeared surprised. 'It's been taken as evidence and will be analysed by our people.'

'I need the images from that cell,' Allison said. 'You can do what you like with the phone, but those images are the linchpin for my entire investigation!'

'The cell phone is evidence in a homicide investigation and cannot be released at this time,' Cleaver told her with ingratiating slowness, as though he was enjoying the process.

'I don't need the *phone*,' Allison repeated slowly, as though addressing a small child. 'I just need the images from it.'

Cleaver watched her again for a long time before he replied.

'Any evidence on that cell is part of the homicide investigation and cannot be compromised in any way. As the cell isn't by your own admission yours, I doubt that it can be released to you at any point.'

'It was given to me!' Allison repeated.

'So you say.'

Allison bit her lip as she tried to control her anger. She had been shot at and risked her life to get hold of the damned phone and now it was being kept from her by a detective who didn't have the faintest clue what was going on here and...

Allison looked at Cleaver and made a snap decision.

'The victim was part of a gang who were hired by Russians, operating in the Maryland area to smuggle computers and equipment into the country and safe haven. It's my belief that those Russians and computers were here for the purpose of conducting cyber–warfare against the United States and may have been used to corrupt the presidential election.'

Cleaver sat still and watched her as though waiting for something more.

'The kid's cell had images he took of the gang leaders and the Russians meeting with senior administration officials,' she said finally. 'The connection would be hard to dispute and would probably lead to convictions of high ranking politicians and a scandal that would make Watergate look like a joke.'

Cleaver stared at her for a moment longer before he replied.

'Your former boss said that you were fired mainly for focussing too much time and resources on conspiracy theories and not enough on daily news stories.'

'Daisy is a celebrity–obsessed idiot and is talking out of her as...'

'As likely as that may be, I cannot and will not place a conspiracy theory above a homicide investigation.'

'The pictures are on the cell,' Allison almost wailed, 'go take a look if you don't believe me!'

'I don't doubt that there will be pictures on the cell, but that's all there will be. Pictures in isolation don't qualify as evidence these days, Miss Pierce, and any official would likely brush them off as a spontaneous community outreach meeting.'

Allison refused to meet the detective's eye, unable to argue with his logic. 'They're still enough to ensure media interest in what happened, maybe enough to uncover a money trail that will lead back to the bigger fish in Russia who organized it all.'

Cleaver smiled tightly as he stood up and tucked his notebook back into his pocket.

'I'll be back when I've got confirmation from ballistics over which gun fired what and where. You're not under arrest Miss Pierce, but I would recommend not leaving the country any time soon, is that clear?'

Allison shot Cleaver a dirty look, and the detective turned and walked away from her at a sedate pace and with his hands in his pockets. The desire to call him back and tell him about Mitchell and Jarvis and the DIA was almost overwhelming but she held her tongue and instead cursed silently to herself. Now she was jobless, hospitalized, had lost all of the evidence she had gathered and was a suspect in a homicide investigation, and all of it was down to Aaron Mitchell.

***

XXI

Gunung Padang,

Indonesia

The heat of the sun was intense as Ethan walked along a dusty track that ascended the side of a hill amid vast tracts of rain forest. Despite the early hour his shirt was already drenched in sweat as he labored along with Lopez alongside him and Hellerman just behind them, his mind focussed on events far away over which he had no control and no influence, except, bizzarely, for what he did out here.

'Tell me what we know,' he asked Hellerman as they walked.

'They're still missing,' Hellerman replied. 'That doesn't mean they're necessarily in danger.'

'How long?'

'Two days,' Hellerman informed him. 'Your sister Natalie was picked up from her office by individuals that the witness, somebody working for Jarvis, suspected of being government agents. Your parents were picked up the following day; there were no witnesses but local security cameras detected them being guided into an SUV running government plates.'

'You got any idea what department?' Lopez asked.

'No, the plates matched in color and design but the image resolution wasn't sufficient for us to make a positive identification of the agency responsible for the arrests, if that's what they were.'

Ethan knew that with the closure of the ARIES program the new administration had been denied the opportunity to pick up from where their predecessors had left off. That meant that they would have to use any means necessary to come up to speed in the chase for the remarkable artifacts that they sought and that Doug Jarvis had been able to liberate from the DIA before his spectacular disappearing act.

The new administration had no need to start questioning Ethan's sister unless they had somehow made a connection between them when it came to matters of national security. Natalie had once become embroiled in a conspiracy at the Government Accountability Office where she had then worked in DC, when a Majestic Twelve assassin had infiltrated the office in order to tamper with and destroy evidence that could expose members of the cabal to prosecution for their crimes. But Ethan's parents had never had any direct involvement in the work Ethan had done for the government. To arrest or otherwise detain them was something that occurred in other countries, in fascist states, not the United States.

'It's a witch hunt,' Lopez said, having learned recently that her own family had been detained in Mexico. 'They're not being held for any other reason than to flush us out and make us look to be enemies of the state, fugitives.'

Ethan nodded. 'The administration is willing to lie to the people on a daily basis, even when they're on the record as doing so. Who knows what they're willing to do behind the scenes when nobody's watching?'

Lopez spoke softly.

'Not racing back to DC was the right thing to do,' she said. 'We'd have walked right into their arms and they'd have been able to connect us to Lucy Morgan, to Jarvis and Garrett. It would have brought the whole thing down before we're finished, and all of it because of emotional blackmail.'

Ethan nodded but said nothing. That a country such as his own could experience such a political collapse in such an incredibly short time stunned him as much as it had stunned millions, perhaps billions of others around the world. There was nothing that they could do about it except forge ahead and hope that they could find Atlantis before either the Russians or the administration's people could get there and remove the only bargaining chip that they had.

'Are you sure this is the right spot?' Lopez asked Hellerman, who was following them with a map under his arm and an enthusiastic grin on his face.

'Without a doubt,' he replied. 'And it makes everything we've been taught about the origins of civilization plain wrong. Those aren't my words, but those of a senior PhD geologist at the Research Center for Geotechnology at the Indonesian Institute of Sciences who has been working this site for some years. It's just up here.'

Hellerman pointed up a narrow track amid the trees that led to a hill top overlooking the surrounding valleys that had been cleared of trees.

As Ethan and Lopez emerged onto the hill top so they realized that it was covered in blocks of stone that formed a series of terraces, unmistakeably formed by human hands.

'The formations are blocks of columnar basalt,' Hellerman explained, 'arranged to form the terraces. The site was first discovered over a hundred years ago and was called by the local people the "Mountain of light". It's believed to have had a purpose of being some kind of retreat or place of meditation as there is no evidence of crop cultivation on the terraces. The terraces have been reliably dated to around four thousand years old.'

Ethan looked at the terraces, which although arranged in unmistakeable geometric patterns were otherwise unremarkable. But the site beyond in the distance interested him.

'Is that a volcano?' he asked Hellerman.

'It is,' came the reply, 'Mount Gede is a local point of worship and may be the reference to the light that is associated with this site.'

'I don't get it,' Lopez said. 'Four thousand years old isn't enough to be of any significance, right? Why would a much older temple point to a site that didn't exist when that temple was built?'

Hellerman grinned and pointed back the way they had come.

'Because the hill we just climbed was not natural,' he said. 'You're standing on top of the world's oldest known step–pyramid, older than those in South America, older even than those in Egypt. When the team of scientists dug down deeper and began carbon–dating artifacts from below the surface, they found material as old as *twenty thousand* years, man–made megalithic structures that pre–date even the most rudimentary civilizations known to man today.'

Ethan looked down over the edge of the hilltop in the direction of an area that was mostly devoid of trees, and to his surprise he could see that the hill was somewhat angular in shape and was surrounded by rings of terraces and what looked like a sort of grand staircase that led up from the very bottom of the hill, similar in appearance to those he had seen at ancient Aztec sites

'Just like Teotihuacan,' Lopez said, recognizing the same basic structure now concealed beneath the soil and foliage of millenia.

'Precisely,' Hellerman agreed, 'and we know that the Aztecs didn't build the great temples in South America but inherited them from much older civilizations. A place like this confirms that an ancient people were building near–identical structures on opposite sides of the planet and that they knew about the location of the other sites, thousands of years before man was supposed to have been capable of travelling by sea.'

'Lucy must have found her sundial somewhere around here,' Lopez said. 'I'm guessing it must have been deep down, right? To be old enough to be relevant.'

'Yeah,' Hellerman agreed. 'If Lucy was able to extract some kind of artefact from this site then she must have somehow done so alone and then covered her tracks. There have been reports of ground penetrating radar detecting buried chambers deep inside the hill but nobody has ever been down there.'

'And nor could Lucy dig herself down,' Lopez said. 'So she must have found some other way in.'

Hellerman nodded and looked around them, but Ethan could tell that they didn't have a clue where to begin. Ethan thought back to the star maps that they had seen in the temple at Dwarka.

'Didn't the Egyptian pyramids have shafts that looked up directly at certain stars?' he asked Hellerman.

'Yeah, they looked up at major bright stars like Sirius and others. Why?'

Ethan felt the heat of the Indonesian sun on his skin and the dense moisture in the air around them. 'The interior of a major structure like this would need ventilation of some kind,' he said. 'Shafts would achieve that, allowing air to move.'

Lopez smiled. 'If Lucy found a shaft entrance…'

Hellerman reacted at once and pulled out the star map from the Dwarka temple, then orientated it to the position that the stars would have been over Indonesia at a time roughly ten thousand years ago.

Without a word Hellerman led them across the hillside, his face buried in the map until he reached a small group of rocks arranged in a neat square on one side of the hill. Ethan looked about for any observers before he lifted a boot and nudged one of the rocks. It leaned easily under his weight and he could see the exposed earth at its base, not densely packed like the rest of the site but loose as though recently disturbed.

'There must be a capstone under the soil,' Hellerman whispered, even though they were alone on the hillside at this early hour. 'Lucy must have covered it back up before she left the site.'

Ethan and Lopez positioned themselves inside the square of rocks and Ethan could see right away where a shovel or spade had been used to carve a neat square of soil and grass right out of the ground. He crouched down opposite Lopez, forcing his fingers down into the soil and beneath the loosened square of earth, and with a heave of effort he and Lopez hoisted the chunk of earth up. The dense grass roots held the earth mostly together in one chunk as they set it down alongside the stones and looked back to see a square of shaped black rock sitting within the stones. Maybe two feet across, the edge was chipped and scraped where Lucy had worked it free.

'She used her spade to wedge it up and get it open,' Ethan said as he crouched down alongside it. 'This would be far too heavy for her to have lifted it all alone.'

Lopez nodded. 'She was working with somebody else.'

Ethan grabbed the edge of the slab, Lopez alongside him, and with another heave of effort they lifted the slab to one side as though they were opening a hatch. The slab broke away cleanly and they leaned it against the wall of stones surrounding the opening before them.

The shaft was barely eighteen inches square, and Ethan could see a ladder strapped or bolted into the side which descended into the depths of the hill. There was no way to tell how far down it went, but the ladder looked far less than twenty thousand years old.

'They came prepared too,' Ethan said as he pulled out his cell phone and activated a small but bright LED light. 'Whatever we need to do it had better be quick, I don't want the Russians following us down here.'

'This is a popular tourist site,' Hellerman warned, 'before long there will be people up here and I can't keep them away from this shaft.'

'Lower the capstone after us and replace the soil,' Lopez said to him. 'Then head back down to the village and buy or borrow a shovel and a decent length of rope. We might be able to call you when we're ready, but if not we'll wait until sundown and you can help us out of here under cover of darkness, got it?'

'Got it,' Hellerman promised. 'And if the Russians show up?'

'Hide,' Ethan ordered him as he climbed onto the ladder and began descending into the shaft. 'If they identify you, they'll find us. Get out of here if it gets too difficult to stay hidden. We'll figure out a way to escape once we've got what we came here for.'

'Which is what, exactly?' Hellerman asked.

'I don't know,' Lopez replied as she too vanished into the shaft. 'I'm just doin' whatever he does.'

Moments later, they vanished into the darkness as Hellerman lowered the capstone back into place. The light from the bright blue sky was gradually pinched off until suddenly Ethan and Lopez were plunged into blackness as the capstone thumped back into place amid a torrent of loosened soil.

**

XXII

'Damn, it's cold in here,' Lopez said.

Ethan could also feel the creeping cold as they descended deeper into the shaft, the light from their cell phones the only illumination. The weak lights flashed this way and that as Ethan carefully descended one step at a time, always searching for the bottom of the shaft and wondering how the hell they were going to get out of here when they were done.

The light from his cell reflected off the glistening abdomen of a spider as large as his hand that scuttled up the wall of the shaft as it tried to escape the light. He heard Lopez utter a muffled obscenity as it made its way past her.

The base of the shaft became visible beneath Ethan, a floor of soil and rubble that he stepped carefully onto before crouching to one side to give Lopez room as she joined him in the cramped confines at the bottom of the ladder.

'Well, this is cozy,' she quipped. 'I saw a millipede on the way down that was as long as my damned arm. At least you haven't forgotten how to show a lady a good time.'

Ethan shone the light from his cell phone down a tunnel that descended away from them into the depths of the hillside.

'I've seen things like this before.'

'What, two–foot long millipedes? Seriously, that thing was all kinds of gross.'

'Tunnels like this one,' Ethan replied. 'The pyramids in Egypt have internal tunnels like this that descend at an angle.'

'You think the same people who built the pyramids came over here and did the same thing?'

'Maybe not the same people, but people who perhaps remembered the same things. We just descended about sixty feet into this hillside, and Hellerman said that material dug out of here at ninety feet was twenty thousand years old.'

'Which means we're already at a geological age of ten thousand years or so,' Lopez replied as she looked at the walls of the tunnel, built from perfectly shaped and fitting blocks of stone. 'Those walls look like the ones we once saw at Machu Picchu in Peru.'

'Same construction method,' Ethan agreed. 'Dry stone blocks, no mortar, irregularly shaped. This place is like a mix and match of half the world's most famous archaeological sites.'

Ethan crouched slightly as he moved off down the tunnel, his six-foot frame several inches taller than the people the tunnel had presumably been designed for. He recalled that the stature of human beings in the past had been considerably less than today due to the daily struggle of survival, the number of calories available to a Neolithic human a mere fraction of those available to people in the western world today.

The tunnel descended deeper into the hillside and the temperature began to rise a little once again, the deeper tracts insulated against temperature changes above ground. Ethan peered ahead using the feeble light of his cell phone and saw the walls of the tunnel end as they reached a more open space ahead of them.

'There's an opening up ahead,' he said.

Lopez followed close behind and together they walked out into a chamber that was perhaps thirty feet wide and forty feet long. The walls were of polished stone and Ethan could see sunken revetements in the walls, while every inch of the temple was laced with ancient climbers, roots and vines that had forced their way inside over countless centuries. Above the scent of foliage and soil he could smell the faint odor of burnt wood.

'She was here,' Lopez said as she turned this way and that, sensing where the odors were coming from and then slowly walked across to where an old torch of dense fabric and wood was propped up inside one of the revetements. She lifted it down and sniffed at it.

'Gasoline,' she reported. 'This was used just days ago.'

Ethan pulled a cigarette lighter from his pocket, a gift from years before and a sort of good–luck talisman that he always carried with him. Lopez held the torch out and Ethan lit it. The flames coiled weakly at first but then took hold as the gasoline still inside the old wood burned.

Ethan switched off his cell phone light as the torch illuminated the interior of the chamber, flickering flame light shimmering off shaped stones and shadows dancing like demons across the walls.

'Very Indiana Jones,' Lopez remarked as she looked around them. 'Now what?'

Ethan turned a full circle and saw at one end of the chamber a raised platform with what looked like a sarcophagus on top of it. He edged his way toward it and saw at once that it was a sundial, buried far beneath the surface where no sun ever shone.

'I don't get it,' Lopez murmured with a frown. 'What good's a sundial down here?'

Ethan stood for a moment as he wondered what the hell the ancient builders of such a chamber were thinking when they placed a sundial about a hundred feet inside a mountain. The dial was set atop the sarcophagus–like rock, the surface of which was randomly pitted and lumpy, as though the people who had constructed it had forgotten to sand it smooth.

'There's gotta be a reason for it,' Ethan said as he looked around them. 'They wouldn't have gone to all this trouble for nothing, and neither would Lucy.'

Lopez stood back from the dais and looked at the surrounding walls, and then she looked up.

'I got it,' she said as she pointed upward.

Ethan looked in the direction she had indicated and saw a small, rectangular shaft that was angled to look directly down on the dais. The shaft was perhaps the size of a house brick and was filled with soil and the debris of ages.

Ethan recalled his own mention of shafts in the pyramids of Egypt that looked out at the stars, and he fumbled in his pocket for his compass as he checked the orientation of the shaft to the dais. He grinned as he looked at her.

'Good spot,' he said. 'The shaft points out of the hill due east, and I'd be willing to bet that at the time of the summer solstice the sunrise would shine directly through that shaft and hit the dais and the sundial here.'

Lopez nodded. 'And that would somehow give us the direction we need.'

Ethan glanced around at the chamber. 'But not the distance, presumably.'

'And it's not the summer solstice,' Lopez added. 'Apart from that we've got this covered.'

The walls of the chamber were covered in engravings, but this time he could see no star maps or anything that immediately jumped out at him as suggesting a map or directions of any kind. Still, Lucy had been here recently and she would not have left before finding out what she needed to know.

'Whatever happens, before we leave here we need the sun to shine down through that shaft.'

*

Hellerman reached the bottom of the hill and the shabby line of corrugated iron shacks that passed for a shopping district in Gunung Padang. The occasional local clattered by on a battered scooter trailing white smoke as they labored up the steep hillside, usually with a stained cigarette clasped between their lips.

Hellerman crossed the dusty street, and then to his amazement he felt his cell phone buzz in the pocket of his shorts. He pulled it out and saw a message from Lopez.

FLASHLIGHT AND RODS TO CLEAN SMALL SHAFT ON EAST SIDE OF HILL BY SUNRISE

Hellerman stared at the message and rolled his eyes as he wondered how on earth he was going to find anything that would be long enough to clear a shaft that would probably be more than a hundred feet long and filled with thousands of years' worth of accumulated soil and debris and…

The sound of another approaching vehicle got his attention, this one not the clattering whine of a moped but the growl of powerful engines. He looked between the shacks to the south and spotted a convoy of big, black SUVs maybe a mile away on the track climbing toward the site.

'Oh no.'

Hellerman turned as he surveyed the shacks, but he could see nothing that would clean a hundred–foot shaft and no sign of any flashlights.

Desperate, he wondered for a moment how Lucy could have done whatever she had done to get the information she needed out of the subterranean site.

Hellerman saw his reflection in a grubby old mirror propped up in a stall nearby, the sky behind him bright blue–white. He checked the position of the SUVs and he knew that he had no time and little choice.

Hellerman dashed toward the man with the stall and the mirror and hoped that he could finish the task before the Russians arrived. He grabbed the mirror and stuffed a wad of cash into the surprised vendor's hand, and then he attempted communication with the Indonesian. 'Do you have any black market materials?'

The old man stared blankly at him and shook his head in confusion.

'You know?' Hellerman tried desperately. 'Things that you shouldn't really stock?'

The old man's eyes narrowed and he said nothing.

Hellerman rolled his eyes, and then made out with his hands the form of somebody pressing down on a plunger and then swung his arms up and shouted a single word.

'Boom!'

The old man's eyes lit up and he chuckled in delight. 'You wan' trinitrotoluene! TNT, no? Why din' you say? I got no TNT, but I have this.'

The old man proudly produced an M14 landmine that looked as though it had probably been left by American forces in the Vietnam War and somehow made its way here on the black market.

Hellerman blinked and glanced at the convoy of SUVs now closing rapidly on the site.

'How much do you need?' the old man asked.

'One will do,' Hellerman said.

He grabbed the mine and handed the old man two hundred bucks before he turned and sprinted back up the hill, wondering whether the mine in his grasp was functional, which then led him to belatedly wonder whether it was safe at all. He figured that the Russians would make it to the site within five minutes, which didn't give him much time to make his escape and there was no way he'd be able to conceal the blast.

He labored up the hillside, and finally clambered up the terraces toward the ranks of rocks standing in silent vigil as the rising sun glowed through the veils of mist drifting among the hilltops.

*

'There it is,' the driver pointed as Konstantin Petrov peered up into the misty hilltops and wondered how many more of these remote and godforsaken locations he and his men would be dragged to in pursuit of the Kremlin's obsession. With Valentin Kurov dead he had no choice but to take direct leadership of the operations – reporting such a loss back to Moscow before they had recovered what they sought was not something he was prepared to do.

'Pull up here and prevent anyone else from accessing the site,' he ordered.

The SUVs pulled up and immediately Konstantin's men poured from the interiors, their muscular bulks dwarfing the local villagers who scurried away from them and vanished from the street. A young boy on a scooter turned back the way he had come and wound the throttle open as Konstantin stepped out into the humid air and surveyed the site.

A tall and vaguely pyramidal hillside rose up to his left, signposts indicating the presence of a Neolithic site. Warner and Lopez had both been tracked here, and now the men Konstantin had employed to assist him in finding them had a personal reason to do so; they had lost friends off the coast of Dwarka, some of them to the sharks that had cruised the waters of the Arabian Gulf. They had not reached the site quickly enough to save the injured troops, and even Konstantin's hardened heart had been wrenched by the carnage he had witnessed on those churning blood–red waters.

'You and you,' Konstantin pointed to two of the men, 'you come with me. The rest of you, stay here and don't let anybody off that mountain.'

The men nodded obediently as Konstantin set off up the track and into the forest. The heat was already unbearable, the sun rising above the mountainous forest to the east and glorious to look at. He ignored it, pressing on up the hill with his two bodyguards right behind him. Konstantin glanced around and, satisfied that they were alone on the hillside, he pulled out a 9mm pistol and pushed harder up the hill as he saw ranks of black stones jutting from the soil and grass on the summit.

***

XXIII

Hellerman knelt down on the hillside as he searched frantically for the opening that he presumed would be somewhere here on the eastern slopes. He could see the rectangle of stones surrounding the shaft entrance over the brow of the hill and he figured that Ethan and Nicola were maybe a hundred feet down in the interior. That Nicola's text message had reached him was amazing enough, but he figured that the hillside must be perforated with empty chambers and shafts that had allowed the signal to escape the hill and reach the nearest tower.

He judged the rough location of any shaft entrance that would both be visible to the rising sun and also angled to reach a spot one hundred feet inside the hill and then began scrambling about looking for a needle in a haystack.

The Russians would be at the village by now and would probably block any exits to escape routes. Hellerman could not hope to slip by them, so all he could do was find the shaft and blast it clean and hope that the Russians would let him live.

He was on his knees in the mud and the grass when, quite suddenly, he smelled woodsmoke on the morning air. He glanced down the hillside, expecting to see a farmer burning waste or similar, but there was nobody to be seen. Hellerman sniffed the air and shuffled across the hillside and then he saw the faintest tendrils of smoke drifting up amid the long grass some twenty feet from where he knelt. He got up and bolted to the smoke, dropped to his knees and pushed the grass aside.

There, in the hillside, was a narrow opening no larger than a house brick.

'I'll be damned.'

He could see that the opening was filled with a loosely packed decaying leaves and crumbs of soil, but if that smoke could get out then the blockages must be loose all the way down. Hellerman grabbed the landmine and pushed it into the opening, then reached in carefully and pulled the safety pin from the top of the mine.

Hellerman gently removed his arm from the shaft, and then reached out for a length of tree branch nearby as with his other hand he pulled his cell phone from his pocket. He tapped a quick message and sent it as with his other hand he eased the stick into the cavity and probed for the mine's pressure–senstive detonator.

Even as he did so, he heard footfalls on the summit of the hill nearby and a soft whispering in Russian.

*

'It's too high,' Lopez said.

She stepped down from the wall, where she had been trying to set the foliage clogging the shaft alight with the flaming torch to help clear it.

'Any word from Hellerman?' Ethan asked as he continued to survey the walls of the chamber.

'Nothing yet,' Lopez said as she checked her cell. 'I only asked him to get a flashlight and something to clear the shaft with.'

Ethan shrugged as he looked up at a series of engravings on the walls of the temple, visible now in the torch light. They looked like nothing that he had ever seen before, the icons of gods and suns and angels both familiar and yet different to those of other religions and temples he had seen.

Each of the images was accompanied by lines of script that seemed to be a mixture of ancient cuneiform and Egyptian hieroglyphics.

'You ever seen anything like this?' Lopez asked as he took photographs of the engravings.

'Never,' Ethan said. 'If Lucy was here she couldn't have failed to have noticed all of this and yet she never mentioned any of it in her video recording.'

Ethan could see figures that reminded him of the Greek god Neptune rising from the sea, bearded and with his famous trident in one hand. Others seemed to depict Zeus and other famous gods who roamed the Underworld, great storms raging over the oceans and gigantic waves crashing over shorelines. There were ships on the oceans, and Ethan suddenly realized that he was looking at evidence of ancient seafaring thousands of years before mankind was supposed to have been capable of planting crops, let alone setting sail for other continents.

'They were travelling,' he said.

And then he saw it, on the western wall of the chamber, a carving of three concentric rings with a cross through the middle. Ethan turned to stare at the engraving, carved from the living rock, when he heard Lopez's cell phone buzz in the pocket of her shorts.

Lopez pulled out the cell, took one look at the screen and then she hurled herself at Ethan and crashed into him.

*

Hellerman finished sending his text and then he laid down out of sight of the shaft opening and with the bent branch he probed in the opening. He pressed one ear down against his arm to protect his hearing and used his other arm to shield his right ear.

The branch pressed against something and then a deafening explosion reverberated through the ground beneath Hellerman as the landmine detonated and blasted a cloud of debris out of the passage to flutter into the sunlight around him.

Hellerman leaped up and grabbed the mirror he'd bought from the shopkeeper, turned it and deflected the brilliant rays of the sunrise into the shaft.

*

Ethan staggered upright as Lopez climbed off him, clouds of debris fluttering down around them as the torrent of filth from inside the shaft poured out into the chamber. As he got up he realized that he could see a bright shaft of light beaming down into the chamber, light enough that they no longer needed the flaming torch.

Lopez set it aside as she showed him the message on her cell phone.

FIRE IN THE HOLE

She turned and yelled up the shaft at Hellerman.

'A couple of yards of bamboo would have done the job! Why'd you try to blow us all up?'

To Ethan's amazement, he heard Hellerman's voice snap back down at them.

'Hurry up, they're here!'

Ethan felt a pinch of concern as he realized that the Russians must already have caught up with them. He was about to suggest getting out of the chamber when a fearsome beam of sunlight burst through the shaft into the chamber and Ethan forgot about Hellerman and the Russians and pretty much everything else.

The sunbeam struck the top of the sarcophagus and instantly both the undulating top of the structure and the sundial cast their shadows across the chamber's west wall. Ethan turned as he saw the moving shadow cast there, Hellerman somehow deflecting the rising sun's rays to mimic the sunrise at the solstice.

The engravings on the wall burst into relief, the moving shadows seeming to breathe life into the ancient carvings as though they were moving with the sun. As the light strengthened so Ethan noticed that the uneven surface of the sarcophagus now appeared in shadow on the wall as rolling hills and mountains, the unmistakeable horizon of a landscape cast in sunlight as the sundial cast its vertical shadow down on a singular point on the horizon.

Lopez flipped her cell phone over and snapped an image of the vivid display just before the sun moved out of alignment and the light began to fade. Ethan looked up the shaft for Hellerman, but instead he heard a different voice call down to him from far above.

'Comrades! I believe that you have found what we are looking for.'

Ethan did not know to whom the voice belonged but he could detect the Russian accent with ease.

'Sure, why don't you come down here and take a look?' he called back.

The Russian laughed, no sound of genuine humor in his voice.

'I think that we have all we need up here, don't we?'

Ethan heard Hellerman shout down at them. 'Don't do what they say! Tell them to go to hell and...'

Ethan heard a faint thump and the sound of coughing as Hellerman was silenced by one of the Russian thugs. Their leader called down to them once more.

'I have your friend's cell phone here, and he has been in contact with you already. Send me everything you have or I will have to fire this pistol I have pressed to his head, understand?'

Ethan swore under his breath but he nodded at Lopez, who was already sending the images they had taken as Ethan began backing away toward the main chamber exit.

'You'll kill him anyway!' he shouted back up at the Russian.

The reply that came back down was as cold as ice.

'This young man? No, he is far too useful. But the two of you? Trust me, the next time somebody lays eyes on either of you, it will be you who is ten thousand years old!'

There was a long moment of silence, and then Ethan heard something rattling down the shaft and before he could say anything two grenades dropped out of the shaft and clattered onto the floor of the temple just inches from where he and Lopez stood.

Lopez whirled and vaulted over the top of the sundial and sarcophagus as Ethan hurled himself over behind her with far less grace. They slammed down together and covered their ears as the two grenades detonated with a deafening double blast that sent shrapnel flying across the chamber to clatter against the rocks.

Ethan remained crouched where he was as he looked at Lopez.

'They'll find the entrance and seal it shut,' he said in a hushed whisper.

'We can't get there quickly enough anyway, it must be visible from that shaft. The Russians will shoot us on sight and take Hellerman with them.'

Ethan listened intently to the sounds coming from outside the shaft. He heard what sounded like walking boots, and then a shadow was cast over the shaft as somebody tried to peer down into the chamber. Ethan saw the feeble glow of a flashlight probe down the shaft and then the Russian's voice taunted them once again.

'You may hide if you wish, but your wait will be a long one.'

There was a cackle of laughter and then the sunlight returned and the sound of men vanished.

'They've got Jo',' Lopez whispered harshly.

'One thing at a time,' Ethan said as he looked about. 'Most of these temples and pyramids have more than one exit.'

Lopez nodded as she too looked around them. 'That may be true, but we don't know anything about this place. How can we possibly find hidden exits from in here?'

'Because we are in here,' Ethan grinned in reply. 'They normally hide entrances to stop people *getting in* to tombs, not to stop them from getting out.'

Lopez couldn't argue with his logic, but a faint crackling sound and the smell of burning caught their senses and they turned to see burning debris tumbling into the entrance shaft, the flickering light of flames lighting the corridor in a ghoulish glow.

'They're gonna suffocate us,' Lopez said.

Ethan got up and hurried to the back wall of the chamber, searching the surface for any possible means of escape. The builders, if they were in any way influenced in the same way as the Egyptians, would have probably used carved blocks to prevent access to the chamber by grave robbers.

Ethan searched the entire back wall but he could see nothing but smoothly cut and positioned stone. There were no doorways, no loose bricks, nothing. The acrid stench of smoke filled the chamber as Lopez backed out of the entrance passageway followed by clouds puffing on the air.

'They're too thick and too many, I couldn't stamp the fire out,' she coughed as she joined him.

The Russians would have used green foliage, which burns with thick smoke, tossing it down into the shaft and then sealing it once more. Ethan knew that there was no need to try to burn them alive down here: most victims of fires were dead from asphyxiation long before the first flames scorched their skin.

'Make it fast, Ethan,' Lopez warned. 'You don't get us out of here I'm gonna dock your pay check.'

'Get low to the ground,' Ethan ordered as he crouched down, the veils of choking smoke drifting up to the ceiling. As he did so he found himself looking at the floor of the chamber, the stones as smoothly cut and placed as those of the walls.

There was no way that he and Lopez could dig their way out of here, but if there was some kind of passage like the entrance they had used that would lead out of the chamber then it would probably be on the opposite side to the one that they entered: *one passage to the world of the living, another to the underworld.*

Ethan looked down again at the stone floor. 'It goes down.'

'Say what now?'

Ethan scanned the floor of the chamber as the smoke lowered further, the air thick with it and stinging his throat. Ethan's eyes blurred as he squinted and tried to see a pattern in the stones. There, barely six feet from where he crouched, he saw a faint rectangular shape where the stones had not been modified to fit each other but instead had been cut with straight lines.

'There!'

Ethan crawled across to the rectangle and instantly saw that the gaps around its edges were just a little wider than those around the rest of the stones. His chest heaved and he began coughing, sweat and prickly heat tingling on his skin as he grabbed the edge of the rectangle and pulled with all of the strength he could muster.

Lopez moved alongside him and heaved at the block, managing to get her smaller fingers down into the crevice around it as she too began shaking with convulsive coughs. With a heave of effort Ethan felt the block rasp and lift as the smoke finally blinded him and his vision swirled with light and color as his brain began to shut down from a lack of oxygen.

Ethan's fingers dragged along the edge of the block and he felt them scrape on the stone as he lost his grip and his balance with it. The heavy block slammed down into place once more and the thick smoke enveloped him as collapsed onto his side.

***

XXIV

Konstantin Petrov climbed into the rear of an SUV and settled in as the driver turned the vehicle around and pulled away from the ancient site. He turned and looked over his shoulder through the window at the forested hill behind them. Despite the thick foliage they had forced into the chamber entrance and the ferocity of the flames, the perfect seal of the replaced stone had prevented even a wisp of smoke from escaping from the chamber. By now, Warner and Lopez would probably be dead and roasting nicely.

He turned to the young and nervous looking man sitting next to him, his wrists manacled in his lap and Petrov's pistol pressed into his side.

'Now then,' he began, 'the image on that cell phone. How would you determine what it tells us? I should add that if I detect any hint of deception, I will respond by shooting off your kneecaps.'

The young man known as Hellerman trembled visibly but he picked his chin up and clenched his fists.

'You may as well kill me, I won't tell you anything.'

Petrov chuckled. It was always amusing to him how people always managed to put a brave face on when confronted with the threat of violence and pain, presumably inspired by the courage of television heroes or imagined peer pressure. In reality, there was little to be gained by withholding information that could almost certainly be gained by other means. Confessions merely shortened the amount of time it took to obtain the required information, and Petrov was an impatient man.

'Joseph,' he replied softly as the SUV descended along the track toward the coast, fifty miles to the south, 'we have a long and uncomfortable journey ahead of us. When I get back to our people with this information, I will have them working on it and they will reveal everything I need to know. Your assistance will merely save us time. Your friends are dead by now and you will be serving no purpose by trying to be a hero. Save yourself a lot of pain for no ultimate reason, Joseph. Take a look at the photograph on your cell and tell me what these shadows on the wall mean to you.'

Hellerman glanced down at the image that Petrov showed to him, and his eyes briefly shimmered with light and life as he saw something there. In an instant Petrov knew that Hellerman could decipher whatever was hidden in the image and that gave the American some leverage, at least for now.

Hellerman looked up at Petrov. 'I know what it means to me.'

'Then tell me,' Petrov urged.

Hellerman smiled. 'It tells me that my friends died rather than reveal to you what it means, and that's what I'm going to do too.'

Petrov looked into the young man's eyes, saw them filled with a volatile mixture of apprehension and determination and pride and fear. He had seen that look before in many interrogations, and although he knew the young American would break with the impact of the very first bullet through his kneecap, he knew also that he would probably try to deceive and delay as long as he could just to keep himself alive in the hope that rescue would somehow come from somewhere.

Petrov glanced at his driver. 'Pull up here.'

The SUV slowed as Petrov holstered his pistol and then reached down and with a small key unlocked the American's manacles. Hellerman looked up at him in confusion.

'You're letting me go?'

Petrov looked at him for a moment. 'In a manner of speaking.'

*

Ethan lay on the stone and coughed as his vision blurred into life and he turned to see Lopez standing over him, a length of wood in her hand, her fingers smeared with blood that looked black in the harsh glow of the flashlight.

Veils of smoke swirled all around her, her vest off and wrapped around her face as she tossed the length of wood aside and grabbed his hands.

'Get the hell up!'

Ethan pulled his legs in and managed to stagger to his feet, and as he swayed unsteadily he saw that Lopez had been able to wedge a chunk of tree root beneath the stone block before grabbing a length of wood to prize it open. A black rectangle of darkness awaited them as she pointed down into the shaft.

'Get down there!'

Ethan staggered down a set of stone steps into the darkness and away from the choking smoke, his head clearing rapidly as clean air filled his lungs and his vision cleared. Lopez followed him in, and he saw her reach up and haul the heavy stone block back into place on its mounts. The glow from the crackling fire vanished and Ethan used his cell phone screen to illuminate Lopez as she sealed the stone back in place.

'Good work,' he coughed, his voice hoarse.

'If a job needs doing, it needs doing by a woman,' she replied. 'Lead the way then.'

Ethan smiled to himself as he descended the steps, which led onto a ramp which continued downward. The walls of the passage were roughly hewn, not dressed and polished like those of the chamber above them. Ethan eased his way down and spotted the ramp levelling out as it headed roughly due south.

Thick vines began to appear in the ceiling of the passage, evidence of the forest growth above them as they moved.

'The passage must end somewhere just up ahead,' Lopez said.

Ethan kept moving and pointed the light to where he could now see a slanted block of stone maybe two feet square in size at the end of the tunnel, roots growing around it in dense coils like the fingers of some grotesque creature.

'We're on the south side of the pyramid,' Ethan said. 'This should bring us out in the forest somewhere near the village.'

He stopped before the giant stone and felt around the edges but he could find no immediate means of moving the block. He was about to consider digging out and around it through the walls of soil and stone when Lopez pushed past and looked up at the stone.

'Step back,' she said.

Ethan eased to one side as Lopez felt around the edge of the stone until she was able to get her fingers into a narrow seam across the top edge of the block. Ethan moved the cell phone's light to illuminate the area and he saw that the block was sitting on a ridge of smaller stones arranged around its edge. Lopez levered the block this way and that, wincing as she did so but shifting the block bit by bit until Ethan could get his hands into the same seam.

Ethan pushed and pulled and the stone shifted in position until he could get his fingers beneath its edge. Chunks of soil and debris broke away from behind the stone slab, freeing it further, and Ethan reached down with both hands and grabbed the bottom of the block. With one great heave he lifted it clear and dropped it onto the floor of the passage behind them.

For a moment he thought that they had been duped and that there was no exit here, the space behind the block as dark and dank as the rest of the tunnel. Then Lopez turned sideways and drove one boot into the thick soil and instantly several inches of mud tumbled into the tunnel followed by bright light and a waft of blessed clean air. Two more kicks and the rest of the soil collapsed and revealed the forest outside.

Lopez dusted off her hands and smiled up at him. 'Ladies first.'

She ducked out of the tunnel, Ethan right behind her as they stood up and breathed in the sweet fresh air. Ethan could feel the tropical heat on his skin and the air may have been humid and dense but right now it was like a drug and he breathed it in deeply before looking around and getting his bearings.

'There's the village,' he said, pointing to their left.

Lopez turned and headed straight for it, crouching low and with Ethan following close behind her. He could see the shanty town on the dusty track, and the rows of tuk–tuks and mopeds lined up nearby. A few locals were walking up and down, going about their daily business. Ethan could see no sign of any other vehicles on the road and no sign of any Russians among the villagers either.

He followed Lopez to the edge of the treeline and they crouched there for a moment. Ethan noticed in the dust before them thick tire tracks, of the kind he might expect to see on SUVs or similar American gas–guzzling vehicles. His eye traced the tracks into the village, and then signs that they had turned around and left again.

'They're already gone,' he said as he looked down toward the south.

'And they've taken Jo' with them,' Lopez said urgently. 'They won't need him for long and we know what they'll do with him when they're done.'

Ethan nodded and looked at the old mopeds lining the shanty buildings. They were all ancient but they'd get them back to the coast far quicker than the tuk–tuks that had brought them here.

Ethan followed Lopez across to the mopeds. An elderly man watching over them shook his head and waved a stick at them, the mopeds hired by people to bring them here and parked for safe keeping. Ethan produced a wedge of green notes and handed the old man a hundred bucks. The old guy's eyes almost popped out of their sockets and he instantly pointed to two of the newer looking machines nearby,

Ethan jumped on board one of them as Lopez grabbed the other and moments later they clattered away, leaving trails of blue exhaust smoke behind them as they accelerated down the hill in pursuit of the Russian vehicles.

Ethan yanked out his cell phone and began dialling, waiting for the signal to pick up. He got Jarvis on the third ring.

'The Russians have got Hellerman,' he reported above the sound of the wind rushing past. 'We're pursuing them now but we're unarmed. We need back up!'

'I'll send some of Garrett's people,' Jarvis promised. 'They can intercept them when they reach Ratu Bay, or Gardu if they head further south.'

Ethan shut off the cell phone and was tucking it into his pocket when he saw Lopez begin to slow down. Ethan slowed behind her as she rode up alongside something in the road, and as he joined her his heart sank. There, lying in the dust, torn and shredded, were the remains of Hellerman's shirt.

Lopez said nothing, just stared at the shirt for a long moment and then pulled away and continued down the hill. Ethan followed, and as they travelled he saw a discarded sneaker that had been Hellerman's, then another, then a belt.

Lopez slowed down ahead of him and pulled her moped up in the center of the road as she climbed off. Ethan pulled in alongside her moped and saw beyond a body lying in the center of the road. Even from thirty yards he could see that it was Hellerman, his body torn to shreds where it had been dragged for several miles down the track.

Lopez was standing over the body and looking down at it, and Ethan knew without a doubt by her posture that Hellerman was already long gone. Slowly, Lopez knelt down alongside the young man's body and lifted a small envelope that she opened and read. Ethan did not approach her but instead waited until she finally turned and walked toward him, not meeting his gaze as she handed him the piece of paper in her hand and walked silently past.

Ethan looked down at the paper and saw a name and a time written upon it, a location that he knew was down in Ratu Bay on the coast. The brief note was signed with a single name.

Petrov.

***

XXV

Washington DC

Allison Pierce walked out of the hospital and hailed a cab as quickly as she could, making sure that it was a random cab pulling in and not one of those waiting in the ranks nearby that could have been placed there.

'The Capitol,' she directed the driver as they pulled away.

The driver eased out into the flow of traffic as Allison pulled out her cell phone and switched it on. There were a handful of messages, most from her former work colleagues updating her on other stories or office gossip that now seemed vacuous and trivial. She skipped past them all and instead accessed her cloud folder, the one that contained all of her files on the DIA case.

The folder opened on the screen, and was completely empty.

Allison felt her heart sink as she realized that she was experiencing something that she had believed only happened in the movies: the complete erasure of evidence and the planting of new evidence used to discredit and deny. She closed the folder and switched back to her messages and one of them caught her eye.

You're on TV!

Allison opened the message and read it:

Your face was on the news last night, hope you're okay! Nick.

Allison clicked on a link at the bottom of the message and moments later she saw a television article detailing her car crash of the night before. Even before she got to the end of it she felt nausea rising up inside her.

'Police were last night called to the scene of a shooting and automobile accident in Bellvue. Local residents reported shots fired and the crash, when a sedan crossed the intersection here in town and hit the local fire department wall before coming to a stop. Police have identified the vehicle as belonging to freelance journalist Allison Pierce,

and detectives believe that Ms Pierce was involved in a drug dispute that led to the fatal shooting of a seventeen–year–old youth prior to the automobile accident. Police are now investigating Miss Pierce, a known conspiracy theorist who recently lost her job due to reported inconsistencies in her investigative work that her former employers considered both disturbing and false."

Allison shut the web page down and stared into the middle distance, aware that her life was coming apart at the seams and that there seemed to be little that she could do to prevent it. She closed her eyes and slumped back in the car seat as the vehicle crossed the 11th Street Bridge over the cold waters of the Anacostia and then eased down the off ramp toward Capitol Hill.

Allison realized that there was nowhere she could go, nowhere she could run to. Her friends would by now be aware that she had been fired, and half of DC and Maryland would have seen the news report and likely would now not trust a word of any investigative journalism she did. To add insult to the injury, she knew damned well that she would be blacklisted by networks across the country keen to distance themselves from the fake news and lies peddled by the administration. The irony of the fact that the lies of the men of power in DC was the reason for the media's obsession with "alternative facts", and that it was now being used to silence the truth, was not lost on her. She recalled how the Nazis in Germany had risen to power by undermining public trust in the free press, labelling any negative press as "fake news" while consolidating their power over those same networks and building the foundations of their power base.

That the same thing was happening to America, and to her, was too heartbreaking to even contemplate.

'Pull over here, please,' she said to the driver.

The cab pulled into D Street and she paid the driver and got out. The cab pulled away, her cell phone tucked deep beneath the rear seats and still switched on. Allison turned and began walking in the opposite direction, turning onto 10th Street and heading north. She kept to the residential areas, avoiding any buildings that looked like they might have CCTV in operation as she weaved her way toward the Capitol.

She was half way there when a sedan pulled in alongside her and the window wound down to reveal Mitchell. Allison cursed and refused to meet his eye.

'How the hell did you find me?'

'I've been watching you the whole time,' he replied in his sombre, gravelly voice, 'in case they tried to take you out again. Get in.'

'Go to hell.'

Allison kept walking.

'Where are you going?'

'The Capitol. I know people there, people who can help me.'

'Nobody is going to help you. If you try to trust the system, they'll use it to chew you up and spit you out. You're already being discredited on national news, how long before you wind up in jail on a murder or drugs charge?'

Allison stopped walking, staring straight ahead but struggling to see through the tears blurring her eyes. Mitchell's car stopped alongside her and he spoke somewhat more softly as he realized the depth of her distress.

'Have you ever noticed that when a political scandal breaks it always ends up growing larger as more and more details are revealed and the accused finds themselves on the end of further charges? The media whips up a storm, not because they're lying but because they're being fed information all the time to inflame the situation.' Allison sucked in a ragged breath as she listened. 'This is what they *do*. This is how they get what they want and how they suppress resistance. They lie, and make liars out of honest people. If you walk into the Capitol they will make damned sure they bring down anybody who tries to help you.'

Allison said nothing, but she turned and walked around to the passenger door and climbed into the vehicle. She sat for a long moment before she spoke.

'They're going to charge me with murder, aren't they?'

Mitchell shook his head.

'I actually doubt that. They have you right where they want you. Anytime they feel the need they can leverage you with the threat of arrest. You're vulnerable, weak and devoid of options and right now all that you want is for your life to return to normal, right?'

Allison blinked, shocked at Mitchell's insight into her tangled state of mind. She realized that she would give anything to roll back the clock by just a few days and go back to her job and carry on as though nothing had ever happened. Mitchell noted the wistful look in her eyes.

'Then they have done their job well,' he rumbled as he pulled away from the sidewalk and swung around to head south, away from the Capitol. 'Now ask yourself: what did you do wrong?'

'I opened my goddamned mouth,' she uttered, her words thick with self–loathing.

'That's true,' Mitchell conceded. 'But what did you actually do wrong, to deserve everything that's happened since?'

Allison thought for a moment. She had merely been trying to find out about the result of a closed session congressional hearing on the loss of billions of dollars of public money after a political scandal that had been swept under the carpet by the administration.

'I didn't do anything wrong,' she said finally. 'I was doing my job.'

'That's right,' Mitchell agreed. 'So tell me, do you want to go build a new life knowing that at any time these people could destroy it again just to get what they want? Do you want to be looking over your shoulder every day wondering if some detective is going to arrest you for homicide? Do you, an innocent person, want to do time in jail for the crimes of politicians?'

Allison's fists clenched into tight balls and she shook her head.

'No, but I don't have any way to fight back and they've told me that if I leave the country that I'll be considered a homicide suspect, and they've emptied all of my files! I have nothing left to work with!'

Mitchell looked across at her. 'Then you have nothing left to lose. Toss your cell phone, right now.'

'I've already done it,' Allison uttered.

For the first time, she saw a bright smile appear on Mitchell's face as he handed her an SSD Memory stick. 'Now you're learning.'

'What's this?'

'Your files,' Mitchell replied. 'I hacked your cloud account and backed the folders up once every hour until the folder was emptied, while you were in the hospital.'

Allison stared in surprise at the memory stick as she felt a rush of delight. 'I'll be damned.'

'If you want your life back and your reputation returned, you're going to have to do what we do to beat the system.'

'What's that?'

'Get ahead of the game,' Mitchell replied. 'You need to assume that everything and anything that you do could be compromised. You need to be certain that somebody is always following you, and you need to put your trust in me and the people I work for because we're the only people on earth right now who know what you're trying to do and want you to succeed. Everybody else wants you to either spend the rest of your life afraid to speak out or to be silenced, preferably permanently.'

Allison said nothing for a moment as she considered her options and realized that they really were few and far between.

'What happens next?' she asked.

'If you're in, you're catching that plane out of the country.'

'They'll put out a warrant for my arrest!'

'They'll do that anyway, one day,' Mitchell promised her, 'but if you leave this too long I might not be around to help and then you'll really be on your own. It's your call.'

'I only have your word to take for all of this. You're asking me to risk the rest of my life on what you say is the truth, when you could be the enemy yourself! How do I know that I can trust you?'

Mitchell smiled as he drove.

'You can't,' he replied, 'but I know someone who you can. You can meet them, listen to what they have to say, and then you can decide.'

***

THE ATLANTIS CODEX

Dean Crawford

XXVI

'It's a trap.'

Ethan stood with Lopez on the deck of Garrett's yacht, the sea around them sparkling in the bright sunshine, but somehow the idyllic scenery and warm wind seemed colder and darker now in the wake of Hellerman's murder.

Jarvis and Garrett stood near the laptop that Hellerman had been using before he had joined Ethan and Nicola ashore. Garrett had already begun the search for someone with the necessary skills to replace Hellerman, but none of them expected the billionaire to find anyone quite up to the task. Hellerman had been unique, his skills honed over the years he had worked for the DIA, and his loyalty had been unquestionable.

'We know it's a trap,' Lopez replied to Garrett. 'That's why I'm going.'

Jarvis sat down and dragged his hands down his face as he stared at the deck of the yacht. Garrett was also subdued and distracted, as though suddenly the danger that they now faced was becoming a reality for him, the threat to life no longer something discussed in whispers but bare for all to see.

Garrett's men had been sent to recover Hellerman's body before local law enforcement got to it. Hellerman was technically out of work and still back in DC so his body showing up in Indonesia would immediately connect him to Garrett's yacht and risked exposing their location for all to see. Hellerman was now at rest below decks while they worked out a way to get him home and arrange for a private burial, not to mention a way to explain what had happened to his family.

Ethan leaned against the wall of the yacht's bridge and folded his arms, more focussed now on Lopez than any of the others. She had remained unusually silent and subdued, and Ethan knew that wasn't a good sign. Despite her diminutive stature, her fiery temperament was capable of provoking a self–destructive instinct and now that Hellerman had been killed by the Russians she would likely charge headlong into any possible avenue of retribution with little or no regard for her own safety.

'What do we know about this Petrov?' he asked Jarvis.

The old man looked up blankly at Ethan for a moment, and Ethan realized that Hellerman's death had affected even his normally resilient determination to get the job done. Jarvis sighed and gestured to the laptop.

'I did a search for him but I'm not as good with these things as Jo was,' he replied. 'The only Russian who fits the bill is a Konstantin Petrov, assigned to the SVR in Moscow and likely also secretly aligned with the *Mat' Zemlya* unit modelled on our own at the DIA. He showed up in Indonesia right after we did, on a private jet that I was able to trace through a couple of shell companies Jo had identified, right back to Moscow itself. He's travelling light but in company, and the same jet landed in India the day after you two arrived in Dwarka.'

Ethan nodded as he moved across to the laptop and accessed the page Jarvis had mentioned. The stern, angular face of a Russian officer stared back at him, the image taken as the officer climbed out of a vehicle somewhere in Moscow. Petrov had a squat, muscular frame and a small goatee beard and his expression was one of stoic servitude to Mother Russia.

Ethan turned and saw Lopez glaring in silence at the image.

'Maybe I should go,' he suggested.

'Like hell,' Lopez uttered. 'I want to look that guy in the eye when I perforate him.'

'Killing Petrov won't get us any closer to Atlantis,' Garrett pointed out.

'To hell with Atlantis,' Lopez snapped, the cauldron of seething rage inside her starting to bubble over, spitting and scalding. 'This is what's going to happen: I'm going to meet with Petrov and let him talk. Once he's done talking, I'm going to make sure he tells us everything we want to know. Then, I'm going to tie him to the back of this yacht and have him towed out to sea at the head of a chump line and watch him get chewed on by whatever takes the bait.'

Before Ethan could reply Lopez turned and stalked away into the yacht. Ethan watched her go and then looked at Jarvis.

'This has gone far enough,' he said finally. 'You knew this day would come. We've lost people before, but not one of the people we've worked with since the first days at the DIA.'

Jarvis nodded, his reply soft.

'It was easier when we were up against Majestic Twelve. At least we knew our enemy and were fighting for the right side. Now, I don't know who we can trust.'

Ethan looked across at Garrett. 'Do you have people who can keep safe the money that we took from MJ–12, and prevent either the Russians or the administration from getting their hands on it?'

'The money I can keep safe,' Garrett confirmed. 'But the rest of us I'm not so sure. Hellerman kept our movements concealed, helped veil where we were and what we were doing so that third parties couldn't link us together. We won't be able to continue that work for long and with the Russians here it's only a matter of time before they expose us, and when that happens…'

Ethan nodded, well aware of what would happen next.

'International arrest warrants, Interpol notices, the works. The government will have the whole world looking for us and we won't be able to use your yacht as a place to hide any more.'

'And they'll locate the MJ–12 hoard,' Jarvis added. 'Right now that's all they're interested in. I think that it's time to initiate the Distribution Protocol.'

'The what?' Ethan asked.

'It's a virus that Jo created,' Garrett explained, 'that will take the various accounts holding the assets of Majestic Twelve and scatter them in small amounts to charities across the world. That scattering will be so wide and complex that it would take centuries to track it all down. Besides, if the Russians or the American government went after them it would be soon noticed and the seizing of assets from charities across the globe would be the kind of negative press that neither government can afford right now.'

Ethan smiled. 'Nice touch.'

Jarvis turned to Garrett. 'Do it now, but quietly. As long as the Russians think that there's still money to chase we have some leverage over them.'

Ethan frowned.

'There's still the chase for Atlantis,' he pointed out, 'which is idealogical to the Russians. If Hellerman spoke of Atlantis or anything else to Petrov before he died then it could send them on an entirely different course.'

Ethan moved again to the laptop.

'Do we have any idea of what the images we took in the chamber up there mean?'

The laptop showed an image taken using Lopez's phone of the wall of the chamber, and the shadows cast across it. Ethan knew that Hellerman had on occasion used software that was capable of matching topology to landscape images but he wouldn't know where to begin to find such software, let alone use it.

'Jo would have used a computer program or something to figure out where we need to go,' he said as he looked up at Garrett. 'You got any idea what that might be?'

Garrett shook his head was about to answer, but the reply came instead from behind them.

'You need a program called PlaNet.'

Ethan turned and saw Amber Ryan walk onto the yacht's deck, a laptop of her own under her arm. Despite the gloom that had settled over the team since Hellerman's death, Amber's smile and infectious enthusiasm for their cause was a welcome ray of sunshine. Lopez hurried out from the yacht and embraced Amber, barely out of her teens and the daughter of the late Stanley Meyer, a man who had created a free energy device known as a Fusion Cage. He had intended to give the device away to humanity for free, an act of selflessness that cost him his life at the hands of Majestic Twelve.

'Amber, what are you doing here?' Jarvis asked as he hugged her. 'You should be laying low back home.'

'Yeah, sure,' Amber replied. 'Laying low just got Natalie Warner taken into custody and Ethan's parents too. I figured I wasn't going to wait for someone to come pick me up, so I hightailed it out here.'

Ethan saw her set her laptop on the table. Amber saw Hellerman's computer there and looked around. 'Where is Jo?'

Nobody spoke, and when Amber looked at Ethan he just offered her a slight shake of his head. Amber turned to Jarvis, the old man speaking softly.

'The Russians got to him,' he said. 'The war has started, Amber. You should know that they didn't hesitate to kill Hellerman.'

Amber stood in silence for a few long moments as she digested the information. Ethan could see that she was struggling to adjust to the reality that one of their team had been executed by their enemy. Amber closed her eyes, took a deep breath, and then opened them again and lifted her chin a little.

'Then let's make sure that he didn't die for nothing,' she said. 'You need a landscape identified?'

Ethan moved to her side as she opened her laptop and he showed her the image from the chamber at Gunung Padang.

'It's this one. The shadows presumably describe hills and valleys.'

Amber nodded as she worked.

'PlaNet is a deep–learning program developed by Google that was trained to recognize locations by looking at over ninety million geotagged images from around the world. Most people can do that too if there are recognizable landmarks in an image, like the Statue of Liberty for instance. PlaNet is different though because it can identify areas based on nothing more than topology, the terrain itself.'

'What's the accuracy?' Jarvis asked.

Amber tilted her head this way and that as she fed the shadowy data from the chamber into her computer.

'It depends on the scale that you're working on,' she replied. 'On a country wide scale it's very accurate, but if you try to narrow it down to street level the accuracy goes down. The image you have here looks like a regional level terrain mask, so this is gonna be a fifty–fifty kind of thing.'

Ethan watched as the computer began to work and started churning out a few locations, most of them scattered across the globe in various mountainous regions.

'There's not enough data to make a match right away,' Amber said. 'We don't know what scale the hills and valleys were, so the computer can't differentiate between mountain profiles and those of hills.'

Ethan looked at the shadowy image once again.

'None of the high ground points have defined peaks,' he noticed. 'That kind of rules out mountains, right?'

Amber nodded as she adjusted the program. 'The peaks are all rounded, so that means that high mountain peaks formed by the collision of tectonic plates is unlikely. Erosion like that typically means older peaks worn down by millienia of wind and rain.'

The hundreds of locations tagged on the map on the laptop screen were abruptly halved. Lopez moved closer to Ethan's side as she looked at the screen.

'What about scale?' she asked. 'That sarcophagus that bore the engravings that cast the shadow might have held the key to how large the hills were.'

Amber brought up an image of the sarcophagus and looked at it for a moment. Then, she pointed to the edges where Ethan noticed faint lines carved at equal intervals all around the edge.

'Those look like distances that could be Yojana, the ancient Vedic measure of distance,' Lopez said.

'Raz mentioned the use of Yojana at Dwarka,' Ethan confirmed. 'He said that a Yojana was about ten miles or so.'

'That's about right,' Amber agreed. 'Nobody knows the precise measurement but on this scale it should be close enough to narrow the search. If not, we could try the smaller measurement of a Kosh, which is about two miles.'

Amber input the new scaling information and abruptly every single location on the map vanished as the computer program failed to come up with a match.

'There's nothing,' Amber said. She tried again with the Kosh measurements, but came up empty once more. 'Either nothing quite matches or we're missing some important piece of data that will complete the picture for the program. Trouble is, without an actual photograph of the area in question we don't know what we're really looking for.'

Ethan stared at the image and shook his head, out of ideas now. He was about to walk away to try to think when he noticed Lopez looking out across the bay toward the forested mountains of Indonesia. She looked as though she were a million miles away, her gaze unfocussed, lost perhaps somewhere on that lonely jungle road where Hellerman's spirit had left them.

'You okay?' he asked.

Lopez didn't respond for a moment, but then she blinked and turned to Amber.

'Hellerman was a games freak, kept playing with those virtual reality headsets and stuff, right?'

'Sure,' Jarvis replied for Amber with a faint smile, 'usually when he was supposed to be working. But we can't use virtual reality because we don't know where to start yet.'

'It's not the VR I'm interested in,' Lopez replied. 'Hellerman designed games, and he used to use something called normal maps.'

Amber's eyes lit up as she looked at the image of the sarcophagus. Instantly she began working as Ethan looked at Lopez, mystiftied.

'That's the first time ever I've heard Hellerman and normal in the same sentence. What's a normal map?'

'It's a 3D map built using a light source,' Lopez said. 'By using a photograph, you can build a 3D model of terrain or whatever, using the way light hits objects to define high and low points. He explained it all to me once and nearly put me in a coma.'

Ethan frowned.

'We already know the topography of the site we're looking for.'

'No, we don't,' Lopez said as she watched Amber working.

Amber took the image of the sarcophagus lid with the light shining across it and dropped it into an art program. Moments later, she produced a gray–scaled image that she moved left and right, the light hitting it and revealing every tiny detail of the terrain.

'Now what?' she asked Lopez.

'Now, make it taller by about ten percent.'

'Say what?'

Lopez gestured back toward Gunung Padang. 'Hellerman said that the chamber and site up there could be as much as ten thousand years old. Sea levels were lower at the time because half of the northern hemisphere was covered in glaciers that were miles thick, heavy enough to compress the ground. I read once that when the glaciers melted it took centuries for the land to bounce back. When this map was engraved, the people who made it would have seen a different skyline to the one that PlaNet program would be familiar with.'

Ethan stared at Lopez in amazement as Garrett smiled.

'That's genius. Hellerman would have been proud.'

Lopez said nothing as Amber tapped in the adjustments and ran the program once again. Within moments a single location flashed on the screen and Ethan knew in his guts that they had found it, for it was on an ancient coastline far from where anybody had ever thought to even consider searching before.

'That's it,' he said. 'That's the one.'

'That's not possible,' Jarvis uttered. 'It doesn't make any sense.'

'It does if you think about it,' Amber replied. 'We all know the legend of Atlantis and of how it was swallowed by the waves, but that occurred at least ten thousand years ago.'

'And a lot's changed since then,' Lopez said.

'It's incredible,' Garrett said, 'that nobody ever thought of this before.'

Ethan nodded as he looked at the location on the map.

It was flashing on an ancient coastline.

Atlantis was no longer beneath the waves. It was buried beneath the *land*.

***

XXVII

Washington DC

Allison Pierce walked along a path that followed the Mt Vernon Trail alongside the slowly churning waters of the Potomac River, the sky a perfect bright blue and the winter sun rising over the panoramic view of DC to her left. The air was crisp and cold enough to stiffen her cheeks and force her to push her hands deep into the pockets of her coat.

The nearby rush of traffic on the parkway was the perfect foil to listening devices, she figured, having been told to come here by Mitchell after a brief and cryptic phone call in the small hours. Things had changed. Time was running out. If she did not leave soon, there would be nothing that he could do to help her.

Allison had no idea what she was doing here. Her job was in tatters and she couldn't help the feeling that she was somehow being set up, that this whole thing was a ruse by the government and the administration to silence her for once and for all. Without access to a major broadcaster her abililty to report the news, *real* news, was gone and now she was following the orders of a man who was an assassin, if everything else she had heard about him was true. Common sense told her to run to the Detective Cleaves with everything she had heard and witnessed so far, and hope that they could unravel it themselves. Curiosity however still drove her toward the memorial before her, brilliant white in the light of the morning sun.

Allison stopped in front of the granite hemicircle that honored all of the women who had served in the armed forces of the United States. She had visited the memorial twice before in her life, both times as a child with her mother, who had proudly served as a cartographer for the United States Army. Allison smiled to herself as she recalled the visits, her mother regaling her with tales of military life while they watched the changing light inside the memorial cast the shadows of quotes into a hall filled with relics of women's military service. Then they would ascend the staircase to the terrace and look out over the Potomac at DC and her mother would tell her of the great things done there, that one man ruled over the whole country and fought for the right of Americans to live in peace wherever they may be around the world.

Allison felt some of her old resolve return. Long gone now were the days when the country's leadership could be said to have the wishes and needs of the American people at heart. It was the corruption and polarization of politics and the rise of corporate influence in Congress and the Senate that had fuelled Allison's mission to defend the honor of men and women like her mother, who had served their country only to see it become the soapbox for businessmen who cared more for their profits than the people who elevated them to office.

'Do you agree with my choice of location?'

Allison turned in surprise. She had been so lost in her memories that she had not heard the approach of the woman who now stood so close to her. She was in her forties, Allison guessed, but it was tough to tell for sure. Her skin had a luminous vibrance to it, barely a crease or wrinkle to be seen and her long mousy hair looked as perfect as that of a teenager.

'Lillian Cruz,' she introduced herself with a handshake and a faint New Mexico hint to her tones. 'Thank you for coming.'

'I'm not sure why I'm here,' Allison replied.

'I am,' Lillian said as she looked at Allison appraisingly. 'You will have met Aaron Mitchell by now.'

Lillian gestured to a nearby bench and they walked toward it and sat down with their backs to the traffic and the urban sprawl of DC before them on the far side of the Potomac.

'Aaron Mitchell is a patriot and is helping us with our work.'

'*Our* work? Who are you?'

'I have a story to tell you, and while some of it will seem familiar, much of it will blow your mind. These things are not the kind of stories you can broadcast on the television and expect to keep your job.'

'We're already past that,' Allison said.

'Your time will come.'

'Quit the jabbing and get me to the right hook, 'cause right now if this story of yours doesn't convince me I'm not getting on any flight out of here.'

Lillian smiled at Allison's tone and spoke softly, as though even here somebody might be listening.

'Over seventy years ago, in the aftermath of the Second World War, a small commitee of a dozen powerful industrialists and military figures was formed by President Harry Truman. Their purpose was the investigation of a series of impactor sites and sightings of inexplicable aerial phenomena that had become increasingly common and prevalent during the course of the war, culminating in a crash and recovery operation in Roswell, New Mexico in 1947.'

'The supposed UFO crash?' Allison asked.

Lillian nodded. 'The committee was named Majestic Twelve, and the only reason it ever existed is because of a leaked document that has since been denounced as a hoax by the FBI and the CIA, despite the fact that the document was dated as having been created in the 1950s, and contained names that no civilian would have known about at the time. Majestic Twelve was formed under intense security at a time when paranoia over Russia was at its height. It wouldn't have been possible to just stumble across something like that, nor to accurately forge it many decades later.'

'Everybody has heard of MJ–12 to one degree or another,' Allison replied, 'what's the story behind the story?'

'After major investigations into the CIA's secret programs in the 1970s, the CIA destroyed the vast majority of its documents pertaining to anything that could have exposed its agents or directors to any kind of legal action. During this purge, everything else containing information about Majestic Twelve was also destroyed. This left the cabal still in existence but without any paper trail or other evidence that they ever existed, and that's where it all went wrong.'

'They went off the range?'

'They went off their heads,' Lillian said. 'Free of any kind of oversight but still closely connected to the military industrial complex and the administration of the time, MJ–12 ceased to be an investigative operation and became one of the most dangerous and brutal cabals the world has ever not known. In their pursuit of power they murdered, pillaged and oppressed without fear of opposition for almost forty years, until another small and covert unit was created to investigate anomalous phenomena, just as MJ–12 had been so many years before. This unit was a part of the Defense Intelligence Agency and was codenamed ARIES. It was led by Douglas Jarvis.'

'Jarvis,' Allison said. 'That's the man who I'm supposed to meet in Indonesia.'

'The same,' Lillian confirmed. 'For several years, the ARIES team worked on some of the most bizarre cases the intelligence community has ever seen, picking them up when local law enforcement couldn't solve mysterious events or when other intelligence agencies rejected reports as fantasy or unworkable. The ARIES team investigated alien remains in Israel and Peru, poltergeists, free energy devices, orbital satellites of unknown origin, even small groups of Civil War survivors alive in New Mexico, their bodies immune to the effects of ageing.'

Allison's eyes widened as she listened and then she realized that Lillian Cruz was watching her, as though waiting for something. Allison peered at her for a long moment, and then she noticed again her flawless skin and hair, the twang of her accent and…

'No,' she gasped, then chuckled and shook her head. 'I'm not buying that.'

'I know,' Lillian replied, 'that's why all of this is between you, me and the river. Nobody would believe any of this and yet it all happened. Majestic Twelve pursued me for years before I was able to secure my freedom, as the last survivor of the Battle of Glorieta Pass in 1862.'

Lillian handed Allison a small, clear plastic bag, inside which was a vial of what looked like blood and a yellowing photograph of several soldiers leaning against an old cart. Among them was a woman, and Allison took only a moment to recognize the woman in the image as Lillian Cruz.

'The photograph of course could be faked,' Lillian said, 'but my blood cannot. You would require Non Disclosure Agreements from any laboratory you send the blood to but they should then tell you what you need to know. I was born in Montrose, Colorado, in 1824. My blood contains a bacteria ingested when I, my husband and his fellow soldiers hid in a cave near Misery Hole, New Mexico in 1862. The bacteria is called *bacillus permians* and is found in salt crystals in underground caves, where it has been revived after over two hundred million years in laboratories in Los Alamos. You can Google the damned things if you want.'

Allison stared at the vial and then at Lillian and suddenly she realized that this was no deception, that this was something real that she could have tested, find confirmation of the story that she was being told.

'Of course, you can't go public with any of this yet,' Lillian cautioned her. 'The public need to know not just about this but about all of the things that Majestic Twelve either bought, killed for or suppressed over the past few decades. There are countless inventions that would have changed our world for the better that have been buried because their emergence would have affected the profits of major corporations or upset the balance of world power.'

'That's what I've been trying to expose!' Allison almost wailed. 'Our country is not governed by people who want the best for us, the whole system keeps the wealthy safe, riding on the shoulders of the countless workers beneath them who are the ones who have to pick up the pieces when it all falls apart!'

Lillian inclined her head in agreement.

'That's the way that it's always been, but over the many decades since the Second World War the quality of life for the average American has greatly improved. Most of us see that as due progress, the result of democracy working for us, but in truth mankind's advancement has been held back by world government. We should have long ago been able to eradicate poverty and diseases, found natural ways to power our world, found ways to overcome our differences with other nations and so on. Now, on the verge of being able to shake off the shackles of corporate interference in politics, we have an administration determined to imprison us beneath the cosh of billionaires once again. Our plan is to prevent that, Allison, and the only way to do it is to hit the news with so many stories at once of how the government has screwed the people over for so many years that no administration would be able to take the heat. The people have a right to know, Allison, and what we have to share with them will make Watergate look like a brief irritation. If you want to, you will be the voice of that broadcast, but you must make your decision quickly, for the governments of America and Russia are searching for us all, and if we're found before we can complete this mission, everything we have done, everything we have lost and sacrificed will have been for nothing.'

Allison stared again into Lillian's clear green eyes and she sensed the fire of righteous vengeance burning within. She took the vial and photograph and put them in her pocket.

***

XXVIII

Ratu Bay, Indonesia

Nicola Lopez walked along the beach, strolling casually near the glistening white rollers nearby as though she were merely a carefree tourist taking in the spectacular view of the tropical paradise island. Her eyes were hidden behind her sunglasses, allowing her to surreptitiously scan the movement of everybody within a hundred yards of her.

Lopez knew that she was being watched, and although she also knew that Ethan was somewhere nearby and watching over her she had the sense that their enemy was close. Lopez had insisted that she meet with them alone, the memory of Hellerman's battered corpse burned into her mind and provoking a primal fury that seethed inside her like cauldron of molten rock as she searched for the Russians.

As she was walking she spotted a bulky, squat looking man sitting at a table beneath an umbrella. He had closely shaved, dark hair and a small beard and was watching her with an intense gaze. Even if she had not seen an image of the Russian she would have known by instinct that the man was Konstantin Petrov. Lopez changed direction, walking away from the shoreline and up to the tables. She could see no evidence of Petrov's entourage of security personnel, but she knew that they would be close by. The fact that Lopez was carrying a concealed Berretta 9mm pistol and could put a round through Petrov's head long before they could reach her suggested a bold, brazen confidence in the man before her, and likely the presence of a sniper within a hundred yards of the table.

'Miss Lopez'.

Petrov stood and bowed slightly in a gentlemanly manner that was not reflected in the black eyes that watched her like those of a great white shark with a smile to match, flat and without emotion.

Lopez kicked a chair clear of the table and sat down opposite the Russian, waiting expectantly as Petrov sat down and regarded her for a moment.

'You and your friend, Warner, have a remarkable ability to avoid dying.'

'Not something you share, believe me.'

Petrov uttered a brief chuckle, as though surprised by her aggression.

'I think that we've got off on the wrong foot, don't you?'

Lopez stared back at him for a long moment before she replied. 'Bit late to start over, Petrov.'

The Russian offered her a hurt look and tutted as he shook his head. 'Come now, that's water under the bridge. Your colleague had something that I wanted and he refused to part with it. I knew then that his courage meant that I would not be able to rely on anything that he said, even though I do recall him begging for the chance to recant as he was dragged behind our vehicle.' He smiled again. 'Such a pity, but he had lost a lot of blood by then so how could I trust anything he might have wanted to say?'

Petrov leaned forward, folded his hands together as he spoke again.

'You're hurt and angry that the young man died at our hands, but you completely ignore that fact that just days ago you killed several of my men in India. We found their corpses floating in the sea of Dwarka, what was left of them anyway. You do know that some of those you left behind were still alive when the sharks attacked them, no?'

'They shouldn't have tried to kill us,' Lopez shot back. 'Don't blame us for the brutality your grim little team of killers mete out to anyone who gets in their way, Petrov. If we were left to our own devices nobody would die and we would have found Atlantis by now.'

Petrov leaned back, drumming his fingers idly on the table.

'I doubt that very much,' he replied. 'Either way, the existence or otherwise of your lost city does not interest me in the slightest.'

'And yet you killed Joseph,' Lopez observed, suppressing the urge to pull her pistol and blow Petrov's kneecaps off, 'over something you now claim to have no interest in, and dismiss the murder as water under the bridge.'

Petrov shrugged. 'We cannot change what is done, only what we do next.'

'Damn right,' Lopez hissed, 'so why not pull your team off the site and we won't have to kill each and every one of you.'

Petrov chuckled again.

'I'm afraid that will not be possible, Nicola,' he replied. 'You see, you have something that we want and it's not the crumbling remnants of some Neolithic slum you and your little band want to dig out of the seabed.'

Lopez raised an expectant eyebrow.

'Thirty–two billion dollars,' Petrov said to her, his black eyes glistening now with delight. 'That is how much we estimate the people we *know* you're working for stole from the United States government. Such a lot of money, far too much for five or six people to hoard all to themselves, don't you think?'

Lopez watched Petrov with a silent, emotionless glare. *Five or six people*. Petrov probably knew about Jarvis, herself and Ethan, maybe Mitchell and Garrett too. It wouldn't have been that hard to connect Garrett to them as they could have traced the yacht's movements, and both Jarvis and Mitchell would be well known to the Russians as a result of their exploits over the years. That told Lopez that Amber Ryan and Lillian Cruz might yet be unknown to Petrov and the Russians.

'You're in it for the money,' she said finally. 'And there was me thinking that you didn't have a good reason for killing Joseph.'

Petrov shrugged again.

'Quid pro quo,' he replied, 'you killed eight of my men, I killed but one of yours, but who's counting? We can call it even and start acting like grown ups. It's not like you don't have reasons of your own to walk away from this considerably wealthier than you probably are right now. Look at you; you're on the run from your own government, who also want the money back and will stop at nothing to track you down. You don't think that as soon as they find you they won't take it all back and throw you, Warner and the others into some CIA black prison in Yemen and toss the key?'

Lopez did not react to the Russian, who sat back in his chair as though in exasperation.

'You amaze me, you Americans,' he said. 'Your own country repeatedly treats you worse than mangy dogs and yet you maintain such loyalty to your flag, to leaders who don't even know your names and yet will see you dead for the money that you hold, money that belongs neither to you or to them.'

'Stones and glass houses springs to mind.'

Petrov sighed and shook his head.

'My government wants the money that your government wants, but right now I don't care about any of that. You, and your friend Ethan Warner, you're much like me in that...'

'We're nothing like you.'

'... in that you'd like for all of this to be over, no?'

Lopez said nothing, and then to her amazement Petrov produced a photograph that he laid before her on the table. The image was of a manuscript, written in what looked like Greek, and it appeared to be very old.

'You have heard of the Greek mariner, Pytheas?' Petrov asked her.

'What of him?'

'He was following another mariner who had preceded him, and that man was called Heliosa. Heliosa was a Greek seaman who travelled widely and was reputed to have obtained a cargo of immense value that was lost in a freak storm somewhere off the coast of what is now Portugal. The crew managed to salvage some of their lost cargo, but most of it remains below the waves.'

Lopez frowned. 'You're after the cargo?'

Petrov shrugged.

'It would be nice if it were to fall into my hands,' he replied. 'The thing is, Heliosa had a slave girl called Jaela, and she recorded his voyages and kept his records for him. Jaela writes that when the ship was lost, they witnessed a city beneath the waves.'

Lopez peered at Petrov uncertainly. 'Go on.'

'The descriptions are vague, but I am reliably informed that the girl's decriptions involved a city of great temples and docks arranged in three concentric circles, the same layout that Plato and others ascribe to your lost Atlantis. Lucy isn't searching just for the lost city, she's following in the path of Pytheas, who was himself searching for Atlantis by seeking Heliosa's lost ship. The difference is that we have the document that Lucy excavated, whereas Pytheas did not.'

Suddenly, Lopez realized why Petrov was here.

'You're going to get lost once you have your hands on that cargo.'

'You and your friends could end this too, right here and right now,' Petrov growled. 'You could relieve yourself of the burden of hiding all that money and we would let you continue on your way with no further interference from us. Think about it. I would let you and Warner leave with half of any of the cargo of Heliosa that we find, a more than generous offer. And before you think that I would betray you, I am a man of my word, Nicola. If you agreed to my terms I would honor them and I would never pursue you or your people again.'

Lopez smiled faintly.

'And I'm sure that Moscow is fully on board with all of that, and that you'll return all of the money to the Kremlin and then just walk away like a good little boy.'

Petrov's eyes hardened.

'Let's not play games, Nicola. We both know that neither of our governments knows precisely how much money went missing after your DIA team dismantled the cabal known as Majestic Twelve, and certainly none of them know anything about any missing Greek gold. There is enough money at stake here for all of us to end our careers with more wealth than we could ever need and for both of our countries to believe that they too have achieved their aims. Everybody wins.'

Lopez glared at Petrov.

'You want to work *with* us?'

'A business partnership,' Petrov urged. 'We both want the same thing. We all labor beneath the corruption and greed of the elite, Nicola, and this is the best way to ensure that we deny them a prize that they ill deserve.'

'By becoming as greedy and corrupt as they are?'

Petrov exhaled noisilsy, his fists clenched now on the table before him.

'I am not an unreasonable man,' he growled at her, 'but I am an impatient one. Your friend Hellerman could have walked away had he told me what I needed to know, and yet he died because he thought that obstruction was the smarter move. He died because he was stupid. Don't make the same mistake.'

Lopez lifted one boot and kicked hard at the edge of the table. The thin metal table between them flipped up and over and crashed down onto Petrov. The Russian threw his arms up to hurl the table aside, and as he did so Lopez smashed her boot down to pin the table in place over him, the Russian peering at her over the rim and his face flushed with impotent rage as she aimed her pistol down at his face.

A small number of nearby tourists and locals scrambled away from their tables and fled as Lopez glared down at Petrov over the barrel of the pistol.

'I'm neither reasonable or patient,' Lopez snarled as she saw two armed men leap into view and run toward her.

Petrov turned to shout to his men to shoot, when Lopez gestured to the Russian's shirt.

'They shoot, you die.'

Petrov looked down and saw a tiny, bright red dot hovering on his shirt. He turned again to his men and waved them down. The guards skittered to a halt twenty yards away, both of them glaring at Lopez but coming no closer.

Lopez down at Petrov over the pistol.

'I wouldn't deal with you for all the money in the world. Before my time is done, Petrov, I'm gonna look down at you like this again just before I pull the trigger and blow your brains out.'

Lopez lifted her boot off the table and tucked her pistol beneath her shirt, the bright red speck still hovering over Petrov's chest.

'Any of you move before I'm out of sight, you all die,' she said.

She turned and walked away from the Russian, her heart pounding in her chest as she made her way out across the beach. She forced herself to walk casually, showing none of the fear she felt as she awaited the pain and shock of a bullet in her back.

She did not dignify the Russians by looking back as she walked out of range, but as soon as she was clear she pulled out her cell phone and dialled Ethan's number. He picked up instantly.

Jeez Nicola, I thought you were going to put him down right there and then!'

'I already wish I had,' she replied. 'They're onto us, Ethan. I'm pretty sure Petrov knows about Garret and Jarvis, and he might even have some awareness of Mitchell. Whatever we do next, we have to consider the possibility that he could sell us out to the CIA in return for kickbacks. He tried to strike a deal with me, to work with us, can you believe that?'

She heard Jarvis reply.

'They're getting desperate, but it's only a matter of time now before they strike, so we have to stay ahead of them. I'll take care of everything, you guys get the hell out of here and on to wherever Lucy's research takes you next.'

'What are you going to do?' Lopez asked Jarvis. 'If Petrov decides to ally himself to the CIA then we're all for the chop.'

'That's why you need to disappear so that you can finish the job,' Jarvis insisted. *'I can handle Petrov and the CIA. Get back here as quickly as you can and I'll explain everything.'*

***

XXIX

Ronald Reagan International Airport,

Virginia

Allison Pierce made her way through the departures lounge and checked the time of her flight before she headed for the bustling waiting area and chose a seat. The chorus of anonymous voices all around her and the sea of unknown faces for once was a welcome veil of cover that she could hide behind as she awaited her flight.

The fact that her cell phone was still probably cruising around the streets of DC was an additional comfort to her. Detective Cleaves would not yet have any idea that she was intending to leave the country and there would not be an APB out for her arrest at this time. Still, she knew that she would only feel comfortable when she had left the plane at her destination and vanished into the anonymous crowds of another country far from the district and its corruption and lies.

Allison buried her face in the pages of a magazine and crossed her fingers that she would make it out of the country without being intercepted or recognized.

It was only three minutes later when she knew that she wouldn't even make it out of the airport.

The security guards gave themselves away first, nonchalantly appearing at the exits to the waiting area and hovering conspicuously to anybody who might be looking out for them. Allison watched them over the pages of her magazine and hoped against hope that they were waiting for somebody else: maybe a drug mule from Colombia, or a suspected terrorist from the Middle East.

Before she could see whom they had come to arrest, a tall man with dark skin eased himself into the seat next to her.

'They're looking for you,' he said simply.

Allison looked at the man, his back straight and his hair neatly cropped. The suit he wore was tight on a muscular frame but he was not a body builder, just somebody in excellent physical condition as any military man might expect to be. Allison recognized the face as that of the man she had filmed entering the offices of Bright & Warner only two days ago to leave with Natalie Warner in the government vehicles.

'It's a free country,' she replied. 'I can leave it if I want to.'

'You're a suspect in a shooting incident in Bellveue,' the man replied. 'One call is all it will take to have the officers arrayed throughout this terminal arrest you and drag you to a jail cell.'

Allison peered at the man. 'Who are you?'

'Who I am doesn't matter, but the people you're getting into bed with are a whole different story.'

Allison said nothing, unwilling to provoke the man into giving her up. That he had not yet apprehended her was a surprise, but she could not fathom why he would even hint that he might intend to let her go.

'You're flying to Athens,' he said finally.

'Lovely city,' she said, 'the birthplace of democracy, in case you didn't know? Democracy is where people vote leaders into power to do their bidding, unlike today, where people are given limited choices, and vote for the least bad choice, who then gains power and fails to deliver anything but corruption and lies.'

The man smiled. 'My, we are a bitter little journalist, aren't we?'

'Try seeing the lies of people of power collapse your life overnight and see how you feel about it?'

'The only people I'm interested in right now are the former DIA agents who made off with a few billions of dollars and committed treason in the process.'

'The only people I'm interested in are the ones who stole that money in the first place and are now covering it up so that they can recover it for their own use instead of returning it.'

The man turned to look at her and his expression changed to one of intense interest.

'You say that your life has collapsed, and you seem to blame it on us? That sounds a little unreasonable.'

'This all began when I tried to confront Congressman Milton Keyes on the results of the congressional investigation into the Majestic Twelve scandal. Since then I've lost my job and been set up for a homicide charge, and all of it's because Keyes and his people were dallying with Russian hackers! Sorry if it seems I'm being unreasonable!'

The man watched her again for a long moment and seemed to make a decision.

'My name is Lieutenant Colonel Foxx, and I'm charged with recovering the money that we're speaking of here. However, I can assure you that I have no intention of it going into the pockets of administration elected officials and I know nothing of congressional meetings with Russian hackers.'

Allison refused to look Foxx in the eye.

'You would say that. Why the hell else would you start abducting people like Natalie Warner?' Foxx's eyes widened and Allison allowed herself a pyhrric victory. 'Surprise, not bad for a bitter little journalist?'

Foxx sucked in a breath as he spoke softly.

'I don't think that you understand the bigger picture here.'

'I understand enough to know that there is more corruption now in DC than there has ever been, which is saying something. I almost got shot forty–eight hours ago and yet now I'm in the frame for a homicide and all of my on–line data has been either seized or erased, including my footage of you and your little team arresting Natalie Warner, so congratulations, you win.'

Foxx took another breath.

'We didn't hack your accounts,' he said finally. 'I got your name from Natalie herself, and that led us to track you down. We found your cell in a cab in DC and figured you'd try to take off somewhere so we had a watch on the airports. We spotted you the moment you walked through the door and came here immediately. You're not under arrest Allison, and you're free to leave the country, although I can't guarantee it will look good to the detective handling your case.'

'If that's so, then who the hell hacked my accounts and stole my...'

Allison understood immediately and suddenly she felt more vulnerable than ever.

'You mentioned Russian hackers?' Foxx pressed.

Allison nodded.

'Congressman Keyes met with them before the elections, known hackers who were smuggling computers and equipment into the US and using street gangs to handle the goods. Keyes has something to do with it but I don't know what yet.'

'And who put you onto them?'

Allison was about to speak but then she silenced herself. 'I can't tell you that.'

Foxx watched her for a moment and then his eyes narrowed.

'Jarvis? Or maybe Mitchell?'

Allison looked at Foxx sharply, and the government man leaned closer.

'They're playing you, Allison. They will use you for whatever they want and then they'll spit you out the other end and forget that you ever existed.'

'Funny, that's what they said about you.'

'They would,' Foxx admitted. 'Jarvis and his colleagues were once patriots who have without a doubt been failed by their country, but that does not give them the right to hightail it out of the country with billions of dollars' worth of assets. Nor does it give them the right to associate with known killers and deem it acceptable in the pursuit of their own brand of justice, no matter how noble they might believe their cause to be.'

'They brought down Majestic Twelve.'

'Yes, they did, and now they're a secretive cabal of powerful and experienced men and women with billions of stolen money to their name, avoiding justice while working with murderers and seeking to undermine and influence the power of elected officials and governments. See anything familiar there, Allison?'

She looked away from Foxx and scanned the crowds, wondering how the hell she got into this mess in the first place. Her mother would not have known whether to be proud or appalled.

'I checked you out on the way here,' Foxx said. 'I can see what you've been trying to do with your career and that's why we didn't call the police about you being here.'

Allison glanced sideways at Foxx. 'What's that supposed to mean?'

'It means that I can help you, if you can help me.'

'Jeez, not you too.'

'This is the right thing to do, Allison,' Foxx insisted. 'Leaving the country to join an alliance of international fugitives doesn't scream innocent to me and it won't to the police or the media when they get hold of the story. You of all people should know that.'

Allison bit her lip. 'What do you want?'

'I want Jarvis and his crew in custody, back here in America where they can face charges for what they've done.'

Allison closed her eyes and slowly shook her head.

'I don't know who to trust any more.'

'I'm not the one who's fleeing the country with billions of stolen dollars.'

'You're forgetting that you just admitted that their hands were forced.'

'They had a choice,' Foxx persisted. 'They chose badly. What are you going to do, Allison?'

She bit her lip more tightly but her mind was a fog of uncertainty and she could not figure out who was telling the truth and who was trying to bend her to their will. Foxx seemed to be in earnest but then he wasn't up against the impossible odds that Mitchell and Lillian and the others seemed to be.

Allison's thought of Lillian gave her an idea and she turned to him. She reached into her pocket and retrieved the vial of blood that Lillian had handed to her, but kept the photograph out of sight.

'This will prove, one way or the other, if Jarvis and his people are lying.'

Foxx frowned as he took the vial. 'What the hell is this?'

'Proof of honesty,' Allison said. 'Run the sample and you'll see. If the results seem impossible, then I will need your help to expose the greatest conspiracy this country has ever seen. If the results are normal, then I will need your help to bring Jarvis and his people to justice.'

Allison stood up as her flight was called to boarding. Foxx stood also, and with one hand he forced a small cell phone into hers.

'GPS tracker,' he said. 'It's active all the time. If you want to help me, just switch it on when you meet Jarvis.'

Allison took the cell phone and looked at it for a moment, then slipped it into her pocket.

'Can I trust you to do the right thing?' Foxx asked her.

Allison said nothing as she turned and marched away toward the boarding ramp.

***

XXX

Oia, Santorini

The PBY Catalina's twin radial engines clattered noisily as Arnie and his wife flew the big amphibious aircraft around the north coast of the island. From his vantage point inside the rear of the aircraft Ethan could see through a bulbous, teardrop shaped Perspex blister a panoramic view of the island amid the shimmering azure Mediterranean Sea.

The sunlight swept through the aircraft as it descended, Arnie lowering the flaps as the Catalina bobbed and gyrated on the air currents rising up off the steep slopes of the island. Ethan could see the main town of Oia perched on the northern coast, the entire shape of the island formed from the edges of a massive, ancient volcanic caldera.

'Santorini was once known as Thera,' Amber explained as the aircraft descended toward the glittering waves, 'and is the site of one of the most powerful volcanic eruptions in history.'

Lopez peered out at the immense view afforded them by the clear plastic blisters, where once long ago there had been mounted machine guns, the Catalina a survivor from the Second World War.

'A volcanic island,' she said as she glanced at Ethan. 'Jo mentioned how supposed visitors to Atlantis described it as a city beneath a volcanic cloud.'

Ethan nodded as he watched the waves rushing up to meet the fuselage beneath them and he checked his harness one more time.

'That may explain why nobody has ever found any evidence of Atlantis. If the city was alongside a massive volcano that blew its top, there would be nothing left.'

'You're seeing the pattern here though, right?' Amber said. 'Several of the sites associated with Lucy's research have involved ancient civilizations that thrived on the slopes of volcanoes. Although none of them yet appear to have been Atlantis, they're sharing the same characteristics.'

Even as the aircraft was about to touch down, Ethan could see that the northern hook shape of Santorini was abruptly cut off where the huge volcano's caldera had collapsed. To the south west another smaller island of steep cliffs and barren rock marked the southern curve of the caldera, cut off again in the south before the bottom tip of Santorini emerged from the waves.

'The ancient city of Akrotiri was located on that southern tip,' Amber said as she noted the direction of Ethan's gaze. 'That's where we'll find whatever the hell Lucy was looking for.'

Ethan felt and heard Arnie cut the power to the two engines and for a brief moment the big airplane seemed to hover in the air just inches above the waves flashing by her hull. Then she settled onto the water with a crescendo of vibrations that thundered through the fuselage until the aircraft slowed down and Arnie turned her toward the docks nearby, where jetties poked out of a natural harbor called Amouni Bay.

'We'll moor here,' Arnie called back down the fuselage as they taxied in toward the shore. 'If anybody comes looking for you at the island's main airport this'll slow them down some, but it's only a matter of time as we had to file a flightplan to get here.'

The endless rattling of the engines mercifully coughed into silence as Arnie shut them down, and his wife threw mooring lines to a pair of helpful fishermen on the jetty alongside them. Ethan punched his harness and stood up, hauling open the Catalina's big side door and letting in a waft of clean air that replaced the odors of metal, grease and aviation fuel.

The Catalina bobbed gently on the water as Ethan and Lopez made their way ashore, Ethan scanning the buildings of the nearby town high above them for any sign of Petrov or his goons. Perched on the cliffs that had once been the edge of the immense volcano's caldera, the town was built entirely from brilliant white stone that shone in the sunlight with such an intensity that Ethan slipped his sunglasses on in order to survey the scene.

The doors and shutters of all the buildings were painted a deep blue that matched the cloudless sky above them as they began climbing up a series of rock–cut steps leading to the town. Behind them, Amber chatted enthusiastically.

'The island was occupied for thousands of years by the Minoan civilization, which is considered to be the very oldest and first European civilization to ever have existed. They preceded the ancient Greeks by some margin and yet the source of their knowledge and their technology is unknown. The Minoans effectively sprung up out of nowhere with a fully–fledged society, city building technology and a script that was fully developed and yet is undeciphered to this day. It also has no known origin. Literally everything that came afterward in human history owes its existence to Minoan culture.'

Lopez looked back over the bay as she climbed and gestured out to the nearby island of Thirasia behind them.

'Look at the size of this thing,' she said. 'The volcano must have been five miles across.'

'At least,' Amber agreed. 'The blast that sent this civilization into the history books created a tsunami that hit the island of Crete to the south and entirely obliterated the volcanic caldera itself, just leaving the rim that we see now. It hurled fourteen cubic miles of debris into the atmosphere when it erupted five thousand years ago and buried the Minoan city of Akrotiri in dense ash. The remains of the city are being excavated as we speak.'

Ethan knew that any excavations conducted at the site by official archaeology would be a painstakingly slow and careful process, taking time that they could ill afford to spend here on the island with the Russians equally keen to take the lead in the race to the city and find the key to Atlantis. However, Lucy had possessed the advantage of being a scientist herself and might have been able to access the site using her credentials.

'Do we have any idea if Lucy was here?' he asked Amber.

Amber shook her head.

'I don't know how she was doing it but Lucy has been travelling incognito for weeks. I couldn't find any evidence of travel by land, sea or air.'

Ethan frowned uncertainly. Lucy would have had Garrett's fleet of vehicles, aircraft and vessels at her command should she have needed them, so why would she have chosen to vanish off the radar unless…

'She might have realized the Russians were a threat,' he said as he climbed the steps.

'You think that Petrov and his people approached her?' Lopez asked.

'He came to you offering you a deal,' Ethan said. 'Maybe they tried Lucy first and somehow she saw the danger and went underground. She might have been concerned that the Russians could connect her to us if she went back to Jarvis or Garrett.'

Lopez nodded.

'That means only the people working the site at Akrotiri would know if she came through here. If the Russians come here then they're going to have the same idea.'

'They don't know what we know though, right?' Amber said.

'They know enough,' Ethan replied. 'They'll figure out the rest soon and that will lead them here. The less time we spend figuring out our next move, the better off we are. Can we be sure that the topographical data from India is a match for ancient Akrotiri?'

'It's as close as anything we've got and I've run the same data four times now. It keeps coming back to the same location, and this island is by far the closest match to Plato's description of the city of Atlantis as anything we've ever heard of.'

Atop the hill, a car awaited them, a travel representative booked in advance by Jarvis handing them the keys to the vehicle. Amber kept talking as they got into the car and Ethan drove out of the parking lot.

'Discoveries at Knossos on Crete and here at Akrotiri have revealed that the Minoans possessed very advanced engineering technology, capable of building multi–storey buildings with complex water piping, air flow management and wood and masonry highly resistant to earthquakes, all of which was far ahead of contemporary Greek technology. Plato's description of Atlantis as being a circular city surrounded by three rings of sea water and two earth rings connected by a canal matches a fresco found in the ruins of Akrotiri that was believed to be a landscape of the city before its destruction. The city is in the center of the caldera's lagoon with a narrow entrance from outside the caldera that would match the layout precisely.'

'So you think that this is it?' Ethan asked as the vehicle travelled south toward Akrotiri. 'This is the source of the legend?'

'Well, it was destroyed by a major environmental catastrophe, much of it has now sunk beneath the waves and there's no better place to hide the remains of a city than beneath a few metres of ash and pumice that's nearly three thousand years old…'

'But?' Lopez added a word to Amber's sentence.

'Well, if Atlantis really is here then where's Lucy?'

Ethan did not have a reply for her as they drove for twenty minutes across the island toward the site of ancient Akrotiri, which was preserved from the elements by a series of large structures that completely contained the site. Ethan slowed and pulled into a parking lot opposite the entrance and Ethan climbed out and surveyed the area as Lopez and Amber joined him.

The site was open to the public and therefore tourists were milling about in the parking lot, which Ethan figured would go some way to preventing the Russians from launching any kind of major surprise attack against them. That said, they had not been afraid to draw their weapons in Dwarka, so their time would be limited here.

'Did Lucy have any contacts here?' Ethan asked Amber.

Amber shook her head. 'Nothing that I could find, but she was doing some research into one Greek artefact that might have had something to do with the search for Atlantis, something called the Antikythera Device.'

'The what now?' Ethan asked.

Lopez replied as they walked toward the main entrance.

'It's an ancient computer found on the island of Antikythera, just over a hundred miles west of Akrotiri, which was constructed in Corinth, near Athens, over two thousand years ago. It is widely recognized as the world's first analogue computer.'

Ethan stared at her as they walked. 'A computer, in ancient Greece?'

'It wasn't exactly a PC,' Amber said, 'but a mechanical device used to calculate the orbits of the heavenly bodies and solar eclipses. It's very complex and has over thirty mechanical bronze gears machined with exquisite precision, something believed to be beyond the engineers of the time although the gears are marked with inscriptions in Koine Greek that suggest it may have had something to do with the Greek engineer Archimedes.'

Ethan knew enough about the famous mathematician to be aware that he was able to think far ahead of his time, but building a working computer seemed beyond even that man's prodigious intellect.

'They couldn't have done that, could they?' he asked as they entered the interior of the ancient city, sheltered beneath its elaborate enclosure. 'I thought that people back then believed the earth to be flat and at the center of the universe.'

The voice that replied was heavily accented Greek.

'A common myth.' Ethan turned to see a slim, bespectacled man watching them, his shirt bearing an official identification patch. 'The Greeks knew well that the earth was a sphere and that the other planets orbited the sun, and nobody but a handful of cranks has ever thought otherwise in the past three thousand or more years.'

Ethan shook the man's hand and saw that his ID badge bore the name Andres Gabris.

'Do we know you?' Lopez asked.

'No,' Andres replied, 'but I was told that you would come here sooner or later and that I should keep an eye open for you.'

'Who told you that?' Ethan asked, glancing warily around for any sign of Petrov's murderous thugs.

'Lucy Morgan told me,' Andres replied. 'She said that you would be following her and that you would need my help.'

***

XXXI

'Lucy was here? When?'

Andres beckoned them to follow him into the interior of the city as he replied, the whole of Akrotiri concealed beneath a vast roofed enclosure. Ethan could see ranks of semi–excavated buildings stretching into the distance, tourists milling and pointing at the ancient structures.

'She was here less than a week ago, and she came straight to me. I'm the researcher in charge of a section of the excavation called the West House. Lucy asked me if she could examine one particular part of the area in great detail.'

Andres led them through the ancient remains of the city, and despite the fact that the buildings were now effectively indoors due to the protective canopies erected over the entire settlement Ethan was stunned at how easy it was to visualize how life might have been for the people who had lived here so many thousands of years before.

The walls were incredibly smooth and the windows inside them were fitted with thick frames, no doubt to strengthen them against the earthquakes that would have frequented the volcanic island. Many of the buildings were still half buried in the ancient ash that had fallen on the site during the eruption, but Andres gestured to the floor as they walked.

'What befell ancient Akrotiri is very similar to what happened to the Romans at Pompeii, with one major difference: the leaders of Akrotiri managed to evacuate their people before the city was consumed. That suggests they had plenty of warning that life was about to become impossible here.'

'Solon's description of Atlantis being beneath a plume of smoke and flame,' Amber said softly as they walked. 'The island might have been under the threat of an eruption for years, decades perhaps, enough time for the word of its appearance to get around to other cities and civilizations.'

To Ethan's surprise, Andres overheard Amber's hushed words.

'The Egyptians spoke of a land far away where the people lived with great technology but also under the threat of great danger,' he said without looking around at them. 'The descriptions matched closely some of the lesser known beliefs about Atlantis.'

'Lucy mentioned that she was searching for the city?' Lopez asked the Greek.

'Of course,' Andres replied. 'It was one of the interests that we shared in our work. People think that we Greeks frown upon the legend, and it's true given that we have such a rich history that represents the birth of democracy in the ancient world: we have much to be proud of without relying on an ancient legend. But that does not mean we wouldn't like to find the remains of perhaps an even greater Greek society somewhere out here.' Andreas grinned back at them. 'As my colleagues like to say, the Greeks were civilized when much of the rest of humanity were still living in caves.'

Before any of them could reply, Andreas gestured for them to follow him into one of the buildings, the entrance to which was cordoned off to the public. Andreas lifted the cordon and Ethan ducked beneath it and then through the low door frame and inside the building.

To their surprise, in contrast to the bare external walls the interior of the building was alive with stunningly colourful and well preserved frescoes on every wall that detailed life in the city before its violent demise. Ethan turned as Andres joined them and beckoned for them to follow them into another room, which had a single long image emblazoned across a strip around the walls.

'This is the Flotilla Fresco,' Andreas said.

The artwork was only about a foot and a half high but it wrapped around three walls of the room in which they stood and was about forty feet long. Ethan could see ships sailing between islands, people hunting in the hills and dolphins in the seas in a panoramic view of life from millennia before.

'This is what Lucy was interested in?' Lopez asked.

'This is *all* she was interested in,' Andres replied, 'and she spent several hours in here before she suddenly took off with a real excitement about her. I think that she learned something but she never said anything about what it was.'

Ethan walked up to the fresco, examining it closely as Lopez and Amber likewise began searching for clues within the elaborate artwork. There was no way that they could spend hours here, the Russians would not be far behind them, so whatever Lucy had managed to work out in hours they would have to achieve within minutes.

'Did Lucy say anything about why this fresco interested her?' Ethan asked Andres. 'Was there anything specific about it that you noticed?'

'No, nothing,' Andreas said, 'she just told me that she was following a lead that an old mariner had passed on to her.'

Ethan and Lopez exchanged a glance. 'Pytheas?'

'She didn't mention a name,' Andres said, and then he recognized it. 'You think that she meant the Greek mariner Pytheas?'

Ethan looked again at the fresco stretched around the walls. Pytheas had made one of the most extraordinary voyages of the ancient world, travelling as far north as the Norwegian fjords, close enough to the Arctic Circle to witness pack ice and the Aurora Borealis. As Ethan looked at the fresco he could see sailing ships leaving Akrotiri, visiting islands and voyaging long distances, sometimes amid flames and smoke before finally reaching a grand looking city with towering spires atop flights of steps. Ethan noticed that the depictions of dolphins in the seas stopped about half way along the fresco.

'Pytheas sailed north around Europe and the British Isles,' he said out loud as his eyes traced the line of the fresco. 'If he left something of his journey behind in this fresco, part of his legend if you like, then maybe Lucy recognized something in the artwork that denoted a location, a place where she needed to travel to next.'

Lopez squinted as she scanned the fresco from one side to the other. 'The locations could be anywhere, there's nothing that makes them stand out enough that we could match them to a current location.'

Amber hurried along the bottom of the fresco, leaning in close and searching for any sign of text or markings that might betray even a hint of latitude or longitude, but even after a thorough examination she stood back from the wall and sighed.

'There's nothing here,' he insisted.

'There must be,' Ethan replied. 'Lucy found it and we need to as well before Petrov and his men find us'.

'Petrov?' Andres echoed as he looked quizzically at them. 'There are others searching for Lucy?'

'Yeah,' Lopez replied, 'and they're not real friendly.'

'If they show up, tell them everything,' Ethan said to Andres. 'Don't try to conceal anything about us or what we're looking for.'

'And if I don't?' Andres asked.

'You don't want to know.'

*

Konstantin Petrov climbed off the deck of the yacht that had sailed into the harbor at Athinios, just a couple of miles north of ancient Akrotiri. He watched as his men handled their paperwork at the port office, the Kremlin ensuring that diplomatic immunity protected both himself and his entourage from any unwanted attention.

The sun beating down on the island was unfamiliar to him, as had been the cloying heat of India and Indonesia. He preferred the cooler air of Moscow in summer, much of his life having been spent to the east of the city where the forests and the winter snows painted a different canvas than the brilliant blue sky and bright sand and rock of these remote volcanic islands.

'Have they been seen?' he asked one of his men as they returned from the port office.

'Neither Warner nor Lopez have been through here yet and the yacht they were on in Indonesia is not here.'

Petrov nodded to himself thoughtfully. It had taken the experts back in Moscow a while to figure out what the images on Hellerman's phone meant, and a while longer to find a suitable match, but it was possible that they had made an error. The thousands of years that had intervened between the creation of the relief map at Gunung Padang and one gigantic eruption event meant that they could be in the wrong place. Conversely, Warner and Lopez were unlikely to be travelling legally from country to country and could even now be wandering the streets of ancient Akrotiri in search of Atlantis.

'Maintain a watch on all radio frequencies,' he ordered his men, 'boats, planes, everything. I don't want anything leaving this island without our knowledge until we either find Warner and Lopez or we find Atlantis itself, is that understood?!'

His men rumbled a muffled affirmation and hurried to their duties as Petrov turned to look south, where he knew the remains of ancient Akrotiri perched on the clifftops.

'I want that place surrounded,' he growled. 'Let's go!'

***

XXXII

Ethan swept his gaze across the fresco as he searched desperately for something that would indicate what had sent Lucy almost running from the site. Andres too began walking up and down the fresco, examining it as he sought an explanation for Lucy's excitement.

'Perhaps she made a connection between more than one thing in the artwork,' he said. 'We might not be looking for a single piece of evidence at all.'

'Thanks Doc, that makes our lives much easier,' Lopez said with a grin. 'Let's face it, we don't know enough about this to figure out what Lucy knew. She's a scientist, an expert in this sort of thing.'

'She's not an archaeologist,' Andres replied, 'her degree was in palaeontology. But she is widely read and apparently became obsessed with the search for out–of–place artefacts a few years ago.'

'Yeah, we know about that,' Ethan replied. 'Lucy has a real knack for standing back and looking at the bigger picture when it comes to finding things that should't be there…'

Ethan broke off as he heard his own words. He thought of how Lucy had been able to consider the impossible in her career despite the strictures of science, and in doing so been able to make discoveries that other scientists would never have had a chance of locating. Suddenly, he stopped looking closely at the walls and stood back. He paced away from them until his back touched the opposite wall of the room, and then he just stared at the fresco.

'What?' Amber asked. 'You see something?'

Ethan didn't reply as he stared at the fresco in its entirety and began to see things that he hadn't noticed before.

'Why is the fresco only on three walls?'

'There were windows on the west wall, looking out over the Aegean Sea,' Andres said. 'You can see where it was, looking out to the north west.'

Ethan noted the position of the window and then orientated himself to it as he looked up again at the fresco. The image began on his left with the ships sailing from a recognizable Akrotiri, as it was before the volcano erupted and blasted half the island into the history books. He realized that the three peaks matched well with the relief map in the chamber at Gunung Padang. As he swept his gaze to the right he saw the ships sailing through the Mediterranean Sea and then, strangely, a series of small islands that looked out of place amid the rest of the scene, right below the large smudged area. To the right he saw another island, this one surrounded by four suns that shone with different intensities as though describing the passage of the four seasons. Then there was the burning ship, and finally the vessels arriving at the palacial city that they assumed represented Atlantis.

And then he saw it.

'The Eyes of the North.'

The others looked at him, mystified, as Ethan pointed to the strange smudge about half way along the fresco.

'That's not a smudge,' he said finally. 'This fresco tells the story of Pytheas' journey into the north, and the Phaistos Disc speaks of a face that looks to the north; *The sun in azimuth, the dawn star aloft, the eyes of the north shall gaze ever toward their goddess, where a land of fire bleeds toward the underworld."*

'The quote from the disc,' Lopez said, recognizing the verse. 'There must be another icon somewhere out there where Pytheas sailed, that of a face.'

Lopez looked at the smudge and frowned.

'She's looking north, out of the windows.'

Andres stared in amazement at the image. 'The West House is set at an unusual angle compared to the rest of the buildings in Akrotiri. If you're right, it is possible that the building was constructed purposefully to be directed in a certain way for that fresco to be pointed at something far away.'

Ethan pulled out his cell phone and within moments he had a map of the world on the screen with their location marked with GPS precision in the center. He turned until he was orientated north and then looked along a line to the north west as he got a handle on where the face might be looking.

The line on the map crossed Europe in its entirety and extended up through the British Isles and on toward Iceland and Greenland.

'That gives us a line,' Lopez said, 'but again there's no distance.'

Ethan looked up at the fresco again.

'Yes, it does.'

Ethan realized that the islands marked on the fresco beneath the image of the face were not islands at all, but one island as mapped by the cartographer during Pytheas' voyage as they circled the British Isles. The channels separating the islands were the great rivers and estuaries, and in an instant he knew that their location on the fresco and the appearance of a single island to the north of the British Isles gave him the approximate location of the face.

'This is it,' he said. 'If we align the markers we found at Gunung Padang with this line and if we can find the Face of the North, we can pinpoint the location of Atlantis.'

Ethan could now see the map of the northern hemisphere as it was known to Pytheas after his voyage stretched across the fresco around the room, and at one end not the image of a glorious homecoming but a veiled message: the location of Atlantis as recorded by the only person who might have actually figured out where it was.

'Is it possible that Pytheas could have sailed east as extensively as he sailed west and north?' he asked Andreas.

The Greek shrugged and nodded. 'There would be nothing stopping such a man but time, tide and the land crossing from the Nile River to the Gulf of Suez. From there, Pytheas could have reached Arabia and from there, India and beyond. There is no record of him doing so, but that of course does not mean it didn't happen.'

'You think that Pytheas could have followed the same route that Lucy is?' Lopez asked.

'Defintely,' Ethan replied. 'Lucy's following Pytheas, using the same ancient references that he had access to in order to track Atlantis down. Now we have what we need, it's time to leave.'

Ethan turned and marched from the West House with Lopez and Amber right behind him, and as they walked out of the building so Ethan came to an abrupt halt and Lopez almost plowed into him.

Ethan looked south down the line of buildings and saw men walking into the enclosure, and even from this distance he could tell by their movement and their posture that they were not tourists come to marvel at the ancient wonders around them. Then he saw a squat, stocky man with a small black beard stride into the enclosure.

'Petrov. Get back inside.'

They backed up into the West House and out of sight as Ethan turned to Andres.

'Is there any other way out of here?'

'There are three exits to the east and one to the south that uses a subway to the main road,' the Greek replied.

'Petrov would have covered the main exits,' Lopez warned.

'His men will be outside,' Ethan confirmed.

Andres gestured for them to follow him. 'Then if you cannot go out, you will have to go under.'

Ethan followed the archaeologist without hesitation as they filed out of the West House and hurried toward the eastern side of the enclosure. Andres walked normally as Ethan, Lopez and Amber variously hugged the walls and crouched low, ignoring the bemused stares of the handful of tourists milling around the exhibits.

Andres turned into a building near the eastern entrance and Ethan followed him inside with Lopez and Amber close behind. They walked through the excavated ruins, the walls helping to conceal their passage as Andres led them to a craggy opening in the ground near one of the walls and gestured to it.

'This tunnel is an old sewer that ran beneath the city. It connects to more excavations on the hillside between the excavation and the car park. Follow it to the end and it joins a staircase that comes up on top of the hill. There's only a chain link fence to cross to reach the road and the car park. Hurry.'

Ethan shook Andres' hand and ducked into the darkness with Lopez and Amber right behind him. The relative gloom of the enclosure meant that his eyesight swiftly adjusted to the dark confines of the tunnel and he hurried along with his hands brushing the walls of the tunnel either side of him for balance.

It was unlikely that Petrov would have placed any of his people to watch these ancilliary tunnels, but Ethan had no doubt that he would have somebody watching the car park. He called back to Amber as they moved through the darkness.

'Amber, you head for the car and get back to the plane as fast as you can. We'll divert and get away from Petrov's team.'

'They might see you. I could pick you up.'

'We can't risk Petrov connecting us to you,' Lopez insisted. 'You have the same knowledge that we do now. As long as you get away and are not identified, you can carry on no matter what happens to us.'

Ethan smelled fresh air in the darkness and saw a faint light ahead as the tunnel emerged at the bottom of a shallow ramp that climbed away from him and then doubled back on itself, heading toward the surface. A bright rectangle of perfect blue sky was visible above that cast bright sunlight down the ramp, the entrance not easily visible from the road or the site. Ethan peered out and could see no guards above the entrance and no shadows cast from anyone who might have been directly above them.

Ethan eased his way out into the sunlight and checked above them before he ran up the two ramps in a low crouch and squatted near the top of the entrance. He peeked over the top toward the enclosure and saw two men standing by the main entrance to the site, and others further away toward the eastern entrance.

Ethan turned to Amber as she joined them.

'Head directly to the car. The Russians don t know who you are and won't be looking for you so don't run, just walk in there as if you're leaving the site and you do this every day. If you walk with a sense of purpose, you won't stand out and any Russians watching the site will ignore you. If we don't get back to the airplane before you see the Russians, tell Arnie to take off and get the hell out of here. Now, go!'

Amber stood up and moved to join a nearby path that led back toward the enclosure and the main exit. Ethan waited in position until she was crossing the road toward the parking lot and then looked at the Russians again. None of the men had moved and none seemed to be taking much notice of Amber other than a cursory glance and then another to something they held in their hands, probably photographs of himself and Lopez.

'Okay, now what?' Lopez asked. 'We've got no way out of here except by road.'

Ethan glanced at the vehicles in the parking lot and noted three of them, each with one man inside all watching the enclosure. Amber started up the hire car's engine and pulled out of the lot, and Ethan smiled to himself as she drove away and none of the watching Russians followed her.

'Amber's away, so all we need to do is get back to Arnie and fly out of here before the Russians can catch up with us.'

'We could hijack a car,' Lopez suggested.

Ethan shook his head. The island was only lightly populated, the traffic was sparse and they could hardly walk into the lot and break into a vehicle with the Russians watching. Besides, there were enough of them about that Ethan seriously doubted their ability to get away from the site without being spotted. Therefore, the roads were out.

Ethan caught a glimpse of something on the waves off the coast and he heard the faint whine of an engine. He turned his head fractionally and saw the source of the noise, and in an instant he made his decision.

'We're gonna get wet again, right?' Lopez said as she noted the direction of his gaze.

'Let's go.'

Ethan broke cover and hurried down to the chainlink fence that enclosed the site, using the cover of the trees to conceal their position from the watching Russians. He knew that it would only be moments before they were spotted, but he could tell that if they could make a break for the shoreline at the bottom of the hill, the Russians would not be able to easily catch them.

Ethan slipped over the chainlink fence and then pulled his sunglasses over his eyes as Lopez dropped down alongside him and they moved to the edge of the road. Ethan stood up, took a breath, and in customary style Lopez slipped her arm through his and they strolled casually out onto the road and turned toward the hill.

They had done this a hundred times in the past and now their easy rhythm concealed their identity as they moved down the hill. All three of the Russians were parked at the back of the lot to give themselves the widest possible field of view, which meant that at this distance they would not immediately be certain that they were looking at Warner and Lopez.

Ethan pointed up to the site alongside them, Lopez smiling and nodding happily as though they were two tourists just strolling toward the site or perhaps the hotel and Bar Akrotiri at the bottom of the hill. They walked without hurry, Ethan not looking at the parking lot directly and in fact mostly keeping an eye on the enclosure entrance as they approached it, appearing to be excitedly discussing their visit while also keeping his face concealed from the Russians in the parking lot to their right.

'They're taking notice,' Lopez said, her keen eyes seeing the Russians talking in their vehicles, probably to each other using concealed microphones.

Ethan nodded and chuckled, gesturing as though he were explaining some of the wonders of ancient Greece.

'I'm hoping that one of them will move in for a closer look.'

As if one cue, one of the Russians climbed out of his car and began crossing the lot toward them, an intercept course that Ethan knew would result in their entire team moving to apprehend them.

'Turn here,' he said, and gently turned Lopez into the enclosure entrance once more.

'You wanna go back in?' she asked him, smiling brightly.

Ethan stopped and pointed to the site, and then he shrugged as though uncertain about whether they should go in and pointed instead down the hill toward the hotel and bar. Ahead, the Russians guarding the exits were watching them closely.

'I want our backs to the nearest guy for as long as possible.'

Ethan kept talking, switching his accent to British as he heard the Russian's approach. Lopez matched the accent, striving to maintain uncertainty in the Russian until the last possible moment.

'But if we go to the hotel now we won't make it back to Oia in time for *tea*.'

Ethan shrugged again as he heard the Russian's footsteps on the asphalt behind them, felt the hairs on the back of his neck rise up as the man came within arm's reach and then suddenly he was shouting into his microphone in Russian as one hand moved toward the pistol concealed beneath his shirt.

***

XXXIII

Jeddah, Saudi Arabia

Allison Pierce knew that she was out of her depth and that her fate was in the hands of people she had never before met, and she felt more vulnerable now than even when the street thugs had been shooting at her back in DC.

The coast of Saudi Arabia crouched low on the horizon to her right, and she knew that the deserts of Sudan and Egypt were somewhere to her left, which meant that she was travelling north and entirely alone but for the two men piloting the privately hired boat now surging through the crystalline waters beneath a savage equatorial sun.

The trail that she had been required to leave behind her had been complex to say the least, and she no longer feared that anybody would be following her, and in many ways that was the source of her concern: nobody knew where the hell she was and if somebody decided to toss her overboard she would be dead long before anybody knew that she was even missing.

Mitchell's instructions had been precise and clear: at Jeddah a boat would be waiting, and it would bring her to Jarvis and his people, where she would finally learn her role within whatever grand plan they had to expose Congressman Keyes and anybody else currently in power in the US they'd been able to attach to Russian hackers. Allison had her new cell phone in her pocket but as instructed she had not switched it on, nor had she attempted to make contact with home or Foxx. The soldier's warning to her echoed through her mind but she forced it from her thoughts as she focussed on hearing out whatever Jarvis and his cohorts had to say for themselves.

Against the hazy horizon she saw a large yacht cruising north, and it was immediately obvious that the tourist vessel was aiming to intercept the ship. She watched as it slowed, the tourist boat catching up swiftly and the vessels coming together gently on the ocean swells as an enormous hatch on the yacht's stern opened up and the boat eased in closer. Lines were tossed to the yacht's crew, and Allison was beckoned aboard the yacht as she saw the boat's crew being paid in cash before the lines were cast off again and the tourist boat turned away and headed back for Jeddah.

Allison was beckoned by a smartly dressed member of the crew who led her through the huge vessel as it got underway once more, cruising more swiftly now but still heading north toward the Suez Canal.

The crewman led her up onto the yacht's upper decks and out into the sunshine once more, the brisk wind from the boat's speed deflected by pristine clear windshields before a row of white recliners, the white deck almost painful to look at in the bright light.

An old man dressed in casual slacks and a shirt stood to meet her as the crewman left, and he shook her hand.

'You must be Allison.'

'You must be Doug Jarvis.'

Jarvis gestured to a seat and Allison took it, uncertain of how to begin the conversation. Jarvis pre–empted her easily.

'You must have many questions, and I would love to answer them all for you but I'm afraid that we don't have much time. I take it that your work with Aaron Mitchell has uncovered at least some of what we've been up against these long years passed?'

'I'm aware of Majestic Twelve,' Allison acknowledged, 'and of the recent interference in US elections from overseas. I'm also aware that I can't trust any of you and that almost everybody seems to be lying about something.'

Jarvis smiled and inclined his head.

'Absolutely correct,' he agreed. 'The fact is that everyone is lying. However, some lie to protect themselves while others lie to protect those who cannot protect themselves. There is a difference, Allison. While you may not be able to tell the difference between the good guys and the bad guys, we know it well and we can prove it all.'

Allison sighed.

'I've heard pretty much all I can take,' she said. 'Everyone has proof of their own story, and that proof discounts the other side of the story until nobody knows what to believe or in whom to place their faith. The media has been hit with so much fake news that now politicians across the world are pouncing on that uncertainty in an attempt to show that they are the only fountain of truth in the world. Why should I believe you over all the other people who seem intent on tracking you down and the billions you have stolen, especially when your own military record states that you are a master manipulator of others? Where are Warner and Lopez, the two people who work for you that I keep hearing about?'

Jarvis said nothing for a moment, watching her in the sunlight as though assessing her.

'The DIA contacted you before you came here,' he said with clairvoyant precision, 'and would have tried to convince you that we're as bad as the people we claim to be hunting.'

'You understand my dilemma,' Allison replied.

Jarvis nodded. 'And yet you are here, alone.'

'I believe that every story has two sides.'

'Good, then you won't mind hearing ours, but before I tell it I should point out that even in this day and age of uncertainty, there remains one voice that cannot be silenced, and one way of proving the truth that will always win out over any political rhetoric.'

'Do enlighten me.'

Jarvis leaned forward in his seat and folded his hands before him.

'Actions speak louder than words.'

Allison narrowed her eyes at him. 'Well, what are you going to do?'

Jarvis leaned even further forward, and he whispered something in her ear. Allison's eyes widened and she looked at him in shock.

'Why?' she asked.

'Because to do so is the only way to bring an end to all of this, and to bring peace back to those who most deserve it, yourself included,' Jarvis said. 'This ship is heading for the Mediterranean at full speed but it is unlikely that we will reach Greece in time to help Ethan and Nicola. Our role in their search is over.'

'I don't get it, why bring me here at all?'

'Because I'm about to make a phone call that will bring Congressman Keyes out to the Meditteranean with all possible haste. When he arrives, you're going to follow him as closely as possible and produce the evidence you need to bring him to justice by the time he returns to America.'

Allison felt her pulse quicken. 'And what happens to you?'

'That will depend on just how tightly you can turn the screws on Keyes and the administration and how far the DIA is willing to go to push through any charges against the guilty parties.'

Allison gripped the arms of her seat. 'Keyes is up to his neck in this and that's probably why he was picked to lead the congressional investigation. I'm not about to let him walk away from what he's done and when his house of cards falls, I'd bet that he'll take everyone else down with him.'

'Then we need this to work smoothly, and for that to happen you need to trust us and do the right thing. In an hour, a flying boat will collect you and fly you across to the Meditteranean. From there you will meet with Lillian Cruz.'

'And do what?'

Jarvis smiled. 'Just do what comes naturally.' With that, he stood and gestured to the open ocean. 'Enjoy this while you can, because everything's about to get ugly for us all.'

Jarvis turned away from her and walked inside the yacht.

Allison waited until he was gone, and only then did she retrieve the cell phone that Foxx had given her. She stared at it for a long time, and then she took a breath and switched it on.

***

XXXIV

Akrotiri, Santorini

Ethan whirled as the shouting Russian pulled a compact 9mm pistol from beneath his shirt as Lopez pulled off her sunglasses and tossed them into the Russian's face. The Russian flinched in surprise as Ethan pivoted on one heel and rammed his boot into the guard's belly.

The Russian folded over at the waist as his eyes bulged and all the air in his lungs was expelled in a loud rush. Lopez drove her own boot deep into the man's left knee and he collapsed sideways as the tendons in his leg popped as loudly as snapping twigs. She caught the man's gun arm and twisted the pistol in his grip against the direction of his fall.

Ethan broke into a sprint as Lopez hopped over their victim with the pistol now in her hands, pursued by the shouts of Russians scrambling from their vehicles and running in pursuit. Ethan dashed down the hill past a row of coaches parked by the sidewalk, elderly tourists staring in surprise as he thundered past with Lopez close behind, the 9mm clutched in her hand.

Ethan heard the ripple of shocked gasps but he didn't break his stride as he ran down onto the lot outside the bar and saw a small boat out on the water and heard the whining engine of a jet–ski as it plowed through the water with a crest of sparkling white foam in its wake.

Lopez dashed up alongside him as the jet ski roared toward them, the owner showboating his skills to the tourists. Lopez dashed out into the water as he thundered past and raised the pistol to point straight between his eyes.

The driver's expression collapsed into shock and terror and instantly he hurled himself from the jet ski and crashed into the waves. The jet ski coughed and spluttered as it slowed down and Ethan dove headlong into the waves and swam across to it. He hauled himself into the seat and gunned the engine, swinging in toward Lopez as she waded out with the pistol held aloft out of the water.

Ethan grabbed her hand and hauled her into the seat as he saw the Russians running down to the shore behind them. He twisted the throttle and the jet ski reared up and accelerated away as he turned for open water. No sound of gunshots followed them, and Ethan figured that the Russians would be reluctant to open fire with so many witnesses standing on the shore all around them.

'They'll be on the move and can beat us back to Oia!' Lopez shouted above the noise of the engine and the crashing water.

'They don't know that's where we're going! If we can get around the headland and turn north we can get Arnie to pick us up off the water!' Ethan yelled back. 'We know things that they don't now and this is the best chance we'll get to completely disappear!'

Ethan guided the jetski out alongside the coast, but despite his getaway plan working perfectly he knew that Lopez was right. Petrov had too many vehicles and men and would certainly have left a couple of guys at the airport who could be re-routed to just about anywhere on the island long before they could make it back to Oia.

As they rounded the headland he saw the north coast of Santorini unfold before them, nearly ten miles away in the haze. He was about to turn toward it when he saw the smaller island of Thirasia to the west. It was almost as far as Oia, but he realized that heading there gave them one distinct advantage: the Russians didn't have any boats and would not be able to send their full force to intercept them.

'I've got an idea!'

*

'Where?!'

Konstantin Petrov stormed out of the enclosure surrounded by four of his men as he held a cell phone to his ear.

'They're on the water, heading north!'

Petrov jogged down to the bottom of the hill and squinted in the sunshine just in time to see the speck of the distant jet ski vanishing as it rounded the headland over a mile away.

'Move everybody to the east side of the island and track their movements,' he ordered, and then turned to his senior bodyguard. 'Wherever they end up, grab them and bring them to me. Don't let them escape again or I swear you'll become a permanent resident of this miserable rock.'

The guard turned and hurried away as Petrov turned back and walked up to the enclosure. Warner and Lopez had emerged from an entrance to the site that was perched on top of a hill nearby, which meant that they had to have already been inside the ancient site and therefore may have learned something new before their escape.

Petrov walked back into the enclosure and toward the curator, an elderly man whom he had learned was named Andres. The curator was currently being held inside his office by two of Petrov's men.

Petrov walked inside the office and closed the door behind him, then turned and closed the blinds on the window so that nobody could see inside. He turned again to look at Andres, who was sitting on a chair with a Russian hand pressed down on each shoulder to keep him in place.

'Andres,' he said, not interested in playing games. 'Do you enjoy your work and your life here?'

Andres nodded but said nothing, watching Petrov with a cautious expression. Given that the Greek man should not have any knowledge of who Petrov was and should not have any real reason to yet be concerned, Petrov could assume that Warner and Lopez had already been in contact with him and warned him of the danger that he faced should the Russians catch up with him. Petrov decided to take maximum advantage of that concern.

'Andres, the Americans you recently spoke to are fugitives from justice in two countries and may be interested in the work of a missing scientist who we believe is searching for Atlantis. I do not much care for their archaeological cause, but they represent a group of individuals who have stolen several tens of billions of dollars from governments around the world and I am attempting to apprehend them and recover the lost money.'

Petrov squatted down in front of Andres.

'There is nothing that I will not do to extract whatever information I require from you. Nothing. But I promise that you will leave this office without a scratch upon you.'

Andres frowned in confusion, and Petrov inclined his head toward a framed picture on the wall of the scientist's wife and children. Andres blanched as he realized what Petrov meant.

'Now,' Petrov went on, 'if you do not want to spend the rest of your life grieving over the unimaginable pain they went through before my men and I finally cut their throats and deposited their bodies far out to sea, I suggest you tell me absolutely everything that I need to know.'

*

Jarvis heard the helicopters long before they reached the yacht as it cruised north through the perfect blue ocean. Out here, apart from the wind and the hum of the yacht's engines there was almost no sound and the powerful rotors thumped the air and broadcast their approach from literally miles away.

Jarvis had served long enough in the military to know the distinctive sound of the heavier, more powerful blades and engines of military helicopters. When he spotted them, two gray specks flying low over the water, he knew that his time was up.

Although he no longer had access to military data, he knew that American warships were always present in these waters, and finding a luxury yacht in the middle of the Red Sea was not a difficult mission for the United States Navy. Jarvis knew at once that Allison had betrayed them, although she was already on her way to the Mediterranean on Arnie's Catalina, and although he reached for his cell phone to check he was not surprised to see that its signal was supressed, probably by electronic jamming from the two helicopters.

Rhys Garrett ran out onto the deck and looked out at the fast approaching helicopters.

'How did they find you?' Garrett asked, horrified.

'It doesn't matter,' Jarvis replied, surprisingly calm considering the fate that probably awaited him. 'When they land, they will take control of the ship. Do what they say, when they say, and deny all knowledge of my misdoings at the DIA. We are friends, nothing more, understood?'

Garrett nodded.

'Slow the ship to help them land,' Jarvis advised, and then reached out and shook Garrett's hand. 'Thank you, for all that you've done for us.'

'They're going to lock you up and toss the key, Doug.'

Jarvis smiled and as the roar of the helicopter's rotors grew and reverberated through his chest, he replied, his words barely audible.

'Not everything is as it seems, Rhys.'

Garrett stepped back and then hurried toward the bridge as the helicopters thundered past the yacht, their side doors open and heavily armed soldiers waiting to throw rappel lines out to board and take control of the yacht.

Throughout it all, Jarvis balanced easily on the deck with his hands folded calmly behind his back and a quiet smile on his face.

*

Ethan guided the jet ski into the beach at Agistri, a small resort on the northern coast of the island of Thirasia, on the opposite side of the ancient Thera caldera to Oia. The jet ski thumped up onto the beach and Ethan stepped off with Lopez in perfect unison, abandoning the vehicle and ignoring the bemused glances of tourists as they hurried up the beach.

'We've got no way off this rock that Petrov can't track,' Lopez said. 'He'll have his men watching us and waiting to intercept us the moment we try to get out of here.'

'I know.'

Ethan pulled out his cell phone and dialled Doug Jarvis's number, the old man picking up the line on the second tone.

'Doug, we've found it.'

There was a long pause on the line and then Jarvis answered, speaking in an oddly slow accent as though they were talking over a broken line.

'That's absolutely fabulous news, very well done. Where is it, Ethan? Where are you now?'

Ethan hesitated, suddenly uncertain. Jarvis never spoke in that way, his inflection altered in a strange way and Ethan could hear what sounded like a helicopter somewhere in the distance…

'South America,' Ethan replied. 'South of Rio. We don't have an exact location but we've narrowed it down to a few square miles. The fresco we found here in Menorca gave us the clue we needed.'

Lopez shot Ethan a confused look but said nothing as Jarvis replied.

'That's brilliant Ethan, keep doing what you're doing and report in when you can. Send Nicola my love.'

'Will do.'

Ethan cut off the line, switched off the cell and then turned and hurled it into the nearby rollers.

'What the hell?' Lopez asked as she saw the phone splash into the waves.

'Doug's been compromised,' he said by way of a reply.

'How do you know?'

'He sent you his love.'

Lopez blinked. 'Okay, I'll buy that. Garrett?'

'No idea.'

'That means we could all be up the river,' Lopez said. 'Enhanced interrogation won't be beyond the current CIA Director and the President won't blink an eye at extreme rendition.' Ethan knew that she was right and that there was nothing that they could do for Jarvis. They would also now not be able to approach Garrett for fear of providing any further links to the billionaire who even now might be in the hands of either the American government or, worse, the Russians.

'Call Arnie, tell him to come get us before Petrov and his men get here. Then trash your cell. We're on our own.'

Lopez dialled a number and spoke briefly to Arnie, then shut the cell off and tossed it into the waves.

'We don't know where to go next and we don't have any real way of getting there,' she pointed out. 'Arnie's plane is slow and Petrov can easily get ahead of it.'

'We can lose ourselves in the crowd,' Ethan said, 'maybe on one of the islands nearby and start hopping across Greece and out of here. Petrov is working under the radar and can't man every port, he'll be forced to scatter and hope for the best.'

'I'd love to share your enthusiasm,' Lopez said as she squinted across the bay behind them, 'but I think his men are already on their way.'

***

XXXV

'Move, now!'

Konstantin Petrov shouted the order as his men tumbled into a speedboat, the owner of which was laying on his back inside the boat with his wrists and ankles bound tightly and his mouth gagged. The pistol pressed to his skull ensured that he complied with Petrov's men as they fired the engines and the boat surged out of the tiny harbour.

'They're on Thirasia!' one of Petrov's men yelled above the wind and waves as the boat roared out into open water. 'There's no airport and no way out of there!'

Petrov looked across the bay at the island of Thirasia, jutting out of the waves and separated from mainland Santorini by less than a mile. Warner and Lopez must have figured that he would have the airport and major towns covered, including Oia, which irritated him but was hardly surprising. What he couldn't understand was why they had decided to virtually strand themselves on another island that they must surely know he could surround and swarm with his men in short order.

'Can you see where they've gone?' he demanded of his men.

Two of them were scanning the bright horizon with binoculars but both men shook their heads.

'They've gone ashore, we can't see them!'

Petrov cursed under his breath as he tried to figure out where the hell they were going. It was possible that they had an escape boat harbored somewhere on the island but it seemed a far stretch to believe that they would have had time to prepare an escape plan so thoroughly. Petrov's men were only hours behind the Americans at best, and the Greek in Akrotiri had told them everything without even a hint of deception: they had seen something in the fresco at the site that had led them to hurry out, just like Doctor Lucy Morgan the week before. The old man had believed that it had something to do with an ancient Mariner named Pytheas, which tied in well with what Petrov already knew, but the Greek man had insisted that the Americans had refused to share with him what they knew. When Petrov had asked why, the Greek's answer had been entirely acceptable to him.

Because they said that you would come here too, and if I knew anything that you would use torture to extract it. Ignorance would be my only shield.

Petrov had considered killing Andres for good measure but had let the man go as soon as his men had reported spotting Warner and Lopez attempting to flee the island. Now, there was nowhere to run and nowhere to hide and…

The sound of thundering engines roared overhead and the speedboat bucked and weaved on the waves as the helmsman ducked instinctively. Petrov crouched down as a huge shadow raced over the boat and he looked up to see a massive airplane soar overhead, its broad straight wings high atop a fuselage that had a curved underside like a boat's hull, marking her out as an amphibious aircraft.

The huge aeroplane turned gently and Petrov could see her flaps deploying as she turned to land alongside Thirasia's north–west shore.

'Go faster!' Petrov yelled at the helmsman.

The man at the wheel threw the throttles open and the speedboat surged at maximum velocity across the crashing waves, Petrov's men struggling to stay in their seats as the vessel was hurled this way and that. Petrov hung on to a railing for grim life as the speedboat rounded the headland and he saw the flying boat turning away from the shore to face out to sea once again.

'Take her down!' Petrov screamed in fury as he stood up and aimed at the aged aircraft and fired his pistol.

The gunshots were snatched away by the buffeting wind and sounded as useless as firecrackers as the airplane's engines thundered again and the plane accelerated away from them across the waves. Petrov's men opened up with automatic weapons and pistols, the speedboat tossed violently as it crashed into the airplane's turbulent wake on the water.

Petrov let out a howl of frustration as he saw the aircraft lift up off the waves, veils of sparkling water spilling like clouds of diamond chips from her shining white hull as she climbed away from them and turned gently toward the west.

Petrov stamped his boot on the boat's deck as the speedboat slowed and his men ceased firing.

'Get us back to Oia and contact the airport!' he roared in fury. 'Find out where that plane is going and then get our pilot to prepare to leave immediately!'

The speedboat turned back toward the distant shore of Santorini as Petrov sat down on a damp seat and cursed silently to himself over and over again. The aged aircraft Warner and Lopez had departed in looked to be a Catalina, an aircraft with great range but low airspeed. He knew that by law such an aircraft could not fly far without either a flight plan or contacting an arrival airport with their details and expected time of arrival, therefore it would be only a matter of time before they were able to figure out its destination and then take off and beat them to it.

The speedboat reached Oia's small harbor within a few minutes, although to Petrov it seemed to take an age. As soon as he was ashore his men clubbed the speedboat owner unconscious and then removed his restraints before hurrying up the beach and heading for their vehicles, as the rest of Petrov's men descended on the small town.

Petrov felt his cell phone vibrate in his pants pocket and he yanked it out angrily and answered. 'Petrov?'

'Konstantin,' came the calm reply, *'an update.'*

Petrov recognized the voice of his superior, General Sergei Olatov, instantly and he forced himself to remain calm as he replied.

'We are closing in, comrade,' he said. 'They have just left Santorini, we watched them go and decided to hang back.'

There was a long silence on the phone. *That would suggest that you remain behind them, comrade. That is not where I would expect you to be after so long.'*

Petrov clenched his jaw before he replied.

'The Americans are leading us where we need them to,' he said. 'Right now if they keep going we will be able to simply follow them all the way to their destination. We will have in our sights the means to ensure the Americans don't double cross us.'

'Then you had best be certain that they cannot slip away from you again, Petrov,' came the reply. *'Your diplomatic immunity relies on your success, or your failure…'*

The line went dead and Petrov slipped the cell into his pocket, and wondered if his superior officer would be so bold with his threats were he standing before Petrov here and now on the beach.

He turned as one of his men hurried up to him.

'They're flying to a small airport called Naxos, on an island eighty miles north of here. The airport is too small for our jet to land on.'

'Hire something smaller from the airport at Santorini!' Petrov snapped. 'Anything, at any price, and get us there ahead of that plane!'

*

Allison Pierce crouched alongside the harbor behind a low, white wall as she watched the Russians disembark from the speedboat while she filmed all of it. She zoomed in carefully and was able to capture footage of Petrov's henchmen clubbing the unfortunate speedboat owner into a stupor before abandoning the vessel and marching up the beach.

She tucked her camera away and stayed out of sight as she watched Konstantin Petrov stalk up the beach to a pair of vehicles that hurried down to meet them. There was no doubt who he was, Petrov a known figure in the KGB and later the Russian Defense Ministry, renowned for a fearsome temper and a near–fanatical devotion to his mother country, but this was something different. Even armed only with the footage she had now, she knew that at the very least she could raise hell across the world and likely have Petrov arrested on any number of charges regardless of his diplomatic immunity. However, her gut instinct told her to hold back and wait. There was no telling what he would do next and it was patently clear that whatever Petrov wanted, it was worth maiming and perhaps killing for.

She waited out of sight until Petrov and his men were gone and then pulled out her cell phone and dialled a number. The line picked up almost instantly, Mitchell's voice calm but uncompromising.

'What do you have?'

'Petrov, he's here and he's in company. Mostly goons, no other faces I recognize but sooner or later he'll have to tip his hand. He can't keep hopping from country to country like this without somebody's palms being greased and he's not beyond violence and intimidation to get what he wants. This guy's virtually sleepwalking into an international incident.'

'Stay on him,' Mitchell advised. *'He'll follow Ethan Warner and Nicola Lopez out of Greece and he'll try to apprehend them the first chance he gets. You need to be there when he does.'*

'How do you know where he's headed if….'

The line cut dead in her ear and Allison shoved the cell angrily in her pocket as she watched the vehicles heading off into the distance. She got up and hurried across to her hire car, fumbling with the keys and trying to shrug off the suspicion that she was still nothing more than a pawn in a game played by men of immense power.

'How long?!'

Petrov was crammed into the rear seats of a Beech Baron 58 twin-engine light aircraft as it soared four thousand feet above the sparkling waters of the Aegean Sea.

'Ten minutes,' came the response from the pilot through the headphones Petrov wore. *'We're on final approach now.'*

Petrov sat alongside his guard, facing forward toward the cockpit. Opposite him sat two more of his most trusted men, both of them staring into the middle distance in an attempt to avoid his attention. The small aeroplane bucked and weaved on the wind currents as the pilot gently weaved between fluffy white cumulus clouds the size of small towns that cast deep azure shadows over the ocean far below.

'We're looking for a sea plane, a Catalina that flew out of Santorini a half hour ago.'

The pilot frowned as he listened and then replied, somewhat mystified.

'I can't be certain, but I think I heard a call sign identify themselves as a PBY about ten minutes ago on the approach frequency.'

Petrov leaned forward in his seat and his dark eyes focussed on the pilot as he produced a thick wad of American dollar bills and waved them near the pilot's face.

'I have two thousand dollars here for you if you can get us on the ground before that Catalina.'

The pilot looked around at Petrov and regarded him for a moment, and then he smiled in reply.

'For that I'll crash the damned plane if you want me to. You'd better strap in.'

Petrov moved back to his seat and fastened his belt as he heard the pilot contacting the airfield tower.

'Naxos Information, pan–pan–pan, November Golf One Seven Niner, ten miles to the south at four thousand feet, QNH one zero two one, rough running engine and low fuel, request straight in approach onto active.'

Petrov heard the tower's reply clearing the aircraft for an immediate approach as two other call signs near the airfield were ordered to reposition in the circuit and the overhead. Petrov immediately recognized the second registration as one that his men had learned of back in Oia, that of the Catalina.

The Baron 58 suddenly slowed and began descending rapidly as the pilot made a high speed dash for the runway now visible dead ahead on the island's west coast. Petrov watched as the pilot waited until the last moment before drawing back the throttles and slowing the aircraft down, gradually extending his flaps one stage at a time and then finally the undercarriage, which whined down beneath them as the pilot called finals onto the runway.

Petrov leaned out of his window and saw a couple of miles to the east the big Catalina, still at one thousand feet altitude in the circuit and flying downwind as it awaited its chance to land. Petrov grinned in anticipation as he turned to his guard.

'As soon as we're down, arrange accommodation for us and our American guests, somewhere remote where we will not be disturbed. They won't be leaving this island until we're finished with them.'

The guard grinned as he got his cell phone ready, the aircraft turning off the main runway as Petrov leaned forward and handed the pilot the money.

'How will you explain the fault?' Petrov asked.

'Carburettor icing,' the pilot replied. 'Mysteriously it appears to have cleared itself.'

The pilot shut down the engine and Petrov climbed out behind his men as they dispersed away from the Baron 58. Petrov turned and saw the Catalina's landing lights shining brilliantly even in broad daylight as the aircraft touched down amid the trembling heat haze on the runway and slowed before it turned off the runway and taxied toward the parking area.

Petrov's men fanned out near the airport terminal building, keeping their weapons out of sight but ensuring the nobody could leave the Catalina and make it to the terminal building without being spotted and intercepted. Petrov watched as the Catalina's pilot taxied to an allotted parking space and applied the brakes, and moments later the clattering of the twin radial engines spluttered out and the big airplane sat in silence on the dispersal ramp as the pilot shut down the systems and vacated his seat.

Petrov strolled to the port side of the fuselage as the pilot opened a large side door and lowered a set of steps before he stepped out into the sunshine.

'Captain,' Petrov greeted him, 'I am here to meet your passengers.'

The pilot was a tall, cranky looking man with slightly graying hair who could have been thirty or fifty years old, it was hard to tell. He peered down at Petrov as though he were examining something he had scraped off the sole of his boot.

'We didn't order an escort.'

An American, his voice rough with age. Petrov saw a middle–aged Asian woman step out of the aircraft, her long black hair tied back in a pony tail and her eyes hidden behind sunglasses as she moved to stand alongside the pilot.

'Two Americans boarded this aircraft at Oia,' Petrov smiled at them, trying to hide the rising impatience festering inside him.

'That's right,' the pilot confirmed.

'Where are they?'

'They're here,' the pilot confirmed as he gestured to himself and the woman. 'This is our airplane.'

Petrov clicked his fingers and four of his men hurried forward. 'Search the airplane.'

'Hey,' the pilot snapped, 'you can't go in there.'

The four men ignored him as Petrov pulled up the corner of his shirt to reveal the pistol in its holster there.

'I'm sure you won't mind,' he uttered with contempt.

The pilot shrugged without concern, and within moments Petrov's men climbed back out of the aircraft and shook their heads.

'She's empty.'

Petrov struggled to contain his fury as he seethed at the pilot. 'You took off from Oia and landed outside Thirasia before departing to here. Why would you land right again right after taking off?!'

'Selfie,' the pilot shrugged. 'We're touring, and the wife's just crazy about taking pictures of *everything*.'

Petrov felt himself trembling with rage and was about to reach for his pistol and drag the pilot and the woman back into the airplane when the pilot gestured over his shoulder toward the terminal.

'We've got an appointment booked with a customs official, if you're done?' he said.

Petrov glanced over his shoulder and saw an official in a blue shirt and black pants, and in the office right behind him was at least one police officer who would be armed and able to call back up to support him.

Petrov turned back to the pilot and then blinked in surprise as the tall American loomed up and glared down at him.

'You've got a problem with me, *Ivan*, let's sort it out with him right now. Otherwise, you're done here, agreed?'

Petrov fumed in impotent silence and then mastered his anger and stood aside to let the American through. As the pilot passed by, Petrov heard a cell phone's camera click and he saw the woman snap him as she passed by before tucking her cell phone back into her bag.

Petrov whirled to the nearest of his men and barked an order.

'They're still on Thirasia! Get back there and find out where they went!'

***

XXXVI

St Kilda Island,

British Isles

(Two days later)

A brutal wind gusted in over endless slate grey waves flecked with white rollers that marched relentlessly in from the west as Ethan leaned into the gale and forged his way up a bleak hillside. Rain splattered his coat and stung the raw skin of his face as he squinted at a tiny map in one hand and a compass in the other.

'This is insane.'

Lopez's voice was almost torn away by the buffeting gale as Ethan paused and glanced over his shoulder at the endless ocean stretching away into a horizon consumed by hazy veils of rain. In his time he had served variously as a United States Marine and a journalist in some of the most dangerous and remote places on earth, and seen things that even now he struggled to believe let alone understand. But right now, he could not ever recall feeling so completely isolated.

The island on which they trekked was located forty or so miles from Harris, part of an island chain off the coast of the United Kingdom known as the Outer Hebrides. Scotland was a full one hundred miles away and the island itself had been deserted for close to a century, abandoned by hardy islanders who were simply unable to cope with the brutality of life this far from the rest of humanity.

'I'm not going to disagree,' Ethan replied finally as Lopez struggled up to his side. 'Greece was a hell of a lot more inviting.'

Lopez stared at the barren, windswept cliffs nearby, the highest in the entire United Kingdom.

'I can't believe anybody ever actually chose to live in this hell hole.'

A gust of wind blasted rain across her face and she flinched away, wiping it off angrily as Ethan checked the map again and shook his head.

'None of this makes any sense,' he said. 'If there's any evidence left on this island of what we're looking for I'm guessing it's long gone.'

He lowered the map and shoved it into his pocket.

'We've been at this for six whole days now and we've come up with nothing,' Lopez muttered as they started clambering back down the hillside. 'Come on, admit it, we're chasing rainbows here.'

Ethan stopped on the side of the bleak hill, the wind buffeting the hardy grasses as the clouds scudded low over the immense slate gray ocean. Above, brief rays of sunshine broke through the cloud cover and drifted in shimmering veils, lighting the turbulent seas in pools of glittering light. The scene was as beautiful as it was desolate, and the sensation of hopelessness that crept upon him now matched the vista perfectly. They were out of options, out of time, out of money and out of leads. The fresco in Santorini had led them here to this bleak isle off the coast of Scotland, in search of a cryptic clue penned by a Greek Mariner, who may or may not have reached this spot several thousand years ago, and might or might not have identified a piece of evidence, that might possibly or possibly not send them on another leg of a journey toward a city that existed only in legend and perhaps only in myth.

Ethan sat down on the hillside.

'I can see why nobody has ever found the damned place.'

Lopez flopped down alongside him on the damp grass and they sat together staring out over the dramatic panorama.

'Did you ever think it would come to this?' she asked him as another squall of driving rain pummelled them, the drops rattling against their jackets. 'That this would all end with us sitting wet–assed on a hillside in Scotland with no friends and no money, looking around for something that probably isn't here?'

Ethan shrugged. 'I guess it's as fitting an end as any other.'

'That's defeatist.'

'It's realistic,' Ethan replied. 'We've gone over the figures a hundred times and we're sitting right on top of whatever damned clue it is that Pytheas said was here. We've walked this hill and every other over and over again and we've found nothing and even if we had, what the hell would we do with it? We can't announce it to the world without exposing ourselves to Petrov and his men, who will no doubt do what they can to ensure we end up taking a swim wearing concrete flippers, and that's if our own government don't lock us up first in some foreign prison and toss the keys.' Ethan sighed and shook his head. 'We just don't have any plays left.'

Lopez realized that in all of the years they had worked together, across all of the countries, in the face of all the incredible things that they had seen, she had never seen Ethan Warner defeated. The realization shocked her but it also flooded her with an unexpected relief, that perhaps now they really could consider giving it all up. Maybe they could just head out into the wild again, back to Indonesia and spend the rest of their days soaking up rays and catching dinner by pole and line. People didn't need money so much out there, on some remote island where the only taxes were those demanded by nature herself.

'Let's get out of here,' she said finally, and grabbed Ethan's arm to heave him to his feet.

They trudged together back the way they had come. As Ethan descended the hillside he could see various ruins scattered about alongside the few tracks that wound their way across the bleak hills. Many were ancient *cleits*, stone huts dotted around the valley into which they were descending, known to the long–gone locals as Village Bay. The dome–shaped structures were constructed of flat boulders with a cap of turf on the top, enabling the wind to pass through the cavities in the wall but keeping the rain out. Used for storage, they were known to have existed on the island since prehistoric times, and Ethan figured that perhaps some of those ancient people might have witnessed Pytheas's trireme visit this bleak spot of land amid the Atlantic's wild rollers. What had caused the Greeks to leave the warmth and light of Akrotiri to travel north to this bleak and inhospitable corner of the world could only have been a treasure like that of Atlantis, but Ethan was beginning to wish they'd just turned around and headed back the way they had come.

Ethan led the way down toward an old house near Village Bay that had been restored by enthusiastic volunteers who travelled to the islands during the summer months. Along with a small military radar post on one of the island's far flung corners they represented the only visitors to this lonely island, and even they evacuated during the winter months due to the storms that could envelop the island for weeks on end.

Lopez virtually kicked the door open as they reached the building and charged inside as Ethan closed it behind him to shut out the gales.

Lopez wasted no time in dousing firewood in the hearth with kerosene and lighting it. A crackling fire roared into life and illuminated the building's shadowy interior as Ethan hauled off his thick winter coat and gloves and warmed his hands in the glow of the fire.

'That's enough, Ethan, I'm done with this place and this whole caper,' Lopez said as she warmed her own hands alongside him. 'First flight out, use what identifications we have left to head east into Asia and then we just vanish into thin air. Everyone else has either been arrested or disappeared, and we'll be next if we hang around here much longer.'

She fluttered her hands demonstratively like butterflies fluttering into eternity. Ethan smiled and thought about it, and then about his parents and sister, the government holding them somewhere and Petrov and his people perhaps searching them out one day in the future as leverage against them. He sighed and closed his eyes, weary of the burden on his shoulders.

'If we run, we will never truly leave all of this behind.'

Lopez scowled angrily. 'This isn't *our* responsibility. We didn't bring all of this upon ourselves, it's the greed of others that drives this whole circus: Majestic Twelve, the administration, the wars and the secrets. It's all about the damned money, so why don't we hand the lot back to them and let them fight over it? With luck, they'll annihilate each other and remove themselves from the equation.'

Ethan stared into the flames of the fire, watched them coil and writhe like demons trapped in Hades, and in an instant he realized that once again Lopez was right. All these years, all of the investigations had all been about pursuing those who wanted power and money, and to keep it all for themselves.

'You're right,' he said finally.

'I am?'

'I'm done with this,' Ethan said and promptly stood up, Lopez getting to her feet beside him. 'I'm done with all of it.'

Ethan turned to Lopez and grabbed her by the shoulders, the flames lighting half of his face in a dancing light while the other half was consumed by shadow.

'We give them exactly what they want. Garrett is still out there, and he's only acting as the custodian of the billions that the Russians and everybody else are so keen to get their grubby little hands on. Let's bring it all into one place and ensure that they're all there too, and then let them destroy themselves fighting for it.'

Lopez smiled nervously. 'That's what we were trying to avoid, right? A military clash between Russia and America?'

'We don't pit the countries against each other, Nicola. We send the people involved up against each other. We draw them into something and then we hit them hard.'

'Trouble is that Garrett won't just hand over the billions, he'll see it as us giving up the fight, or worse getting him tied into it. You've seen what the Russian courts do to billionaires who challenge the Kremlin – what's to say our administration won't do the same to him? He's not going to openly admit his involvement in this.'

Ethan knew that she was right and that Garrett, brought into their fight due to the murder of his father in Montana so many years before at the hands of Majestic Twelve, had no reason to further risk the fortune he had made since in trying to find Atlantis.

Atlantis. Ethan now hated the word more than anything in the world. The search had in a short period of time cost them everything, and for what? The right to piss off some of the most dangerous, spiteful and self–centered people the human race had ever seen? Ethan wished that he had stayed where they were in Indonesia, and for once done not the "right" thing but instead what he had needed to do for a long time and put himself first. He looked down at Lopez. *Them* first.

'If we can find it, Atlantis, how do we get the Russians down there?' he asked.

Lopez shrugged. 'Petrov won't be hard to find. We just call him down there and make a deal. Accounts, reassurances, something to cover our backs before we meet.'

Ethan nodded. That, of course, would be the location of the money and perhaps the ancient city itself. He sighed again, withered by the helplessness of the situation.

'I guess we go with handing them the money and letting them fight over it then,' he said finally. 'Let's face it, Atlantis isn't going to walk in here and help us, is it?'

A knock sounded at the heavy door, and Ethan's heart flipped in his chest as he reached for a Berretta 9mm pistol tucked into his jacket.

Lopez pulled her own weapon out as they eased their way to the door. Lopez covered Ethan as he reached out and then yanked the door open and aimed out into the gloomy half darkness.

A woman stood before him, her long blonde hair tucked into her hood and a bright smile on her face that was only slightly withered by the sight of a pistol aimed at her.

'Lovely,' Lucy Morgan greeted them as she reached out and pushed Ethan's gun down. 'Haven't you found the final codex for Atlantis yet? You're practically standing on top of it.'

***

XXXVII

Ethan stared at Lucy in amazement as she hurried into the tiny abode and hauled off her hood as Ethan shut the door behind her.

'Were you followed?' Lopez asked.

'Are you kidding?' Lucy replied as she sat down on the narrow couch and warmed her hands in front of the fire. 'The ferry only runs back and forth twice each day and I was the only passenger they had for the afternoon. About the only things following me were seagulls.'

Ethan moved to a nearby chair and sat down.

'Where the hell have you been? We've been chasing you for weeks.'

'I know,' Lucy said. 'It was the only way to get you here, and I knew that if I went back to Jarvis then my cover would be blown. The only way to finish the search was to do it alone while you two took the flak from the Russians.'

'Gee, thanks,' Lopez uttered.

'You're welcome.'

'You knew about the Russians?' Ethan asked.

'It's why I went underground,' Lucy replied. 'They showed up in India when I was working, looking for the same things that I was but not asking nicely. The locals warned me that they were snooping around and I figured it was safer to disappear than to just run back to Doug for help. Where is he, anyway?'

Lopez averted her gaze, and Ethan took a breath before he replied. 'Doug was arrested in South Africa.'

'By whom?'

'Our own,' Ethan replied, 'we haven't heard anything from him since.'

Lucy stared into the flames for a moment. 'What about the others?'

Ethan replied, keeping one eye on Lopez as he did so.

'Mitchell and Lillian are still at large but out of contact, Amber and Garrett are fine but they're not able to help us any further for fear of being identified. Hellerman… Hellerman was captured by the Russians.'

Lucy's face fell and she stared at them in shock. 'Have you heard from him?!'

Ethan stared at Lucy for a long moment, and his expression said it all. Lucy's hand flew to her mouth and her gaze shifted to Lopez, who glowered down at her from where she stood.

'It's what happens when you disappear and let others *take the flak.*'

'It wasn't like that,' Lucy protested, tears welling in her eyes. 'I'm not a soldier or cop like you two.'

'Nor was Hellerman.'

'But I didn't...'

Lucy broke off and Ethan put a hand out to forestall Lopez. 'Lucy didn't kill Joseph, the Russians did, okay?'

Lopez shot him a hot look but she turned away from the confrontation with her arms folded across her chest as Ethan turned back to Lucy.

'This whole thing is about archaeology for you,' he said, 'but for the Russians it's all about the money and they'll kill anybody who stands in their way. You're lucky to have made it this far alive.'

Lucy nodded, wiped a tear from her cheek. 'I was searching for the city, not trying to get people killed.'

'People *are* getting killed,' Lopez said from nearby, 'so how about canning the riddles and the wild goose chase and telling us what we need to know so that we can find this damned city, draw the Russians into it and then blow them all to hell?'

Lucy looked at Ethan in confusion.

'We're done,' he said by way of an explanation. 'Doug is under arrest, Garrett can't help us and right now the three of us are fugitives and will likely be arrested or killed if we're found. Like it or not, if you know how to find Atlantis then now would be a good time to share and tell us what we're doing on this rain–soaked rock of an island in the middle of nowhere.'

Lucy took a moment to compose herself and order her thoughts before she began speaking.

'This rain–soaked rock of an island in the middle of nowhere represents what I believe to be one of the last strongholds of a people who once lived in the city we know of as Atlantis.'

Ethan glanced at Lopez, who rolled her eyes but said nothing.

'The people who built a flourishing and technologically advanced civilization ended up here?' Ethan asked.

'I believe that everything I've found in this journey, and which you have also seen, indicates that the survivors of some ancient society that suffered a cataclysmic disaster managed to voyage to other locations around the world in search of new homes and they brought some of their knowledge and technology with them. Their skills resulted in the birth of the civilizations that we regard to be the first, in ancient Sumeria and the Indus Valley.'

'Why would they come here?' Lopez asked, reluctantly joining the conversation.

'Why would they go anywhere?' Lucy countered. 'If their city was indeed consumed by the waves then they could have been scattered to the four corners of the globe in search of new homes. This island holds secrets that no archaeologist can explain, evidence that it was settled far earlier than even these old homes would suggest.'

Lucy pulled from her backpack a map of St Kilda that she unfolded and lay on the floor between them as she got to her knees and began pointing out landmarks.

'There are structures here called *An Lag Bho'n Tuath*, the Hollow in the North, some five thousand years old, the purpose of which is unknown. In Gleann Mor, to the north west of here, there are the remains of similarly aged structures that are unlike anything else seen in Britain or Europe. But the most telling evidence is that of something called the *Taigh na Banaghaisgeich*, or "The Amazon's House".'

'The what now?'

'A legendary female warrior who supposedly lived on this isle in the depths of recorded history,' Lucy replied. 'The story is also known across other isles in the region, that of a strange warrior who lived and hunted here, and who built a home in an unusual and innovative way. Its remains still stand, built from stone with no wood, earth or mortar to cement it, just like some of the world's most famous and ancient megalithic remains. It's pyramidial in shape, and seems to match the much older structures in other parts of the island, suggesting a common origin.'

'So what?' Lopez asked, losing interest already, 'some spear-throwing savage showed up here thousands of years ago. It's not the radical breakthrough we were hoping for.'

'How about the Face of the North then?' Lucy asked. 'Would that be breakthrough enough for you?'

Ethan sat back and shook his head.

'We've walked up and down this isle for days searching for anything that some ancient culture might have left behind, and we've come up empty. It's either no longer here or we can't find it because it's buried.'

Lucy smiled as she looked at them both 'Well, you can relax because I know precisely where it is. I passed it on the way here.'

'You do, huh?' Lopez murmured.

Lucy got up and grabbed her coat. 'You know, for two super-smart DIA field operatives with all your gadgets and gizmos and guns, you sure do miss the obvious sometimes.'

She tossed Ethan and Nicola their jackets and zipped hers up.

'You're gonna tell us that we could have left here days ago, aren't you?' Ethan said miserably.

'Yup,' Lucy acknowledged. 'I was waiting for you down at Gatwick. I thought that, given all that you'd solved up to now, you'd have no trouble figuring this final piece out. How wrong was I?'

'I've gotta see this to believe it,' Lopez said as she pulled her hood up and followed Lucy out of the house.

The sky was darkening, the bleak hills foreboding in shadow and the ocean crashing against the cliffs nearby as the endless rollers marched in from the Atlantic, but the rain had stopped as Lucy led them at a brisk pace up the hillside once again. However, this time they travelled east, following the coastline and climbing up until Lucy stopped and gestured to the bay below them.

'And there it is!'

Ethan stared down at the bay and the headland known as Dun but he could see nothing that suggested any kind of monument at all. The sunset behind them was piercing the clouds with fiery strips of molten metal that cast brief, drifting patches of light to contrast starkly with the darkening skies.

'I don't see it,' he said in confusion.

'Not down there,' Lucy replied. 'Out there!'

Ethan saw her pointing not at the bay but out into the open water where a huge, jagged chunk of rock loomed from the ocean. Then, Lucy held out a photograph of the rocks taken from the opposite side of them, probably from the deck of the boat she'd arrived on. Ethan held the picture up and he almost coughed in disbelief as he saw the huge rocks forming the image of a man's face staring out towards the south across the ocean.

'I don't believe it,' Lopez uttered. 'We passed it on the way in here.'

The features of the face in the rock were unmistakeably ancient Greek, a long straight beard with angular eyes and even a small nose that was somewhat eroded by the passing of thousands of years.

'Could it be chance?' Lopez asked, huddling against the cold wind. 'The rocks look volcanic.'

'They are,' Lucy replied. 'That rock is called Stac Levenish and this entire isle is formed from the rim of an ancient volcano.'

Ethan looked at her sharply now.

'Another one?' All of the Atlantis legends refer to islands beneath smoke and flame.'

'It might be that the Atlanteans preferred outposts on volcanic islands because they're formed of rich soils ideal for cultivation. That's the reason that so many cultures grew up on or near volcanoes, to take advantage of those soils despite the risk from the volcanoes themselves. This area could have seemed like a home away from home to the people of Atlantis. And get this; this area was above water ten thousand years ago, which meant that…'

'Stac Levenish could be reached on foot, and they would have been able to see the face from the other side,' Ethan said as he pulled out his map and then he hesitated and looked at Lucy. 'You've already done this, haven't you?'

Lucy nodded, her features beaming in delight at him from inside her hood.

"The sun in azimuth, the dawn star aloft, the eyes of the north shall gaze ever toward their goddess, where a land of fire bleeds toward the underworld."

'The face looks to the south, *toward their goddess,* which from historical reference I concluded was the site of Atlantis. Stac Levenish is only visible when approaching the islands from the east, *with the dawn star aloft,* which again I concluded to mean with the sun behind you as you sail, illuminating this side of the rock face and enhancing the shadows in relief to make the face more visible. From the island of St Kilda itself, there is nothing visible at all.'

As Ethan watched, Lucy produced a map onto which she had plotted lines that stretched all the way across the globe from Indonesia all the way to India, beyond through Egypt and into the Aegean Sea, and from there thousands of miles north to the British Isles. At Stac Levenish, a further final line ran south down across Europe and intersected all of the other lines at a single point on the map.

'I'll be damned,' Lopez uttered.

In the lonely darkness of a remote and windswept isle far from the rest of humanity, Ethan, Lopez and Lucy huddled in a tight group and looked down at the map where the lines intersected. Against the lines Lucy pressed another image, this one on transparent plastic so that the map was still visible below, that appeared to show some kind of ground–penetrating radar shot that was overlaid across the same part of the world where the lines intersected.

Three concentric rings, with a line pointing out of the center.

'On a continent the size of Asia,' Ethan said above the howling winds.

'Beyond the Pillars of Hercules,' Lucy acknowledged.

'A city of three concentric rings,' Lopez said, shaking her head in wonder.

Lucy folded the map and the image up to shelter them from the wind and the rain as she grinned at them.

'We've done it,' she said. 'We've found Atlantis.'

***

XXXVIII

USS Bataan,

Persian Gulf

The cell was tiny, barely providing enough room for a man to sit. There was no bed, no sink, no latrine but for a small grill in the deck that probably drained into the bilge pump exhaust. The heat was intense, the cell located close to the engine room and denied any proper ventilation. The cell door was of metal bars, the locks impossible to break even if the prisoner could reach them, which he couldn't as one wrist was permanently manacled to the deck.

Doug Jarvis sat in silence with his back to the hot metal wall behind him and his mind somewhere a thousand miles away. The crew of the Wasp–Class amphibious assault vessel had taken his clothes and replaced them with cheap, paper thin overalls designed to make the prisoner feel as vulnerable as possible. Jarvis cared about none of this. He sat with his head hung low to feign the slump–shouldered pose of a man suffering complete and utter defeat and instead allowed his mind to wander free and unbidden into the oblivion of dreams.

He had known, of course, that this time would come. All that he could hope was that he had given Ethan and Nicola and the others enough time to escape and continue the search for Atlantis and whatever might await them there. They had come so far, seen so much now that it seemed impossibly cruel that they would be crushed when within a hairs' breadth of the ultimate goal: an explanation of everything, of an answer to the many anomalous discoveries they had made over the years. Jarvis cared not for the money that the Russians and the administration were so obsessed with. Instead, Jarvis was possessed by an overpowering need to *know,* to understand what they had been dealing with all these long years. Ultimately, all paths led back to Atlantis or the legend thereof.

The sound of approaching boots alerted him and he slumped a little lower, his chin almost touching his chest. He knew what would happen next. Contrary to popular belief there would be no horrendous torture or "enhanced interrogation" although such methods had been used in the past by previous administrations. Jarvis was an old hand at this game and nearing the end of his life. His heart would struggle to survive any such physical traumas and it was likely his interrogators would know already that Jarvis would not easily give up any information this late in the game.

No, they would find another angle, something subtle and yet all the more effective for it. The boots reached the cell doors, which opened as Jarvis watched from the corner of his eye. The manacles were removed and then rebound behind his back as Jarvis was hauled to his feet and guided out of the cell.

The USS *Bataan* had become known in the US Navy as "Cell Block Five", a reference to her operating number and the fact that she had been used as a mobile black prison numerous times since she had been commissioned in 1996. Jarvis himself had ordered suspected Daesh fighters and other terrorists to be sent to her decks to be detained when due process was something that needed to be ignored, although he would never have believed that he too would one day be confined aboard her.

He was marched to an interrogation room, the ship's decks silent, indicating that the crew were being kept away from him at all times. Both of the men escorting him bore the insignia of officers, men trustworthy enough to maintain their silence. Jarvis was sat down and manacled to a table inside the room, and then the officers left and another man entered the room.

Jarvis did not reocgnize the man, but although he was wearing the standard disruptive pattern material uniform typical of the American soldier and there were stars on his collar denoting his rank as a Lieutenant Colonel, there were no unit insignia or patches identifying which part of the American military machine he was currently working for. Tall, with dark skin and an erect bearing, he closed the door to the room and took a seat in front of Jarvis, folding his hands before him with an appraising look in his eye.

'My name is Lieutenant Colonel Foxx, and you're a hard man to find, Mister Jarvis.'

'I'd like it to have stayed that way.'

'I'm sure you would,' Foxx replied as he opened a folder and examined the contents, 'but the State Department and the Pentagon all felt that the world would be a safer place with you tucked behind bars.'

'They have a warped sense of right and wrong, more now than ever.'

'Let's not play games,' Foxx replied. 'You may see yourself as a modern day Robin Hood, stealing from the rich to fight crime in your valiant little fantasy world, but when thirty billion dollars is spirited away into the night by an employee of our own Defense Intelligence Agency, I don't care if you're the lovechild of Nelson Mandela and Mother Theresa. The moment you absconded with those funds you became a criminal and nothing more.'

Jarvis said nothing as Foxx laid out a series of images before him on the table. Jarvis peered at the pictures, presumably shot by investigators on Foxx's team shortly before they had swooped and arrested him. He could see photographs of Rhys Garrett's yacht, of the man himself on the deck. Nearby was another image, this time of his granddaughter, Lucy Morgan.

'Now,' Foxx began, 'thirty billion dollars takes some serious laundering, and although I suspect that the cabal known as Majestic Twelve was already likely to have done so, you would still need new accounts and ways of hiding such vast sums of money in places that it would be difficult for my people to find. I would imagine that the owner of a major corporation with assets already in the billions would be a good place to start, agreed?'

Jarvis shook his head.

'Rhys Garrett is a benefactor, not a bank, and he knows nothing about any of this. You know that his father was murdered by Majestic Twelve?'

'I do,' Foxx acknowledged, 'a powerful motivator for him to join forces with you against what you see as corporate and political corruption.'

'What do you see it as?'

Foxx hesitated, just for a moment, caught off guard by the sudden question. 'I see it as my job to bring traitors like you into custody to face the justice that you deserve. Your motivations are not my business.'

'They should be,' Jarvis said as he sat up a little straighter in his seat, sensing something in the man sitting opposite that he had not expected to find.

'I'm not interested in your crusade.'

'You're the cause of it.'

'What's that supposed to mean?'

Jarvis took a breath as he looked down at the images. 'You've been hunting us for some time now, and yet what have you seen happen to the money that we allegedly stole from the government, even though the government doesn't actually own the money in question?'

'You can sell your line to the courts, right before they send you down to a security max for the rest of your life. I want to know the location of the money, all of it: account details, transfers, everything.'

Jarvis smiled quietly and watched Foxx for a long moment before he replied.

'That's their overriding concern, isn't it,' he said finally. 'The money. They're not interested in justice or the return of Majestic Twelve's ill-gotten gains to the people they variously robbed, extorted or murdered over the past sixty years. No, all that doesn't matter to them. They want the money, while it's untraceable, so that they can keep it untraceable and take it for themselves.'

Foxx ground his teeth in his skull.

'The details,' he repeated, and tossed Jarvis a pen and a pad of paper. 'From the first dollar to the last.'

Jarvis didn't move, didn't take his eyes from Foxx.

'When you were assigned this case, you were working for your country. I can assure you that things have changed and you're now working for a business whose sole interest is to take advantage of the cripplingly slow judicial and political system in order to make as much money as possible. You are merely an instrument of that new policy, and anybody who cannot see that is merely blinded by their own dogma.'

Foxx leaned closer to Jarvis, his voice low.

'And your dogma, Jarvis? You really think that I'm going to sit here and believe that it's in the best interests of the country that you took off with thirty billion dollars of government assets?'

'The money didn't belong to the government.'

'It sure as hell didn't belong to you.'

'That much is true,' Jarvis conceded, 'which is why I don't have it. I never have had any of it, and if you had the slightest inkling of how the modern world worked you would understand that *nobody* has any of it.'

Foxx squinted at Jarvis. 'What the hell is that supposed to mean?'

'The money,' Jarvis replied. 'It's worthless. Billions of dollars, but it's all digital, it's all in an Internet ether of transactions and assets, each valued for its potential and not for its physical worth. That's how cabals like Majestic Twelve stayed under the radar of the IRS and other government bodies: on paper, their only assets were properties and investments that had no taxation that remained outstanding on them. All of their financial accounts were represented by shares, stocks, mineral wealth and so on whose value was dependent on the markets at any one time. There was no physical money and there never has been. The government seized anything physical after we exposed the corruption of Majestic Twelve by leaking what you now know as the Panama Papers. Everything else…' Jarvis smiled again. 'It's just digital money, numbers, and we've let them all just spill away back into a monetary system that is as corrupt as the politicians back in DC trying to leverage it for their own profit.'

Foxx sat for a moment as he tried to digest what Jarvis was saying.

'You're telling me that it's all just *gone*?'

'It's recoverable,' Jarvis corrected him, 'some of it anyway, but most of it was dispersed widely by our IT expert. I happily allowed him to recover what he could and promptly donate it to thousands of charities around the world. Right now, and over the past six months, you would be amazed at how much money has found its way into the hands of people who actually *need* it, rather than those who would hoard it all for themselves even when they're already wealthy beyond avarice.'

Foxx wrote swiftly on a pad, then looked up at Jarvis. 'This IT expert, where is he now? We'll need to talk to him.'

Jarvis leaned forward on the table.

'He's dead, murdered by the same people who were hunting us.' Now Foxx's expression changed and Jarvis went in for the kill. 'They're Russians and they're heavily invested in the current administration. The victim's name is Joseph Hellerman, formerly of the Defense Intelligence Agency, and he was a patriot who died to protect the welfare of two of my operatives who even now are out there doing what they can to prevent Russia and America from facing off over billions of dollars that don't belong to them and that they'll never be able to find. And now here we are, you interrogating me for crimes committed to try to prevent corruption in our own government, and you abducting the families of American patriots being hunted by their own people.'

Foxx glanced down at his notes, and Jarvis saw Hellerman's name written there among a list of others: Ethan Warner, Nicola Lopez, Natalie Warner and more.

'Who says that we've abducted anybody?' Foxx challenged.

Jarvis allowed himself a small smile of victory as he kept his eyes fixed on the soldier.

'Because we've got you on film taking Natalie Warner into custody in DC just a few days ago.'

Foxx looked up sharply and Jarvis tapped the images before them on the table, not giving Foxx time to think, keeping him off balance. 'You think that you were tipped off, and found us, don't you?'

'We received an anonymous tip off from a…'

'Cell phone off the coast of Jeddah, Saudi Arabia in South Africa, yesterday. The cell was supplied by you and equipped with a GPS transmitter with a unique signal that pinged off a satellite at half past noon local time, right when I asked Allison Pierce to switch it on.'

Foxx stared at the old man as he realized what had happened. Jarvis sat back in his seat and smiled.

'I know about Allison and I ordered her to switch the cell on so that you would find us. It had to look like we were captured, not surrendering, and it had to happen out here and not in a city where we could easily be repatriated. Now, you need to listen to me very carefully, because if we get this wrong a lot of people are going to die.'

***

XXXIX

Donona National Park,

Andalusia, Spain

Ethan crouched low in the small boat that he had hired from a local store just a few miles away from the silent Guadalquivir River on which he and Lopez now rowed, their oars slipping through the silky water in silence.

The sun was not yet up above the horizon, the dawn little more than a faint glow to the east as they made their way up the river. Lucy Morgan guided them from the center of the boat, her gaze affixed to a GPS device into which she had loaded an image of the ground penetrating radar data she had shown them on St Kilda island. Ethan watched the glow from the screen illuminating the look of permanent wonder on her face as they eased their way further inshore toward a destination that had lain unknown beneath the feet of mankind for millennia.

Ethan looked around them and could admit to himself that this was not the kind of place he would have considered as a possible location for the mythical lost city of Atlantis. The Donona National Park was a wildlife refuge and protected by numerous laws designed to prevent human intrusion into the wetland habitat. The park was filled with marshes, shallow streams and sand dunes and formed Las Marismas, the delta created by the river where it flowed into the Atlantic Ocean. Reasonably flat and with scattered tree cover, the area was a haven for scientific research and ecosystem study and neither Ethan, Lopez or Lucy had any right to be there at all.

'This area did not look like this ten thousand years ago,' Lucy whispered as the boat advanced silently. 'It was still filled with the same brackish marshes and sand dunes, but the central feature of the area was a series of concentric rings of bedrock with a single channel out to the coast, as it was then. The radar data is incontrovertable: if this is where the city that we now know as Atlantis stood, then it was built upon a natural formation and not constructed purposefully as Plato seemed to suggest.'

Ethan frowned as he looked around them.

'How the hell can an entire city be hidden beneath a handful of dunes and ponds?'

'Because the area holds geological evidence of several high–energy events, including major storms but more importantly tsunamis. Geological evidence from this area reveals that repeated tsuanims reached miles inland, suggesting enormous power that could easily have swamped a coastal city like Atlantis, and with tsunamis come not just water but also debris from the land and immense quantities of silt.'

Lopez gave a snort from the bow of the boat. 'So, it's under the mud.'

'In a sense,' Lucy agreed, 'although some areas should remain accessible. The park area here has become an aquifer over many thousands of years, and so if Atlantis is down there it will be effectively under water. However, any structures down there would also likely provide shelter from both water and silt if we can find a way into them.'

Ethan shook his head.

'And if we do? What then? It's not like we can excavate anything here, we wouldn't last a minute before the Russians or the local police are alerted to our presence and we find ourselves in a jail cell.'

'The joy of discovery is all the justification that we need,' Lucy said as she glanced over her shoulder at him. 'It's out here Ethan and it's waiting to be found, and I know who lived here.'

'You *know* them?' Lopez asked.

'We know this place as the mythical city Atlantis, but this area was the location of an extremely ancient culture and city known as Tartessos.'

'Never heard of 'em,' Ethan admitted.

'Not many people have, because they're so ancient that even today some refer to the Tartessians as a mythical culture, a people that may have never even existed. The city of Tartessos was a semi–mythical harbor city described by the Greek Herodotus as being just beyond the Pillars of Hercules. The culture was said to be rich in metals and mineral wealth, just like Atlantis, and even gold and copper from Celtic lands, according to the fourth century historian Ephorus. They traded with the Phoenicians and there have been tremendous treaures discovered in this area, including the El Carombolom hoard of gold now on display at the Museum of Seville.'

'So the people were real enough,' Ethan said. 'How come everyone isn't aware of them then?'

'Their language and writings have never been classified because although they have been compared to both Celtic and Indo–European scripts they have never been fully deciphered, and they also share commonalities with both Sumerian cypher and Egyptian hieroglyphic scripts which suggest them as the common originator of both. Most archaeologists aren't willing to cross that line as it suggests a link to an advanced pro–genitor civilization on the Iberian Peninsular, and that sounds too much like Atlantis for anyone to go ahead and stick their neck out and say it.'

Ethan said nothing as they rowed along the river and began to approach an area of dry land that looked little more than a spit of sand poking out of the water, trees silhouetted against the dawn sky.

'It's just ahead of us,' Lucy said excitedly.

Ethan and Lopez stopped rowing and let the boat's momentum carry them into the shore. The prow bumped up onto the sand and Lopez leaped out and with their help hauled the boat out of the water and onto the beach.

'Now what?' Lopez asked.

Lucy held up one hand to silence them as she turned on the spot, her eyes still fixed to the screen as she orientated herself and then promptly marched off into the woods. Ethan grabbed a backpack they had brought with them and pulled it onto his shoulders before he set off in pursuit of Lucy.

'This place doesn't look like it could contain a lost city,' Ethan said again, 'and for that matter it doesn't look like anybody ever lived here.'

'The area has been occupied for thousands of years,' Lucy contradicted him as she walked, never taking her eyes from the GPS screen. 'Until about seven thousand years ago the area was flooded after the melting of the glaciers when the Ice Age ended, but over the millennia since it has gradually emptied, the silt and sand dunes building up over time. That terrain has supported the Phoenician cultures, the Phocaean Greeks and the Tartessians. Remnants of their presence have been found across the breadth of this area but nobody thought to look deeper *underground* for evidence of older settlements, which is why this data has remained hidden until now.'

Lucy kept moving for another few minutes and then she stopped near a clearing that was surrounded by trees and bushes and seemed a little higher than the surrounding marshes. Ethan realized that they had followed what he had assumed was a game trail between the bushes but that had in fact become suddenly dead straight and much wider, the foliage around them concealing the pathway that now seemed so obvious.

'Are you seeing it yet?' Lucy asked, and he realized that she had been watching him.

Ethan looked ahead and saw a long mound rising up from left to right before them. Although it was not high, it protruded enough from the surrounding land to be noticeable, and then beyond it he saw another more conical formation of land that rose higher still, like a mound surrounded by a...

'Concentric circle,' Ethan blurted as his mind suddenly grasped an image of where they were standing.

Lucy gestured to depressions between the mounds that were filled with sand.

'These are known locally as *lucios*, and are depressions in the ground where sand and silt has been left behind as waters have receded over hundreds or even thousands of years. The higher ground has been bound together by vegetation, and has something beneath it upon which soil and silt has been able to cling, allowing it to stand against the elements.'

Ethan stepped forward and realized that the vast clearing upon the edge of which they stood was in fact a depression that was filled with the barely discernible form of a mound surrounded by the broken shape of three concentric circles of raised land, all of it almost perfectly concealed beneath the shifting sand and the foliage.

'I'll be damned,' Lopez said. 'It's right under there?'

'It's right under there,' Lucy confirmed, 'and there's enough of it above the water table that we might be able to get in there and take a look.'

Lucy set off along the narrow path at a swift pace, driven now as much by conviction as evidence. Ethan followed her over the first of the rings and then across the depressions of sand, Lucy aiming instinctively for the main mound in the center and no doubt already thinking about how to get inside.

Ethan and Lopez kept pace with her as she approached the central mound and then she slowed and surveyed the surface of what to any observer would have appeared to be a perfectly natural formation. Lucy stared at it for almost a full minute, long enough that Ethan began to wonder whether she was just soaking the moment up, the glory of being on the verge of a discovery like no other.

'This is how Howard Carter must have felt, just before he opened the tomb of the Pharoah Tutankhamun in the Valley of the Kings,' she whispered.

Lopez glanced at Ethan. 'I'm pretty sure Howard Carter didn't have the Kremlin pursuing him when he got there, but even then he would have got the hell on with it. Do you know where the entrance is?'

Lucy gave Lopez a withering look and gestured with her thumb to the south west side of the mound. 'The entrance would have faced the port and the main route into the city, but that entrance will be buried deep down right now. Any major temples and other structures often had ceremonial purposes and were orientated toward the equinoxes. My guess, based on other cities from antiquity, is that there would be a structure close to the surface and with some kind of cavity that would be used to overlook the city, right about here.'

Lucy thumped her heel against the edge of the mound. She knelt down and pressed one hand to the sloped ground as though she were trying to sense the presence of something below her, and then she switched off the GPS device and began pushing mounds of sand away to the sides.

Ethan and Lopez moved alongside her and began likewise shifting the sand into piles either side of them. Lucy dug down, the sand becoming damp as she burrowed and revealing dark soil, and then Ethan saw the soil wiped clear of what looked like smooth stone or rock.

'Here,' Lucy said in delight as she frantically began clearing space beneath them and expanding the exposed surface of the rock.

In the pale light of dawn Ethan saw more rock appear, and then all at once he saw that the rocks were individual bricks that were perfectly aligned with each other, pushed together so closely that it was not possible to wedge even a piece of paper between them. He began to work harder, yanking bushes out of the soil and hurling them aside as they burrowed down and to the sides in search of an entrance.

'The stonework is like that of the Egyptians, but the cut has more in common with Incan sites,' Lucy said as she worked. 'It's the upper level of some kind of temple.'

Ethan could see that although each of the stones bore flat edges in the manner of Egyptian temples, the angles were randomized rather than uniform, more like Inca temples such as those he had seen at Macchu Pichu some years before. The stones there had been selected as close fits to the next and then shaped to fit perfectly.

Lucy scraped at the soil with her bare hands and finally encountered a flat, square panel of smooth cut stone, some two feet square, that was set into raised blocks. Ethan stood back and guessed that the stonework was of sufficient quality here that it might be considered very nearly water tight.

'We need to get in there,' Lucy said.

Ethan pulled out a pair of folding metal shovels from his backpack, the handles of which formed wedges perfect for prizing stubborn rocks from compacted soil. Ethan shoved the handles in at two points along one edge of the stone and then he and Lopez pressed their boots down on them as hard as they could.

The handles bowed under the pressure and then Ethan heard the tell–tale rumble of rock scraping against rock. The stone shifted and Lucy shoved a third shovel into the opening gap to pin the stone open. Ethan moved to one side and then got his fingers underneath the stone as he and Lucy heaved it upward.

The stone flew up and toppled over onto the side of the hill as a waft of stagnant air puffed out into their faces. Ethan looked down and saw nothing but an impenetrable darkness before them.

'What was that stone for?' Lopez asked.

Lucy stood up and brushed herself down as she looked at the perfectly cut stone now lying nearby on the hillside

'This area might have been prone to tsunami for many thousands of years, and the best defense would have been stone blocks in recesses in the windows. The people might have set it and others in place in the hopes that they could return, but they never did.'

Ethan was about to ask another question but he didn't have time. Lucy pulled out a small torch and then grabbed the lower ledge of the opening and tucked her legs beneath her before hopping into the opening and vanishing into the darkness.

Ethan shrugged and followed her in, Lopez right behind him.

***

THE ATLANTIS CODEX   Dean Crawford

XL

Cadiz, Spain

Allison Pierce hurried across the street outside the terminal of Jerez Airport and got into a hire vehicle. Her eyes were concealed behind sunglasses and she wore a summer hat with loose clothes that did as much to conceal her shape as her identity. Mitchell had warned her of the dangers of facial–recognition software employed at major airports and other hubs, and therefore she had also plugged her cheeks with cotton wool and wrapped her waist with spare clothes beneath her blouse to further conceal her identity.

The fake passport and other documents that Mitchell had supplied her with had functioned perfectly and to her relief she had passed through customs without a hitch. She knew, of course, that it was possible that she was being followed but she could only leave as difficult a trail as possible and hope that it was enough.

The car was hot and she wound down the windows as she waited, a gentle breeze wafting through the vehicle as she checked her burner phone and selected an app that showed her various aircraft travelling into and out of Cadiz. She picked out the one she wanted and smiled to herself as she recognized the picture of a private jet inbound from Ronald Reagan International. The flight had landed twelve minutes previously and had disembarked only moments ago.

As she watched the terminal she saw two smart white sedans with tinted black windows cruise effortlessly into the sidewalk outside the terminal. Within moments, two smartly suited men stepped out of the terminal and were followed by two more either side of a man whom Allison recognized instantly.

'Well, hello there Congressman Milton Keyes.'

Allison shrunk back into the shadowy interior of her car as she filmed the senator climbing into the second of the two white vehicles as the suited men all climbed into the first. The vehicles pulled smoothly away again and Allison started the engine on her little hire car and pulled out to follow them from a good distance behind.

*

'Thank you for agreeing to meet with us, congressman.'

Konstantin Petrov sat inside the plush interior of the vehicle and regarded the man before him.

'This is a dangerous precedent,' Keyes uttered. 'Congressmen have lost their jobs and been imprisoned for less. Why am I here?'

Keyes was older than Petrov and it showed. His jawline was flabby and his skin blotchy from what Petrov imagined was too many late nights sipping liquor with his congressional pals. Keys represented something that Petrov and all commoners despised: the rich man who lorded over the masses, who passed legislation that favoured corporations over the common people and who knew little of life in the real world.

'I would not have brought you here were it not of paramount importance.'

Keyes appeared unimpressed.

'There is nothing out here that warrants my time and effort. This is something that we agreed would be handled by your people.'

'My people?' Petrov asked, unable to prevent himself from taunting the congressman.

Keyes faltered. 'By that I mean, that you.., I mean that…'

'You mean Russian,' Petrov replied calmly. 'You mean ordinary person, commoners.'

Keyes reared up in his seat a little. 'I didn't mean it like that.'

'But that is what you wanted to say, no?' Petrov pressed, still presenting an affable air despite the contempt now boiling inside of him. 'That I am something less than you are?'

Keyes seemed to suddenly notice the muscular frame beneath Petrov's shirt and the cold gleam of a killer lurking somewhere in his eyes. The congressman shook himself from something that might have been fear, remembering that he was an American lawmaker.

'I am here because you asked me to be,' he snapped. 'I want to know why. Threatening me with the exposure of our accord was unnecessary.'

Petrov smiled, no warmth in his eyes as with one hand he slowly produced from beneath his shirt a long, highly polished blade. The combat knife was serrated on one edge that glittered like diamonds encrusted in a shark's tooth.

Keyes immediately reached for the door handle and yanked on it, but the door remained firmly shut as Petrov leaned forward and glared into the congressman's eyes.

'We're in this together, Milton,' he snarled, 'down here on the street, and until I say otherwise you belong to me.'

Petrov's hand shot out and the tip of the blade pressed against Keyes' belly. The congressman sucked in a deep breath as he tried to pull his stomach in and away from the blade and he reared up in his seat. Both of his hands wrapped around Petrov's and tried to push the weapon away but his feeble arms were no match for the soldier's raw strength.

'Now,' Petrov murmured as he kept the blade pressed against the congressman's flabby stomach. 'Tell me, about how you intend to renege on the deal that we agreed.'

Keyes quivered and his eyes wobbled in horror as he shook his head.

'No. No, that's not true! We have said no such thing and…'

Petrov shoved the blade hard against Keyes and the weapon pierced his shirt and sank an inch into the fat of his stomach. Keyes screamed in terror and pain, but Petrov kept the blade in place with immovable strength.

'Every time you lie to me this blade will sink another inch into your guts, and I'll keep pushing it until the tip severs your spine and pins you to this seat, do you understand?'

Keyes nodded, sweating profusely.

'We were tipped off,' Petrov growled. 'We know that you intend to betray us. How?'

Keyes whimpered and his words spilled from his lips in a torrent.

'They're going to corner you inside the site and kill all of you! There's nothing that I can do about it! I didn't want any part of this, they made me cover up everything and bury the evidence!'

Petrov leaned even closer, the knife ready.

'This blade will puncture your intestines if I push it any further, and they will begin to leak bodily waste directly into your bloodstream and ensure a long and agonizing death as the contents of your guts swill through your body. You won't be able to escape, because the last push will sever your spine and render you incapacitated. By the time anybody finds your remains, the animals and the birds won't have left much to identify you by.'

Keyes began to blub incoherently, the strength fading from his flabby arms as he capitulated entirely to his fate, knowing that there was nothing he could do to prevent his death at the hands of a Communist psychopath. Petrov saw in him a man of great power who now found himself facing up to who he really was – a weak man.

'When will they come?' he demanded.

Keyes blubbed his unintelligible answer amid a stream of spittle and Petrov twisted the blade sharply. Keyes screamed, more in terror now than pain, and shouted his reply.

'They are tracking us! We are expected to travel to a site that has been located in the marshes somewhere, where we were told that money from Majestic Twelve has been hidden! Then when you're all there, they will attack!'

'Who?!'

'I don't know!' Keyes wailed. 'Special Forces or something, they have a ship off the coast!'

Petrov nodded slowly, and patted the back of Keyes' hand as though consoling a child. Then he yanked the blade out of his guts, the serrated edge ripping flesh and skin on its way out. Keyes groaned and folded over his wound as Petrov thought for a moment.

The Russian tip–off had been anonymous, and now suddenly there was an American warship off the coast of Spain, conveniently positioned to intercept them. Petrov examined the blade of his knife for a moment, the shiny metal smeared with the congressman's blood.

'Jarvis,' he uttered to himself.

The American had, so Petrov had been reliably informed, arrested aboard a luxury yacht matching the description of one that had been seen near both Indonesia and Santorini and was now somewhere in the Red Sea. Jarvis had evaded arrest for many long months, but suddenly finds himself in American hands…

Petrov made his decision and nodded to the driver.

The vehicle was already well out of the city and travelling swiftly north. The driver found an old track near a church, which was standing alone near a forest surrounded by endless miles of wilderness shrubland.

The driver cruised into the woods and pulled up at a lonely spot where the sun beat down in silence.

Petrov reached across Keyes and pushed open the door, then looked the congressman in his quivering and bloodshot eyes.

'I am a man of my word, and so for coming clean I will spare you your life,' he said, 'or rather I will allow you the chance of survival, however slim that may be. If you speak of me, ever, it will be your family who will suffer the consequences.'

Keyes opened his mouth to protest and then Petrov's blade sliced across the back of the congressman's heel in a line of white pain. Keyes screamed again as his Achilles Tendon was severed and Petrov shoved him out of the vehicle to crash down onto the lonely desert road, his hands clutching his mauled belly.

Petrov hauled the door shut and the vehicle drove away from the scene, Petrov cleaning his blade as the driver glanced over his shoulder.

'If he survives and makes it back to America, he'll feel safer and might open up to the courts and identify us. It's risky to let him go.'

Petrov smiled as he worked.

'He will not survive, Victor,' he replied calmly as he worked. 'It's not just blood that I'm cleaning off this blade but Epibatidine. It's the poison of an Ecuadorean tree frog and is lethal in even the smallest doses.'

The driver chuckled to himself and shook his head as he looked in the mirror and saw the form of the Congressman's body curled up in the road amid a cloud of dust.

Petrov pulled out a cell phone and dialled a number. When it was answered, he could hear the sounds of a busy vessel's bridge deck in the background as he spoke.

'It is confirmed,' he said. 'The Americans intend to betray us. Sail at maximum speed for Cadiz and we will meet you on the coast.'

'Understood, comrade. You should know that there is an American warship within a few miles of Cadiz.'

'Understood.'

The line went dead and Petrov pocketed the cell phone. The Americans would never reach the site in time to protect their people, and Petrov would be long gone before they arrived. All that he needed now was to gain access to the site, take what he needed, and then escape and vanish into thin air.

*

Allison slowed as she saw the two vehicles in the distance, still headed north as they turned right and joined another highway headed out toward the national parks area. Her vehicle had closed on them unexpectedly as they had slowed rapidly in a cloud of dust, and she figured that they had stopped for some reason, and she realized why when she saw the form of a man kneeling in the center of the road as the dust cleared.

Allison slowed as she recognized the figure and her heart leaped into her throat as she realized that Congressman Keyes was raising his hand toward her, trying to flag her down. Allison looked up to see the Russian vehicles disappearing in the heat haze far ahead and she cursed as she wondered whether Petrov and his men had picked her up on their tail and sought to distract her from following them.

Allison stopped her car and got out of the air–conditioned interior into the heat of another blazing Spanish dawn. The sight of Keyes on his knees in a foreign country with none of his entourage to protect him inspired in her a moment of grim delight that lasted only seconds as he realized the state he was in.

'Help me,' he gasped, one bloodied hand over a messy wound in his guts.

Allison hurried across and tried to help him to his feet. Keyes staggered weakly upright, one leg dangling weakly beneath him, the sock soaked in blood as they shuffled to the vehicle and he slammed his hands down onto the hood for balance, Allison unable to bear his weight any longer.

'I asked you for help once,' she said. 'That fell on deaf ears.'

'You hadn't been stabbed and beaten,' Keyes snapped in reply, his face still blotchy with pain and shame and his eyes puffy and damp with tears.

'Tell me everything,' she insisted. 'Who did this to you?'

Keyes peered sideways at her as his addled brain finally conjured a thought. 'What are you doing out here?'

'It's a long and tragic story and most of it's been caused by people like you,' Allison shot back. 'Thanks to you and a media who care more for sensationalism than truth I'm now a fugitive on the run and you're half dead! Who did this to you?!'

'The Russian,' Keyes gasped, 'Petrov.'

Keyes slumped a little more on the hood of the car and Allison noted the sweat beading on his face and an unhealthy palor to his skin.

'I'm feeling real bad,' he gasped, his hands trembling and his one remaining good leg quivering beneath his weight.

Allison pulled out her cell phone to dial for an ambulance and immediately realized that she could get no signal. She cursed and slammed her hand down on the hood of the car as she looked again at Keyes. She was no doctor but she knew a dying man when she saw one. Petrov might have punctured the congressman's stomach with his knife, but he might also have done more than just that and she knew that if she left Keyes here he wouldn't last much more than an hour.

'Tell me what happened!' she insisted. 'There's no time to argue! If you don't talk then Petrov will kill everybody he finds out there!'

Keyes struggled to stay focussed and blinked, then spoke.

'The Russians were involved in a campaign to spread fake news during the presidential election,' he gasped. 'They set up a control room in downtown DC and used cybercrime to influence the way people think. They've been doing it for years inside Russia but have now spread their work to the United States. Militarily, Russia isn't the force it once was and so the Kremlin has resorted to other means to project their influence into world events.'

Allison shook her head. 'How do you fit into all of this?'

Keyes lowered his head further, sweat dripping from his brow onto the hood.

'They wanted me to act as a go–between for the Russian hackers, and to ensure that the investigation into Majestic Twelve did not reveal the lost billions but only that which had already been declared to the public.'

'Damn it!' Allison cursed again and hit the car hood. 'I knew it! It's all about the damned money and you people don't care whose lives get destroyed in the process! How much were you in for, Keyes? How much did they promise you?'

Keyes shook his head. Allison took one last look at him and knew that if they didn't move now, they would never make it back to Cadiz and a hospital in time.

'Blood money,' she snapped as she hauled Keyes off the hood and helped him to the passenger side. 'You're as bad as the Russians you were stupid enough to deal with, and now more patriots will die because of what you've done.'

***

XLI

USS Bataan

Lieutenant Colonel Foxx strode down a corridor inside the warship as it sailed north out of the Straits of Gibraltar. They had been at full steam and had crossed the Mediterranean in record time, and all of it on the word of a man who had a reputation for being able to twist anybody to his will.

That said, everything Jarvis had claimed had checked out, although there was no way that he was going to let the old man go. It had taken months to track him down, and regardless of his motivations Foxx was determined to complete his mission and bring Jarvis back to America to face trial for his actions.

Foxx entered a small interrogation room, where Jarvis sat manacled to the table.

'Is it done?' the old man asked as Foxx closed the door and sat down.

Foxx took a deep breath before he replied, perhaps because he couldn't quite believe what he had now witnessed with his own eyes and ears.

'A call was placed to a member of congress,' he said, 'after we tipped off the Russians through a DIA source in Moscow. The information we placed resulted in the congressman and the Russians arranging to meet in Cadiz, just as you said they would. We're tracking them now. How do you know that the area contains what they're looking for?'

'My granddaughter, Lucy Morgan, identified it some days ago and sent me the details,' Jarvis replied. 'We've sat on it because the Russians were tailing my operatives. Sending them there would also give the Russians what they needed.'

'Well, they're on their way now.'

'And my testimony?' Jarvis asked. 'You have filed it, exactly as I gave it?'

Foxx sighed. 'Despite my better judgement, yes. I have recorded that your team is searching for Atlantis, which you believe ties in to several prior DIA investigations that involved discoveries including, but not limited to; alien corpses in Israel and Peru, a device known as *Die*

Glocke recovered by the Germans before World War Two that's rumoured to be some kind of alien craft, and a satellite that had been in earth orbit for the past thirteen thousand years that you recently recovered from Antarctia?'

Jarvis nodded, not the slightest trace of deception in his voice.

'The entire catalogue of artefacts recovered by the DIA as part of my ARIES program points to the conclusion that our planet has a longer history of civilization than we know about and that someone, somewhere wants that knowledge to remain secret.'

Foxx nodded as though he understood. 'And these artefacts, where are they now?'

'I managed to hide some of them before the new administration took over,' Jarvis explained. 'But most were taken away and hidden. I believe that the new administration is determined to recover them, regardless of the risks to life and limb and national security.'

'You're telling me that the Russians are colluding with our own leadership in this, that they're working together?'

'Only on the face of it,' Jarvis replied. 'They may have colluded to ensure that they both gained the election result that they wanted, but beyond that I don't believe that they intend to trust each other and in fact my best guess is that when it comes to crunch time they'll deploy their forces against each other anywhere in the world they choose.'

That got Foxx's attention.

'They'll go to war over this?'

'When was the last time you ever heard of the Russians being true to their word or our current administration being lauded for honesty and integrity? As soon as either side thinks they have the winning hand they're going to drop rocks on the other and get out of dodge as fast as they can. That might be fine if either side had a reputation for anything approaching competency but my biggest fear right now is that the whole thing will go south, and before you know it we'll have a military flashpoint between east and west right here in Europe and there'll be nothing we can do to stop it getting out of hand.'

Foxx stared at his notes. Even if Jarvis was off his head and the entire tale was some kind of veil fabricated to cover some deeper truth, he knew well enough that the ship on which they sailed had just passed through the Straits of Gibraltar and that just a hundred miles to the south the Russian Udaloy–class destroyer *Severomosk* was sailing on international waters at maximum speed toward the Spanish coast. As far as he could recall the Russians had nothing more to do with Spain than booking it as a holiday destination.

He thought for a moment.

'The Russians that you say are behind all of this. Had you identified them yet?'

'Only their leader,' Jarvis replied. 'He showed up in Indonesia and is the man responsible for the murder of one of our team. His name is Konstantin Petrov and he operates under Diplomatic Immunity.'

Foxx felt a tingle of shock at the mention off that name. Petrov was a man who had been mentioned many times in communications chatter picked up by Foxx's team. Deployed after his predecessor had been killed in an anomalous incident in Egypt that had also involved DIA operatives assigned to Jarvis before his disappearance, Petrov was believed to have been operating as part of some kind of exotic unit called…

'Mat' Zemlya,' Jarvis said for Foxx, 'Russian for "*Mother Earth*". The unit is modelled on the DIA's ARIES program and generally hunts for the same things that we do. It's why we so often found ourselves up against Russian operatives around the world. Listen, the people out there working for me are patriots and they're trying to prevent a war from being sparked. Get your people onto this instead of arresting our family members and you'll see that I'm telling the truth. We're tired of this now and want it brought to an end as much as you do, but if you don't deploy forces to support Ethan Warner and Nicola Lopez, this is going to end with the Americans and the Russians betraying each other and starting a conflict that could lead to World War Three. Is that something you want on your conscience?'

Foxx did not reply for a moment, but then he spoke softly.

'We haven't arrested your family members,' he said. 'We took them into protective custody.'

Jarvis raised an eyebrow, but said nothing as Foxx went on.

'We knew they were being targeted by the Russians and that if captured they might be harmed in return for information. You're right, Mr Jarvis, this will end here and now because we can't risk the exposure of the kind of information you're in possession of to Russian thugs like

Petrov. Your families are all safe and will be returned home as soon as this matter is resolved.'

Jarvis nodded.

'And Ethan and Nicola? They're in the company of my granddaughter, a civilian. They'll be in the firing line if your people don't get to them first.'

Foxx looked at Jarvis for a long moment.

'I will inform our people of friendlies on site,' he promised. 'If this process results in the complete recovery of materials stolen from the DIA and the prevention of a major international incident then it will go a long way in clearing your name. However, the government has no interest in your crusade and every reason to oppose it. I will do what I can to protect them, but sooner or later we're going to be back in the United States and things will be out of my hands.'

Jarvis nodded, looking as though he was in deep thought.

Foxx stood from his seat, turned and marched out. He closed the door behind him and knew that most of what he had just heard was so incredible that he could not hope to present it to his superiors and expect them to do anything except lock Jarvis up and throw away the key. He would have to tread lightly or this whole thing would explode in his face, not to mention across the whole of southern Europe. Any confrontation between Russian and American forces here would demand the intervention of the United Nations and the NATO alliance, which would mobilize forces within moments of any clash to lock the Russians down on the borders of Poland and Germany. Poised for open conflict, the rest of the world would be forced to take sides. China would ally with Russia, allowing Communist North Korea the support its deranged leader craved, while Iran and Syria would oppose America and Israel. Even if the European situation were diffused quickly, neither Israel nor Iran would deny themselves the *righteous* opportunity to strike their neighbor. From there, all bets were off.

Foxx hurried to a communications suite deep inside the ship. From here, he could use secure satellite links with Washington DC to determine from his superiors the best course of action and ensure that this flashpoint was extinguished before it could even begin. Within moments of accessing his high–security account, Foxx was linked to the Pentagon and was explaining to a four–star general only the parts of

Jarvis's story that wouldn't get him sent to a private hospital ward in Vermont with padded walls and soft music.

'And you can verify this information?' the general asked.

'It matches everything we know so far, and with the Russian destroyer *Severomosk* within hours of our position and Konstantin Petrov already in Spain, I'd say the likelihood that this is a false alarm just went out the window. If we don't act to intervene and prevent the Russians from linking up with Petrov, this whole thing could go south real fast sir.'

The general nodded thoughtfully.

'I'll have to clear it with the Joint Chiefs of Staff, but that means that the administration will be in the loop. If what this guy Jarvis is saying turns out to be true, they may attempt to prevent any US military action that might endanger their goal or expose further evidence of their collusion with Russian activists inside the DC area.'

'Their goals are not in line with United States national security sir,' Foxx said. 'Right now, I'll take a tongue lashing from any elected official rather than a potential global military clash on the soil of an allied nation of the NATO alliance.'

'Agreed,' the general replied. 'What allied assets do we have on the ground there right now?'

'Several Americans, former DIA operatives who have worked to uncover this conspiracy.'

'Civilians?'

Foxx nodded, and he could see the general working through his options.

'These former DIA, are they the same operatives assigned to Jarvis, who colluded to escape with classified artefacts and documents, not to mention finances, in the wake of the Panama Paper and the Majestic Twelve scandal?'

'The same.'

Again, a long pause, and then the general appeared to make a decision.

'Deploy what forces you have available to covertly infiltrate the site and take control of it with extreme prejudice. There are to be no mistakes, Foxx. I want this whole thing cleared up before that destroyer reaches the area.'

Foxx lifted his chin. 'Yes sir. What about the joint chiefs?'

The general shook his head.

'We can't risk any of them attempting to derail this before Russian support is forthcoming to Petrov on the ground. Get your men in, hit the area hard and remove any trace of evidence that any American serviceman ever set foot in the Donana National Park, is that understood?'

'Yes, sir!'

Foxx shut off the communications line and let out a long sigh that was something between relief and regret. He knew he had no choice and that to some extent neither did the general, but he also knew that he could not bring himself to think about the people on the ground who had no idea of what was about to happen.

Foxx left the communication suite and walked down into the Wasp–Class carrier's loading bay. He saw there a small knot of men who were camped out amid the gigantic CH–53E *Super Stallion* helicopters stowed below decks, their rotors folded back on themselves to save space.

The eight soldiers were all members of a United States Navy Seal Team, and most of the other crewmen moving around the hangar gave the Special Forces soldiers a respectable berth as they busied themselves preparing their kit. Each man was equipped with diving gear and an impressive array of weapons designed for combat both above and below the waves.

The team leader saw Foxx approach and snapped to attention. The rest of the team followed suit but Foxx waved them to ease as he spoke softly enough to avoid any of the ship's crew from overhearing.

'The mission is a go,' he reported. 'You'll be inserted into the location off a routine flight from a CH–53 to Rota Naval Base north of Cadiz. The same helo will pick you up on the way back. We have ground penetrating radar data of the site and have identified several subterranean cavities near the coast that you can use to exit the area. The timing has to be tight – you're operating on the soil of a sovereign allied nation without their knowledge or that of the United Nations.'

'Understood,' came the reply, brisk and business like. 'What's our window?'

'Two hours,' Foxx replied. 'That's all we have to give. The helo will report engine trouble and land at Rota. Our people have buried a minor problem deep enough for it to take that long to identify, but once its fixed the pilots will have to leave. Be sure that you and all of your men are on that flight.'

'We will be. Collateral?'

Foxx sucked in a deep breath and shook his head.

'All entities in the vicinity are to be treated as hostile,' he replied. 'There are no allied entities in the area that we're aware of.'

'Understood.'

With that the SEALS returned to their work and Foxx mentally placed an image of Ethan Warner and his team in a box and filed it away into some deep neural tract where it would no longer bother him.

***

XLII

The interior of the mound was dark and the air laden with the stench of rotting vegetation and brackish water. Ethan's flashlight barely penetrated the deep gloom as he edged along behind Lucy Morgan, feeling his way mostly by touch along what felt like a narrow path of smooth stone slick with moss and slime.

'This isn't the glorious capital of ancient technology I was hoping for,' Lopez said as she followed them.

Lucy's voice reached out in reply from the darkness.

'This city has been buried for perhaps ten thousand years, it's not going to be in tip–top shape for your grand arrival. I'm sure the people who built it would be deeply sorry for your inconvenience.'

Lopez said nothing in reply as Ethan ran his hand along the wall beside him and felt the smoothly interlocking stones, the surface of each shaped until it was perfectly smooth to the touch.

Their flashlights illuminated what appeared to be the upper gantry of some kind of temple, and Ethan could see the vague outline of pillars and steps across the gloom to his left. The sound of their voices hinted at a large open space and a drop somewhere to their left to lower levels. The entire temple was filled with the sound of dripping water coming not from above but from somewhere below, where the levels of the city remained below the water table.

Across the temple floor he could see thick streams of shaped silt and sand, dry now but revealing the flow of water as it slowly drained away perhaps thousands of years ago and left in its path rivulets through the silt. The walls were dry but he could feel countless tiny grains of silt encrusted into the stones.

'The city must have been underwater for some time, perhaps thousands of years,' Lucy said as they moved, sensing the same things as Ethan. 'Now the water is draining away due to climate change and the human use of water from the aquifer, which is why we were able to get in here at all. If Spain had been of a less temperate climate and hadn't formed a nature reserve in this area, erosion would probably have exposed this city centuries ago.'

Lucy suddenly began descending and Ethan found himself on the edge of stone steps that descended down from the upper gantry and onto the temple floor. Behind him Lopez cracked two glow sticks and tossed them out into the void, the glowing tubes bursting into life as they spiralled down thirty feet and landed with soft thuds in thick silt.

As they fell so they cast light on the temple, its perimeter filled with fluted columns reminiscent of ancient Greece and a huge statue of what to Ethan appeared to be the Roman God, Neptune. The muscular, bearded figure stood some twenty feet high and loomed at the head of the temple, one thick arm pointing out toward the temple entrance while the other held a towering trident that almost reached the ceiling above them.

'Neptune?' Lopez asked as they descended the steps. 'What's he doing here?'

'I very much doubt that the founders of this city knew that figure as Neptune,' Lucy replied as she hesitated at the foot of the steps. 'The Romans would have adopted the figure to fit their own legends and myths, the Greeks likewise and later the Christians.'

'Christians?' Ethan asked.

Lucy gestured to the gigantic trident in Neptune's hand. 'Where do you think Satan got his trident from? Every legendary or mythical figure of our time has its origins concealed by much older civilizations. The Christian anti–Christ, Satan or Lucifer, has its origins in Neptune and the Roman's worship of the goat. The Romans revered the goat as a sign of spring, a happy and energetic creature that provided milk and meat. When the Christians took over Rome, they re–cast all the popular Roman gods as evil and pagan creatures. In Lucifer's case, they gave him Neptune's body, his Trident and the head of a goat and made him the ruler of the underworld, the embodiment of evil, which was the opposite of what the name Lucifer actually meant.'

Lucy stepped gingerly onto the thick silt on the temple floor and her boot sank some six inches into it before it reached the stone below.

'What does Lucifer actually mean then?' Ethan asked.

'It means "bringer of light",' Lucy replied. 'The term was Caananite in origin although the word Lucifer comes from the Latin. It was the name the ancient world gave to the morning star, that which heralded the *end* of darkness, and what we know today as the planets Venus, Mercury or the star Sirius, all of which rise just before the sun at certain times of the year and are extremely bright. Christian mythology just twisted that on its head to bury the memory of older gods and bring new generations into their cult. Children today are taught in schools to fear Satan as a great evil but in fact the figure is as ancient and fictional as any other deity, a mythical creature invented by early Christians and nothing more.'

Ethan stepped into the silt as Lopez tossed more glowsticks toward the corners of the temple and for the first time in thousands of years it once again glowed with light. Ethan could see thick sloping mounds of silt piled up where ancient flowing waters had deposited them, and high up on the gantry edge were rows of symbols and what looked like letters that made Lucy gasp in awe.

'That looks like Linear A script,' she said as she stepped closer to the nearest line of text, some fifteen feet above them and carved into the rock in letters six inches high.

'They look like hieroglyphics,' Lopez said.

'And they're identical to the symbols we saw on *Die Gocke* in Antarctica,' Ethan said, 'the Black Knight satellite.'

'The what?' Lucy asked after a moment, confusion on her face.

Ethan figured that since they were no longer working for the DIA and that the government they had once served was now actively hunting them, there was no longer any real reason for he and Lopez to abide by the non–disclosure agreements that they had signed.

'On one of our previous investigations we were sent south to Antarctica to pick up the remains of an artificial object that had been orbiting earth for at least thirteen thousand years,' he replied. 'That led us to find another object that matched precisely an alien craft rumored to have been captured in Germany a few years before World War Two. Both carried the same markings around the rim, just like those up there, and they also match well–regarded and witnessed UFO encounters with similar objects in Kecksburg, Pennsylvania in 1965 and Rendlesham Forest, England in 1980.'

Lucy still appeared confused until Lopez spoke.

'The people of Kecksburg built a giant model of the UFO complete with the markings,' she said, 'that still stands outside the town to this day, and the Rendlesham Forest incident was witnessed by dozens of US military serviceman and even audio recorded by the base commander who led the team that encountered the object. These cases aren't your run of the mill, lonely forest road encounters – these things happened and were witnessed by dozens and even hundreds of people, and they saw those symbols on the UFOs they encountered.'

Lucy looked up again at the symbols and began photographing them as they moved through the temple. Ethan could hear the sound of running water nearby, and ahead he could see in the faint glow of the sticks an archway that was half–filled with silt that descended away from them into the darkness down more steps.

'How far out do you think we can get?' he asked Lucy as her camera flashed behind him.

'Not that far,' she replied. 'The silt and debris will have buried the city long ago, and what isn't buried beneath silt will be beneath the water table and inaccessible to us. The only way we'll ever see the entire city again is if the entire park is drained, and there's no way that's going to happen, it's far too large.'

Ethan frowned as he looked around them. The city that so many had searched for, for so long, was now so deeply entombed beneath millennia of accumulated silt that it was unlikely that anybody would ever know the true extent of its depths. That so many had come so far, and that so many others had lost their lives for what amounted to nothing more than old stone buildings half–buried in a lonely marsh appalled him, and he wondered again why so much of what he and Lopez had investigated over the years had led to so much loss and bloodshed.

'So this whole thing was for nothing?' Lopez uttered.

Lucy looked around them at the temple, searching for some sign or means of delving further into the ancient ruins.

'There may be passages or tunnels through the silt, channels dug out by fast moving water that might follow the streets and alleys of the old city, and we might be able to access some of the larger buildings but it's hit and miss and highly dangerous. Any part of this place could collapse at any moment and there's no guarantee that Heliosa's ship is going to be within reach.'

Ethan peered into the darkness and could see the forms of steps and tunnels moving away from them, the old passages dried now like mining tunnels but their floors still glistening with moisture.

'We've come this far,' Ethan said. 'There's no sense in turning back now.'

Lucy looked up at the texts. 'They appear to be some earlier form of Tartessian script, which itself would give a very ancient date of origin to this city.'

'The ship we're looking for was lost here during a tsunami, right?' Lopez said. 'Ships have a habit of floating, so what's the chances that it would have settled somewhere higher inside the city rather than lower?'

Lucy sighed and looked around them.

'It's possible,' she conceded, 'but I'd be concerned about travelling deeper without support from the outside world. If something happens, a collapse of some kind, we could be buried alive down here.'

'You said you wanted to find this place,' Ethan said, 'well, now you have. You've found Atlantis.'

'Tartessos,' Lucy corrected him.

Lopez gestured at the immense temple surrounding them. 'I don't care what it's called. Let's jut see if we can find Heliosa's ship and snatch Petrov's prize from under his nose, okay?'

Ethan heard something from above them, a faint sound that was not the rush of water nearby but more mechanical and coming closer with every passing moment.

'Whatever we're going to do, we'd better get on with it or we're going to become permanent residents down here. Which way?'

Lucy flustered for a moment as she got her bearings, and then she pointed toward the largest of the subterranean tunnels to their left.

'That way,' she said. 'If the ship survived the tsunami then it would most likely have been dragged out to sea when the waters receded. If we're going to find it, it's going to be in there somewhere.'

Ethan didn't hesitate as he turned and began trudging through the ankle–deep sludge toward the cold and inky blackness before them.

***

XLIII

Konstantin Petrov hurried along the animal trail with his men surrounding him, heavily armed and running to keep up. At this early hour and this far out into the park there was no chance of them being observed by anybody, the remote marshes and lagoons far from the nearest towns.

Petrov followed the team's point man, a former soldier and tracker who was tracing their quarry with an ease that betrayed the fact that it must be Lucy Morgan and perhaps Warner and Lopez with her, moving fast and not expecting Petrov to be this close behind them.

'They're not covering their tracks,' the point man said. 'They don't know we're here. At least three people.'

Petrov nodded in satisfaction, then glanced behind him to see the twenty armed men jogging along behind, equipped for whatever met them when they located Warner and Lopez. Most carried grenades in black webbing slung on hastily when they had arrived at the location, and all were armed with AK–12 assault rifles. Further back, another six men were carrying diving equipment with them, ready for the possibility that their destination might be submerged beneath the lagoons.

Petrov followed the tracker out toward a mound and over it toward another and then finally a third, larger mound and the tracker waved his extended left hand up and down as he slowed. The tracks followed the circumference of the mound and then all at once Petrov saw an area of disturbed ground and beside it a slab of shaped stone that appeared to have been discarded there.

As they closed in, he saw the blackened maw of a narrow opening in the sloping ground and he pushed past the tracker and hurried to the edge before looking in. He could see that the tracks ended here, and that the soil and sand had been shovelled hurriedly out of place to expose the entrance to whatever lay inside. Petrov turned to his men and pointed at four of them.

'The four of you set up observation posts at all cardinal points around this site, make sure nobody gets close without us knowing about it. The rest of you, with me.'

The four soldiers scattered to maintain a watch on the site as Petrov checked the magazine on his pistol. Then he holstered it and poked his head carefully through the cavity and into the darkness. Quickly, he tucked in his legs and dropped into the opening as his men filed in behind him with military efficiency.

*

Allison Pierce sat inside a waiting room at the Hospital Universitario Puerta del Mar in Cadiz and tried calling Jarvis, Ethan and Nicola once again but there was no response from any of the lines and she knew without a doubt that something major had already gone down. She figured that Foxx had moved on Jarvis and perhaps his entire team and that everything had gone south long before the Russians had reached the area.

The ward was quiet, located in a corner of the hospital reserved for private patients. Allison had gone out of her way to call every single elected official she knew to inform them that Congressman Keyes was in critical condition in a Spanish hospital, and then she had called a journalist colleague in New York City and informed them of the same before sending him footage taken with her cell phone of the congressman being rushed into an operating theatre surrounded by surgeons and nurses all jabbering away in Spanish. The chances that Keyes would ever be able to deny that he had been here at all was now completely removed, and that was when she had decided to drop the bombshell to her colleague and send him the images of Keyes meeting with the Russians in DC during the election campaign.

Her colleague had almost hit the roof when he saw them, proof positive that Keyes had lied on oath and that of all the people that could have been chosen to lead the inquiry into Majestic Twelve and its international associations, he was the least reliable to perform the work. Then she had asked her colleague to sit on the information and not go public with it until both she and Keyes were safely back in the United States, for their own safety. Once back on home soil, she would take the reins of the story in order to both clear her name and restore her reputation.

She was still sitting there figuring out her next move when a surgeon appeared and walked toward her. She stood up and he smiled.

'He'll be fine,' the surgeon said in heavily accented Spanish, 'you saved his life. Can I ask how you know this man?'

Allison shrugged. 'We worked together back home in America.'

The surgeon nodded as though he understood, and gestured behind him. 'He's out of anesthetic now so you can go see him if you wish.'

Allison thanked the doctor and walked swiftly into the ward, where she saw a series of doors to the private patients' rooms. Keyes' name was on one of them and she made sure that she took a picture of it with her cell, ensuring that the rest of the ward was visible in the shot before she made her way into the room.

Milton Keyes was propped up in the bed on pillows, an IV line in his arm and with his eyes closed as though asleep. She noted the heart monitor and the steady pulse and pressure it recorded as she made her way around the side of the bed.

'Congressman?'

Keyes opened his eyes, focussed on her and then winced and looked away.

'Are you never going to leave me alone?' he rasped weakly.

'You're welcome,' she replied. 'Surgeon said that without me you'd have been dead.'

Keyes chuckled bitterly. 'I might as well be. I got a call five minutes ago from my wife informing me that Congress is asking questions about why I'm half way around the world in hospital. I take it that you've been up to your handiwork again?'

'I'm covering myself,' she replied. 'I wouldn't want you to start worming your way out of all this now, would I? Or worse, asking your Russian friends to arrange an accident for me.'

'I don't have any Russian friends,' Keyes spat angrily.

Allison held up her cell to him, the screen filled with the image of Keyes meeting with a small group of men in DC months before. Keyes' eyes widened in shock and he looked at her, and she could tell that it was not shock at seeing the image but surprise that she still possessed a copy.

'I have friends in high places too,' she purred softly. 'They backed up my files before your people got to them.'

Keyes looked away from her. 'I don't know what you're talking about, and those people were nothing to me, street kids being helped by congressional initiatives, nothing more.'

'Half the country knows you're lying,' Allison went on, 'the other half won't believe it until they see these images being beamed into their living rooms in the next twenty–four hours.'

'What do you want from me?'

'What does anyone want from their elected leaders? The truth. Honesty. Integrity. Try bucking the mold and manning up.'

'That's naïve in the extreme,' Keyes uttered.

'Only if corruption is considered the norm,' Allison replied. 'I have back ups of everything, Milton, and more evidence than just what I'm carrying now. I'm giving you the chance to get ahead of this, despite everything you've done. Go public, expose the truth behind the election and the lies, show people what's really going on and you'll get clear of the coming storm.'

Keyes chuckled bitterly.

'You don't think that the administration wouldn't hesitate to act against me, to deny my claims and then end my career? My life would be over, I'd have nothing and then the world would move on and forget about it all.'

'Two hours ago your life was already over,' Allison pointed out. 'The Russians threw you under a bus Milton, and congress will do the same. This is your only play: come clean and let the American people hear your voice. There are people here who could die if you don't do the right thing! Tell the Spanish authorities that there are armed Russian gunmen here in the country, that they did this to you and will attack other American citizens if they're not stopped!'

Keyes grit his teeth and squirmed but she could tell that he was beaten, that he had nowhere else to go. The congressman opened his mouth to speak, and then suddenly four suited but bedraggled men strode into the room.

Allison turned and saw Keyes' guards rush to his side. One of them grabbed her arm and hauled her away from the bed.

'Get them off me,' Allison snapped at him.

For a moment she thought that Keyes would call his bodyguards off, but then he smiled and snarled at them,

'She's not welcome here and she has illegally obtained sensitive information while I was incoherent under anaesthetic. Her people attacked us! Take her cell phone and throw her out of here!'

Allison writhed as the guards yanked her cell phone from her hand and she twisted away from them.

'You're making a mistake! People will die if you don't act now!'

Keyes said nothing as Allison was forcibly pushed from the private room and the door was slammed in her face. The surgeon who had spoken to her looked across in surprise as Allison cursed and stormed away from the ward.

She was almost out of the main exit when a woman stepped in alongside her and handed her a fresh cell phone. Allison looked up and saw Lillian Cruz walking beside her, talking softly in her distinctive accent.

'Keyes won't be turned, and fortunately you won't have to.'

'How the hell did you know I was...'

'I've been following you the entire time,' Cruz said. 'That's my job here, to cover your ass and make sure that people like Keyes get what they deserve.'

'His people took my cell again.'

'You have it backed up this time.'

'Yeah, but he'll already be making calls to track it down.'

'Doesn't matter,' Allison replied, 'you only sent out the still images as instructed, right?'

'Well, yeah, but we don't have anything else on him and he can claim the images are forgeries.'

Lillian patted the back of Allison's arm as they walked.

'The stills aren't all we have,' she promised. 'Where are Ethan and Nicola?'

'I can't reach them and they were being tracked by the Russians!'

'Then we need to move fast,' Lillian said as she took out her cell phone. 'Come with me.'

***

XLIV

'It's this way.'

Lucy ducked down as she led them deeper into the subterranean system forged by the passage of flood waters over thousands of years. Although the surface of the city street was buried beneath a foot of compacted silt Ethan could still get a sense of the streets and the buildings around them, many of which were visible protruding from the walls of silt like ghostly apparitions entombed in the soil of ages.

The street was descending, and although the passage appeared smooth and solid in the flashlight beams Ethan could see areas where the upper sections had collapsed, mounds of rubble and silt now half–blocking the passage beneath the marshes above.

'Any of that comes down while we're here and it's goodnight one and all,' Lopez said as she observed the debris, the air rank with the odor of rotting vegetation and brackish water. 'How come the water isn't just flooding straight down into here?'

'The vegetation and the city are acting like foundations,' Lucy said as they picked their way through the debris. 'It's holding some of the surface material up, but it could collapse at any moment and frequently does. Fortunately for us, the marshy land fills in any collapses and they then drain slowly again, keeping the city concealed and these pathways open.'

Ethan saw what looked like the front of a house to his left, the structure eerily similar to those they had seen at the excavations at Akrotiri. Flat fronted stone walls held a single, low door with a heavy frame, much of which was rotting in place as the water and minerals slowly got the better of the thick timbers. Ethan could not see inside but he imagined that within would be a treasure trove of Tartessian archaeological wonders, relics from an age of human civilization that existed five thousand years before the beginning of recorded history.

Lucy slowed as she reached an area where the passage ended in a junction that offered them the choice of forking left or right. Both channels were low and precarious, debris scattered across their path betraying countless collapses and the flood waters that had then partially swept the debris away.

'The records that Pytheas kept suggested that the trireme was lost somewhere in the inner channel during the tsunami,' Lucy said. 'The crew were able to access it only for a few days before the debris and silt settled enough to completely bury the wreck. If it's still here in any recognizable form we must be within a hundred yards of it. If it's been dragged too far by water flow and debris over the centuries then it's lost forever.'

Ethan glanced left and right and could see no difference between the two passages.

'Better make a choice while we still can,' he urged her. 'It's pot luck whether we find anything anyway.'

Lopez's sharp eyes picked something out in the darkness that Ethan had not noticed.

'The tunnels slant downward to the right,' she said as she pointed ahead.

Ethan saw that she was right and that the tunnels were running slightly downhill to their left, and that would mean that any debris and silt would likewise have flowed in that direction. Ethan could mentally picture a flow of water out of the lagoons flooded by the tsunami that Pytheas had witnessed centuries before, and his men fighting to recover valuables from their lost ship before she was consumed.

'The water flow out would have dragged silt and debris with it,' Ethan said, 'so it must have flowed from our right to our left, leaving less and less behind it as it travelled further out from the land.'

'Anything large like a ship would presumably have been left behind.'

Lucy nodded and turned, heading to their right. The tunnel climbed upward slightly, the ceiling a low crevice that offered little comfort and appeared to be glistening with moisture. The fact that it was standing at all was a miracle, and Ethan knew that countless tons of material could plunge down upon them at any moment.

Lucy led the way, her flashlight beam slashing through the darkness, and then it caught upon something half buried in the silt. As Lucy advanced upon it so Ethan saw the shape of some kind of ornate vase glinting in the harsh light beam. Lucy crouched down alongside it and examined the surface, which was decorated with ornate images of bare–chested warriors wielding spears and shields.

'Andokidean amphora,' she identified it, 'red figurines, so around the fifth century BCE. This would have been a valuable item at the time.'

Ethan peered ahead into the gloom and saw more similar artefacts littering the silt around them. Lucy eased forward, crouching down as the silt passageway narrowed further to a slim crevice, beyond which her flashlight beam penetrated a larger area that Ethan could not see from where he was. As she moved, she saw another item in the silt at her feet and picked it up.

The object looked like a pitcher of some kind, and was wrapped in geometric patterns dominated by the same arrangement of three concentric circles and a central line extending from the bottom.

'It's Cypriot,' Lucy identified it, 'probably more than three thousand years old and covered in icons that historians normally identify with the so–called Holy Grail, the cup of Christ.'

'Yeah,' Lopez replied, 'we got that lecture back in India. The cup is the real myth, and the icon represents the layout of Atlantis.'

'Tartessos,' Lucy corrected him again, and then turned and walked for a few more yards before she slowed again. 'There's an opening up here,' she whispered back to them, getting down onto her belly and slithering through the gap.

Ethan and Lopez exchanged a reluctant look and then wriggled through the same opening and promptly slid down a bank on the far side. Ethan tumbled down and found himself sitting alongside what looked like a row of long, low buildings buried deep into the walls of the cavity, and then he heard Lucy's gasp.

'There!'

Ethan turned to their right and his flashlight beam reflected off what looked like old wood. As his eyes adjusted to the gloom he realized that he was looking at the stern of a vessel that was almost completely concealed within a wall of ancient silt and dried mud. Ethan got to his feet as Lucy bounded across to the vessel and ran her hand along the base of her hull.

The ship was lodged at an angle in the debris, her rudder long gone and her stern high. Ethan could already see that she had been crushed by the immense weight of the debris that had been deposited on top of her and compacted over millennia. However, her angle had protected the stern from the flood waters that must have regularly swirled through the cavity and her timbers did not look quite as rotten as others they had seen down here. Even so, she was black with age and he could smell that rotting wood from where he was on the far side of the subterranean cavern.

'You think there's anything still aboard her?' Lopez asked.

'Only one way to find out,' Lucy replied as without hesitation she clambered up the side of the ship's stern and carefully climbed over shattered beams and onto her deck.

Ethan followed Lopez up and onto the deck, and instantly he could see the gaping, jagged hole hacked into her upper decks where Pytheas and his crew had attempted to salvage what they could from the wreck. Much of the ship was rotting away and he didn't trust any of the beams to hold his weight.

'They left most of it behind,' Lucy said as she peered down into the interior.

Ethan placed his flashlight in his teeth and then crouched down as he grabbed the lip of the deck and gently lowered himself into the darkness, trying to spread his weight as much as possible to avoid snapping the timbers as he stretched his arms and felt the briefest touch of a deck beneath his boots.

Ethan released his hand hold and landed softly on the lower deck. The scent of ancient wood and dislodged dust wafted around him as he crouched down and used the flashlight to peer into the ship's interior.

The ship's middle deck had been where the rows of oarsmen had been sat or chained, hauling the vessel through the water by force of combined effort when the winds had not been favorable. Ethan could see rows of benches where they would have been seated, several men to an oar, in rows that ran the length of the hull.

The interior was intact to almost the hull's mid–section, but beyond that Ethan could see that the ship was crushed flat by the debris, her timbers snapped and twisted like the gruesome fangs of some ancient beast bared in the darkness.

Just ahead of where he squatted Ethan could see another opening in the deck, this one square and uniform. Pytheas and his men must have accessed the trireme's holds through it and relayed the contents out until the build up of debris became too dangerous and they were forced to abandon the wreck.

Ethan slid downward toward the deck hatch, and saw Lopez drop down behind him and follow until they were either side of the hatch.

'Ladies first?' he suggested.

'Who said chivalry was dead?'

'You're lighter,' Ethan pointed out. 'Plus I can pull you up again more easily than you'd be able to lift me.'

Lopez winced but she could not deny the logic as she shuffled into position and then turned and lowered herself down. Ethan readied himself to lift her at a moment's notice as Lucy joined him at the edge of the hatch.

'You see anything yet?' she asked.

Ethan heard Lopez land on the hold deck and then there was a long pause before he heard Lopez utter something from the darkness.

'Whoa.'

'What do you see?' Lucy demanded.

Ethan peered down, and then Lopez reappeared with a bright smile on her face as she held something up to them. In the glow of the flashlights Ethan saw it reflect pure gold at them, a braclet of some kind that was thick and heavy and glittering for the first time in countless centuries.

'Is there any more down there?' Ethan asked as Lucy carefully lowered herself down into the hold.

'Are you kidding?' Lopez called back. 'I think we hit the mother lode. There's no way the three of us could get all of this out of here!'

Ethan ducked his head down into the hold and saw Lopez's flashlight reflecting off a dazzling array of gold, silver and other materials that were haphazardly piled amid countless broken wooden crates and thick mounds of silt that had entered the rear of the hold when the ship had been consumed by the waves.

'We're gonna need the flotation bags,' Ethan said as he scanned the array of priceless golden artefacts. 'I want all of this out of here as quickly as possible.'

Lucy nodded eagerly and with Lopez began lifting the gold out of the ship's hold as Ethan scrambled back up the deck toward the jagged entrance. If he could get just a half dozen bags out of the ship and away to safety, he and Lopez would become independent once again and could start thinking about building a new life somewhere far from the US Government, the DIA and the damned Russians.

Driven by excitement, Ethan hauled himself up out of the ship and stood up to come face to face with the barrel of a Kalashnikov rifle.

'Greetings, Mister Warner.'

Konstantin Petrov stood on the ground below the ship with fifteen or so heavily armed men, four of whom were surrounding Ethan and keeping their weapons trained upon him.

***

XLV

Ethan said nothing as Petrov and his men climbed up onto the trireme's slanted deck and four of them descended into the ship. He knew that there was little point in calling out a warning as there was nowhere for Lucy or Lopez to run.

Petrov came to stand face to face with Ethan and smiled.

'I've heard so much about you,' he said. 'I'd so like to get to know you better, but unfortunately I'm in something of a hurry so we'll have to dispense with any formalities.'

Petrov stepped past Ethan and called down into the ship.

'How many are there down there and what's the cargo?'

The reply came up from the depths of the ship. 'Two women, and the cargo is priceless, just like you said!'

Petrov nodded in satisfaction. 'Have the women pass the cargo up to us.'

Lopez's voice echoed through the cavern.

'Petrov, get down here and come unload this stuff yourself, you lazy son of a bi...'

'Bit touchy, aren't we?' Petrov cut her off with a smile as he glanced at Ethan. 'You two make quite the couple. I don't have time for any heroics though, so this is the deal. For every ten seconds that you delay in unloading those goods, I will slice off a piece of Ethan Warner.'

Ethan was instantly grabbed by two of Petrov's men and forced to his knees on the deck as Petrov drew a combat knife from a sheath on his belt. The Russian grabbed Ethan's hair and yanked his head to one side as with the other hand he pressed the edge of the blade against Ethan's ear.

Ethan grinned up at the Russian. 'Go ahead, it'll mean I won't have to listen to you, or them.'

Petrov laughed, then turned and saw one of his men place a solid gold statuette of what looked like an ancient Olympian on the deck of the ship, followed swiftly by more items as Lucy and Lopez began emptying the holds of their cargo.

'There,' Petrov said as he released Ethan's head, 'many hands make light work, no?'

Ethan said nothing as he watched the Russians packing the artefacts into flotation bags that Ethan had brought with them and handing them down to Petrov's men below the ship. They worked for almost a full half hour, until all thirty of the bags were full to bursting with the precious cargo and one of Petrov's men turned to him.

'That's all we can carry,' he reported. 'There's as much again inside there but we'll have to come back again.'

Petrov shrugged. 'That is not a problem. Our ship will be here soon and we will be able to take everything with us. I would suggest, Anatoly, that you and your men grab something for yourselves before we leave. It would not be prudent to hand over everything to the Kremlin, agreed?'

Anatoly's features lit up and he bellowed to his men in Russian.

'Two objects to a man, no more. Move, now!'

The soldiers dashed up onto the deck and began filling their jackets with the artifacts being passed up from below. Petrov turned to Ethan and offered him an apologetic look.

'I'm afraid that your delightful companion Nicola declined my offer to share in the wealth that we've found here, Ethan,' he lamented. 'Therefore there won't be enough for you, and besides, you won't be leaving here now anyway.'

Petrov lifted his pistol to point at Ethan's head as he smiled down at him.

'It's been a pleasure hunting you all down,' he said. 'Rest assured that before being shot, your companions below decks will be given to my men before they leave. I'm sure they'll show them all of their Russian hospitality.'

Petrov's men sniggered in grim delight as Petrov pressed his pistol to Ethan's forehead and squeezed the trigger.

A deafening gunshot rang out and Ethan's vision blurred as the air around his head seemed to explode. Petrov staggered to one side as a hail of bullets plowed into the Russians and cut them down as they struggled to bring their weapons to bear.

Ethan hurled himself away from the Russians and rolled off the deck as he glimpsed shadowy figures dressed in black fatigues pouring toward the ship, their rifles firing in controlled bursts as they advanced.

'American!' Ethan yelled at them, his hands in the air. 'Allied aboard!'

The advancing soldiers appeared not to hear him and Ethan threw himself back into cover as bullets splattered the silt wall near his head. He ducked down alongside the ship's hull as a Russian toppled over the edge of the ship's deck and landed with a thud at his feet, his skull punctured with two bullet wounds. A pair of grenades rolled beside his body and Ethan grabbed one and pulled the pin as he hurled it out toward the advancing soldiers.

'Grenade!'

The warning echoed above the clatter of gunfire and Ethan covered his ears and ducked down as the grenade detonated with a thunderous blast and the advancing soldiers hurled themselves into cover. Ethan heard a new noise even as the soldiers recovered from the grenade attack and began firing again, and he felt the earth shift beneath his feet and saw veils of material spilling like falling curtains from the vault ceiling.

The shockwave from the grenade blast, confined within the cavern, had destabilised the area and Ethan realized that they had only moments to escape before the entire place came down upon them.

He turned and grabbed the fallen man's Kalashnikov and the second grenade, but this time he turned and tossed the grenade under the ship as he yelled at the top of his lungs.

'Lopez, fire in the hole!'

Ethan threw himself clear of the ship and up against the buildings embedded in the wall of the cavern and lay flat on the ground as the grenade detonated. The ship's timbers groaned under the blast as the weakened and rotting hull shattered, the grenade opening a four–foot wide hole from which poured a stream of dusty silt and ancient gold relics. Right behind the dirty pile of material tumbled Lopez and Lucy, Lopez dragging the scientist behind her and running for cover as the Russians opened up on the soldiers now pinned down inside the cavern.

The trireme shuddered as more of her broken hull collapsed, and the wall of silt and debris in which she was half–buried trembled as the delicate balance of support was disturbed and the wall began to fail.

'Where's Petrov?!' Ethan yelled above the din.

'I didn't see him go down!' Lopez snapped as she joined him. 'We were inside the damned ship, in case you hadn't noticed!'

Ethan turned and saw the row of buildings had doorways, some filled with silt but others open and accessible. He could see that they ran down the length of the cavern and that they could possibly represent another way out.

'Let's go!'

Ethan took aim and fired over the heads of the advancing soldiers, who were moving by sections toward the boat in orderly fashion that betrayed them as well trained troops. Ethan could see that they were carrying M–16 rifles as Lucy and Lopez dashed to the nearest open doorway and plunged inside.

Ethan backed up, firing as he went not at the soldiers but at the Russians atop the stern of the trireme. The bullets smacked into two of the men and they dropped as the rest fought for their lives, and Ethan saw the advancing soldiers change their aim and start focussing only on the Russians. The soldiers' bullets impacted the ship in a hail of deadly fire, the ship's ancient timbers no defense against modern ammunition, and as Ethan backed up he saw two of the soldiers switch to their underslung grenade launchers.

'No!'

Ethan's warning was lost in the din of battle as the grenades were fired. The two weapons rocketed across the cavern and smacked into the trireme's stern and exploded with brilliant flares of orange light and tongues of flame. Ethan ducked aside as the shrapnel cut through the Russian gunmen like a scythe but it was the ceiling of the chamber that drew his attention.

The entire subterranean cavern seemed to shudder and then Ethan saw the hull of the ship twist sideways. Russian gunmen fell to either side and he saw the entire edifice of the rear wall of the cavern subside downward across the ship's decks. Even as the vast tide of silt and debris came crashing down so Ethan saw in the darkness a black jet of dark water blast down from the rear of the cavern and crash across the trireme.

Ethan whirled and sprinted down the front of the buildings as Lopez and Lucy emerged two doors down and ignored the remaining gunfire as they sprinted for the narrow fissure that led back out of the cavern to the surface. Ethan glanced sideways and saw the American soldiers turning to flee as the single jet of water became a sudden and terrifying wall of filthy dark water that poured toward them, consuming the entire trireme once again and rushing with a deafening roar of thousands of tons of force.

Lucy and Lopez wriggled through the gap as Ethan leaped and rolled through behind them and they started running down the uneven tunnel outside, reaching the fork and turning left to start climbing toward the surface.

'Keep moving!' Lopez yelled.

Ethan heard the wall of the tunnels behind them collapse as the force of the breach hit it and the tunnels flooded with millions of gallons of water. The silty earth beneath his boots trembled as the water rushed up behind him and he saw the soldiers sprinting to get clear, the water rushing past them and swallowing them whole.

'We're not going to make it!'

Ethan could see the rising tunnel before them in the near–darkness, and in the distance the faint beam of sunlight illuminating the temple they'd used to get down into the tunnels, and then the water hit him from behind and he stumbled and fell as it rushed past and swallowed them all.

Ethan fought to keep his head above the surface of the frigid, filthy water as it carried him in a tumbling vortex through the tunnel and then into the temple. He swam hard for the side, seeking in the darkness some sign of the stone steps they had used to descend from the temple gantry to the lower levels.

'Over here!'

Lopez yelled to him and he saw her and Lucy clambering out of the water and staggering up the stone steps, their clothes drenched and muddy as Ethan swam to join them and pulled himself out of the churning water. His legs felt suddenly weak and a chill enshrouded him as he staggered in pursuit of Lopez, the deluge behind them losing its impetus as the level of the water equalized and settled.

Ethan could see several of the American soldiers swimming toward the side of the temple and looking up at him as he forced himself upward toward the small square of brilliant light that was their only escape. Lucy and Lopez reached it first and climbed through as Ethan staggered after them, stunned by how cold the water had been and how he was shivering now as though on the verge of hypothermia, and then his legs ceased to function and he collapsed to his knees.

Ethan put one hand out to steady himself, confused, and then the cold bit deeper into his bones and he realized that he must be losing blood. In the faint light he looked down and he realized that amid all the mud and water there was an oozing of fluid from somewhere in his stomach.

Ethan put his hand over the wound as the pain finally hit him. His vision blurred and stars whorled in front of him and he sucked in a deep breath as he realized that there was no strength remaining in his body and that he could't keep himself upright any longer, even on his knees.

'Ethan?!'

Ethan slumped over his wound, his breath coming in short gasps as he heard Lopez calling for him, but he could not move his head to look at her even when he heard the soldiers' rifles clatter rounds that sounded as though they were hitting the stone walls around the entrance.

Ethan closed his eyes and then he heard the stone block that they had removed from the entrance shoved back into place and the interior of the temple was plunged into an absolute blackness that matched the cold darkness that now overwhelmed him.

As gentle as a lullaby, Ethan felt the last of his strength leave him and all around him fell silent and still.

**

XLVI

Lopez squinted in the brilliant sunlight as she shielded her eyes with her hands and tumbled out of the temple and onto the sand, the heat of the sun on her skin. Lucy staggered alongside her as they stumbled away from the entrance to the temple, trying to let their eyes adjust to the brightness. As her vision cleared, Lopez saw several dead bodies of Russians nearby, shot where they must have been guarding the approaches to the site.

Lopez whirled as she heard the stone cover being shoved back into place behind them.

Petrov slammed the heavy block into position and then turned with a pistol in his hand and aimed it at them. Lopez froze as she saw the look in the Russian's eye, one of absolute fury and the cold–blooded need for vengeance. His left leg was bleeding and he was limping from a wound he must have sustained when the American soldiers had blasted their way into the cavern, but he was still standing despite the damage.

'You,' was all that he could hiss at her, his lips twisted with rage.

Petrov stepped away from the block and stalked toward Lopez, the pistol never wavering from her face.

'You, and those idiot friends of yours, have just lost us all a *fortune*!'

Lucy backed away and raised a hand. 'Killing us isn't going to change anything!'

Petrov grinned, his jaw clenched and his teeth bared. 'No, but it will make me feel a whole lot better about *everything*!'

Petrov turned to aim at Lucy and Lopez swept her boot across the sand and kicked it up into Petrov's face. The fine grains splattered across his vision and he growled as his eyesight was spoiled, turning back to aim at Lopez.

Lopez ducked down and swivelled on her left heel as she struck out with her right boot and slammed it into Petrov's leg, her heel driving deep into his wound. The Russian squealed in pain as he fired and the shot went over Lopez's head. Lopez rushed in and smashed his pistol arm aside with her left fist as she dropped a round house punch right down across the Russian's temple. Her knuckles smacked into his forehead with a loud crack and she saw his eyeballs roll up briefly into their sockets as he plummeted onto his back on the sand.

Lopez kicked the pistol from his grip and fell upon him, straddling Petrov's chest as she punched him in the face over and over again. The Russian's nose broke and two of his teeth flew clear of his splitting lips, trailing drools of blood as Lopez rained down a frenzy of blows that rocked his head this way and that.

The Russian eyes fluttered as he fought to maintain consciousness, and then he thumped Lopez in her side. Lopez barely noticed the blow until she felt something rasp against bone inside her and heard Lucy scream.

She looked down and saw Petrov's serrated blade buried to the hilt in her flank, his hand gripping the handle. She looked at Petrov, saw his eyes glittering with malice through a mask of blood and bruised tissue as he twisted the blade in her side. White pain ripped through Lopez and she cried out in pain as she rolled away from him and the serrated blade tore out of her.

Lopez slumped onto her back on the sand, both hands clasping her wound and her eyes wide as she sucked in a deep breath and tried to master the crippling pain seething through her body as Petrov crawled to his feet. Blood sagged in long loops from his ruined mouth, his eyes already swelling up and his skin torn and bruising heavily as he staggered upright and towered over her. His voice when he spoke was taut with pain and thick with the swelling already affecting his lips and cheeks as he pointed at his own face.

'This will heal,' he gasped as he turned the blade in his hands and gripped it. 'You won't.'

Petrov moved to stand over her, then raised the knife above his head as he made to plunge the weapon down and into her heart.

The gunshot came from behind the Russian, a single round that slammed into his back with a dull thud and exited his chest with a fine spray of blood that splattered across the sand next to Lopez. Lopez squinted in the sunlight and saw Lucy holding the Russian's dropped pistol in both hands, her face a mask of shock and terror.

Petrov stared sightlessly at the horizon, his fractured heart spilling blood down his shirt as he toppled slowly sideways and then crashed down onto the sand with a thud. Lopez looked at him and then she felt the warmth of the sun fading away as a chill began to envelope her.

'Charming,' she uttered as she tried to stem the flow from her wound.

Lucy dashed to her side and forced her hands over Lopez's side. 'Stay still, you're gonna be fine.'

Lopez chuckled grimly and shook her head, her voice tight with pain.

'Oh good, 'cause I was worried I was bleeding out here real quick, miles from any hospital.'

Lucy winced and grief twisted her features, as from somewhere in the distance Lopez thought that she heard the sound of a helicopter coming closer. The beating air reverberated through her chest and shuddered through the ground beneath her, and against the bright sky she saw a huge blue helicopter thunder into view, plumes of sand whipped up into a vortex nearby as it descended toward the ground.

'Stay with me!' Lucy yelled into her face.

Lopez smiled, although she had no idea why. She felt her own hand press down on Lucy's and she could feel the blood slick between them, and she figured that there was nothing much left to hold on for. She'd seen Ethan go down, and if he was still in there now then there was little point in expecting the American soldiers to attempt to save his life. Both of their families were in danger as a result of their work over the years, and really there was only one way to ensure that they weren't caught up in any of this mess ever again.

Lucy didn't fight the cold as it washed over her, nor the darkness that followed.

*

They waited.

The sound of the helicopter outside was not that of the *Super Stallion* that would extract them in less than an hour, for it was to meet them at the rendezvous on the coast. Conscious of the risk that the Russian interlopers might have called in reinforcements, the SEAL team waited with their weapons trained on the exit. They heard the helicopter take off again a minute or two later and then the sound of its rotors faded away into the distance.

Convinced that the way was clear, the leader of the team shoved the stone block out of the wall and brilliant sunlight streamed in as he and his men rushed out into the daylight and secured the area.

Within minutes, they had dragged their cargo of flotation devices out of the temple, the valuable haul having conveniently floated out of the cavern with the flood waters. They then hauled the bodies of the dead Russian guards off the sand and tipped their bodies back into the opening. Finally, they heaved the stone cover back into place and with military efficiency they covered the entrance once again with the soil and sand displaced earlier in the day. Two of the team spent several minutes carefully ensuring that it was impossible to tell where the entrance was.

Satisfied, the SEAL team leader gathered his men together and they hurried toward the coast, each carrying the burden of a single flotation bag packed with untold riches destined for their superiors back aboard the USS Bataan, and four men each bearing the extra load of a field stretcher carrying one of their own. They reached the dunes of the shoreline within twenty minutes, moving at a pace that only trained Special Forces could sustain, and then they settled into the undergrowth to await the arrival of the *Super Stallion*. After only fifteen minutes the *Super Stallion* helicopter, known in Navy terms as a "helo", thundered up the coast on its routine mission, cleared with the Spanish government, and briefly it slowed and hovered just a few feet above the rollers and the dunes, its immense blades whipping up huge clouds of sand that swirled in a diaphanous cloud around it and helped conceal the eight–man SEAL team as they burst from cover and dashed for their extraction.

Sixty seconds later, the *Super Stallion* climbed away from the beach and thundered out to sea, the beach and the park behind it once again returned to the anonymous solitude and silence it had enjoyed for thousands of years.

*

Lieutenant Colonel Foxx watched as the *Super Stallion* touched down on the Bataan's deck, her soldiers disembarking with their concealed cargo on their backs. The men quickly headed for a sector near the stern of the assault ship that had been cordoned off to avoid any prying eyes from examining whatever the SEAL team might have brought back with them.

Foxx did not intend to search the contents of the flotation sacks until later. The fact that they were all filled with something was enough for him to know that the mission had been a success.

Foxx made his way instead to the ship's observation deck and grabbed a pair of binoculars that he used to sweep the horizon until he found what he was looking for. The sleek gray form of a Russian destroyer was looming out of the early morning haze and heading for their position off the coast, and judging by the head of her bow she was at full speed.

'Any communications chatter from the *Severomosk*?' he asked the captain.

'Repeated calls on a high–frequency channel,' the captain confirmed. 'We have heard no response. What do you want us to do?'

Foxx lowered the binoculars and thought only for a moment before he replied.

'Take us out of here, all ahead one half. Make it look like we're not rushing.'

The captain nodded and Foxx felt the ship start to move as the captain gave the orders and the Bataan eased away from her position, giving ground to the Russian destroyer so as to neither help nor hinder her passage.

Foxx watched the destroyer for the next hour as she slowed and cruised along the coast in international waters, but the Russian vessel did not make contact and she did not attempt to follow the American ship as it sailed away into the Atlantic Ocean. Foxx eventually lost sight of her over the horizon along with the European coast, and it was then that he finally abandoned his vigil and headed for the stern.

The SEAL team were prepared for the debrief, and they filled him in with their customary efficiency before showing him the contents of seven of the flotation sacks they had recovered from the site. Foxx regarded those contents with interest before the team leader showed him the contents of the eighth sack, now laying before them on a bed in the sick bay.

Foxx raised an eyebrow as the soldier looked at him. 'What do you want us to do about this?'

'You weren't supposed to bring back any casualties,' Foxx pointed out.

The SEAL remained stoic in his expression as he replied. '*Semper fi*, sir: once a Marine, always a Marine. We opened fire without prejudice, but this one still fired in support of my men. We might have our orders, sir, but we also have our honor.'

Foxx thought for a moment, and then he made his decision.

'I'll handle it when we get back to DC,' he said. 'For now, keep doing what you're doing and tell nobody.'

***

XLVII

Capitol Hill

Washington DC

(Six months later)

Allison Pierce watched from the steps of Capitol Hill as a line of executive vehicles rolled up in the warm summer sunshine. She leaned against a wall and waited patiently as four of the legislators due to deliver the oversight hearing to the rest of congress exited their vehicles and walked up the steps toward the building.

Allison could see that they were all talking together, sharing the odd chuckle here and there, oblivious to the world beyond their cossetted capitol and the miasma of legalese that was their currency in life. She waited until they were almost alongside her before she called out.

'Milton.'

Congressman Keyes looked across at her and his joviality slipped away into something akin to a scowl. He uttered something to his companions and changed direction, moving reluctantly toward her as the other lawmakers hurried up the steps and into the building.

'You just don't quit, do you?' Keyes uttered as he confronted her.

Allison enjoyed watching the congressman squirm, but she had no interest in twisting the knife further into his guts and simply got down to business.

'We agreed upon an open hearing,' she snapped, 'and yet you're all closed doors again.'

'I can't help what the rest of congress wants to do, and besides it was out of my hands the moment the FBI got involved. They kept the investigation under wraps for three months, remember? Right up to the point where *Little Miss Pierce* got all impatient and went global with her report.'

Allison allowed herself a small smile that curled stubbornly from one corner of her lips. Her independent report, which was aired live by all of the major networks and eventually as a documentary that was shown around the world, secured her reputation and revealed many of the lies and deceits used by men of power to influence elections around the world to suit their own business needs. Even she could not have imagined the sheer scope of the corruption that had become a hallmark of democracy, where even the United States was not immune to the influences of other nations with the will and the means to interfere with the democratic process.

Now, as a result of her work and the worldwide scandal that it had exposed, Allison had become one of the world's most respected investigative journalists and her woes of six months before seemed trite and distant now. She had dedicated herself to exposing men like Keyes to the extent that the White House routinely dismissed her reports as "fake news" until it became obvious that they were anything but faked. She had kept Keyes in her pocket however, her evidence against him overwhelming and ready to let go the moment he considered doing anything other than the decent thing.

With the director of the FBI having recently been fired by a president desperately trying to prevent his links to the Russians and the treasures uncovered at the site in Spain from being exposed, not to mention the more expansive links to Majestic Twelve that had been enjoyed by senators and congressmen alike, she knew that she had the halls of power trembling with uncertainty and fear.

'A flawless report,' she warned him, 'with full disclosure afterward, or I'll blow your career into the water.'

'You can't keep doing this,' Keyes hissed. 'Sooner or later it will become old news and by God when it does I will bring down the full force of congress upon you and…

Allison held up her cell phone and Keyes saw that it was recording everything he was saying. Even as he stumbled on his words, Allison pressed a button and a video played. Congressman Keyes' features blanched as he saw himself stagger in front of a vehicle, the camera mounted on the dashboard and looking through the windshield at him, the sky a hard blue and his face sheened with sweat. In the background he could hear Allison Pierce's voice.

'Tell me what happened! There's no time to argue! If you don't talk then Petrov will kill everybody he finds out there!'

Keyes watched himself struggle to stay focussed and then speak in a ragged voice.

'The Russians were involved in a campaign to spread fake news during the presidential election. They set up a control room in downtown DC and used cybercrime to influence the way people think. They've been doing it for years inside Russia but have now spread their work to the United States. Militarily, Russia isn't the force it once was and so the Kremlin has resorted to other means to project their influence into world events.'

'How do you fit into all of this?'

'They wanted me to act as a go–between for the Russian hackers, and to ensure that the investigation into Majestic Twelve did not reveal the lost billions but only that which had already been declared to the public.'

Allison heard her own voice on the recording.

'Damn it! I knew it! It's all about the damned money and you people don't care whose lives get destroyed in the process! How much were you in for, Keyes? How much did they promise you?'

Allison shut the video off and slipped the cell into her pocket.

'I've made more copies of that film than a *Disney* movie,' she uttered as she leaned close to the congressman, 'and we have the records from the hospital in Spain detailing your treatment and my involvement. I'll spill it all in an instant, any time between now and the end of our lives, the moment you even think about hesitating to speak anything but the truth. And I want everyone formerly of the DIA associated with these events and their families *completely* exonerated. It's your call, Keyes: do the right thing, or spend twenty to life in prison for treason.'

Keyes scowled in frustration but Allison turned and walked away, not dignifying him with a chance to reply or protest as she walked down the steps of the Capitol and turned right. She walked along the avenue and a sedan slipped alongside the sidewalk as a door opened smoothly. Allison got into the still–moving vehicle with practiced grace and closed the door behind her.

The interior was cool and dark, and despite the fact that she was doing the right thing Allison realized that her heart was hammering at the inside of her chest as though she had just run a marathon.

'How did it go?'

Lillian Cruz sat in the seat beside Allison, watching her expectantly.

'He's got no choice,' she replied, 'and you were right to hold that video back until the last minute. I think he'd started to get comfortable with the idea that we didn't have anything on film as evidence.'

Lillian glanced out of the window at the city as they were driven by a tall man with dark skin who watched Allison in the rear–view mirror with dark eyes. Aaron Mitchell nodded to her in greeting but said nothing as they joined the freeway and headed south.

'You're never going to tell me what happened to them, are you?' Allison said to Lillian.

Lillian smiled quietly and looked at her. 'Why would you want to know?'

'Because they were patriots, people who really did serve the interests of their countrymen instead of corporations and profits. Their story deserves to be heard.'

'Maybe some people prefer to remain in the shadows. Perhaps they don't want to share their stories, or be known for what they have done. I know that I don't, and I hope that you will honor that.'

'Of course,' Allison insisted, 'but even so, just for my own peace of mind?'

Lillian watched America passing by outside her window.

'Ethan Warner died of a single gunshot wound to the stomach,' she said softly. 'Nicola Lopez passed away after a fatal knife wound to her side. Both of their bodies were repatriated to the United States and they were cremated together in a private ceremony some weeks later, along with Joseph Hellerman. Douglas Jarvis was tried by Court Martial and sentenced to fifteen years' imprisonment in a security max facility in Nevada, solitary confinement, no visitors. No other charges were laid against other suspected members of the group who had at times joined them aboard Rhys Garrett's yacht, due to insufficient evidence of any wrong doing.'

Allison peered at her with interest.

'That's a remarkably clean story with very little evidence to follow if I were to doubt its veracity, Lillian.'

'You're catching on well.'

'And Amber Ryan?'

'She's just sold her late father's fusion–cage technology to a major defense contractor on the understanding that they use it to build transportable nuclear fusion reactors for the benefit of the people. Lockheed Martin made their announcement of a portable fusion reactor a few months ago, which will end our reliance on coal and oil for fuel.'

'Lucy Morgan?'

'Recently led an expedition to Spain that recovered four loads of Tartessian gold from a sunken Greek trireme off the coast,' Lillian replied. 'It's causing quite a stir in the archaeological community, from what I've read.'

'And the money that MJ–12 stole, that the government and the Russians wanted so badly?'

'Let's just say that Amber Ryan managed to gradually leak that money back into the accounts of those from whom it was stolen over many decades, and that she left a trail so clear that if the government had chosen to pursue it any further they would then have been forced to prove how it was lost in the first place. The risk of exposing further corruption in an already corrupt government is far too great for the administration to take. However, the recovery of much of the cargo of the trireme of Heliosa is likely to have been used to grease the palms of most of the players, and ensure their silence at the highest levels. There has been no evidence of any political uproar from the Russians, despite their continued sabre rattling.'

Allison sat back in her seat for a moment and thought about the Russians and their determination to recover the supposed "untold wealth" hidden somewhere off the Spanish coast. She looked briefly at the vehicle that they were in, and the smart clothes that Lillian was wearing.

'I know that Garrett's yacht was in the vicinity of the Spanish coast within days of Ethan and Nicola being there. The media reported that Lucy Morgan's divers off the coast had recovered large quantities of gold and silver from the shipwreck that was studied by arhcaeologists and declared to be ancient Tartessian gold, just like the Treasure of El Carambolo found in Seville decades before.'

Lillian nodded but said nothing as Allison got into her stride.

'Ethan and Nicola took *twelve* of those flotation sacks with them,' she said, 'but the media reported only four sacks' worth of material recovered from Lucy's excavation site.'

Again, Lillian said nothing.

'You dispersed the MJ–12 money but made off with a pile of archaeological gold instead?'

Mitchell's voice reached her from the front seat.

'That is a scandalous accusation with no foundation in reality, and we distance ourselves from any such fake news wherever possible.'

Mitchell's eyes were twinkling with delight as he looked at her in the mirror. Allison looked across at Lillian and smiled.

'That kind of money could be used to disappear,' she said. 'It would last a lifetime, especially if those people were to move away from America and live in some quiet, anonymous fishing village half a world away…'

The car eased into the sidewalk and Allison realized they were parked outside a large colonial house in an exclusive area just outside the city suburbs, the kind of place where the locals raked in six figures from their jobs in the city and spent their weekends aboard yachts in the local marina.

Lillian extended her hand, and Allison shook it uncertainly.

'It's been good knowing you, Allison,' she said in her southern drawl. 'Keep doing what you're doing.'

Allison felt her hand being turned over and a set of keys pressed into her palm, as with the other hand Lillian handed her an envelope, within which she could see papers relating to title deeds.

Allison's eyes welled up and she felt her throat constrict, but before she could think clearly she was getting out of the car as instructed and the door closed behind her. She stood on the sidewalk and watched as the car pulled smoothly away and cruised down the street until it was no longer in sight, as though it had driven into the oblivion of the history books.

*

Lillian Cruz waited until they were well clear of the residential area before she dialled a number on her cell phone. The line picked up immediately, the voice of an elderly man replying, his tones jovial and almost carefree.

'Is it done?'

'It's done,' Lillian confirmed. 'Keyes will do as he's told and the loose ends are tied up. Where are you now?'

'Far away,' came the reply, although she could hear the sound of rollers crashing against a shore in the background. *'In fact, so far away I don't really know where the hell we are. Foxx did his work well. The three of us will disperse from here. Take care of yourself, Lillian.'*

'You too.'

The line went dead, and as Mitchell drove over a bridge that spanned a river Lillian opened her window and tossed the cell over the side and with it any evidence of Jarvis, the DIA, Majestic Twelve, Congress and several decades of pain. The thing that made her smile was the way Jarvis had described his current situation: *"the three of us"*. She closed the window again and saw Mitchell looking at her with interest.

'Where do you want to go?'

'Anywhere anonymous. Anywhere we can't be found, chased, questioned, hassled or recognized.'

Mitchell smiled as he changed gear and headed for the nearest freeway.

'I know just the place.'

***

Sign up to Dean Crawford's Newsletter and get a *FREE* book!

www.deancrawfordbooks.com

ABOUT THE AUTHOR

Dean Crawford is the author of over twenty novels, including the internationally published series of thrillers featuring *Ethan Warner*, a former United States Marine now employed by a government agency tasked with investigating unusual scientific phenomena. The novels have been *Sunday Times* paperback best–sellers and have gained the interest of major Hollywood production studios. He is also the enthusiastic author of many independently published novels.

Printed in Poland
by Amazon Fulfillment
Poland Sp. z o.o., Wrocław